IN TALL COTTON

CHARLES HULSE

IN TALL COTTON

KENSINGTON BOOKS
http://www.kensingtonbooks.com

KENSINGTON BOOKS are published by

Kensington Publishing Corp.
850 Third Avenue
New York, NY 10022

All Kensington titles, imprints, and distributed lines are available at special quantity discounts for bulk purchases for sales promotion, premiums, fund raising, educational or institutional use.

Special book excerpts or customized printings can also be created to fit specific needs. For details, write or phone the office of the Kensington Special Sales Manager: Kensington Publishing Corp., 850 Third Avenue, New York, NY, 10022. Attn. Special Sales Department, Phone: 1-800-221-2647.

Kensington and the K logo Reg. U.S. Pat. & TM Off.

ISBN 0–7582–0121–4

First Kensington Trade Paperback Printing: March 2002
10 9 8 7 6 5 4 3 2 1

Printed in the United States of America

For
GORDON MERRICK
For all the reasons
he knows
and
for
my brother Larry
for reasons he may
suspect . . .

IN TALL COTTON

Chapter One

THE RING SLIPPED OVER my swollen knuckle as if it had been soaped. My hands, although scratched and bruised from the battle for my life this afternoon, were small, even for a fourteen-year-old. A diagonal crack across the face of the turquoise stone was dirt-encrusted but somehow matched the natural black-veined patterns embedded deep in the blue-green stone. They call it blue-green, but that's a limitation of language. There don't seem to be any words to describe that color—the richness, the depth, the little flecks of brownish gold trapped just under the surface that held me spellbound. The heavy silver band needed polishing and one of the little rounded silver beads beside the stone was missing but wouldn't be noticed if I wore it turned out toward the side of my hand. I had never wanted anything so much in my life. I knew that all the rest of Sister's jewelry—the dangling earrings, rhinestone-studded curved combs she used to keep her hair pulled back from her face, the strands of pearls and beads—was pure dime store. Even damaged, the ring was real. Honest. The silver had been hammered by hand by Arizona Indians. The stone had been chiseled out of the rocky earth and polished and hand-fitted into the silver mounting. I'd seen this sort of thing in the tourist shops in Phoenix when we first came west from Missouri almost four years ago, and at first sight that mysterious bluish stone had captivated me and I had longed for a ring. Not a big belt buckle like many of the men wore. I wanted a ring. And here one was, all but for the taking. Not

9

that I contemplated stealing it. I'd never stolen anything in my life. It was difficult enough coping with the names we were called at school—Okie, Arkie, Missouri Mules or worse—without adding thief to the list. Sister would probably give it to me. She wasn't my sister, she was my first cousin and I was her favorite, her baby. Her real name was Virginia—Ginny—but neither of us was called by our real names. After all, the ring was broken and she was so particular about what she wore that I doubted if she'd be caught dead wearing a cracked ring. What she did wear might be Woolworth's, but it was in perfect condition and she wore everything with style.

The ring kept flashing as my fingers rummaged through the dresser drawer and her suitcase. I knew she wouldn't mind if she caught me prying but what was I looking for anyway? I needed a letter, a document, an incriminating secret, anything. Anything I could use to keep her on my side. The word blackmail kept coming to mind, but it surely couldn't be blackmail where Sister was concerned.

Sister hadn't totally unpacked—the suitcase lay open on the floor with bras, stocking suspenders and what she called "half-slips" trimmed with lace frothing up over the edge of the smart case like frilled wrappers in a box of expensive chocolates. I tidied and folded as I held every piece up and examined it—the material often as sheer as the gossamer stockings. The garterbelts too, were lace-trimmed. All impeccably clean and new looking. But something was missing. What was it? I lifted the folded pieces out again. All there. All the elegant underwear necessary for a complete change for every day of the week. Except . . . That was it. No bloomers. No panties. Didn't Sister wear panties? Could that have some special meaning? Something not quite nice? I wouldn't have expected to find the heavy square cotton things that Mom wore, but surely she wore *something*. Suppose a gust of wind, like at the fun fair and the skirt flying up . . . Naw, it couldn't be. She'd probably just washed them all.

Hidden under the underwear was a layer of photographs. Sister was in all the photos—seated at different tables with different glasses and bottles in front of her and different men beside her but she was always smiling with her perfect teeth flashing and her dark eyes glittering with the reflection of the camera's flash, as glamorous as any movie star. Sometimes with bare bronzed shoulders, sometimes with furs—usually silver fox—draped over them. I'd always adored her. She was living proof that the epithets hurled at us refugees from the great Dust Bowl—lazy, ignorant, barefoot hillbillies, moonshine-swillin' no-accounts—were lies. At twenty-three years of age, she was as sleek and sophisticated as anybody I'd come across. She was as beautiful and stylish as any of the women in the picture magazines. And since I gobbled up magazines, particularly movie magazines, I felt that I was a bit of an authority on the subject. It had taken her no time at all to stop teetering on unfamiliar spike heels, learn to order her steak rare and develop a taste for the most expensive whisky and wine. She'd made the leap from Ozark farm to the bright lights of Phoenix, Arizona, with consummate ease, seemingly transformed in flight.

Sister's flight from the farm had been real enough. Six years ago, her mother, my Aunt Dell, simply took her two teen-aged daughters by the hand, told her husband, Jesse Slokum, to *bese ma coula* (the English equivalent) and started walking west. They'd hitched rides and made remarkably good time which is no surprise. Aunt Dell, even though she's my dad's older sister, is no slouch as a looker even now and Mavis, her older daughter, is pretty in a quiet way. The three of them standing beside a lonely road in 1935 must have created quite a temptation for any driver but I always believed that it was Sister's sparkling eyes and smile—not to mention voluptuous figure—that brought the cars and trucks to screeching halts in front of them.

In 1935 it was a fairly daring thing to do—even more so now, I guess—for a woman with two young girls to hitchhike halfway across the United States, but as Aunt Dell said, "It was either that or rot with Jesse. Hell, it wasn't a question of choice, it was a question of survival."

They survived. Thrived, even. It was, after all, not unlike emigrating to a new country where a new language had to be learned, new customs to become aware of and new behavior patterns adopted.

When our family first chugged into Phoenix in '37, embarked on our own flight two years after theirs, they were able to receive us in a reasonably comfortable bungalow, surrounded with all the visible signs of prosperity. At any rate, in the middle of the Great Depression, it looked like prosperity to me. They had all worked hard those first two years and been rewarded. Mavis was engaged to a handsome young lawyer who was her first and last boss. She had him wrapped around her little finger and his impressive Buick was at her disposal. He was ambitious, determined to be the richest lawyer in Phoenix and as Aunt Dell hinted, not too particular how he reached his goal.

Sister was a cocktail waitress—my brother Junior and I exchanged shocked looks at what could only be a dirty word the first time we heard cocktail mentioned—at a nightclub called The Ship. It was a ship. It was a huge wooden cutout painted to look like an ocean liner only I couldn't imagine a ship being that big. There was an immense dance floor and all the big touring bands—the Dorsey Brothers, Benny Goodman, Charlie Barnett—played to packed houses while Sister sidled through the crowds carrying trays of drinks to the thirsty dancers. She'd sometimes make as much as twenty dollars in tips alone. Actually, tips were all the salary the waitresses got and somehow Sister managed to get the lion's share. One night, a man slipped a hundred dollar bill down the front of her blouse as she leaned over to serve the drinks. "For that beautiful smile, honey," he'd said.

So the transplants adapted. They'd settled in and taken on the protective coloring of the city-dweller. Granted, Phoenix wasn't exactly on a par with, say, New York or Boston, in terms of population or sophistication, but compared to Galena, Missouri, it was a big change and a challenge. All three ladies had made the transition and smoothed off the rough edges of the farm except perhaps for the giveaway twangs and drawls left in their voices.

But we—Mom, Dad, Junior, and I—hadn't adapted. We hadn't made the transition from Ozark farm to West Coast city life as gracefully as Aunt Dell and the girls. If we had, we'd still be in California. We'd had four years since our arrival in Phoenix to take on whatever protective coloring the civilized world required, but we hadn't made it stick. Only four years and here we were back staying with Aunt Dell in Arizona—this time in a dusty little copper mining town called Ajo—a stopover in our retreat. Our retreat back to Galena, Missouri, from all the golden promises of the West. We were putting down solid roots there when Dad snapped his fingers, gave the order to pull up stakes and pile back into the Model-A Ford and hit the road. Dad's decision. None of us others had a vote. Pure dictatorship, Junior said. Most dictatorships get toppled but Dad's resisted dissent on every level and grew stronger with each inconceivable edict. The only thing we were taking with us from California was the baby, Becky, who'd been born there.

After that first year in Phoenix, we had settled down in Clovis, California, Dad with a good job, Mom with prospects of reestablishing her schoolteaching career and good schools offering both Junior and me endless opportunities, when all of a sudden the Ford was up on blocks in the garage with Junior underneath it and Dad grinding away at its valves. That could only mean trip. Travel. Back on the road. End of dream.

The baby, Becky, had been a part of the dream. She seemed to round out and enhance our good fortune. Particularly for me. She was mine from the minute she was born—my anguished prayers and talks with God about her safe arrival had given me the right to claim her. She became my charge as Sister had always said I'd been hers. I crowed with delighted pride at school about my new little sister until Junior got me aside and tried to explain to me that it wasn't necessarily something to boast about.

"Why not?" I demanded.

"Well . . ." He was blushing. "You know how babies are made?"

"Of course. 'God plants the seed in the belly of . . .'" I began to recite and he joined me in our old private joke. He cut it short.

"Oh, for heaven's sake." He shook his head with dismay. "You're so dumb. Don't you know they have to do it to make a baby?"

"Who?"

"Mom and Dad, silly."

"Do what?"

"*It*, dummy."

"So?" Why was he so serious? "It wasn't an immaculate conception."

"But . . . Don't you see? You and I are so much older." He blushed again. "Well, if they'd had the three of us, you know, one, two, three—sort of blam, blam, blam—OK. But now . . ." I was beginning to understand. He was embarrassed at the idea of Mom and Dad doing it. Having sex. I suppose the idea of anybody doing it embarrassed him, but I'd never thought of it one way or the other. I had been doing it with somebody myself ever since I could remember so I figured everybody else was too. Except, of course, Junior. And I have to admit that the knowledge that he took such a dim view of it often dampened my own enthusiasm. Indeed, I have such respect for him that on several occasions thoughts of his disapproval were enough to call a halt to activities before so much as a fly-button had been touched. He was my protective skin. Protecting me against myself. "It doesn't matter. Forget it. I just wish you wouldn't scream the news from the housetops. Does everybody have to know we have a new baby sister?"

As far as I was concerned, *yes*. Here she was—thanks to considerable self-sacrifice on my part—whole, healthy, beautiful and mine. And she was at this very minute as I continued my fruitless search for *something* among Sister's innocent belongings, safely asleep downstairs on a pallet on the floor out of direct range of the air-conditioner's fan. It was Sister herself, stretched out on the couch, who was getting full benefit of whatever air was stirring. It would have been fairly difficult to catch pneumonia sitting stark naked and dripping wet in front of this primitive cooler. It was the sort found all over Arizona—a handmade wooden frame holding chickenwire that in turn held excelsior through which water dropped from a trough fed by a delapidated garden hose. A fan then drew the hot desert air through the dampened excelsior and cool air filled the room. It even worked. These boxes were slapped over at least one window of every house, giving them a one-eyed pirate look. Some houses had them at every window, literally blinding the house, the ungainly attachments looking like goiters or giant mud-daubers' nests. Those makeshift boxes underlined and expressed the transitory feeling of the times. People were on the move constantly—looking for work mostly—and the coolers were often empty packing crates superimposed on to the buildings. Junior said they reminded him of carapaces and wondered what sort of beast had left its shell at the window and crawled inside the house.

Downstairs, the cooler managed to make the sitting room bearable, so long as you didn't move. If you sat quietly, the sweat would eventually stop flowing but it never seemed to dry completely.

Here in Sister's airless upstairs room, I was covered in sweat with the simple exertion of putting away the photographs. I noticed that the men with Sister were all swarthy, beautifully if exaggeratedly dressed and usually sporting a diamond ring—they could be gangsters. Was this something I could use?

I stared at the last photograph so long that it began to go out of focus, to swim, even tremble before my eyes. I blinked and ran a hand across my forehead. The photograph was suddenly spotted as though hit by a rainstorm. It was covered in stains as dark as blood. I instinctively lifted my fingers to my swollen lip. Dry, except for a slick of sweat. Not bleeding onto the picture which I wiped on my hip. Now the stains were streaks. And my vision was still blurred—marred by sweat or tears. God knows I felt like crying. Crying and screaming for all that I'd lost. I rubbed my eyes with my shoulders and sat up straight, head up and back, rigid, keeping away from the suitcase to stop the splattering drops falling on the photos and the delicate fabric.

My knees felt glued to the floor and my body ached from the beating it had taken. I held out my arms and turned them back and forth looking for bruises. My legs were unmarked, they just didn't want to support me as I rose painfully to my feet.

"Totsy, honey." I slammed the suitcase lid shut with a bang, and shook my head to clear it of sweat, tears, and fear. What *had* I been looking for? "Where are you?" It was Sister's voice calling. And yep, that's what the whole family calls me. Totsy. Not *Topsy*. She was a girl. And she just growed. I am a boy and I haven't growed as much as I'd like in almost fifteen years. I wondered how old I'd have to get before I outgrew that nickname. Frankly, it was still difficult even for me to think of myself as Carlton. That's my real name, Carlton Woods. The memory of my first day in school still makes me redden with shame. The teacher held up cards with all the first-graders' names printed on them for each to identify and I kept looking at "Carlton" blankly, waiting for a card with Totsy on it. I could spell that.

"Up here," I called. "Be right down." I tugged at the ring. It stuck on the knuckle that it had slipped over so easily before. The knuckle hurt. I started sucking on it as I went down the stairs. I'd learned nothing useful from the room.

"Becky's beginning to stir," Sister said as I went into the darkened cool room. "She was kinda whimperin' a minute ago." Sister propped herself up on one elbow, her dark hair damp and sticking to her wet forehead.

"Uhnumm." I still had my finger in my mouth.

"You still suckin' your thumb?" She grinned. "Come on over here. I thought I broke you of that a hundred years ago."

I leaned in against her and she put an arm around my shoulders lightly. It was too hot for a real embrace but she touched me and caressed me at every opportunity as she always had. It made me melt with joy. Joy mingled with guilt and fear now. Why had everything gone wrong? She felt deliciously moist and warm next to me and smelled of soap and sleep. "I got your ring stuck. It won't come off."

"Well, you'll either have to cut your finger off or just keep it, won't you?"

"Do you mean it? Can I have it?"

"Course you can, honey. It's just an old broken thing. I found it next to a wilted corsage on a table after a party of young kids had left. At The Ship. Remember The Ship? I chased after them, but they'd gone." Her face clouded. "You keep it. It makes me sad."

Becky rolled over fretfully and made little noises of irritation. I ran to her and dropped to my knees beside her on the floor. "Gee, thanks, Sis. I love it. I'll never take it off." I picked up Becky and rocked her in my arms. She was soaking. In every sense of the word. Her little plump body was glazed with perspiration and her diaper sodden. I put her back on the pallet and started to change her. "Hey, Sis, I tried your method of putting her to sleep this afternoon. Didn't work worth a darn. You said it was surefire for me."

"All I did with you when you were that size was just blow gently on your eyelids. You'd be asleep in minutes. Not even your mother could figure out how I did it so quickly."

"This little rascal just squinches up her face and starts to howl."

"It all depends on your technique. I'd start so softly that I'd hardly be letting any air out at all. You'd start to blink and then I'd increase the pressure." She chuckled. "Of course, those damned eyelashes of yours helped. Just look at 'em now. As thick as caterpillars. Once I got some air on them, they were too heavy to lift. You'd be out like a light. Ooohhh, what I wouldn't give to have them. Boy, are you going to drive the girls crazy—if you aren't already. Crazy with jealousy for them bits of fur you wear around your eyes."

I could feel myself almost arching my back and purring with pleasure like a cat being stroked. Her words oozed over me like honey, soothing my jangled nerves. No wonder I adored her. She'd managed to make me forget—for a moment—my slip of the tongue this morning. Why couldn't I learn to keep my mouth shut? Junior had pointed out to me several times—kindly and with strained patience—that one of my worst faults was blurting out things without thinking of the consequences. When I thought of the consequences I faced now, my body began to tremble. How in God's name was I going to face this alone? If Junior were here, we'd work it out together somehow. This was one hell of a time for him to get sick. He'd never been sick before. He'd always been right there—right *here* beside me, as close and familiar as a second skin. That second skin protected me from getting cut or scratched or scraped. Now he was in a hospital and I was a walking contusion. A contusion that wouldn't be walking much longer if I didn't straighten out some serious misunderstandings.

I went on absentmindedly dusting powder on Becky's bare bottom until there was a white crust filling the pink cleft that seemed to continue unbroken in a semicircle from front to back. Like a scar made by a single blow with a sickle.

"Honey, you're going to clog her up," Sister said. "Thank God that's powder and not cement."

We laughed as I pinned Becky into the fresh diaper, deft experienced fingers inside the cloth protecting the delicate skin from the pin's sharp point. The ring flashed.

"It *is* a sort of girlie ring." Sister's voice had changed. I glanced up over my shoulder and noted a frown between her brows. "Hope nobody'll call you a sissy."

"Don't care if they do," I said a bit too prissily and turned my attention back to Becky. Could Sister be making further reference to my slip of the tongue this morning about Roy. *Uncle* Roy, I reminded myself. After all, he was Aunt Dell's husband. But for only a couple of years. He was only a relative by marriage. New to the family. We didn't know him very well. Dad thinks he's the greatest thing since the V-8 engine just because he's a cowboy and can do sixty-five push-ups. Talk about your hero-worship. I think I know him better than anybody. Any of us, that is. Except maybe Aunt Dell. But I doubt if she knows he's dangerous. I mean *deadly* dangerous in the way that I know. I could actually see my heart pounding against my ribs. Had Sister noticed? I looked back up at her and went on quickly, "I've been called that before. And lots of other things besides." My laugh stuck in my throat. "Why, at some of the schools I've been to . . ."

"Oh, honey. *School.*" She made school sound like a leper colony. "Oh lordy, the things kids say. They'as always the cruelest things. Why, back home . . . oh me, oh my . . . I used to wonder where they *heard* the things they'd call us. And each other."

"I sure never heard some of the things they called me out in California," I boasted to Sister, anxious to rid the air of the sissy references. "I'll bet you haven't either. I couldn't even repeat them to you. Boy. I've had more fights about . . ."

"Oh, you're a tough one," she laughed, ruffling my hair. "I'll bet you knocked all them guys naked and then hid their clothes." I was stunned and must have looked it. "Don't you know that old expression, honey? It's like knockin' . . . no, that's not it. It's *turning* somebody every way but loose." She laughed and I joined in. "Your daddy's always sayin' things like that." She tugged at my hair and lifted my face up and peered at me. "And what's that? There. Your lip looks swollen. Somebody turnin' you ever which way but loose?"

I jerked my head away. "Oh, that's nothing." I grinned up at her. "I cut it shaving."

"Whoeee," she threw her head back and laughed as she headed for the hall. "Honey, you need a shave about as much as I do." She paused and turned back to me, a small frown between her brows. "It'd be pretty darn queer if I did have to," she said evenly.

There it was. The subject. The word. QUEER. The *trouble.* The whole trouble just dangling in the air between us. It filled the room. There was no way of avoiding it as we had this morning. I glanced quickly at Becky. Go on, I begged, do something. Throw up all over me or scream bloody murder, for God's sake. You managed to get this conversation stopped this morning by somehow covering yourself in dog shit. Create another diversion, please, please, please, and save me from this. I shook her slightly and squeezed her hopelessly. I resisted a temptation to pinch her painfully to make her yell. She giggled and gurgled happily. I placed her on the pallet with her favorite toy—an empty cigarette package of Dad's—and prepared to meet my fate.

I lifted my eyes slowly to Sister's hard and questioning ones. Our eyes held so deeply and for so long, my eyeballs felt dry and hot. I pulled my back up straight, took a deep breath and started talking. I talked a blue streak. I explained, denied, cajoled, swore on stacks of bibles, professed to only rudimentary knowledge of sexual facts and acts, made jokes, danced, did imitations while launching into an ancient cowboy story whose stale punch line had some relevance to the point I was trying to make. I kept my eyes on her, holding her gaze as much as possible. It was as though I were trying to hypnotize her or convert her to some weird religion with my own wild fervor, like an hysterical evangelist with a new recruit to convince, to baptize, to have born again a new mind clear and clean and unmarked by what I'd blurted out this morning that had turned our world upside-down. Mostly I wanted her to laugh. If I could just make her laugh, I'd be halfway there. And then, there it was. A twinkle in the dark eyes, a twitch at the corners of the voluptuous mouth and with one last wild antic on my part, a guffaw, a great cascade of laughter bubbled up and spilled over me like a soothing shower. We both laughed until she waved a limp dismissive hand at me and started up the stairs. I'd won. At least this first round. I dropped my head—it weighed a ton as my chin hit my chest—and let my entire body go slack with relief as I offered up a silent thankful prayer and a hurriedly slurred apology for the contortions the truth had been forced through.

Sister's voice came to me from what seemed a long way off. "Where's Momma and Roy?"

"Went shopping," I called back, instigating a howl from Becky. She wanted her bottle.

"Your mom and dad still at the hospital?"

"Yeah. They stay later today. Saturday. Visiting hours last till six." I was talking to her from the foot of the stairs now, on the way to the kitchen to feed Becky.

"Then I'd better hurry." I could hear her head for the bathroom just as a car came up the drive. "Oops, there's Momma now. I'll help 'em unload." She clattered down the stairs and brushed past us and was out the door before I'd started preparing the baby's bottle.

The car doors slammed when I was testing the temperature of the milk by squirting a drop on my inner arm and looked out to see Sister and Roy talking and laughing on the far side of the car. The sight of the two of them together, in cahoots, froze me with terror. It was up to her. She held my very life in her hands and probably didn't know it. She couldn't possibly know, but she could make it all right if she'd understood the point of my clownish cowboy performance. One word would do the trick. She had no idea how far this "slip of the tongue," this little "misunderstanding," this schoolboy "revelation" had gone. If I'd told her where I'd really got my swollen lip, my life would be worth even less than it was now.

Aunt Dell was yelling at them to unload and get the shopping into the house. Thank God Aunt Dell wasn't being brought into it. At least not yet. If that happened, I was a real goner. Aunt Dell burst into the kitchen first, panting and laughing. Sister and Roy still had their heads together outside, nodding and glancing back toward the kitchen windows, surely—I hoped and prayed—turning it into a harmless joke just between us three.

"Whoooeeee!" Aunt Dell cried with a wide smile. Sister's smile. No question about their being mother and daughter—they shared the same square high-cheekboned face and the flashing teeth and eyes. "The *heat!*" She turned and screamed out the back door. "Roy! For God's sake get in here and get us a beer." They were already like an old married couple and I fervently hoped they'd stay that way for the next hundred years. Please God, don't let anything I've done come between them.

Roy came in, followed by Sister, both laughing and smiling at each other knowingly. He put an overflowing cardboard box down on the floor and headed for the icebox with a broad wink at me which I refused to acknowledge except with an inner sigh of relief so great I almost dropped Becky. Sister put a bulging paper bag on the table. "OK. Done my chores for the day." She winked at me too. "Off to soak." She shot a last conspiratorial smile at Roy and went out into the hall.

"You'd think we'as feedin' an army. Look at all this stuff." Aunt Dell sank into a straight-backed chair and wiped her forehead with a limp hand. "Well, we'll be needin' every mouthful once that big brother of yours gets out of that damned hospital. That boy eats like a horse. Not like you, you puny little thing. Go lay that chile down, Totsy. It's too hot to touch anybody. Even that sweet thing. Look at her suckin' away. Lucky thing." She swung around in the chair. *"Roy!*

For Christ's sake! Beeeeeerrrrrr! Before I die." She let her mouth drop open and her tongue hang out and panted comically like an exhausted dog. Roy plunked an open bottle down in front of her and she lifted it and drank thirstily. "Couldn't even wait for a glass. Aahhh! That's better. I may even live."

"And how's old Ah-ho-ho treatin' you, son?" How could he go on making that silly joke and move around perfectly normally after what happened? How could I go on staying under the same roof with him, let alone talk to him or look at him? This was grown-up stuff and I was growing up forcibly. If he didn't know how old Ah-ho-ho was treating me, nobody knew. "Hot enough for you?" Another brilliant bit of grown-up repartee. There was plenty of reasons for me to doubt the joys of the mysterious inner grown-up circle.

"Plenty." I could speak if I didn't have to look directly at him. "With the fiesta on, the town was really pretty last night when I walked around after supper. They had lights strung up to that central fountain all the way around the square. There were four or five Mexican bands—singers and dancers—moving around in the crowds." I was talking to Aunt Dell as though there was nobody else in the room. "One group even asked me to join in the dancing . . ."

"Oh, they always do that," Aunt Dell said. "That's all part of the fun of the fiesta. They sure can sing and dance, them wetbacks."

"One boy was showing me steps. Very difficult ones, too. You have to beat your heels and clap your hands at the same time but the rhythm is so sync . . . synco . . . well, complicated. I couldn't get the hang of it."

"Aw, you're just like your daddy. A little practice and he can do any kind a dancin'," Aunt Dell declared with a wave of her hand.

"Well," I said, daring to boast a bit, "they did say I was pretty good. Maybe I can go back tonight. It was fun." Out of the corner of my eye I felt more than saw Uncle Roy regarding me with a funny expression. Suspicion? "But I still haven't seen much of the town." I rolled my eyes at Becky who kept me housebound. "Only the bit we came through when we arrived and the central square."

"Poor kid's only been here three days, for lord's sake," Aunt Dell said as if defending me from some accusation. "And that's been spent baby-sittin'. Soon's Junior gets better, we'll show you around. Not that there's all that much to see. I don't know much about it neither. And hope I don't have to. The damned Arizona State Meat Department's plumb lost its mind. They transfer Roy down here—him a inspector of meat on the hoof, for Christ's sake—to a copper minin' town where they ain't a herd of cattle within a hundred miles. Ah-ho-ho-ho, indeed. More like ha-ha-ha." Jokes on the pronunciation of Ajo were apparently irresistible. "All these Mexican names just about got me running backwards. *Caliente* ain't so bad. I'm just about to git *Quijotoa* but wouldn't you know we'd rent a house on *Xochimilco?*"

"You should have seen Dad asking directions for this street. Funniest thing I've ever seen."

"I can just see that no-account brother of mine. OOooeee, gets purple and chokes when he gets mad, don't he?" She roared with laughter and slapped her thigh.

"I better get rid of this sweaty load," I said heading with Becky to the sitting room.

"Your folks not back yet?" Aunt Dell called after me. "It's after six."

"Not yet," I called. Then I caught sight of our Model-A Ford pulling up in front of the house as I passed the hall door. "Oh, yes, here they are now." I walked down the hall and opened the front door. I could hear Aunt Dell and Uncle Roy moving in behind me and Sister almost bumped into them descending the stairs that gave onto the hall. I stepped out onto the porch. Sister stepped out behind me while Aunt Dell held the screen door open with Roy peering over her shoulder. The cement paving slanted from the porch steps down to the sidewalk along the street so we were looking down at Mom and Dad as they got out of the car. At the top of their heads, really, their faces hidden. Becky jerked her head away from her bottle, bounced in my arms and reached toward the approaching figures. "Momma!" she called.

Mom stopped, head still down. Dad took two quick paces and took her by the arm. They didn't look at each other, they looked up at us. It was written on their faces as clearly as if they'd shouted. "Oh my God," Aunt Dell gasped, almost inaudibly.

Junior was dead. Their set faces and the stiff extra-straight way they walked declared the news.

Mom's eyes didn't look like she'd been crying as she walked toward us, floating up the steps as though they didn't exist, and took Becky from me. Mom's eyes didn't register that we existed either. They didn't seem to register anything. Becky glued herself to Mom like a breastplate, a shield against the world. It was on Becky's bare back that Aunt Dell's tears fell when she flung her arms around Mom.

My face was buried in Sister's soft bosom where I could feel her heart pounding so loud that I scarcely heard Dad when he said, "You're all we've got now, son," and ran his hand roughly over my head and squeezed my shoulder until it hurt.

I don't know how I got through the next few days. They are a blur. A blur of disbelief. Grief overlaid everything like volcanic ash. They *said* Junior was dead but that didn't necessarily make it so. It had to be some sort of mistake, a miscalculation, a misjudgment—one tiny heart beat skipped that they'd made a snap judgment about. What would happen when his eyes fluttered open as it happens in films when the poison, the sleep potion or the wicked witch's curse has worn off? I was driven wild by the horror of the idea of his eyes opening where they said he was now.

"What a place to be buried." Junior had said that. The words echoed through me as I remembered exactly when I'd heard them. We had crossed the border over into Arizona for the first time and were driving along near a place called Tombstone. We'd stopped for gas and had seen some rattlesnakes and a Gila monster down in a viewing hole or pit. The poor beasts had looked more dead than alive and I remember he'd shuddered when he said, "What a place to be buried." He couldn't possibly have had an inkling, a premonition that he'd be buried in the Gila Desert.

I refused to accept the fact that he had been buried. Here or anywhere. I refused to accept anything that had happened since we'd left California. Junior couldn't be dead any more than I could be alive without him. We'd always been together. It was inconceivable that I could go on breathing when he had stopped. I wouldn't be able to look at myself in the mirror without knowing that I had no right to have sight, heartbeats, feelings. I didn't deserve to be the one alive. I wasn't worthy and I knew it. I also knew that I'd see my unworthiness reflected in Dad's eyes as long as I lived. Mom's too, perhaps if they were ever able to reflect anything at all again. I'd lost my second skin. Like a snake. I was that expression Dad saved for unspeakable people: Lower than a snake's asshole. I felt like a snake, sliding silently around where I wasn't wanted, where I had no right to be. I was a pretender. I wasn't the one who should be here at all.

I didn't want to believe that I had gone back to the Fiesta in the town square the very night they said Junior had died and had danced wildly with my Mexican street musicians. Had drunk Tequila. Had loved it, what's more. Had even puffed on a Mexican cigarette Juan rolled by hand in his room that caused me not only to fly, to lose touch with the earth and defy gravity, but to also lose touch with all restraints and controls. I had openly defied God. I defied God's existence and His Son's teachings by willfully performing acts that I knew by any definition—not just Southern Baptist definition—were abominations. Acts that that same afternoon I'd been brutally forced to commit in the backseat of a car in broad daylight, I performed that night with abandon. Acts of humiliation and degradation in the afternoon became flights of ecstasy with a chosen partner that night.

I'd lost my mind. Did I think by denying God's existence I'd cancel out Junior's too? Just because he wasn't beside me, was his watchful presence no longer to be considered? Were Junior's standards no longer valid? Was I shaking off all traces of decency to prove to myself that Junior was truly dead? If he were no longer there, I didn't have to seek his approval anymore? The magnitude of my loss was beginning to become apparent to me. Without seeking his approval, without having his restraining reasonableness at hand, I could go whole hog. Whole unmentionable hog. And had. Was this what my life was going to be without him? I couldn't make myself believe that all that was left of him was his spirit.

Could I believe that puffed-up waxen doll in the coffin in the funeral parlor had anything to do with Junior? Those rouged cheeks and the funny smile on the too-full lips had nothing to do with anybody I'd ever known. I wanted to scream at them all when I saw it. I wanted to scream, "It's not Junior! Can't you see? Just *look*, for Lord's sake. Look at the hair for one thing. That's not Junior's. It's a wig. Don't you know a wig when you see one? See, the color's all wrong. It's too light and it looks like straw. Dead like straw. And there, *there*, the parting! See? It's on the wrong side. What more proof do you need? It's on the right instead of the left." I wanted to call out to Mom, "Mom, don't you know your own son? Your first born?" And to Dad, "Dad! Listen, Dad. Can that be the greatest ball player of his generation? *Look*, for Christ's sake. A trick is being played on all of us. Don't you know it? That *can't* be Junior. Junior's off somewhere. Somewhere else—maybe he's gone to that military academy he always longed to go to. Maybe he's back in Clovis, marching in the high school band. But he's not *here*. That pathetic facsimile is about as convincing as the little matador dolls on sale at the Fiesta. Look! Please, just *look*, for God's sake. Don't be taken in . . . It's some sort of hideous joke . . . Can't you see, for God's sake? Are you all blind. All blind but me? Why do you *accept* this . . ."

Then, a funeral. Ostensibly for Junior. Thank God, it too was a blur with only certain moments clearly etched in my mind. Fleeting pictures of our little knot of people—swollen to about a dozen with the arrival of Mom's sisters, Aunt Bill and Aunt Elsie—all crowded together in a stunned clump listening to a preacher straining to think of something to say about a dead boy he'd never even seen. Had never known his sparkling eyes or his sweetness. He was just standing up there sweating, that poor preacher man, making up words, words he thought we'd like to hear. Empty words. Nice words. Worthless words. Words meant to console. But what is consoling about ". . . it's God's will." Or "God calls his children home . . ." What kind of a God is that? Certainly not the God that I'd felt on such comfortable and friendly terms with until I turned my back on Him the other night.

There was some organ music that was just loud enough to stir some dust motes around the organist who also sang a couple of hymns and ended up with "Jeannie With the Light Brown Hair." That had been a request of Mom's because she'd heard Junior whistling it with one of his last breaths. That was the clearest moment of all for me. That was the moment I thought my heart would break. I'll never be able to listen to that song again as long as I live. Or bear to hear anybody whistling. Whistling any tune.

The pallbearers were volunteers from the local Boy Scout troop. They sat off to one side of the church uncomfortably rigid in their stiff uniforms covered with badges. They were embarrassed by this unfortunate ritual for somebody unknown but tried valiantly not to show it. (I just looked up "pall" in Junior's dictionary that I've been carrying around with me like he did. Only for me it's a talisman, a connection with him as intimate as if I were holding his hand. Mom handed it to me without saying a word when his things were brought back from the hospital. I'd had difficulty figuring out the connection between "to pall—to lose interest" and "pallbearer—a coffin atten-dant." I'm beginning to understand now.)

From one minute to the next, it was all over. Aunts boarded trains for Missouri. The Model-A was packed and we moved to it like ro-bots, easing ourselves silently into our accustomed positions and drove off.

Drove off. We just drove off. Heading back the way we'd come four years ago. Along the same roads. We could, with some sort of time warp and imagination, wave at ourselves passing in the other direc-tion. We drove off. Headed east. Leaving behind the most important part of ourselves. Of each of us. Our lives. Behind in a grave. An unmarked grave. Just a typed-out name with dates in a metal frame that stuck into the sandy earth on a wire prong. We didn't have the money or the time to have a tombstone cut here in a place not too far from Tombstone. When we first started west, we left Oak Grove, Arkansas, on the day after Grandma Idy had been assigned her hole in the ground. History was repeating itself. Would we go on forever, back and forth on these endless roads, never having a real home, just depositing members of the family in holes all over the fucking place until there was none of us left?

I felt considerable relief getting out of Ajo although it hadn't been easy for me to make proper farewells to anybody except Aunt Dell. She was the only one in that Ajo house untouched by my sordid little story and I hoped she would remain untouched. As for Sister, I could hardly look at her. I was sick enough with guilt without assuming any of hers. She'd stirred the sordid little story into a froth of fear that still stuck in my throat and made it difficult for me to embrace her with my usual warmth. It choked me to know that she was instrumental—however inadvertently—in having me fear for my life. It was as though gangsters had a contract out on me and the terror I was living with constantly kept my blood icy. So did the very sight of Roy. I shrank from him as from a coiled rattler. His winks and knowing smiles were meant to calm my fears but only fed them. I could do without him for the rest of my life. But that other one—that irreplaceable one that we were leaving—how could I possibly live without him? There was no way to say farewell to him. Ever. He'd be with me always.

We were a sorry lot bouncing along in the Ford. I was huddled in the backseat, way over on my side staring out my window trying to put the inconceivable happenings in Ajo out of my mind, terrified to turn my head from the window to face the awful emptiness next to me where Junior had always been.

Nobody would have guessed that Dad had been crumbling away inside ever since Junior's illness's first warnings months ago. Looking at the back of his head now, seeing his hands firmly on the wheel in their customary position, he seemed solid enough. Perhaps the steering wheel was his crutch, the thing that held him together. God knows at every possible opportunity he found reasons to seek its support.

As for Mom's withdrawal, if it got any deeper, she'd turned inside out. We were all afflicted. Maimed and wounded in our various

ways, left scarred as if by the removal of a vital organ. I felt particularly crippled. Crippled and crutchless. I tried to close my mind to
the horrifying fears—wrapped in layers of shame—I had for myself.
Fears about what I thought I might become. Or had I become it already? What was *it?* Was it *my* flaw? We all have at least one. Having
embraced the forbidden was I doomed forever? If so, whose fault
was it? Could Junior have saved me from performing loathesome
acts? Could anybody be blamed? Maybe Dad? No, you can't blame
others for your own flaws. Or actions. It's something you have to
live with by yourself. But Junior wouldn't have let me face it alone.
He'd have understood—he actually said as much in the car: "I
couldn't hate you, Tots. I couldn't possibly hate you, no matter
what you did. Or how you turn out." How much had he known? Or
guessed?

If for nothing else, I could still blame Dad for our present predica-
ment. Looking at the back of his head now sent a searing flash of resentment down my spine that was almost thrilling. Being able to
blame him for something was soothing. I could tell by the thickness
of Dad's head and neck, the stubborn set of the shoulders, and the
arrogant command of the car and its occupants that he and I'd come
to the parting of the ways. I knew he'd never help me realize my
dreams or ambitions, let alone help me face or fight this curious
demon I felt within me. I was on my own—a bit blemished, soiled
and scarred, but not ruined. Just fifteen years old and I was con-
fronted with the awesome task of single-handedly making something
of myself. If I got into any trouble—particularly the sort I sensed I
might be headed for—he'd turn his back and simply consider it another example of the inequities of life. Verifying conclusively that
God had really got his wires crossed and whisked the wrong victim
"home." Dad could have borne—oh, so philosophically—my being
whisked "home." But not Junior. For Dad it was a soul-wrenching ca-
tastrophe. I could see him eventually wishing me dead, if he didn't
already. Captain J had said that it was normal to wish your father
dead, but was it normal the other way around? I don't think I wished
him dead, but I let my new resentment of him take hold and root itself in the core of my being. With some nourishment, it could become hate.

Just how much over the years could I blame Dad for? All I know is
that we'd been fine, just the three of us; Mom, Junior and I. Happy
and getting along fine back at the beginning in Galena. Long before
I even knew who Dad was. We'd managed perfectly well without him

since right after I'd been born. If he'd just stayed away, we'd all have been better off. We might even all be alive. If he hadn't come back and started us out on this tragic journey, Junior wouldn't be dead. Yes, it looks like it's going to be easy to work up a case against him. Even hating him. But when you know you are hating yourself too, it makes it easier to spread it around.

Chapter Two

DAD WAS JUST a dim occasional presence in the early days. Now with us. Now gone. Mostly gone. When gone, his absence wasn't a cloud hanging over us. Our lives seemed to go on whether he was there or not. We went to school when we were old enough and Mom went on teaching at her country schools and finding whatever work she could during summer vacations. When Dad did appear, he provided vivid, lively moments but when away, I for one, didn't grieve or pine.

We lived in several houses in Galena, Missouri—none our own— but the first one I remember was a two-story clapboard house two blocks from the Stone County Court House on the main square. It was down a hill from the square. Well, everything was down a hill from the square or up a hill from it. The town square was sort of a shelf, a semicircular one, natural or hacked out by early settlers with the twisting James River flowing south down below the railroad tracks. Behind the shelf was a hill, steep but as the houses petered out into woods there were footpaths worn through the trees by generations of children climbing up to the schoolhouse at the top of the hill. The crisscross lines of paths was like an intricate carpet design, each making no sense except to the family who used it. Everybody had their rocky route from house to school or house to town square, which was the heart and core of the town.

Memories of that first house are without Dad. There was a long yellow stain under one of the upstairs windows, spreading down the weathered clapboards, as though some previous tenant had been too lazy to go outside to the toilet.

"Why didn't they use a pot?" I asked Junior.

"Maybe they did use a pot," he grinned. "And dumped it out the window."

"That'd be easier than trying to pee out the window. You'd have to stretch way out or have a long toy like a hose and you'd have to be careful not to fall . . ."

"Hush, Totsy," Junior was blushing. You couldn't even say "pee" in front of him, let alone "toy."

But you could sure say toy in front of Bonnie Lou who lived across the street. My thing was called a "toy" and we played with it. Bonnie Lou was fascinated by it and I was fascinated by her. She didn't have a toy for some reason so I guess that's why her interest in my not quite six-year-old one was so unflagging. She did have something that I wanted desperately. Her knowledge of dancing. She could play with my toy until the cows came home, watching it get hard and pointing straight up—we both regarded it as some sort of miracle—so long as she taught me all she knew about tap dancing. And she knew a lot. She'd taken lessons somewhere before moving to Galena and even had black shiny shoes with ribbon ties and silver metal taps on the heels and toes. I was determined to learn everything she could teach me even if it meant letting her put my toy in her mouth which she did once and I knew we'd committed a sin. Anything that felt that good couldn't be allowed. Junior would have had a fit if he knew.

I was an apt pupil—everybody had always said I had natural rhythm—and was soon embellishing the basic steps and developing my own routines to whatever music she'd put on the windup phonograph.

"That silly kid's a dancer," Bonnie Lou's father said one day. He did nothing but sit all day making cigarettes in a funny little hand-operated machine—cigarette paper in one side, a sprinkling of tobacco from a Prince Albert tin, a handle turned, a roller moved across a flat surface and out dropped a perfect cigarette. He made them by the hundreds. Not to sell, he just stuffed them into empty packs of Wings or Spuds and put them away in cardboard boxes. I don't think he even smoked.

They moved away—cigarettes and tap shoes—leaving tingling memories in my loins and the ringing in my ears of "That silly kid's a dancer." I already knew I was going to be a dancer, but Bonnie Lou's father was the first to recognize it. I'm going to be one day. One way or another.

When school let out for the summer, Mom was faced with job hunting. She faced that problem every year. She was paid as much as fifty dollars a month for teaching but only during the school term. It was during the summer holidays that she really worked. She always said she loved teaching so much she'd even pay for the privilege. Obviously a fairly empty boast in the early '30's in the Ozarks.

That year, it must have been '32, Mom found part-time work at the Galena Hotel as room maid, receptionist, waitress, dishwasher and scrubwoman. She ran the place.

The hotel was only three blocks from our house so she felt she could keep an eye on us and nobody seemed to mind me and Junior running in and out of the hotel all the time. It was like having Mom home with us and we all three got our midday meal free. Mom said it was free, but Junior told me that our food was most of her wages. All her hard work was just to feed us.

"Don't they give Mom any money at all?" I asked.

"Not much. They take our food from what she earns." Junior was biting the inside of his lip and his eyes looked misty. "We're eating Mom's wages and it sticks in my throat."

"That's silly. We ought to eat as much as we can. The more we eat, the more wages Mom is making."

"Oh, you . . ." Junior put his arm around my neck and pulled my head down near his chest and gave my scalp a brisk knuckle-rub, chuckling deep in his throat. I could tell that he was pleased and amused by me. I was an outrageous showoff at best, but he was the audience that I wanted to applaud me the loudest.

With nothing much else coming in, in came Dad. We three were a bit cautious as we welcomed him—rather like animals sniffing out a pack member who'd strayed away to make sure he still belonged. Of course he belonged. He was our father. He'd been away enough in my short life for me to feel that I didn't know him very well. I couldn't remember exactly the last time I'd seen him. It wasn't that I didn't recognize him when I saw him, that was easy and pleasurable. He was good to look at. People said I looked like him—which pleased me—and Junior looked like Mom. That wasn't a bad thing either. Mom and Dad were a handsome couple, everybody said so. That is, when they were a couple.

Dad and I had blue-gray eyes—Mom and Junior, huge dark brown pools for eyes. The high cheekbones and broad straight-toothed smile Dad and I share happily with Aunt Dell and Sister. That is certainly a plus, but I'd like to resemble Dad in height. I have to practically do a back-bend to look up at him.

We also move alike, especially when we dance, but I make an effort to imitate Dad in that department—he's the best dancer I've ever seen—in the regular dancing sense, not the movie star tap dancers, although he knows some interesting jig steps he learned from his father that are being passed on down to me when he's in the right mood.

By the time Dad came back to Galena that summer, there wasn't much summer left. Mom went on working at the hotel and we went on eating her wages at noon. Dad apparently wasn't on Mom's payroll because he didn't join us at the hotel table. He was usually on the other side of the square at the Domino Cafe sipping three-point-two beer. That's what they called it then. I didn't understand about Prohibition or what President Roosevelt was doing with the drinking laws, but it was some time before I knew that beer had names like Pabst, Millers or Budweiser. I thought all beer was called three-point-two.

When Dad wasn't at the Domino, he'd be hanging around laughing and talking with the men who gathered around the Court House. Idlers, Mom called them. Junior told me what that meant and said they were also known as "hold-up artists." If they ever stopped leaning against the building, it'd fall down. I guess that Dad was one of them too, because he didn't seem to have much of anything to do.

Dad would sort of pretend that he had business at the Court House because he was a good friend of the sheriff's—Clem Walters—and spend a great deal of time in his office next to the jail on the second floor. He knew all the gossip and would pass it on to his cronies leaning up against the big square brick building. They'd wave and call Dad over to their groups where they'd all have looks of anticipation on their faces. Ole Woody always had a good story to tell. They'd hitch up their striped overalls at the crotch, lift a foot up behind them onto the little masonry edge and lean back with expectant faces. Dad never let them down. He'd talk, shake his head and lead the laughter.

Junior and Dad had a particular bond. Baseball. They talked about it without stopping. They even talked when the radio was blasting out the games. It was then, when I was just six, with a spurt of independence that I decided I hated the game. It came to me in a flash and I knew I'd have to keep it a deep dark secret. Hating baseball was traitorous. It just wasn't done. It was a delicious secret, one I've kept to this minute and the tingling duplicity I feel as I feign interest is as delicious as having Bonnie Lou's hand on my toy. Both are pleasurable secrets. I still play the loathesome game when necessary and my revenge on it is that I'm pretty good at it.

Dad's daily pattern didn't vary much. Mornings, Court House. Me with him running all over the building from the men's room on the ground floor with the writing all over the walls that I tried to understand, up to the fourth floor and the courtroom where the trials were held and back down again by sliding on the slick bannisters. At lunchtime we'd separate. Me for the hotel, he for the Domino Cafe.

Many of the idlers hadn't become that by choice. Dad wasn't the only man out of work. The depression. THE depression. The Depression. THE DEPRESSION. THE *GREAT* DEPRESSION. It was the cause of everything and everything was blamed on it. "That's why your father is away so much," Mom explained. "He's trying to find work."

I don't know what Dad did in the afternoons except just sit there in the Domino. At any rate that's where he usually was when Mom had our supper at home about ready and he still wasn't home. "It's getting on toward six," Mom would say. "Why don't you boys run up to the square and see if your father's ready for supper." She never said in so many words to go to the Domino, but we all knew where to find him.

That first time, Junior had been reticent about going into the cafe and I took my cue from him, holding back when I wanted desperately to see what was going on behind the big window where I could hear laughter and music. It was one of the few places on the square that I hadn't thoroughly investigated. The window glass had been painted white on the inside up higher than a man's head and above the white line, painted on the clear glass was DOMINO CAFE in flowing letters like the Coca-Cola signs. There was a Doctor Pepper clock—Doctor Pepper at 10:00, 2:00, and 4:00. We stood uneasily at the door, glancing at each other until Junior finally eased the door open very slowly and peeked in. I squeezed in under his arm and had my first look.

The lights weren't very bright and there was a lot of smoke and a smell that I heard Mom refer to as "beer, booze and bodies." A long bar ran along one side and a row of empty booths faced it. On the other side of the room. On the wall, facing us was the focal point of the otherwise spartan room, a wondrous jukebox aglow with wormy contorted colored lights and producing scratchy dance music for the two couples who were lazily gliding and turning in the middle of the floor. They were wrapped so tightly around each other they looked more like they were holding each other up rather than dancing. People, mostly men, were spread around the four tables that were lined along the inside of the painted window or dotted along the bar on high stools.

Edging into the room, my back against the wall and tugging Junior in with me, I searched for Dad. He wasn't here. I looked at Junior to find out our next move. He wrinkled his nose and muttered, "Stinky," just as a voice from the table nearest called out, "Hey, Woody, I think you got some company. Ain't these two towheads your'n?"

"Shit," another man's voice answered from another table. "Woody ain't home enough to know his own kids. If they *are* his own . . ."

Laughter hadn't time to get really started nor the man finish his sentence before he was lifted out of his seat by Dad who'd grabbed him by both shoulders in one bound from the dance floor, leaving Marge Davis stranded with a look of such surprise on her face you'd have thought her partner had gone up magically in smoke.

In a flash, Dad was bumping the man against the white painted window making the glass wobble dangerously as he accented each word he uttered with a bump of the man's head against the glass. "I—don't—think—I—heard—that,—did—I, Coot? *You silly son of a bitch.*" On the last words I was sure the glass would come crashing down on our heads as Dad beat a furious tattoo with the man's head against it. Junior jerked me after him toward the bar, away from the window.

Chairs were knocked over. Men jumped from stools and started moving in toward the ruckus, all talking and yelling at once, shoving each other out of the way or tugging and holding others back. The bartender came scooting out on all fours from under the bar through a hatch. Dad's grip tightened as his quarry suddenly went limp as though his bones had been removed and he fell forward against Dad's chest.

"Stand up!" Dad screamed, shaking the man like a rug. "Stand *up*, goddamn it! I ain't finished with you. I want your stupid ass outside where I intend to kick it till you won't be able to use it for a week."

"Oh, Woody," Marge called, trying to elbow her way between Dad and the man. "He's drunk, Woody. Leave him alone. You know Coot. He don't know what he's sayin' half the time."

"*I* know what he said." Dad continued to shake him. "He said too damn much. Now stand *up, goddamn* it!"

Everybody was crushing in on them. The bartender eased Dad's fingers one by one from where they seemed imbedded in the man's flesh and supported the sagging creature toward a back door marked "Toilets".

Dad was surrounded by men who'd pushed Marge out of the way and were congratulating him, patting him on the back, offering him drinks. "Woody had that poor sucker scared shitless, didn't he?"

"I'm still goin' to whip his ass," Dad said, beaming at all the attention he was getting. "That is if he ever sobers up enough to stand up so's I can aim at him."

"Come on," another man yelled as the bartender returned to his position at the bar. "Let's put Casey to work. He ain't had to open a beer in fifteen minutes."

As they all moved to the bar, laughing and jostling each other, none seemed to remember that we were still standing there. Least of all, Dad. As Junior said later, "After all, it was us who started it all."

Marge wasn't the only woman there. There were two others I didn't know. Marge was a friend of Mom's from their school days and I liked her. She usually made a big fuss over me. I moved away from Junior's side and waved at her. She was moving toward the jukebox looking just as she had when Dad had left her in the middle of the dance floor. Stranded. Deserted. Left out. They all looked left out. The other two women and us too. We were all left out. Fighting and drinking were men's sport. Not for women and children. Marge didn't look at me. Junior was biting his lower lip and his eyes had that funny misty look. I knew he was going to take my hand in a second and drag me out of there but I wasn't about to leave. There was still laughter here. Marge put some money in the slot and the jukebox lit up like a Christmas tree and I recognized one of my favorite songs, "Turnip Greens," a lively tune that just made you want to dance. Especially Bob Wills' bouncy rendition.

This time I caught Marge's eye and she threw her hands up in the air and screamed, "It's Totsy!" as if I had just landed from the moon and was really somebody special.

Dad turned toward us grinning. "Are you two fightin', drinkin' and dancin' fellers still here? I'd'a thought you'd be so drunk by now that they'd had to carry you outta here like they done ole Coot Jenkins."

The laughter covered Junior's step forward and whispered, "Mom says that . . ."

"I know. I know what Mom says," Dad said loudly, waving his hand expansively. "Mom says supper's ready. Right?" He leaned down toward Junior from the tall bar stool and almost lost his balance. "But are *we* ready?"

"Fightin's over," Marge called as she bore down on me with open arms and hugged me. "Totsy don't drink, do you, honey?" She squatted down in front of me. "Why don't you show these folks what you really do?" She looked up at the men. "You see this chile? Well, you just see him dance. He can out-dance his old man." She stood up, weaving slightly and clutched my hand. "Although Woody would be the last in the world to admit that anybody could out-dance, out-fight or even out-fu—"

"Whoa!" somebody yelled from the bar. "Hold 'er, Newt. You mean out-drink him, don't you, Marge?"

"*He* heard what I said," she tossed her head and rolled her eyes at Dad who roared with laughter. "Come on, Totsy, show 'em what I mean." She led me to the center of the floor and let go my hand and was backing away, bent forward toward me clapping in time to the music, encouraging me with her smile and her body moving in a way to induce me to move with her.

I couldn't help myself. I mimicked her movements for a moment, moving toward her, my body starting to take over on its own. I glanced at Junior. Should I be doing this? He was grinning as broadly as Dad. OK, then. Nobody said no. As Marge screamed, "Let 'er rip!", I did just that. I'd done this at home and at Bonnie Lou's but here I was on a big empty floor with a lot of people watching me and I was grinning the same satisfied grin Dad had when he was getting all the attention. Having all the attention is heady stuff. It can spur you on. I don't know exactly what I did, but I jigged, twirled, tapped, strutted, threw in some Charleston steps I'd picked up and as the music got faster I only know that my body was moving with it. I could feel it. All through my body. I never felt so good in my life. I don't think I was even touching the floor. When the music stopped abruptly, it was like being slapped in the face.

I came out of my trance feeling sharp stings on my bare legs. It was money! The men were all throwing nickles, dimes and pennies toward me. The coins danced around me, tinkling their own music, and I danced crazily as I scooped them up, making another dance routine out of clearing the floor of the coins that seemed to keep on pouring in while the men whistled and stomped and clapped. I'd had my first taste of performing. And I was hooked. Firmly and forever. I even got paid for it. Even Junior was beaming and looking proud.

On the way home, with one of us on either side of Dad, not balancing him exactly, but holding a hand each, our high spirits ran through our hands and bodies like an electric current between each other. We skipped and hummed "Turnip Greens" with Dad lifting us both high in the air above the curbs when we came to them. We'd become a trio. Just us men. We'd shared an experience that didn't involve Mom.

I continued dancing right into the house, leading the way, rattling the coins in my cupped hands and singing, "Guess what I got. Guess how much I got." We all three were elated and talking at once as Mom leaned a hip against the kitchen table which was set for three. She crossed her arms over her comfortable bosom, nodding and smiling with eyebrows raised into question marks waiting for our explanations.

We gabbled on as we washed our hands at the enamel basin and scrambled into our chairs. Mom served us some cold fried chicken and salad. We all seemed to have a different approach to the events of the evening if not exactly different stories to tell. Junior was saying we'd have been home sooner if Totsy, the showoff, hadn't started acting cute and dancing all over the place. I put in that it was Marge who'd encouraged me but realized that her role in the evening's happenings should be minimized when I caught a particular look flash between Mom and Dad. OK. Registered. No Marge. Above all, no Marge and Dad dancing. That much I knew from somewhere deep down inside. Dad launched into a long account of how he got to discussing the possibility of working for something called the WPA with Ralph Humbard and just lost all track of time. That was Depression talk.

I turned to Junior to try and recapture some of the excitement and fun at the Domino. Our high spirits were sagging. "Hey, and how about when Dad picked that man right out of his chair and his head was banging . . ." They were all three staring at me. All stony and silent. Junior looked up at the ceiling—a signal for me to shut up. Dad pushed his chair back and stood up with a disgusted glance at me. OK. OK. No fights. I didn't realize. My mistake. Give me time, I'd learn the rules. Sorry. I didn't know yet how to doctor a story to fit circumstances and audience.

"And what was the fuss about?" Mom asked quietly. "Who started it?"

"Wasn't anything, Milly," Dad said dismissively. He was washing chicken grease off his hands with his back turned to us. "Just Coot

Jenkins drunk again and smart-assin' around. Shootin' his mouth off."

"What about?" Mom went on in the same even voice.

I sneaked a look at Junior whose eyes shot to the ceiling again. I scrunched down in my chair. How was Dad going to handle this? What was permissible? What was allowed in our newly formed male solidarity?

"I didn't even hear what he said." Dad's voice seemed to be coming from a long way off. "I just moved in to help Casey ease him out before he caused some real trouble. You know how he is." He turned back to Mom, smiling easily and drying his hands. So that's how we men handled it. We lied. If I was going to have to lie, I was at least learning how from a master.

Junior pushed his chair away from the table. "'Scuse me . . ."

"I'm done, too," I said, following Junior into the other room. "I want to count my money again." Not to mention wanting Junior to explain some things to me.

" . . . and Coot drunk as a coot," Dad was saying and I heard Mom's laughter join his as I sat on the floor of the living room and spilled out the coins.

"He's not batting a thousand," Junior mumbled. That was the first time he'd used that expression which was to become part of our private language.

"What? What does that mean?"

"I'll tell you when you get older."

Shit, I thought, even though I didn't dare say it. I wondered just what he thought of Dad's behavior but could tell he was upset so didn't push it.

That had been the first time for me at the Domino. Plenty others were to follow and I relished them all. Junior didn't. He started waiting outside while I told Dad supper was ready. He loathed everything about the cafe. The drunkenness, the sloppy good-ole-buddiness, the melting away of reticences and self-control. He was apparently born knowing how to behave properly and the Domino and its patrons offended him. I looked to him for guidance because I've always had a tendency to go all out on everything. No restraints bothered him. He had control. I tried—am trying—to learn from him because it is something I lack.

Those days of glory were too intoxicating. I was drunk on my new fame as that "dancin' wonder." There were certainly no restraints once I was turned loose on that dance floor. I'd go mad. But the decision to call a halt was not mine. It was Dad's. Depending on how he was feeling, he'd either finish his beer and wave to his buddies or more often yell, "Let's have another one, son!"

That of course was further music to my ears. Dad would sometimes join me. He has some jig steps he's passed on to me and when we both broke into the famous Woods back-shuffle together, we'd bring the house down. There he was, tall and lean facing a miniature replica of himself while I, his shrunken image, mirrored his movements and steps to a tee. We didn't take our eyes off each other—we spoke into each other's smiling eyes and it was only when we danced that I ever saw that particular shining light directed at me. Those Domino nights were soon over and that shining light in his eyes has since been focused solely on Junior.

Then it was over. Summer was gone and so was Dad. There was no reason to go to the Domino. I was no longer in the limelight. I was like a drunk without drink.

As usual, I didn't know where Dad had gone. He just disappeared as far as I knew. Mom made reference to his going to find work in the timber mills, the wheat harvest, the cotton harvest or wherever when anybody asked. She seemed to know where he was and maybe Junior did too, but I never took it in. If there were any letters, I never saw them.

There were other things to take our minds off Dad's absence. We moved from Galena to Crane for a start. Crane's about twenty miles north and close to a school Mom got that fall. She always "got" the school. She never referred to getting a job teaching at a school, she *got* the school. Sort of like getting a cold.

The school was called Cave Springs, a two-room country school with Mom teaching the first four grades. For the first time, we would all three be in school. Junior and I were enrolled in the Crane Grade School which had a room for each grade and was almost as big as the Galena Court House.

My first day in school was the embarrassing day when my teacher held up "Carlton" printed on a piece of paper and I didn't recognize my real name. I didn't think I'd ever live that down, but it wasn't as embarrassing as the little girl who was sitting in front of me who'd wet her pants because she was too shy to tell the teacher she wanted to make Number One. She may not have known the signals. I told the teacher for her since it was I who discovered it. It was running off her seat into my shoe. Maybe I shouldn't have told on her, but I was only trying to help. Everybody laughed at her which I didn't think was right, but it took everybody's mind off the fact that I obviously didn't even know my own name.

School was a revelation and I loved it. My teacher soon had me wrapped around her little finger. Along with her knitting wool. She knitted all the time. She knitted standing, sitting, walking, talking, teaching, correcting, disciplining, reading and somehow even when writing on the blackboard. Before my mesmerized eyes, garments grew from circular needles, from three or four small needles overlapping each other somehow, from biggish ones, from bigger ones that she held under her arms and occasionally from a crochet hook. She'd be wearing one day what she'd just started on the day before. It was magical. The tubular shapeless things seemed to have a life of their own, sliding onto her lap, creeping over the side of her thigh, writhing down to the floor like huge snakes uncoiling mysteriously from her flying fingers.

I *think* I was elected "Postmaster" at Valentines time but whether voted in or appointed or just plain grabbed, I was it. We all made valentines industriously for days. I'd designed and headed the construction of a miniature post office in the corner of the room. We'd rigged a pigeonhole cupboard out of cardboard boxes with the alphabet pasted on each one and I was in business.

I was so proud of my position as Postmaster that I wouldn't leave it even at recess time. Anyone could mail a valentine at any time. I'd cut out and colored stamps and everyone in class had cut out circles of paper of various sizes. That was our money. We all took the game deadly seriously. I more than anybody.

Toward the end of the week, just before Valentine's Day, I was standing at the counter during recess sorting out the last few posted cards when I felt something touch my leg. I jumped back and there crawling behind the counter on all fours was Mary Ann Spritely.

Before I could speak, she put her finger to her mouth, "Sssshhhh. It's a secret. I'm not really here. Don't tell anybody."

There was nobody to tell. Miss Dodge was on playground duty. "Are you hiding from somebody?"

"Yeah. Sort of." She was squatting now, sitting on her heels with her knees wide apart. "Look. I want to show you something." She tugged on the leg of my short pants. "Come down here," she whispered.

I saw nobody coming so I squatted down facing her in the same position she was in. Our heads were touching and she still held on to my pants but her fingers were up inside the leg now and wiggling around. She kept saying "Ssshhh" while her fingers groped around on the inside of my thigh tickling nicely and making me giggle. "Shush!" she hissed. "Look." With her other hand she'd pulled her panties aside to show me a pink slit, just like Bonnie Lou's only I'd never seen Bonnie Lou's open like this. "I've seen one before," I said, trying not to seem too interested.

"Put your finger in," she whispered, as her hand made firm contact with my toy causing me to catch my breath. "Shush."

"I think I hear somebody," I whispered back as I lifted my head over the counter. Billy Joe Carter bounded into the room. I stood up straight and blurted "Post office's closed."

"I don't care. Just want my coat." He disappeared into the cloakroom as the exploring hand took an even firmer grip on my toy and all surrounding parts. I gasped as I squatted down again.

"Come on," she urged. "Put your finger in. I'm playing with you, so you have to play with me." I did as I was told. Rather abruptly, causing her to gasp too. "Easy." She moved her buttocks in a circular motion and my finger slipped in deeper and deeper into a warm moist hole. She continued to move her buttocks and at the same time moved her hand deliciously on me. Our foreheads were touching as we both watched what our hands were doing. She made a funny little sound in her throat and we raised our heads at the same time, bringing our mouths so close I could smell and feel her breath. Suddenly she darted out her tongue and moved it across my lips. I felt as though my hair were standing on end. My toy most certainly was and now she was vigorously moving her buttocks, her hand and her tongue. All three things going with practiced coordination. It reminded me of the game Junior and I played of trying to rub our tummies with one hand while trying to pat the top of our head with the other. It made me giggle.

The bell rang for end of recess. I stood up automatically, breaking contact with her but her hand had somehow got tangled up with my underpants and I was in a slightly bent-over position looking over the counter as Miss Dodge walked through the door.

Caught!

Mary Ann stood up beside me. Both caught. What we were doing couldn't have been more fun and because it was, it stood to Baptist reason that it couldn't have been more wrong. What would Miss Dodge do?

"Here's my dime, Carlton," Mary Ann said with shining innocence. "It blew way over here in this corner." She held up a tiny paper disc. Her lying technique had a professional polish.

"Oh." I was dumb and dumbfounded. "Thanks."

"You're the most diligent postmaster I've ever seen, Carlton," Miss Dodge remarked. "Keeping up the true postal traditions—neither rain nor snow nor recess can keep the mails from flowing." What did "diligent" mean? Dare I ask Mom? Or would that give me away? "We'll deliver all the valentines before school is out today and then you'll be out of a job." She smiled down at her knitting and moved toward her desk.

Mary Ann smiled prettily and said, "I can't wait to see how many valentines I got."

She looked so sweet that I wondered if I'd dreamed what had just been happening. My initiation rites with Bonnie Lou had not included the refinements offered just now—so I couldn't have dreamed it. Or that there were more to come.

That was the beginning of an alliance that was to last through the second grade. Looking back, it could be called an erotic alliance but then I thought of it as an extension of first-grade "creative play."

When school was out, the problem of a job for Mom that summer was solved by her being taken on as a waitress at the nicest cafe—almost a restaurant—in Crane. Her hours would be erratic so off Junior and I went to stay with one of Mom's sisters, our Aunt Elsie, in a town not too far north of Crane.

Since neither of our cousins, Claudine (close to my age) or Helen (a bit older than Junior) gave the remotest indication that they were interested in "creative play," that aspect of my life was dropped for the duration. Not exactly forgotten, however, and since it had been my experience that it was the girl who made the advances, I kept an expectant, but unrewarded, eye open for overtures.

The lazy summer passed playing in the sprinkler on the lawn during the day and trying to scare the daylights out of each other in the evening telling ghost stories.

Mom came up almost every week on her day off and it was a wrench when she had to leave early to catch the train. "If we only had a car," she'd sigh, "all this would be so much easier."

"Let's buy one," I suggested.

"With what?" Junior understood realities.

"Well, we've been making some money helping Mrs. Linthicum in the yard next door." I corrected myself. "Well, Junior has." I'd done a bit of raking and promptly spent my earnings on a root-beer float. A current and everlasting passion.

"We'll get a Packard," Mom teased. "How much have you made?"

"Will eighty-three cents help much?" Mom and Junior laughed into each others' eyes. They had a special way of looking at each other sometimes—a deep secret understanding look—that excluded everybody else. Even me.

"Hey, maybe Dad will come roaring in in a brand new car." With that, I dealt the conversation a death blow. Mom cleared her throat and glanced at Aunt Elsie. The subject was quickly changed. Dad's name—at least as far as I knew—wasn't mentioned again that summer.

Except once and that was when Claudine confided that she'd heard Mom was trying to divorce Dad.

"Aunt Milly told Momma that she'd divorce him in a minute if she only knew where to find him," she said.

That meant several things, but mostly it confirmed my suspicion that Mom never did really know where he was and only pretended when anybody asked her.

Changing rooms at school was like moving to another town. The second grade was just across the wide hall from the first grade room but it was another world. A world ruled by Mrs. Webster, who proved from the first minute to be resolutely immune to my charms. She found me so resistible that there was nothing to do but work extra hard, which I did when not working on recruits for Mary Ann's storm cellar games.

I lacked Mary Ann's self-assurance and confidence in pooh-poohing those threatening recruits who'd leave our magic circle with an "I'm going to tell on you." She apparently hadn't been brought up with the Southern Baptists' conception of sin. Baptist sin is straightforward and pure. Quite simply, it's all-inclusive. Everything is a sin. I was, therefore, primed and ready for damnation and repentance when the Scandal—such as it was—finally broke. As luck—bad luck—would have it, it was Junior who brought it home to me. We met at the kitchen door, both flushed and breathless. He by running up the hill from baseball practice and I up the other side of our hill from Mary Ann's. This was the hour when he was undisputed boss—before Mom got home. Junior had not only made the baseball team, he *was* the team. He'd already led the Fourth Grade Furies to victory over the fifth and sixth grade teams mostly by employing his unique slide into stolen bases and into home plate. He practiced that slide constantly. It was at first alarming—then embarrassing—to see him run a few feet and fall on his side and slide into flower beds, bushes or trees, leaving devastation in his wake and his clothes a wreck. Women and girls were forever screaming with fake or real concern when he'd suddenly hit the ground. There was a rumor for awhile that he was epileptic, fortunately squelched when his baseball fame spread.

He didn't slide into the subject that had given him the angriest face I'd ever seen. He hit it right on the head. "It's written there," he said accusingly. "Right up there where everybody can see it when they come home from school."

"What are you talking about?" I asked innocently.

"You must have seen it. It's chalked up there in letters two feet high on the culvert facing."

"Well, I didn't see it. I don't understand every word I read."

"First you say you didn't see it and then you say you don't understand everything you read. You must have seen it. You had to walk right past it."

"They didn't even know how to spell 'Totsy.' They put an 'e' in it."

"So you did see it!" Trapped. "Why did you say you didn't?"

"I meant I saw it, but I didn't understand it." I shrugged. "It isn't in my reading vo-va-cabolary."

"Cab-*u*-lary." He grinned. "Since you claim to have read every book printed in the English language on the second, third, and fourth-grade levels, how can you not know 'fuck' when you see it?"

"It's not in any of the books I've read."

The grin filled into a smile and he shook his head. "You have heard the word?"

"Yes."

"You've seen it printed?"

"Yes. But I always look away. It's dirty."

"You turned away when you saw it printed today?"

"Yes. Pretty fast."

"But you got the meaning?"

I hesitated. "Not quite."

"It's fairly straightforward and to the point."

"It wasn't very long. No."

"Just 'Totsey'—with an 'e'—'fucks M.A.' Right?"

"Uh-huh." My nickname stuck with me everywhere but in the classroom.

"What don't you understand?"

"Well . . ." This really was going to be an embarrassing admission. "I don't honest and truly know what it means."

"What?"

"Fuck." That was the first time I'd ever spoken the word. I'd heard it, seen it on walls, giggled about it, knew that dogs sometimes got stuck doing it, acted knowingly when it was mentioned, but the truth of the matter was I really didn't know what it was. "I sort of know. I *think* I know, but I'm not sure."

"Oh, for heavens sakes. You do too know. You've seen animals at Grandpa's and Aunt Amy's and well, *everywhere,* do it. What do you mean you don't know for sure?"

"We're not cows or horses. They don't wear any clothes."

"What's clothes got to do with it?"

"Well, you can see what the animals have . . . you know, all the things they do it with. They're all there, just hanging around. That's just nature."

"The point is, *do* you?"

"Do I what?"

"Fuck Mary Ann?" He was raising his voice.

"I don't think so."

"Don't think so!" He resorted to his talking-to-an-idiot voice. "Just tell me what it is you do. You're down there at her house all the time. They say she has a playhouse in the storm cellar. Are you still playing with dolls?"

I had. Not too long ago. "I am eight years old. What a thing to say."

"If you aren't fu—If you aren't doing what was written on the culvert, what *are* you doing?"

"I don't know."

"Then why would anybody write such a thing up there?"

"Jealous?" I was pretty sure it has been Darryl Wilson. One of my major errors in recruiting. His toy had had some skin cut off and consequently wouldn't stand up. Mary Ann had tried everything she could think of and so had I but he was a total failure and Mary Ann might have been just a bit rude about his limitations although I felt sorry for his poor scarred toy.

"OK. Somebody is jealous. They are jealous enough to write that dirty thing up on the wall. What do you do with Mary Ann that would make them write such a thing?"

"We just play." Explaining was difficult. I almost blurted out the suggestion that he come and join us and see for himself. Then I realized that if ever I was going to make the error of my life in recruiting, that would be it. If he saw us all stark naked, writhing all over each other, giggling and tickling and prodding and poking with every appendage into any and all apertures and crevices, he might have been amazed or perhaps even amused, but mostly I think he'd have been appalled. Particularly when we'd got a mixed bag of three or more romping bodies going at once. "It's sort of . . . Well, it's like playing puzzles." That was as close as I could get.

"Playing puzzles? How do you mean?"

"You know. Jigsaw puzzles." He looked stunned. "You know, putting the pieces together. Fitting all the pieces in their places . . ."

"And what do you wear when you play puzzles?" A light was dawning in his eyes. He was beginning to understand. Finally. Now I could really explain.

"Nothing! We don't exactly choose up sides or anything like that, but it's sort of a game like any sport with winners and losers. The winner is the one that can think up the most complicated puzzle and how it fits together. You see?"

"And you yourselves are the pieces. Is that right?"

"Yeah!" He was getting the picture. "And depending on how many we are, it can get very interesting and exciting. Sort of like a wrestling match."

"How many are you?"

"Mostly just Mary Ann and me . . ."

"I."

"I. And . . . well, you know, if somebody comes along and wants to play . . ."

"Play!"

"Yeah. Sometimes three or four. And you know I think it was Darryl Wilson who wrote that up there. His toy was cut when he was a baby and it won't stand up, so it wouldn't fit into . . ."

"It's true." He shook his head and turned away. "I can't believe it. Don't you understand anything?"

I was getting a gnawing feeling of fear in my stomach—that sort of fear you get when you know you're about to be caught in a lie. But I hadn't lied. I'd told the truth. Up to a point. But there was something beginning to emerge from this interrogation—images were floating around in my mind of our swarming bodies on the doll blankets mingled with animals humped on top of each other and the preacher's voice screaming about sin and pointing a finger at me. My stomach churned and my knees felt weak. I slumped in a chair as Junior turned back to face me.

"That was what you were doing. Don't you know that?"

"What? What was I doing?"

"Fucking Mary Ann, like the writing said, you dummy."

"*Was* I?" I was stunned.

"And didn't even know it!" He looked at me slumped in the chair and started to grin. "Games! Puzzles, he calls it." He threw back his head and roared with laughter. Was it going to be all right? Was it just a joke? Had I committed a terrible sin or not? "When did you start this . . . these *games?*"

"First grade. Valentine's Day."

"That's appropriate." He laughed again. "You're eight now. You've been doing this since the first grade. I think I'd better ask *you* what it's all about. I'm going to be ten and I haven't even seen a naked girl."

"No!" I was incredulous. I was totally familiar with the female body. I had done things that Junior hadn't done. "Then how do you know that that was what we were doing? Fu . . . What Darryl wrote up there?"

"Because that's what it is. I know that much."

I had to broach the real problem. "Is it . . . is it a sin?"

He wasn't laughing any more. "Yes."

"Oh." Fire and brimstone were going to engulf me. I was a goner.

"Don't look so pitiful," he said as he pushed me gently upright in the chair. "You didn't know what you were doing. But now you do. So you just have to stop doing it. Just pray for forgiveness and promise that you won't do it any more. Not till you're married. Then it's OK."

"You won't tell on me?"

"Who? Tell Mom? Don't be silly. Just pray that the rain washes off that writing before the next P.T.A. meeting. It wouldn't be very funny if she read it."

That was a terrifying thought. "I'll rub it out," I suggested.

"You could try, I guess." He moved over to the counter where the washbasin was and began washing his hands and face. I sat feeling empty and bone tired as though I'd been up after midnight like on New Year's Eve, and no longer had any control over my limbs. Somehow I'd escaped damnation. Junior had seen to that. I'd learned that what we'd been doing was sinful. That really didn't come as too great a surprise, the suspicion was growing all the time that something was wrong. It was a relief to know for sure. I'd just have to put it out of mind and weather Mary Ann's scorn. I could hear her making fun of me as she had the others who'd left the magic circle. That would be part of my punishment for my sin. I could take it. School would be out for the summer in less than a month anyway.

"Hey, Tots," Junior said through the towel he was rubbing his face with. "What was it like?" He turned around and faced me, still wiping the lower part of his face. "Fun?" His eyes twinkled.

I just grinned and nodded slowly.

Chapter Three

Mom was hired again at the cafe and since she seemed to have run out of sisters—at least in the immediate vicinity—Junior and I were sent to Grandpa Woods' farm for the summer. The farm was the Woods' homestead place in Hi, Arkansas. It could be spelled "High," I'm not sure. There had been a sign on the one-room schoolhouse that doubled as a church but it had faded down to the bare wood. What the population was is a mystery. There were several farmhouses but not one close enough to see the other. Grandpa and Grandma Idy did have a telephone but it rang so rarely that I didn't see much use in it. Mom said it was faster to write than go through the half a dozen operators it took to get the two-longs-and-a-short that was Grandpa's ring. There was no town center. All shopping was done in Oak Grove, Arkansas, some ten miles away. There was a sign on the road there: Oak Grove, Arkansas. Population 30.

Junior and I loved being there, at least for awhile before the loneliness set in. We could sort of understand why Dad had left home at an early age. But it was difficult for us to understand why he was still gone from us. He'd been out of our lives now for almost two years. Grandpa didn't talk about Dad much. They'd had some sort of falling out many years ago. Dad's version of the story was that Grandpa had a violent temper and had once lost it so completely that he lost his most valuable cow along with it. She'd kicked over the milk bucket one time too many and Grandpa picked up an ax handle, hit her between the eyes

47

and she fell dead on the spot. He regretted it, but claimed she deserved it. Therefore, when Dad was in his teens and Grandpa threatened him with a beating for some infraction of the rigid rules, Dad just took off. He's been wandering around ever since.

Grandma Idy spoiled us rotten. She'd never had children of her own, so her stepchildren's children became hers. Particularly Junior and me. She baked cookies and cakes and pies for us every day. Made fudge with peanuts that they'd grown right there on the farm. There was a big bin of them in the smokehouse along with sides of bacon and ham. There was flour they'd ground from their own corn and other grains all in bins with wooden tops that lifted up on leather hinges. It was like going into a country store. The storm cellar was the same—shelves lined with dozens of jars of hand-canned fruit, jams and jellies, relishes, pickles, and sauces. There were crocks of sauerkraut, cheeses hanging in dusty cloth, even meatballs and slices of pork loin were canned in their own juices and fat, all beautifully displayed and enough to feed an army.

In season, in the springhouse, which had a cement trough into which hand-tingling cold water was constantly gushing, there'd be watermelons, muskmelons, or other fruit chilling in the water, along with freshly churned butter and jars of buttermilk and sweet milk and cream so thick you'd mistake it for butter.

They didn't need stores. They made everything themselves. Grandpa and his father had built the log house back in the 1800's. There was a huge stone fireplace in the main room, which was combination sitting room and bedroom. There was a smaller bedroom off the kitchen where Junior and I shared a bed with great thick featherbeds covered in colorful patchwork quilts that Grandma had made herself. We always ate in the kitchen at a big long table. Grandma always served, never sitting down with us. I could never figure out when she ate.

Mom marveled at Grandma's neatness. She wore pretty cotton dresses with long sleeves with lace cuffs and collars winter and summer and no matter how hard she worked or how dirty the job, she always looked clean and tidy. She could wash dishes, clean the stove, polish it with stove black, and never have to roll up her sleeves. Mom said it was a miracle. Mom adored her but explained to us that Dad still held some resentments because she'd replaced his mother. How anybody could resent Grandma for anything was beyond me. I thought she was a saint. Grandpa said Dad was just plain bullheaded. There was certainly no argument about that. The way

Grandpa said it made me wonder if he was all that fond of his younger son.

The long hot summer creeped by. The creek that was one of the boundaries of the property was down to a trickle. Wading and craw-dad fishing had lost their appeal. There was one deepish hole where we could splash around and cool off, but not actually swim. Which was just as well since neither of us could. It was waist deep on Junior and chest deep on me and when we'd go there in the late afternoon, I'd kick off my short pants and underwear—we both went bare-footed—and jump in naked with only Grandma's poke-bonnet on that I'd taken a fancy to and wore almost everywhere.

Junior laughed and said I looked pretty silly stark naked in a poke-bonnet. He was never stark naked. Not if there was the slightest pos-sibility of anybody seeing him. And this miniature swimming hole was sometimes used by the Wilkins boy who lived on the next farm. He was a year or so older than Junior and was dismissed by most peo-ple as being "just about half-silly."

Junior always wore his underwear at the swimming hole and was sitting in them on a big boulder drying off one day when the Wilkins boy appeared.

"Howdy," he said. He was wearing bib-overalls and apparently nothing else because he was out of them in a flash and cannon-balled naked into the pool practically on top of me.

Junior was on his feet. "Watch what you're doing!" he yelled an-grily. "You almost landed on Totsy."

"That's who's under that poke-bonnet?" I scrambled out of his way and started climbing out of the water. "Why I thought that was a pretty little girl." I was standing next to Junior on the rock now, shak-ing out the wet bonnet. "Well, might as well be a little girl for all the pecker he's got. Look at that little thing. Not bigger'n a crawdad."

I glanced down and quickly sat down to hide myself. It didn't look very big. I could think of nothing to say but, "Well, I'm just eight." Ordinarily I'd have said "almost nine."

The Wilkins boy rolled over on his back and let his hips lift in the water until his thing was visible and I saw that there was hair around it. He took it in his hand and waved it at us. "Now, there's a pecker. Just looky here." As he flipped it back and forth it grew bigger. It was the biggest one I'd ever seen. "Hey, Junior. You got hair yet?" Junior was looking up, squinting into the sun, elaborately ignoring the boy who was stroking himself and his thing was getting alarmingly big. He watched himself with a little grin of pride. "Now what about *that?*

That's a real humdinger, ain't it?" I couldn't take my eyes off it. Under Mary Ann's expert tutelage, my fascination with the human body in all its permutations knew no bounds. It certainly was a humdinger and I was aware of a humming in my groin and I felt my own getting hard. Now why in the world was that? And nobody even touching it.

Junior stood up and turned his back and said, "I'm going to find some skimmers." He turned to me. "You better get dressed."

"Hey, Junior, looky here," the Wilkins boy called. "Watch." His hand was traveling back and forth on himself purposefully. "Where you goin', Junior? Hey! Watch!" He was pounding his pecker violently. "Hey! I'm goin' to shoot! Ya' wanna' see it? I'll bet you can't shoot. Hey, *look!*" I was looking. Intently. If it was size that made a pecker, then he had a real pecker.

Junior jumped down on the other side of the boulder calling, "Come on, Tots, we have to get the cows in."

I was riveted to the spot. I couldn't have moved if I had wanted to. The Wilkins boy had an audience of one whose enthralled attention made up for Junior's lack of interest. He smiled up at me as he stood up, thrusting his hips forward, making his pecker look even bigger and stroked it faster and faster until all his muscles tensed and he gave a little grunt as something shot out of his thing. He did shoot. Whatever it was landed on the water and floated on the surface, a white substance like spit.

"There! You ever seen that afore?" I shook my dazed head at him as he rinsed his pecker off in the water. "I'll bet you didn't know that that's where you come from."

"Oh, yes, I do," I said indignantly, misunderstanding. "I come from Missouri. Galena and . . ."

He fell over backwards into the water, howling with laughter. He brought his head up out of the water sending great sprays in every direction with his hair and spurting out mouthfuls with his guffaws. He was choking and laughing and trying to speak at the same time. "Don't know nothin'," he hollered, splashing water as he slapped his hands down on the surface of the water, and jumped up and down. "Dumber'n a mule, I'll swear I never seen nothin' like it." He cackled and splashed. "Don't even know he comes from white stuff off'n his daddy's pecker." His laughter was drowned as he fell back in the water again.

I'd fumbled into my underpants and shorts during this last exhibition. I picked up the bonnet and turned to see Junior on the side of the creek, motioning for me to come on. I glanced over my shoulder and called out, "Bye" as I jumped off the rock. I ran as fast as I could toward Junior. I heard the Wilkins boy calling something like, ". . . dumb little peckerwood . . ." as we both lit out across the field as fast as we could.

We didn't speak until we'd crawled through two different sets of barbed-wire fencing and had swung out and around behind the grazing cows in the pasture.

"Did you see?" I asked.

"See what?"

"What he was doin'." The poke-bonnet acted like blinders on a horse. I had to turn my head all the way around to see Junior's face and then all I got was a non-commital profile.

"Sure. He was playing with himself." He sounded disgusted.

"Is that wrong?" Maybe it was all right if somebody did it for you.

"What do you think?" I could feel him looking at me through the side of the bonnet. I didn't turn my head.

I took the easy way out. I shrugged. "I don't know."

We walked along in silence. The cows had spotted us and had begun to move slowly toward the farm buildings that looked awfully small this far away.

"Can you?" I ventured.

"Can I what?" He'd raised his voice and I knew he was looking at me again. "Take that stupid thing off your head, for pete's sake. How'm I supposed to know what you're talking about if I can't see you. Besides, it *is* sissy. It's a *bonnet.*"

"I know what it is. I can even make one." I'd got him riled. Or at least something had got him riled. If I wasn't careful, he wouldn't answer any of my questions. After a few more paces, I tried again, very quietly. "Well, *can* you?"

"What?" He stopped. "Make a bonnet?" He let out a whoop of laughter.

I ripped off the hat and turned back to him. Good, we could make a joke of the whole thing. "No, silly. What he said you couldn't do. You know." I mimicked the Wilkins boy's motions exaggeratedly and I hoped, comically, "Like he did. Shoot."

He shrugged and moved forward beside me. "I wasn't watching." He didn't sound reproachful. He kept moving but he started laughing. "Is that what he did?" He hooted. "If that's the way he looked, like you, just now, it must've been pretty funny."

I hurried to catch up with him. "Yep. That's what he did." I caught him by the arm and turned him around to face me and did my imitation again, making a moronic face. He was really laughing now. "And then it happened. All of a sudden this white stuff shot right out of his pecker. *Ker-plop*. Right in the water."

"We'd better not go swim there any more." He was laughing but made a face of distaste.

His distaste at the mention of the white stuff was bringing up more questions. I didn't know where to begin. I'd never been so confused. I tried again. "Well. Can you? Can you do it? He said he bet you couldn't."

"I don't know," he shrugged and picked up a rock and threw it toward the last lagging cow. "I never tried."

"You mean played with yourself?" He shot me a quick frowny glance. "Well, that's what you said he was doing."

"It's called jacking-off." He stumbled a bit on the expression and then muttered, "I think that must be it. What he was doing."

He seemed out of his depth, too. I guessed that he couldn't do it and was ashamed to admit it. "Well, I guess you have to have hair to do it."

"Maybe." He didn't look at me.

We were silent once more, plodding along, stepping automatically over the cow patties. I hadn't got very far. Only learned a new expression that I couldn't wait to spring on Mary Ann. She thought she knew everything.

"But he wasn't right about that other thing he said, was he?"

"What's that?"

'just when we were leaving. Something about us coming from that white stuff off our Daddy's pecker." I was having my own trouble saying that. I felt that I was on a dangerous path to knowledge that I wasn't sure I was ready for. When Junior remained silent, I found myself almost pleading. "That's just a lie, isn't it? He was just being dirty. Wasn't he, Junior? That's not how it is, is it?" It *was* dirty. The way the boy'd looked and smiled at me was dirty. "God plants the seed, doesn't He? He plants the seed in our mothers' bellies and we grow. Don't we? We're *God's* children, aren't we?"

Junior stopped and put his arm around my shoulder, hugging me to him. "Well, I'm not exactly sure how it works myself." He squeezed me and chuckled at the admission. "Anyway, he's an asshole." I jerked my head up and looked at him in amazement. He'd never said anything like that before to me. He laughed at my astonishment. "Well, he is. He may be right, but he makes it all sound wrong." He waved both arms at a cow that had headed back to the pasture. "We'll be God's children until I find out otherwise."

"You'll tell me the minute you know for sure?"

"I'll send you a telegram." We both laughed. "Until then," he nodded at me and I joined him as we recited together, "God plants the seed in our mothers' . . ."

That was our private joke. When there was any reference to sex or procreation that we didn't quite understand, we'd look at each other and mouth, "God plants the seed . . ." and nod knowingly.

The summer spiraled down to a close punctuated by Mom's infrequent visits and the occasional late-night electric storm. The storms were a delight to the eye but brought a chill of fright right down to the soles of my feet. One particularly terrifying slash of lightning hit a tree not far from the house and the jolt shook the house like an earthquake. Grandpa loved the storms and was as enthralled with them as a child with fireworks. I couldn't help wondering what the storm cellar was for if we didn't use it.

Mom's visits were not only infrequent, but the last couple turned out to be downright disasters. She'd brought a man with her. A used-car salesman called Lloyd Shults who was obviously trying to sell Mom more than a car. He apparently wanted to be included along with the extras like the spare tire, the jack, the crank and an extra fan belt. Junior liked the car but not him. We both decided that he deserved the epithet of "asshole" for several reasons. One, because he kept calling me "Topsy" even after I'd spelled my name for him. But mostly we resented the proprietary air he had with Mom. He kept touching her all the time in a way that not even Dad did. Well, not in front of us anyway. Granted Dad wasn't around and had never been much of what you'd call a real father, but the idea of Shults replacing him—the idea of the divorce made it seem highly likely—kept me and Junior awake several nights discussing the possibility. We decided that having an asshole for a father was worse than having an absent one.

We needn't have worried. All Mom did was buy the car. The very Model-A that's become almost a home now. She'd be a hundred and ten, she maintained, by the time it was paid off even with the special easy terms Shults had made for her, but she needed it because we were moving back to Galena and she'd have to drive herself to the one-room school at Wilson Run. She'd "got" another school.

Back to Galena! I was thrilled. No more withering looks and sarcastic comments from Mary Ann. When I bowed out of the magic circle, she'd actually suggested that I was worn out anyway and ready for replacement. I could do without that sort of emasculation.

We kissed Grandma and Grandpa goodbye with promises to come for Christmas. We were mobile now, our lives would change. We headed for home the back way past Uncle Jess and Aunt Dell's place to show off the car but disaster had struck there. Aunt Dell had just up and walked out with Mavis and Sister leaving an hysterical Uncle Jesse and a note which read: "Jesse . . . We gone. You ain't got guts enough to find us so see you in court. In meantime you can kiss my ass." That seemed to be that. We realized that part of Uncle Jesse's hysteria was due to the fact he'd lost his three field hands with a corn crop ready for harvest.

Moving back to Galena was moving back home. Scott and Bessie Moore who were old friends of Mom's were our new landlords. They had converted their upstairs into an apartment—kitchen and two big rooms. Everything fitted us to a tee. Even the long trip down the stairs, out the front door, around the front of the bay-windowed dining room, back along the side of the house to the walkway that led to the outhouse didn't seem too much of an inconvenience. At least at first. When winter brought snow and rain it was a trek to be put off as long as possible.

During vacation, just before we went down to Grandpa Woods for Christmas, a card came from Aunt Dell. It was a penny postcard stamped from Phoenix, Arizona.

"Well," Mom said. "At least one of the Woods heard from." She handed the card to Junior. "Here. Read it to us."

"Dear Milly and boys," he read. "Made it this far and just set down. I got work and girls will get. Merry Christmas. Love from the three purtiest—that's the way she spells it, p-u-r-t—purtiest hitch-hickers you ever seen."

"I can just hear her," I said. "She writes just like she talks."

"Hitch-hikers?" Junior looked at Mom with a slight frown. "Do you think they really hitch-hiked?"

"You know your Aunt Dell. When she says she's going to do something, she does it." She shook her head. "I'm sure she did. Wouldn't put it past her. An awful lot of people are heading west. I lost two more children at Wilson Run just before vacation. The Reese children. Mr. Reese came by the school and told me he had to pull out. Couldn't make the farm pay. Jobs not available . . . "

Her face was getting the sad look that was companion to any mention of the Depression. "Hadn't we better hurry?" I interrupted trying to avoid that dread word and the mood it induced.

By the time we got over the James River, bearing to the right on the southbound finger of the "Y" bridge under the huge cliff, it had started to snow. I bounced up and down in the backseat and started singing "Jingle Bells." Mom and Junior joined in and we drove along with the snaking river on our right, its banks cushiony white clouds down to the black water's edge. The leafless trees were having their straggly twisted and broken shapes softened by layers of snow, like cotton bandages. The gray cliffs on the left had turned black and glistened with a wet sheen. Everything was black or white. There was no color anywhere.

Mom never drove very fast but now that there was some chance of ice, it was a very cautiously driven Ford that rounded a sharp bend just outside Blue Eye, Missouri, a tiny town right on the Missouri-Arkansas border. Stopped in front of our slowly moving car was a larger, later-vintage Ford. Just stopped, not parked. Dead in the middle of the road. No attempt had been made to pull over to the side, it had just stopped as though the driver had something better to do than make room for another vehicle. Since there was practically no traffic it was a reasonably safe thing to do.

Mom made the usual and often fatal mistake of braking instead of gearing down and we slid dangerously near the stopped car so that I could see what the driver had stopped for. He was lifting a bottle to his mouth and drinking thirstily until the girl in the seat beside him gave a wild yelp of surprise at our sudden appearance alongside them. Junior's face at his window was staring directly at them, not a foot away. The driver coughed and spilled some amber liquid down the front of his coat. We were oozing by so slowly, it was like slow motion in the movies. I could see a couple in the backseat fly apart from an embrace at the sound of the girl's yelp as though a bomb had gone off between them. The woman in the backseat had bright red hair, so fuzzy and abundant that it obliterated part of her partner's face.

"Hey, wasn't that . . ." Junior swung around in his seat to stare into the backseat of the flashy car.

We came to a full stop just about three feet in front of the other car. Mom was out of the Model-A before I knew what was happening. "Keep the motor running," she ordered Junior in a tight voice as she flew past my window and had the back door of the other car open before I could switch myself around on my knees to look out the rear window.

"What's going on?" Junior screamed from the front seat, struggling with the hand brake and fidgeting around to reach the accelerator with his foot.

"I don't *know*," I screamed back. But I could see Mom's backside perfectly clearly. It was sticking out the back door of the neighboring car, with her upper body inside, one foot on the running board. Her backside was bouncing around in a strange dance, knees bending and straightening up until her foot slipped out from under her on the icy ground. She fell, banging her knee on the running board and at the same time hauling the woman with the red hair out of the car practically on top of her. "She's pulling that woman by the hair," I yelled. And she was. She was hanging on as though she had a huge fish on a line and wasn't about to let it go. The woman was screaming bloody murder, and the man in the backseat pulled the woman back into the car, causing Mom to lose her grip on that great tangle of fuzz. "Now she's slapping at the woman," I reported with the excitement of a sport's announcer on radio. "Wow! She's really working her over!"

With his foot on the accelerator, Junior was stretched out almost flat on the driver's seat, but had his window rolled down and his head out it. "It *is* Dad!" he said with disbelief. "Who's that woman with him that Mom's hitting?"

It was getting more and more like a movie, only now it wasn't slow motion. Mom was back on her feet in a good solid stance and her elbows were pumping as though she were working out on a punching bag. She pulled one arm way back and swung with all her might and we heard a resounding slap as the woman let out a particularly violent scream. The woman in the front seat was on her knees facing the backseat, pushing and tugging at Mom. We could see Mom say something through clenched teeth as she slammed the door with all her strength, almost causing her to lose her footing, and ran back to our car and was in place and had the car in motion in one fluid movement. Junior was the perfect copilot, easing off the hand brake just as Mom let out the clutch and we pulled forward, picking up speed quickly as Mom shifted smoothly from low, to second, to high.

"Finally another Woods heard from." She wasn't even panting. She didn't seem to have any reaction to her brief but violent exertions. It was a fairly short scene, but it seemed to go on forever while it lasted. Now she sat as straight as ever. Her hands on the wheel firm, not tight. Had it really happened? Had we actually seen Mom behaving like that? Creating a real catfight, screaming, scratching and pulling hair? It couldn't have happened, I thought. Mom wouldn't lower herself. But I had to believe my eyes and I had only to glance up at the rear-view mirror to see Mom's triumphant look to know that it *had* happened. Her eyes were sparkling, her cheeks rosy, and a funny little smile was trying to break through her iron control. She looked young and bright and healthy as if she'd just had a bracing run in the snow.

"Maybe it's the cold that's forcing them out of the woods," Junior said looking straight ahead. "The Woods are coming out of the woods."

Mom glanced at him, he turned toward her and they burst out laughing. I joined in, a bit nervously not knowing how much of a joke we could make of this. When *we* got into fights, we were scolded. No matter how much we'd insist that it had been the other person's fault. Mom would always say, "You must have done *something*. Nobody fights for nothing." She'd sure done something. She'd just knocked a woman around and looked positively pleased with herself.

"You know that I'm not particularly proud of what happened back there," Mom said, trying to keep a note of triumph out of her voice. "I saw it was your father in there even before we passed the car. I know the back of his head pretty well." She let out a little laugh. "I've seen it going out the door often enough." I started to laugh, but a look from Junior nipped that in the bud. Mom looked back at me in the mirror quickly. "I meant that to be funny. Sort of. But we all know that it isn't very funny. Well, it hasn't been." She concentrated on the road for a few minutes. "I don't know what came over me. I've never had a feeling like it before. That red hair seemed to turn me blind with rage." She paused. "Like I've read they do at bullfights. They wave something red to get the bull stirred up. Well, something stirred me up and I had to get my hands on that head of hair."

"You just saw red," Junior said reasonably.

"Literally," Mom agreed. "And this is the last time I want this mentioned. Is that understood?" She sounded her stern schoolteacher self.

We two just nodded, both knowing that this was serious and Mom was talking to us as adults. About intimate things that she'd never touched on before and I'm sure neither of us would have done anything to stop her even if we noticed that the car was sliding into a ditch. She went on at length about the necessity for secrecy of this embarrassing encounter. Above all, we were not to mention anything to Grandpa and Grandma. They'd be very hurt if they knew Dad was back and hadn't contacted them.

"The idea that he'd be this close . . . At this time of the year when families are . . ." Mom shrugged and seemed to drift off into thoughts of her own. So did I. And for this time of the year, my thoughts weren't very Christian. This was the most blatant expression of Dad's disregard for his family to date. He was *here*. Right here between Galena and Hi. Down here in this unchartered no-man's land vaguely called The South End of the County where he'd met, married and left Mom with two babies. Here he was with a red-headed floozy. Right in our own backyard, as it were. It was apparent that he didn't give a—well, in his own words—a fuck what happened to us. He really made the Wilkins boy's description of a father's basic role ring with sad truth: We were nothing but the white stuff off his pecker. If whatever he did to create me and Junior he could do with red-headed floozies wherever he found them seemed to diminish our very existence. OK. If he couldn't recognize us, why should we recognize him? It could have been anybody's pecker. Only it wasn't. I look too much like him. No, I'm his. I just wish he'd look after his own a little more carefully.

After Mom had been silent for a while, I asked, "Did you know who . . ."

"Never saw her before in my life. None of them. I have an idea that they all have an inkling who *I* am by now. I just hope I never see any of them again."

"You mean Dad?" I was lining up a lot of questions to put to Junior. Like: Why didn't Mom strike out at Dad? Why only the woman? It seemed it ought to be Dad she was mad at. Unless, of course, they really were divorced and they no longer had any hold on each other. I kept wondering if Junior knew more about it than I did.

"Dad? Oh, good Lord, no." She paused and I saw her eyes in the mirror narrow with concentration. "At least I don't think I meant him. I just wish he'd make up his mind what he's going to do. And with whom. He's been away more than he's been with us since you were both babies. Oh, I have to admit that in the beginning, there was a reason. He was looking for work. And he *did* work. And he even sent a little money home. Well, once or twice. But . . . How can I say it so you'll understand? It's just that . . . Well, *hell*—as Dell would say— I love him. He's your father. And nothing would please me more than for him to act like it."

"At least we know he's in the neighborhood. Even if he disappears back into the woods, the woods are near ones," Junior said softly.

"I was just thinking that," Mom said.

It was a Christmas like others we'd spent on the farm, with the same magic ingredients, only we didn't know it would be the last in that most perfect setting (Mom always referred to it as "story-book"). Grandpa had the tree cut—the tallest we'd ever had—and ready for us to decorate. There was a box of decorations, rather skimpy now, the silver icicles wadded into lumps and broken into small pieces that were difficult to drape over the thick furry branches. Most of the store-bought ornaments had been smashed over the years by us or other grandchildren but we improvised with bits of cotton sprinkled about like snow, colored paper cut into all sorts of shapes, cardboard stars covered with tin foil saved from cigarette packs, and paper chains made quickly and messily with flour and water paste. We made long ropes of popcorn threaded on string and big popcorn balls made by sticking the popcorn together with warm molasses that was being heated up for us to pull into taffy. Pulling taffy was Junior's favorite sport—next to base-ball—and his taffy was the smoothest and silkiest. The final touches on the tree were the miniature hand-dipped candles that Grandma Idy made by melting down the paraffin she used to seal her jam and jelly jars. She always kept everything—there'd eventually be a use for it.

The smells from the kitchen were almost unbearable. On Christmas Eve all the sweet things, the mince pies, the cakes and cookies, would be baking, the smells meeting and battling with the fresh popcorn from the fireplace in the living room. Christmas Day with the turkey stuffed and baking along with a country ham that had been cured in the smokehouse and surrounded by sweet potatoes with marshmallows that we'd bought from Scott Moore's store, I would finally have to be pushed out the door by Junior to race madly around the house in the fresh snow, trying to clear our heads of the maddening odors.

Running reminded me of another Christmas here, all the smells and the snow and the tree much the same, only Dad had been with us. It wasn't as gay as we wanted this one to be. Something had gone wrong between Mom and Dad. Even way back then. I don't know quite what. I did know that Dad had been drinking quite a bit and on Christmas Eve, we could hear Mom trying to shush Dad's angry voice after we'd gone to bed on our pallet on the kitchen floor next to the still-warm range. He was still roaring when I went to sleep and it was his voice that woke me the next morning.

We could feel his unfocused anger when Junior and I went in by the fireplace to dress. Grandma and Grandpa were out doing chores that not even Christmas morning would allow them to put off. We were scuffling around, Junior trying to tickle me which made me squeal—my ticklishness is a family joke and I could become hysterical if someone looked as though they were even thinking about touching my ribs. I had taken off my pajamas and was giggling and stumbling getting into my underpants. Junior was that one step ahead of me, he had his underwear on, but nothing else.

All of a sudden Dad exploded. "You both are turnin' into a couple of sissies. Gigglin' and ticklin'. Ought to be toughened up. And it ain't too soon nor too late. Now git! Both of you. Outside. Right now! Just like you are."

"We don't have our clothes on, Dad," I whined.

"I can see," he bellowed. "I'm not blind. I said like you are. And I mean it. Barefooted and bare-assed. Git out there and run three times around the house. You hear me? I said *now.* Three times and I'll be countin' from the porch."

"Woody!" Mom stuck her head around the kitchen door. "There's a foot of snow out there. They'll catch their death . . ."

"You keep out of this, Milly," Dad's voice was steel. "When I tell my kids to do something, I mean it." He turned a furious flushed face to us. "Now *git.* "

Junior grabbed my hand and pulled me toward the door. "Hey, that'll be fun. Come on, Tots, a race in the snow!"

"But I'm *naked* . . ."

"Make you run faster. Come *on.* "His eyes were imploring me, begging me to go. Dad's explosion had said something special to him. He seemed to know that if we did as ordered—even something as silly as running barefooted around the house—the tension building up between Mom and Dad might be relaxed.

We went. The minute my feet hit the snow, I was away. I've never run so fast in my life. Each step was so painful that the only thing to do was keep the feet off the ground by keeping them flying. The first lap around the house was such a shock that I don't remember it. It was the third one, with the snow feeling like hot coals and the cold air that didn't seem to want to go into my lungs, that I thought I'd never make. Junior was a few feet ahead of me, looking back from time to time to make sure I was all right. His breath was as heavy as smoke in the freezing air. By the time we finished at the edge of the porch, my feet were numb, my nose was running like a valve, and I was choking on each attempt to breathe that wouldn't bring any air with it. Junior pulled me onto the porch and half carried me to the door. We both fell through it, winded and exhausted. Tears of fatigue and cold were mingled with my snot and I'd have cried and screamed if I'd had the breath to do it. Dad was standing by the coat-rack beside the door, putting a bottle back into the pocket of his overcoat. He hadn't even watched! Junior hurried us both over to the fireplace as Mom came running out of the kitchen with two warm towels that felt like they'd come out of the oven. Junior hopped up and down exclaiming how much fun it had been. I made no effort to pretend I liked it. He gave me a look telling me to follow his lead. I tried to laugh but the sound wasn't convincing. Dad just stood grinning down at us as Mom fussed and rubbed us down with the towels. He'd made some sort of point. But what was it? To prove that he was boss? He always seems to assert his authority when he has the least right to do so.

None of us was trying to make any particular point this year except that we were having a wonderful Christmas. We were working at making it wonderful—the best ever, we kept reassuring each other and Grandma and Grandpa. We exchanged our gifts, ate until we couldn't force down another mouthful and sat around the big table in the warm kitchen groaning with satisfaction.

There'd been more snow during the night, completing the perfect picture but we discovered when we went outside to "shake our dinner down" and slough off the sleepiness that the heavy food had induced that the new snow was freezing. We left earlier than we would have ordinarily. Grandpa had agreed that it could make driving hazardous. When we got to Blue Eye and the bend in the road where we'd halted on the way down yesterday, we all three seemed to tense up and strain forward in our seats.

"I hope they drove safely," Mom said under her breath. "Wherever they went."

Chapter Four

MY THIRD YEAR of school—at this new school in Galena—was going smoothly. The teacher, Mrs. Keller, if not exactly in my pocket, didn't seem to find me as repulsive as Mrs. Webster had. I wasn't particularly looking for a replacement for Mary Ann, I was just looking. And enjoying the effect I thought I was having on my classmates. Junior teased me about all the girls I imagined had crushes on me. He pointed out that if anybody so much as looked at me I thought they were flirting. I was so convinced of my charm that when a lady being introduced to me by Bessie Moore said I looked very familiar, I blushed prettily and said, "Thank you."

I felt lost trying to figure out the telegram Junior sent me on my birthday in March. Well, he didn't actually send it, but he had gone to the railroad station and picked up a Western Union form which he filled out as follows:

To: Totsy Woods

Address: c/o Scott Moore
Galena, Missouri

Message: HAPPY BIRTHDAY STOP
WILKINS BOY DEAD RIGHT
STOP JACKING-OFF

GROWS HAIRS ON PALMS OF
HANDS STOP LAST SENTENCE
FROM UNRELIABLE SOURCE STOP
WILKINS BOY'S INFORMATION MOST
RELIABLY CONFIRMED
STOP   STOP   STOP
   LOVE
   J. W.

It wasn't till he explained that "stop" was a period in telegram-talk
that I sort of understood. He refused to explain any further. He just
said he'd promised to send me a telegram when he found out and
what he'd found out. Namely, the Wilkins boy was right. The white
stuff floating on the water . . . I decided not to think about it. Or of
jacking-off, let alone growing hair on the palms of my hands.

There was another new third-grader that year and being two new
town kids we were sort of thrown or lumped together at the beginning of the year, bolstering each other's confidence. The other one
was Reba Jean Bolton and I liked her immediately even though
being "lumped" with her was a bit embarrassing. She needed all the
confidence bolstering she could get. The other kids made fun of her
clothes because they were unmistakable hand-me-downs and some of
the things she wore shouldn't have stopped on their way to the rag-
bag. She wasn't stupid and could hold her own in the classroom. She
read in a flat monotonous voice but didn't stumble and her hand-
writing on the blackboard was clear and neat. What she couldn't
cope with was the playground at recess. The taunts of the other girls
flattened her against the wall. She never joined in any of the games
unless I dragged her with me. My insisting on her being accepted was
also a test of my own popularity and position. I was new too and had
to prove myself. Championing Reba Jean required every ounce of
persuasion and strength that I could muster but then I'd had pretty
good training recruiting for Mary Ann and had quite a bag of per-
suasive tricks.

Reba Jean wasn't the cleanest girl in class but when I went to
where she lived I understood why. She lived in one of the store buildings on the south side of the square—an old haberdashery that had
been one of the first shops to go out of business at the beginning of
the Depression. There was no running water, no sink or wash basin
and I often helped her carry buckets of water from a neighbor's garden faucet down a side street. I'd visited Reba Jean several times in

the big bare room where she and her mother and father slept, ate, cooked, and did what little washing they did before I knew there was another room to the store.

We were doing homework together one day alone—her mother was often out—when we both lifted our heads from our work at a crying sound. I looked at Reba and her eyes grew big and darted to a door in the back wall that I'd never noticed before. The door out the back was in the center of the wall, this one was small and near the corner.

"What's that?" I asked. It could have been a kitten or even a baby.

"Oh, it's Clementine. She'll hush up in a minute."

"Clementine?" The sound was louder, fretful and demanding. Definitely an animal. A puppy maybe. "Does she want in?"

"She can't come in," she said dismissively. She turned her attention to her tablet where she was copying out something from one of our readers.

"Oh." I figured that it was a puppy and it wasn't allowed in the house. Then suddenly there was a wail, high pitched and eerie ending in a whining whimper. "Why don't we go play with it? Maybe it wants a drink of water or something."

"It's my sister."

"Your sister?" I stood up expectantly. "I didn't know you had a sister."

"Nobody does." She went on copying.

"Well, she seems to want something. She's just a baby?"

"Yes. Just a baby." She carefully finished writing a sentence, ground the end of her pencil with a twisting motion into the paper making the period, put the pencil down carefully and stood up. "Come on. You're my best friend." She headed toward the back of the long room. She opened a drawer in a kitchen table and took out a long skeleton key and walked to the door and unlocked it. She looked over her shoulder at me. "I'll let you see."

She had a baby sister that she hadn't even mentioned. That was very surprising. I'd always wanted a baby sister or brother to take care of. When I told Junior I was going to ask Mom why she didn't have a baby, he finally elaborated on his slightly cryptic telegram and reminded me that babies weren't a one-person operation. But if Dad came home one day . . . well, it might still be possible. He wasn't sure how old you had to be to start making babies or how old when you had to stop.

Why wasn't Reba Jean pleased and proud of her little sister? I'm sure I would have been. Why was she kept behind locked doors? I was beginning to be apprehensive as I went through the door into the dark little room. It had obviously been a storeroom for the shop. There was only one small window, high up on the end wall, over a door that had been boarded shut.

The whimpering sounds came from a crib that I could just make out against the wall. Reba Jean moved toward it with sure firm steps and let the side of the crib down with a bang. The sharp noise caused the high-pitched wail to soar out into the darkness and a shiver went down my spine. I pushed the door we'd come through fully open, letting in a bit more light. I followed Reba to the crib side and looked down. On the dingy wrinkled sheet was a baby. She was wearing only an out-sized diaper which made her little limp legs look like sticks coming out of the wide openings. Even in the dim light, I could count her ribs. The slightly enlarged head was made to look bigger by being connected to the emaciated body by a thin cord of a neck. A neck that couldn't possibly have held the head upright.

Reba Jean picked her up, cradling the dangling head in the crook of her elbow to keep it from lolling back over her arm. She turned to face me. "This is Clementine. Say 'hello,' Clementine. This is my friend, Totsy. Totsy Woods." She looked up at me and smiled shyly. "My *only* friend, Clementine." She rocked her like a doll—a boneless rubbery doll—back and forth in her arms.

I couldn't speak. It was a baby and yet it wasn't. Somehow the skin on the pathetic little frame looked withered and old. The head wobbled dangerously and the poor baby's mouth was open showing a few nubs of teeth, just some bumps that hadn't come through the gums yet. I finally managed a "Hello." I tried to say the name but for this lifeless little creature to have a long lovely name seemed wrong.

"Here, Totsy. Hold her." The bony bundle was in my arms before I knew what had happened. "I'll get some water for her." She headed out the door, leaving me holding the smelly little creature. I couldn't think of it as a baby. It had nothing to do with any baby I'd ever seen. The sounds it made and continued to make in my arms were more animal than human. "This'll keep her quiet." Reba Jean was back with a baby bottle filled with water. "Just sugar and water. We don't get much milk."

"I'll put her back in the crib," I said.

"Don't you want to hold her? She's just like a little doll. I dress her up and play with her all the time."

"I think she's a little wet." I thought from the way she smelled she was more than that and couldn't wait to get her out of my arms.

"Oh, she's *always* wet," Reba Jean said, relieving me of the wriggling, grunting body. The wriggling and grunting were the only signs of life. I couldn't see how it could go on breathing down that thin little tube of a neck. "Water goes straight through her."

"She's kinda skinny . . ."

"Always has been," she said matter-of-factly as she put Clementine back in the bed. I wanted to straighten out the sheet but it seemed too late. A nice straight, clean sheet might have made her more comfortable.

"Maybe if you gave her more milk she'd grow some more . . ."

"She won't."

"Won't what?"

"Won't grow."

"All babies grow. Maybe because she's been sick or needs . . ."

"She's nineteen." The bottle in place had stopped the whining.

"Nineteen *what?*"

She turned to me. "Nineteen years old." She bent down and lifted the side of the crib that fitted back into its top slot with a click. "There. Come on." She headed out the door.

I was thunderstruck. *Nineteen?* I stared again at the awful wormy little body squirming lazily, moving almost in slow motion as though under water. *Nineteen?* And this is as far as she'd got? I ran after Reba Jean, trying not to look as shocked as I felt. What had happened? What went wrong? God must have been out to lunch when this seed was planted.

"Momma thinks it's her fault," Reba Jean said, reading my mind. "She cries all the time and says it's her cross to bear. They say Clementine will be just like that until she dies." She said all that in her flat, monotonous reading voice. As though she were repeating something she'd memorized.

"*Is* it your Momma's fault?"

"Papa says it is. When he drinks." She was straightening up her homework. "He wanted to put Clementine in a home, but Mom keeps saying it's her cross to bear."

I gathered up my books. My hands weren't sure of themselves. I dropped things and had to pick them up. "Well, it's very sad. Sad for your mother. I'm sorry . . ."

"Nothing to be sorry about. It's just the way it is . . ."

"Well." I wanted to run home and wash. "I've got to go. See you tomorrow . . ."

"Yeah. 'Bye." She said it as though she didn't expect to ever see me again.

She confessed to me months later that I was the first one she'd shown Clementine to who'd remained her friend. I never told anybody about Clementine. Not even Junior. Not even when the image of her poor misshapen body haunted me. I took on some of Reba Jean's shame about her as my own.

Chapter Five

THE COLD WINTER hadn't brought any Woods out of the woods, but spring did. Dad appeared one Sunday toward the end of April—not too long after my birthday. He was not laden with gifts for me or for any of us. All he brought with him was a raging case of jaundice and the most beautiful pair of riding boots I'd ever seen. The jaundice we had to nurse him through, the boots we had to polish.

We were in our upstairs apartment listening to the Sunday evening radio programs when he appeared. Junior and I were glued to the crackling noise, Mom was correcting papers for her Wilson Run pupils when there he was. Standing at the head of the stairs, looking thin and sick.

"That was quite a rusty you cut, Milly," he said as we all sat staring at him. "Turn that fuckin' thing off," he ordered. Junior snapped the radio off without taking his eyes off Dad.

"You were cutting quite a rusty yourself, Woody," Mom said calmly. "I somehow got the impression you were being held prisoner by a red-headed gorilla."

The corners of his mouth twitched with the beginning of a smile that was cut with a grimace of pain. "Not up to much rusty-cuttin' now." He leaned against the doorjamb and slowly crumpled to the floor. Mom and Junior were both beside him in a flash.

He was put to bed in our room and took over our lives as we tried to save his. He was back. What was left of him.

By the time school was out in late spring, Dad was on his feet. But not his dancing feet. His interest in the Domino Cafe had been dimmed by Dr. Young's pronouncement. "You drink, you die." But he had a new interest. Baseball. Granted, that wasn't new. The new interest wasn't just baseball, it was Junior playing baseball. A new dimension had been added.

"That boy's born to it, Woody." His cronies confirmed his convictions and Dad would beam.

"Looky here, son," Dad would say, holding up the paper. "The Boston Red Sox just signed on a rookie—only eighteen—for ten-thousand dollars. Just look at that! I tell you, boy, that's where the money's at." Their eyes would flash with greed and wonder or perhaps just ambition. Dad had a potential star on his hands. He was sure of it, you could tell by the way he looked at Junior. The fact that I was going to become a dancing movie star seemed of no interest.

For some reason, Mom didn't have to work that summer. As a waitress or anything, I mean. Maybe it was because Dad got a job. He was actually working. Well, for a while anyway. So we spent that summer in Springfield and by some fluke right in the middle of colored town. Being segregated *against*. Mom was taking some summer courses at the Missouri State Teachers College and Dad was driving a truck back and forth between Galena and the Springfield stockyards. Full of livestock going up, empty going down.

We had a very nice big house across the street from a beautiful park with a sparkling swimming pool which we weren't allowed to use. The park or the pool. Junior and I were outraged that just because we weren't black we couldn't go into the park. Watching those sleek beautiful bodies frolicking on the other side of webbed mesh steel fences cut off from us as though in another world was so painful that we stopped playing in our front yard. We even stopped using the front door. We went down the street to a trickle of a creek where we'd dejectedly try to catch crawdads and be called "white-trash" occasionally by passing black children which made us feel even more inferior.

By the time the summer was over, our original trio was restored. Regrouped. Dad was gone. Again. He had disappeared on one of his trips going back down to Galena empty. As I understand it, the boredom of the same fifty-odd miles of road—or perhaps the smell of his untidy passengers—became too much and he just kept right on driving. It sounds rather implausible, but those were the only facts I ever got. Junior and I figured he hadn't stolen the truck or he'd have been in jail.

Back in Galena for the next school year, reality was particularly harsh. Mom had signed her contract with Wilson Run, but there was going to be some problem about payment. More than one school was short of funds. Many teachers were paid with what they called "warrants"—not as good as a check and only a little better than an I.O.U. Now she wasn't even getting real money for teaching.

People who were really down and out (like Reba Jean's family) could get free potatoes—dyed blue so they couldn't sell them but also told the world they were on relief—and some other necessities. Mom's school along with others in the poorest districts, were given loads of free grapefruit. Mom laughed and said most of her country children had never even seen the fruit before but took to it avidly and she swore the citrus intake had cut down absences from colds by over fifty percent.

It was during Thanksgiving vacation—the Sunday before we three had to return to school—that we heard footsteps on the stairs and we all four came together on the top landing. Mom from the kitchen, me from the main room, Junior from *our* room which I was sure we were going to lose again the moment I saw Dad standing there. This had been one of his shorter absences—only about three months and, as it turned out, his last. He was wearing the beautiful riding boots with beige twill riding breeches and a leather jacket. He'd never looked so handsome. Or healthy.

We all just stared at each other and gaped at the splendor of this almost unrecognizable man until Mom said, "Truck have a blowout, Woody?" Her eyebrows arched over twinkling eyes. "Or did you shoot a rod?"

"No. I just sort of blew a gasket." They looked at each other for a long moment and then hooted with laughter as Junior and I dashed to give him welcoming hugs and kisses. Again. Perhaps if we'd been a little less welcoming . . . But we let Mom take the lead on that.

When Dad left this time, we went with him. We didn't go very far but we soon missed those bright airy rooms with the lovely views of James River and the center of town. We moved into one of our views. Not the river. Practically into the courthouse. We had two rooms— tiny, viewless, airless—behind a rundown little diner that very soon had a sign up proclaiming it "Woody's Café." There was a long high counter with twelve stools bolted into the cement floor on the right as you entered and four painted wooden booths on the left. I loved it from the first moment I saw it. Junior and Mom were dismayed. For the first time, Dad and I were in cahoots. And not dancing.

We moved in and cleaned and painted the place during Christmas vacation. We didn't have Christmas on the farm that year and we all regretted it. It was our last chance. Grandpa had made a deal to trade the place for a smaller farm—only forty acres—a mile outside Oak Grove. Oak Grove, Arkansas. Population 30. He and Grandma moved at the beginning of the year. I wondered if they'd change the population sign to read 32.

Woody's Cafe, which had been staked by a friend of Dad's in St. Louis (a horse breeder whom Junior and I dubbed the Stud and who was responsible for the fancy riding togs Dad sported), opened on New Year's Day, 1935. It quickly became the gathering place for Dad's old cronies who never spent a cent. Since we didn't have a beer license, there was nothing we served that they could possibly want to drink. We had soft drinks: Dr. Pepper, Royal-Crown Cola, Nehi in all flavors, Cream Soda (an addiction of mine that Dad swore would bankrupt us before the end of the month), and of course coffee which one of Dad's buddies called horse piss, then changed his mind and said it wasn't strong enough to be horse piss. We didn't have tea.

The plan was for Mom to do the baking—pies, mostly—when she got home from school and Dad would be in charge of the kitchen. We served hamburgers, cheese and ham sandwiches and one blue-plate special every day—roast pork or beef with mashed potatoes and a soggy vegetable. We featured Dad's specialty, chili. A great pot of beans was on the back of the stove cooking all the time. When they were ready, they were transferred to another pot and great hunks of a reddish brick-shaped mass of unidentifiable ingredients mashed together and hardened was cut up into the beans. The brick was wrapped in clear cellophane stamped with red letters spelling out simply: Chili-Bricks. They resembled in size the big bars of yellow wash soap we used in the cafe's kitchen and I often wondered if Dad might not have sliced a bit of soap off now and then by mistake.

With all our efforts to make the cafe pay—I gave up my school lunch hour to wait on tables, Junior learned to scour the greasy chili pots without getting sick, Dad all but lassoed passersby—we had to admit defeat after the Spring court session. That successful six weeks wouldn't be repeated until the next session. By the time school was out in May, Mom had long since stopped baking. Even Dad's chili pot simmered for days before it was empty. We were facing a hot, dead summer. We were losing money just keeping the place open. The exodus west continued. Galena was beginning to look like a ghost town. Stores and shops went out of business from one day to

the next, leaving blank, blind holes in the series of buildings lining
the square. The Domino closed. An era was over. We were part of the
past. And we didn't seem to have any idea about the future. Until
something happened that galvanized us into action and started us on
our travels. Grandma Idy died.

The Woods really came out of the woods for this sad occasion. In
front of Grandpa's new Oak Grove house—a four-roomed clapboard
of a heart-sinking familiarity—were parked cars with license plates
from Missouri, Arkansas, Oklahoma (three), and one from Kansas.
That would be Uncle Ed, Dad's brother, who'd picked up his second
wife in Kansas City where he'd worked for years. His wife had more
than made up for the fact that she had a child already by providing
Uncle Ed with a baby daughter with embarrassing speed. His step-
son, Ronnie, was fourteen now and a particular friend of mine. He
laughed at everything I did or said. A very endearing trait.

We were the last of the immediate family to arrive because we were
going. Going on after the funeral, heading west. I suppose Mom and
Dad had been discussing this move because everything seemed organized. Junior and I were each given smallish suitcases and told we
could fill them and take nothing more. Anything that didn't fit in
that or the trunk we were sending on to Aunt Dell in Phoenix would
be left with our belongings and sold at an auction sometime in the
future. I was amazed at how little we owned once the tags had been
put on the bits and pieces. Just how the cafe was disposed of, I have
no idea. Junior said something about bankruptcy court, but I didn't
understand.

By the time we got to Oak Grove, Junior and I had arranged and
rearranged ourselves in the car, squirmed around in the backseat
like animals preparing nests for a long hibernation—which it eventually resembled—fitting ourselves and the few extra things in we'd
begged to bring: Junior's ball-glove, bat and ball, my shoe box with
DO NOT TOUCH, Private Property of Carlton Woods scrawled on
the lid and for some reason, a Chinese checkerboard with the marbles in a bag that Junior had stubbornly insisted on bringing. When
the awkward size of the board was mentioned, he threw the closest
thing to a tantrum I'd ever seen him resort to. That damned checkerboard was with us for several thousands of miles and drove me crazy
from the beginning. It was either up against the window, cutting out
the view or blocking the door when we stopped so we had to climb
over it. He was impervious to our jokes about it and our screams because of it. He clung to it like a child to a teddy bear.

The funeral took place the afternoon of our arrival. Grandma Idy was laid out in the front bedroom of this house I didn't know but in the big spool-patterned four-poster I'd known all my life, covered with her most beautiful patchwork quilt, looking very much like herself. The lace collar was pinned with the cameo under her chin. Her hair neatly and softly arranged. I had never seen a dead person before. She looked so natural, I had to remind myself why we were here. The solemnity, the hushed voices and tiptoeing around were unlike any family gathering I'd known. Grandma dead? She didn't look dead. What finally convinced me was noticing that powder and rouge had been applied to her face. If she were alive, she'd never have allowed anybody to paint her face.

Chapter Six

THE HOUSE WAS FILLED with hushed confusion; neighbors paying respects—some Grandpa hadn't even met yet in his first six months here—family members in and out the screen doors, children of all ages racing around all over the place trying not to have too much fun seeing each other again. Those voices that were raised were not considered out of order since they were directed at the children—reprimands, threats, admonitions.

Then Grandma's coffin appeared, being carried out the door reminding us all what we were really here for. Babies that were being passed from hand to hand gurgling, cooing or wailing suddenly became as quiet as the grownups. The air turned still—there wasn't a sound, not a cluck from the chicken run, no mules brayed or cows mooed, even the birds were silent. The silence of death. There was something about the way the coffin slid into the hearse that gave me the shivers. The box fit too neatly and smoothly into the rear end, feet first she went, swallowed up silently, disappearing from us. Disappearing in the ass-end of the bus. Everything was moving in the wrong direction. Feet first into the unknown. We were too. We were going from here to the unknown. To the west.

Everybody headed for the cars that were backing and turning to get in line to follow the hearse that had come all the way from Berryville for Grandma's last short trip to the Baptist Church in Oak Grove a mile away. The house emptied behind me as people moved past me, silent except for sibilant whispers, filling the cars, jumping on top of each other as the cars eased down the lane, following Grandma in that long black car with the frosted windows. Was that Grandma? Grandma Idy who'd cooked for us, cared for us, was *alive* for us? Who'd always be alive for me? She had loved us. One less person in the world to love us. I wasn't sure that we had enough of them to spare. I was beginning to get an inkling of what death was all about. Finally real tears were welling up and blinding me.

"That you, Totsy?" I turned from watching the black death wagon creep away with its train of followers to find my Uncle Henry, married to one of Dad's sisters, squinting down at me. "Oh. Thank God. Don't recognize any of these kids. You're the only easy one. You ain't growed at all." He moved myopically away toward one of the last cars as my tears got choked up on laughter. I was coughing and sputtering, blinded and choked when I felt an arm around my shoulder guiding me toward the last car. I was pulled into the car and down onto a lap into arms that held me tight. A new fit of coughing brought a hand to my back, which thumped me gently between the shoulder blades. I leaned back on a chest to catch my breath.

"Tots," Ronnie's lips were at my ear whispering. "You laughin' or cryin'?"

"Both," I gasped.

He started to tickle me but he felt my body freeze and knew this was not the right time. He moved his hands away from my ribs, crossed them on my chest and pulled me back tight against him. We'd been close ever since he came into the family some four years before. Uncle Ed brought his new wife, Edwina, and Ronnie down from Kansas City to meet us when they first married. He immediately became like a new big brother. He hugged me to him often like Junior did, he loved to watch me dance and encouraged me to show off at every opportunity. He didn't think it was idiotic for me to want to be a tap dancer. He was the only one who knew of my ambition. Coming from Kansas City, he'd had the opportunity to see tons of vaudeville shows and movies and assured me I had real, natural talent.

Junior and he got along pretty well, but it was me he'd seek out and lure away from all the other cousins at family gatherings. "You're the only one of this whole outfit that's got anything on the ball, Tots. I can talk to you." He dismissed the rest of the Woods as a bunch of hicks.

He gave me my first cigarette when I was six. I got a bit sick and he held my head and laughed while I retched dryly. "I'm sorry, Tots. Thought you were more experienced than that." I had lied about

how often I'd smoked. When I confessed it was my first time he ruffled my hair and said, "You're a crazy little kid, Tots, but I love you."
He told me proudly when they'd moved down here a few months ago
that he was a bastard. "This ain't no place for bastards, Tots. It's OK
being a bastard in a big town, but down here with all these Bible
hicks, it's going to be hell."

At fourteen, he not only smoked—almost openly—he even shaved
pretty often and I could feel soft bristles on my cheek as I moved to
open the door of the car when we pulled up in front of the little
church. Our car was the last and we had to stand at the back since
there were no seats remaining. I got a glimpse of the coffin covered
with flowers—mostly roses and garden flowers in simple bouquets
spread around on the box with others in vases. I was glad that I
couldn't really see what was going on. Everybody was standing
singing a hymn and from my low vantage point, I got only a sea of
grownups' bottoms unless I lifted my eyes. When I did, I got the back
of their heads or the faces of babies looking at me over shoulders.
During the prayer after the song, with everybody remaining standing, I couldn't see the preacher, only heard a disembodied voice with
quavering tones droning on and on.

When the congregation finally sat down, my view of the coffin was
clearer and so was the awful finality of the occasion. The reading of
verses of First Corinthians whatever through whatever had just been
announced when a darting figure in frilly blue ruffles and white
shoes dashed up the aisle toward the casket. Ruby! I could feel Ronnie stiffen beside me. His little sister. Half-sister. Uncle Ed's pride
and joy. She reached the coffin and was delightedly pulling the flowers off and handing them around to the people seated in the front
rows. Hissed whispers split the hot air. Uncle Ed fought his way over
feet and knees to get out of the pew, motioning frantically at the
happy child who continued to distribute flowers. The preacher had
chosen not to notice her but the congregation was bobbing up and
down with silent laughter or horror. The suppressed titters became
open when Uncle Ed tripped and fell headlong into the aisle.

Ronnie had me by the hand and out the door before I could catch
my breath from the hoot of pent-up laughter that had to escape,
even through a handkerchief, and we were weaving through the cars
toward the main road.

He still had me by the hand, muttering to himself, as we passed
through Oak Grove—all four stores, the filling station, the big old
building called The Mule Barn, and the few houses—and out the

other side. We walked toward Grandpa's new house in the blazing sun, past the town sign which hadn't been changed to read Population 32 and would now have had to be changed again if it had.

Ronnie didn't say anything until we passed the last house and took a shortcut across an alfalfa field between the road and Grandpa's orchard at the back of his property. "What a clod," he murmured.

"Who?"

"Who? Ed, that's who." He shook his head. "Only that dumb hick could turn a funeral for a nice little old lady into a Mack Sennett comedy." I didn't know who Mack Sennett was. "And she *was* nice." His mouth tightened and he looked down at his feet trudging through the dry, short remains of the hay. He looked like he might cry. I'd seen no sign of any feeling one way or the other from him so far today. "*She* was nice. She was good to me. She made me feel that I had a family." He kicked at a lump of dirt. "But that clod! Dumb hillbilly. Why'd Ma have to go and marry a hillbilly, for God's sake?" He stopped at the barbed-wire fence. "Ed and Ed. What a joke! Uncle Ed and Auntie Ed. Mr. Ed and Mrs. Ed. Edward. Edwina. She surely didn't marry him for the joke." He held the bottom wire down with his foot and lifted the top with his hand making a wide opening for me to crawl through. I did the same for him. "Boy, what a joke. Just to give me a name? A last name? I liked our old one. Parks. I don't know who my father was and I'll bet she doesn't either. Parks has some style." He stopped and looked at me. "Not that Woods doesn't. For you, I mean. It's a very good name but you come by it naturally."

"I guess so. I don't think I'm a bastard."

He laughed and put his arm around my shoulder. "Yeah, well. One in the family's enough. See what it causes? She has to go and marry Ed just like she joined that hick hillbilly church." He threw his head back and sang, "To wash my sins in the tide . . ." He stopped and stood in front of me. "You know what her sin is?" He poked his finger in his chest. "Me. *Me.* I'm her sin. She thinks by giving me Ed's name and having *his* baby . . ." He rolled his eyes heavenward. "That *baby.* She sure is his. He's mad about her. Ruby's going to kill us all." He hugged me to him. "Oh, Tots. If only you were my brother . . ."

"I feel like I am."

"Yeah. Anyway we got the same name. Parks to Woods. Not really much of a change."

"Can't see the Parks for the Woods."

He threw his head back and roared. "Totsy, you *are* a crazy little kid." He turned me to face him. "And I *do* love you." He gave me a little shake and looked down at me and smiled. His dark blue eyes changed mood in a blink. "Come on, enough serious stuff. Come on, Tots, let's have a laugh." He bent toward me with his fingers crooked like claws and rushed for my ribs. I let out the expected squeal and rolled my head back and jumped up and down screaming. He tickled me until we were rolling around on the ground, me kicking and squirming to avoid his insistent fingers, he laughing with me, crawling after me on his knees until I rolled under a big persimmon tree and onto one of the fallen soft orange fruit, squashing it messily with my elbow.

"Ugh. What a mess." I was panting and still laughing.

"Come on, we'll wash it in the pond." The pond was almost dry, and the deep holes left by the cows' feet in the mud had dried leaving an uneven bumpy bank all around the remaining water.

"Take your shoes off. It's easier barefoot. Besides, if you slip, you'll be up to your knees in the mud like the cows were."

Ronnie lighted a cigarette when we were settled back under the persimmon tree shoulder to shoulder, our muddy feet stretched out in front of us drying, insistent flies buzzing around us, and crawling on my wet and sticky arm. I shook my head no when he offered me the expertly hand-rolled and lighted cigarette. "Savin' your breath to compete with George Murphy?" I just looked at him out of the corner of my eye and grinned. "Good. It's like being an athlete like Junior. You have to take care of yourself." He took a long drag on the cigarette. "I just want to be rich." He sat forward, drawing his knees up and rested his elbows on them. "And get the hell out of here."

"Like us, huh?"

"What do you mean, like us?"

"I mean like we're doing. We're going to California."

He looked stunned. "Going to California?" It came out in a whisper of disbelief.

"I thought you knew . . ."

"No." He shook his head slowly from side to side. "No. Nobody said any . . ."

"We only decided ourselves—I mean Mom and Dad just decided when we heard Grandma died . . . I can't hardly believe it myself."

"Shit." He hit his knee with a fist and stood up. "Ed drags us down here to that damned farm. Turns me into a Woods and then keeps me in the backwoods." That made him laugh. "That's pretty damned funny, ain't it?" We both laughed. "And listen to me, I'm saying 'ain't' like all the hicks. A bastard Woods in the backwoods. And now both Ed and Ma have turned into holy rollers! They're crying and praying all the time." He raised his arms and looked up at the sky in imitation of religious fervor, "Oh Lord, my savior—forgive me for all my sins . . ." He looked down at me and pointed to himself and winked and went on, "cleanse me, oh my savior. Let me walk in that righteous path. Lead me to your ever-lovin' arms, Oh God . . ." His arms fell limply to his sides, his head drooped. "Oh GooooOOODDD." It was a low moan. "What am I going to do, Tots? I don't get to see you all that much, but I knew you were there. Up in Galena. Or Crane. That's not far. When we moved down here, just knowing that you were there made it better." He grinned. "Not *OK*, but better." He dropped back down beside me. We sat for a time in silence. I was looking up into the tree, counting the persimmons that were almost ripe. "Up there," Ronnie went on as though talking to himself. "Up there in Galena, I could get to you. But California . . ." His voice trailed off.

I looked over at him and he had dropped his chin on his chest and seemed to have his eyes closed. I leaned forward a little to get a better look at his face. Tears were streaming down his cheeks. It was my turn to be stunned.

"Hey, Ron," I nudged his shoulder with mine. "We'll be back. I know that. It's just this Depression and Mom says that in a . . ."

He opened his eyes and grinned at me, our faces so close together that it was hard to focus but I saw tears in his long black lashes and streaks down his cheeks. "I know." He jumped up. "Come on. The cars are coming back. We'd better go." He started running full tilt toward the barn carrying his shoes. I grabbed mine and raced after him. He was holding the barbed wire open for me when I caught up with him. "Besides," he said as I bent down to crawl through, "when I run away, I'll just come and find you."

Now there was a party. A wake I guess they're called. All the women—Dad's three sisters (Aunt Dell naturally was still in Phoenix), Mom and Ronnie's mother, along with neighbor ladies— had been cooking before the funeral and now that it was over, everybody was milling around waiting for dinner. The men were gathered around the cars in little groups kicking at tires, opening and closing doors, lifting the folding hoods from one side or the other to inspect motors or pour buckets of water that the older boys were carrying from the well into radiators. They talked quietly and seriously, the groups changing and moving and regrouping at another vehicle. Sly glances shot over broad shoulders as bottles were passed discreetly around tight circles of wide-backed men who knew they were being observed and everybody knew what they were doing but the ritual was too ingrained, the rules too strict to risk a break from tradition. They had to drink secretly.

This could have been any gathering—a birth, a wedding, an anniversary, birthday or holiday. The women's role was as clearly defined as the men's. They gossiped and glided around in the kitchen, each seeming to have a particular job and knowing instinctively in any house where plates, silver, linen were kept. The toddlers and babes-in-arms created no encumbrances but were natural growths cleaving to the breast or hip of the mother as she circumnavigated the islands of crawlers on the floor, stepping over them or around them with an innate assurance, not needing to glance down to know that a child was between her feet. They moved like fish—sliding gracefully through intricate patterns of movement, never quite touching each other or the new growth on the bottom of the water. It was an underwater ballet, their voices soft, the occasional burst of laughter like bubbles rippling up and bursting on the surface—lost on a cushion of water as were the subdued sounds of plates, platters, bowls as they filled the huge table so completely that you couldn't tell whether there was a tablecloth or an oilcloth underneath the elaborate feast. It did Grandma proud.

The front room was given over to Grandpa as chief mourner who held court from his leather rocking chair, surrounded by an ever-changing group of neighbors and townspeople who'd come to express their sympathies. He sat, puffing on his pipe, rocking almost imperceptibly, accepting the stumbling speeches of condolence with a patient nod of appreciation.

The screen door was pushed open, an aunt motioned and called gently to the men across the sprawled-out bodies of at least a dozen of us children on the wide front porch. We would wait until the grown-ups had eaten before we were allowed at table. I never knew how old you had to be to join the first group—Ronnie seemed almost grown up but he stayed with us. There was some unwritten law.

I was sitting with Junior with our legs dangling over the edge of the cement porch. Ronnie was stretched out flat on his back just behind us. "Where'd you two get off to?" Junior asked in a low voice with a hint of accusation in it.

"When Ruby started strewing the flowers around," I explained, "Ronnie had to get me out. I was about to explode."

"You're lucky," Junior said, turning back to include Ronnie who eased him back so that his head rested on Ronnie's thigh. It was the most intimate thing I'd seen pass between them. I got the feeling Junior was making a special effort to be as friendly with Ronnie as he knew I was. "It got funnier. Or worse, whichever way you want to look at it. You knew Uncle Ed fell down chasing Ruby?" I nodded. "Well, she ran screaming like a banshee, climbing up on the preacher's podium." He lifted his head to look at Ronnie. "Your sweet little sister . . ."

"*Half* sister, don't forget."

". . . started yanking on the preacher's pants leg and chanting "I wann' make pee-pee. I wann' make pee-pee."

Ronnie shook his head, trying not to laugh. "See? See? What'd I say, Tots? That kid's going to kill us all."

It turned out that the organist started a few chords to drown out Ruby and Uncle Ed finally caught her and flew out the back door with her in his arms. Junior sighed heavily. "The rest was even less fun. Ruby's antics weren't all that much fun really. I think we were all . . . well, nervous and everything." He stopped and lay very still. "Then they took the casket outside. Outside into the graveyard." His voice had become flat and matter-of-fact. "When I said you were lucky, I meant you were lucky to miss that part. That last part. I sure wish I had. I hadn't thought about the last part. I guess I wouldn't let myself think about it. We all—all the family (I looked all over for you, Tots) had to stand by that hole." He paused, took a deep breath and went on hurriedly, as though it was something he had to say quickly and get it over with. "That hole looked so dark. And deep. It looked deeper than . . . well, than necessary. She was such a small, little lady . . ." I couldn't hear him any more. His voice broke and his shoulders were shaking with sobs. We both sat up and I grabbed him in my arms the way he'd always grabbed me when I needed him and held him close. Another pair of arms wrapped around us both and held us in an iron grip and rocked us back and forth soothingly. Did it take a death to bring people together?

We were eventually allowed to eat. People discussed at length the difficult sleeping arrangements. Mom, Dad and Junior were going to stay with Grandpa. The Oklahoma contingent was being spread out on pallets at Grandpa's, Uncle Ed's and neighbors'. Ronnie simply put me on the bicycle and that was that. It was a foregone conclusion that I'd go with him and help with the farm chores giving Uncle and Aunt Ed a chance to visit with all the relatives.

There was also a prayer meeting—actually a revival meeting scheduled for that night in the Mule Barn—and two of Dad's Oklahoma sisters were determined to go. So were the newly born-agains, Ed and Edwina.

"That's a real ass-cutter, Tots, on these dirt roads. Want the seat? I can stand-pump." I shook my head no to Ronnie's offer even though my ass was being cut by the bar on his bicycle and we weren't even through Oak Grove yet. We saw that cars were already parked outside the Mule Barn for the revival meeting and it was just after sundown. He finally stopped at the bend past the Baptist church and graveyard which looked closed and deserted and gave no sign of a new occupant. He took off his shirt and folded it as a cushion for me on the bar. "There. No need to have your ass go numb and your legs drop off. I gotta' take care of you." He went into his cornpone act. "In them bib over-halls, you're just about the cutest little shit-kicker I ever seen."

Their farm was about the same distance north on the Blue Eye road from Oak Grove as Grandpa's was south. The steep drive on the right of the house made it necessary for us to dismount and walk. Ronnie pushed the bike while I rubbed feeling back into my backside.

Ronnie gave me the half-bucket of corn to feed the chickens while he lurched off under the weight of a huge bucket of slop that had been prepared earlier for the pigs. We lured the five cows into their stalls, with fresh feed in their troughs, sat on three-legged stools beside them and went to work. I was as fast as Ronnie, drawing the warm white liquid out of the fat teats with an expert hand. I was stripping my first cow, carefully squeezing down from the udder as Grandpa had taught me to make sure all the milk was there frothing in the bucket and not a drop left in the cow, when I got a faceful of milk aimed from under the cow Ronnie was milking.

"Slow down, show-off," he yelled. "You really are a shit-kicker." He laughed.

We raced from cow to cow, milking as fast as we could. I'm not sure our stripping would have passed muster with Grandpa. We were filling our buckets, occasionally spraying streams at each other, at arm-paralyzing speed. My forearms were aching when I finished my last animal and I leaned my head against her flank and the sweet smell of milk and cow filled my whole being with an aching sadness. The beloved old Woods place where I'd learned to milk a cow was gone, replaced by a sadly predictable little gray house. Grandma was gone. We were gone. Practically. What *was* California? They probably didn't even have cows there.

"Hey, Tots!" Ronnie called. "Gone to sleep? Come on." We carried the milk back to the house and into the back screened-in porch where the milk separator was. Ronnie adjusted the pieces expertly and we poured our buckets into the big round receptacle at the top. More buckets were placed under the cream spout and the milk spout. "Tots, you turn this monster while I get some light and things." It was almost dark. I started cranking the handle which moved easily for the first few turns then became steadily more difficult as the spouts started dribbling their liquid into the buckets. Ronnie came back with a lighted coal oil lamp and an armful of quilts and pillows. "God knows where Ma is going to put all the others, but I figured we'd be safe and out of the way of the thundering horde over here in this corner." The separator acted as a separation for the porch, dividing it and creating a private area at the far end where Ronnie laid out quilts for a pallet and covered them with sheets, crawling around on his knees straightening them neatly. "There. I can't wait to get into that. I'm dead." He looked up at me and jumped to his feet. "Let me do that. It gets hard after awhile." He peeked into the big, round, shiny metal bowl where we'd poured the milk. "You've got it more than half done. Good." He grabbed the handle and put his whole body into turning it. The milk began to gush out the nozzle, the cream oozed thickly in one long undulating stream into its bucket, the soft yellow liquid looking almost as solid as Junior's silky taffy.

We folded our clothes beside the pallet and went outside naked. The dim light from the oil lamp made us just barely visible to each other. I could see that Ronnie had some hair down there. I still didn't have any, but I had attained peter or pecker status at last. I couldn't wait to move past that stage because I hated the names. When would I have a cock? Ronnie most definitely had one. He had primed the hand pump and filled a bucket of water and poured it over me as I soaped myself. The water was freezing and I squatted down shivering for the next bucket, noticing that the cold water had made me shrink back to toy size.

"Oh, damn. I left the towels there by the back door, Tots. Go dry and get into bed. Your teeth are chattering. I'll be there in a minute."

I ran gratefully, dried quickly and was on the pallet under the sheet in seconds. I seemed to melt into the floor. I was bone tired as Mom would say. I just lay there on my back, feeling too exhausted to move. I couldn't have turned over if my life depended on it. I seemed to be weighted down. There *was* a weight on me. On my thighs. I'd dozed off. I hadn't heard any sound or realized when the light had been blown out. I opened my eyes to see Ronnie's silhouette sitting across my thighs with arms raised and fingers crooked ready to attack my ribs. "I'm going to get you," he croaked in a spooky voice.

I responded with my usual squealing and squirming like I knew he wanted as his fingers hit their goal and danced up and down my sides. I laughed and rolled about as best I could under his weight. He was chuckling and laughing under his breath. My breath started coming in gasps. "Oh . . . Ron . . . stop it. Stop it, *please.*" I could hardly get the words out. My body went limp. I mimicked his cornpone accent. "Ron, ah'm jest plain . . . tuck . . . tuckered . . ." I sighed with real fatigue, ". . . out." He slowed down. I changed to my own voice. "I really *am*. Tu-uuc–cckker–ed. Oooouuuuutttt." The last word faded away into the dark.

He sat back, still straddling my legs. "OK, Tots. No more ticklin'." He sighed heavily too and lifted himself off me onto his knees. "Then I'll just eat you up." He fell forward catching himself with his hands on the pillows beside my head and buried his face into my neck with a growl and playfully nipped little bits of my skin with his teeth. That was more ticklish than anything he'd ever done. I didn't squeal, my breath had caught. He growled and nibbled, moving his head down over my chest, chuckling between growls, his nibbling teeth and lips and tongue causing my body to feel as if I were being electrocuted.

I tried to speak. "Ron . . . don't . . ." but it came out in such a soft whisper that I could barely hear myself above his funny low growling and chewing. His mouth was moving all over my chest and sides and stomach. Each contact with my skin caused an intake of breath but there didn't seem to be time to let any air out. I grabbed at his curly hair and lifted his head. Our faces were nose to nose, eyes wide and glittering in the dark. "Ron . . ." I could feel his breath on my face. "I feel funny . . . my body . . ." I was gasping more than whispering. I turned my face away. There was such a tingle down my spine, up my legs, through my middle, all through me, racing on electrical currents toward my core, the center of my being, my throbbing hard-on . . .

His head dropped onto my chest again, his mouth open and his tongue and lips moving over me, kissing, licking, nibbling as he moved his head down further and further and suddenly I was inside his mouth, hot, wet, sucking on me, his tongue working around and under my balls. All of me was inside his mouth and then all of me exploded.

I heard a loud, long cry echo into the night as my body thrashed around with a feeling in my groin that went beyond anything I thought my body or any body capable of experiencing. The cry was coming from me and it was suddenly stopped by Ronnie's mouth covering mine. I couldn't breath, I was suffocating but it didn't seem to matter. I was floating in some sort of weightless world. I couldn't feel Ronnie on me any longer, only his mouth and his tongue playing on my lips and then I felt his hand arranging my legs—he opened them—then dropped down heavily onto me as he pushed my legs closed around something hard that was working up and down slowly rubbing against my inner thighs. I tightened the muscles automatically and the movement accelerated. He tore his mouth from mine and began licking and whispering incoherently in my ear. "Tots, oh Totsy. I . . . oh this is something I wanted . . . oh Tots, you're going . . . you're leaving . . ." He raised himself up on his hands, looked down into my face while his hips worked faster and faster and I moved my pelvis up to him, flexing my leg muscles, then crossing my feet at the ankles, instinctively knowing that would make it better and tighter for Ronnie. "Oh Tots, yes . . ." His mouth was on mine again and I felt a warm liquid between my legs, as he turned his head and panted into my neck, taking shuddering breaths and kissing me at the same time.

I started to cry. Really cry. I don't know why. It started and I couldn't stop it. My body was wracked with sobs. Everything was wrong. It had been wrong all day. We'd just done something bad. I knew it had to be bad because the sensation in my body kept on surprising and frightening me. Ronnie's lips on my neck and chest, my cheeks, kissing my tears and whispering, "Oh, Tots . . . I'm sorry, Tots. Listen, Tots. I don't know what happened . . ." My skin was on fire. Everything he was doing to me was wrong. I was sure of that, but I couldn't stop him or my sobs. They were choking me and I was gasping as he went on apologizing. "Oh, Tots. Don't cry, Tots. Please. I'm sorry. I never have . . ." He was reaching behind him and brought a cloth up between my legs, wiping me where the liquid had seeped down to my buttocks. I had no strength. He handled me as though he were diapering a baby. He moved my boneless legs around as he needed, as he cleaned me, all the time muttering. "I'm ashamed, Tots . . . you aren't mad at me, are you? Tots?" I couldn't speak even though my choking sobs had subsided. I just lay there, limp, lost and stupefied by what had happened. "Don't be mad at me, Tots. It just kind of happened. I don't know what . . ."

I wanted to reach up and touch his cheek, but my arms wouldn't move. I wanted to tell him that it was all right, but I couldn't speak. Something earth-shattering had happened to me—that much I knew—something that I knew was going to be important in my life if not change it altogether, but I didn't understand it. I could feel my eyes droop. I had no more reserves. I was used up. Ronnie was busily straightening the sheets, plumping the pillows, lifting my head gently to make me more comfortable, drawing the sheet over us both as he snuggled down next to me, all the time making little comforting noises, apologetic and remorseful. He slipped an arm under my pillow and put his other one over my chest and pulled my limp body close to him. He leaned his face down close to my ear and said barely audibly, "You see, Tots. The problem is . . . well, I wasn't kidding. Tots, can you hear me?" I managed a slight nod. He cleared his throat and his words were so faint—just breath really—that I wasn't sure I heard correctly, but I think he said, "I love you. Tots. Totsy. I love you. I don't understand it either but I *do*. I know I do . . . I love you . . ." I was asleep.

Chapter Seven

I WOKE UP INTERMITTENTLY during the day, looking out my window to check where we were. Names began to melt into one another—Eureka Springs, Fayetteville, Van Buren, and Fort Smith and suddenly over into Oklahoma just at nightfall. Junior had found out the name of the town where Will Rogers had gone to school at a military academy and had been disappointed to learn we wouldn't go anywhere near it.

"I just wanted to see a military school," he confessed to me. "It has nothing to do with Will Rogers."

Dad is one of the world's champion long-distance drivers and he set out to prove it that first day. We stopped only when it was necessary—eating sandwiches Mom had made up whenever we were hungry. Dad wanted to avoid as much as possible the roadside cabins and motor courts on the pretext that they were dirty, full of bedbugs, and just a waste of money. The latter point carrying the most weight. He drove steadily on through the night, our headlights picking up names of towns like Sallisaw, Eufaula, Welecta, and Hanna. This first lap of our trip would establish the fact that I fall asleep the minute wheels roll underneath me and that Junior was undisputed copilot and navigator from the backseat. He too had finally fallen asleep against his checkerboard after repeating that we were to head for Holdenville and then take the first cutoff to Ada. It was a family joke that Mom's brother and his wife got stuck in Ada on their first attempt to get to California because it was his wife's name. Ada. That would be our first stop.

"And they're probably right now at the second night of the revival meeting in the Mule Barn, singin', shoutin', praisin' the Lord and savin' souls hand over fist," Dad was saying. He and Mom talked quietly in the front seat, Mom keeping the conversation going by encouraging Dad to talk to keep himself awake. He had what he called his "eye-opener" in a half-pint bottle under his seat and a slug now and then from that really did seem to pep him up. We've done a lot of driving in the last four years or so and we all marvel that whiskey and driving as far as Dad's concerned mix beautifully. He could drive—and has many times—as much as twenty-four hours straight and swear he could keep right on going. But give him several drinks without a steering wheel in his hands to keep him steady and an endless highway stretching out in front of him and he's glassy-eyed and repetitive—not to mention argumentative—before you knew what was happening. As long as the half-pint had something in it, he was all right. Mom teased that she didn't know which was more important to the running of the car, gas or whiskey.

"All of 'em," Dad went on. "Practically my whole damned family. Beulah and Daisy and now Ed. I never thought I'd see the day that he'd be standin' up in front of people and givin' testimony about how the 'Lord just come straight at me like a big red ball of fire'." He raised his voice to imitate his brother.

Mom darted a look at the backseat, "Shh, Woody, the boys are sleeping."

"Tots hasn't had an eye open all day." He chuckled softly. "Never saw anything like it. He's dead on his feet. That Ronnie probably kept him awake all night telling his bullshit stories about Kansas City." I swallowed hard and shifted my position slightly to hear better but still pretending sleep.

"He's getting better," Mom said so quietly I had to strain to hear. "Better looking too. Working on the farm will do him good."

"That boy ain't goin' to have a easy row to hoe, I can tell you. Both of 'em has gone plumb crazy. Ed *and* Edweeena." Dad always made fun of her name. "Religion's got 'em both chasin' their own tails. Milly, I swear I don't hardly recognize my own brother any more. He's acting plain silly. You remember how he was when he was married to Florence? Why they wasn't a more dancin', drinkin', and havin'-a-good-time couple in the Ozarks than them two. You remember that dance him and . . ."

"He . . ."

". . . Florence give . . ."

"Gave . . ."

". . . when they was livin' on the old Slaughter place down on the creek bottom? That was one of the best dances I'as ever at."

"I miss all those dances." Mom's voice had a faraway sound to it. "The good ones, that is. I didn't think much of the ones that ended in fights. Like the one where you got hit between the eyes with a beer bottle."

"Whoooeee. That was something, wasn't it? Ed was there, too. Right in the middle of that knock-down-drag-out. Remember? I seen . . ."

"Saw . . ."

There was a dangerous pause. "*Seen* him stand up and get knocked down—oh Lord, at least half-a-dozen times. He'as so drunk you couldn't a hurt him with an axe." They both laughed softly. "But look at him now. Wouldn't say shit for fear it'd melt in his mouth. Jesus! I mean not sayin' shit ain't going to get you to heaven any faster than . . . well, whatever it is they're doing that makes them think they are goin' to have a free pass for the Pearly Gates."

"Well, it makes them feel better."

"Feel better? Sheee-it. You know what he done . . ."

"Did . . ."

"Goddamnit, Milly, do you want to hear the story or are you goin' to go on interruptin' me?"

"Sorry, Woody. Second nature. Schoolmarm to my tippy toes."

"What he done this mornin'? Ed?" He paused. "Was it only this morning? Seems like a long time ago already. A long way away." Now Dad's voice had the faraway sound. "Anyway, when I picked up Totsy he hadn't even had his breakfast. Said Ed wouldn't let him set down at the table without no shirt on. How about that for pure horseshit? A ten-year-old kid can't set down to eat breakfast in the *kitchen*, mind you, on a hot mornin' without a shirt." I could feel Dad take a quick look at us in the backseat. He lowered his voice even more. "He had Tots purt'near cryin'. Tots said he couldn't put on the shirt 'cause it was dirty. Hell, we ain't down here for no fashion parade. I seen the shirt. Had milk all over it. It was a mess. The boys had just been doin' what me and Ed done all our lives—squirtin' milk at each other when we'as a milkin'." I couldn't imagine Dad and Ed doing what Ronnie and I did after we finished the milking. I couldn't imagine anybody doing it. I tried to erase the picture from my mind. I'm still trying.

"At least him and Ronnie had done the damned chores so's they could all make fools of theirselves at the Mule Barn revival," Dad continued. Milk wasn't the only thing on that shirt. Ronnie's face had fallen when he realized what he'd used to wipe us up. Poor Ronnie was saying, "I'm sorry, Tots," when we went to sleep and he woke up saying it.

"What'd Ed say to Totsy?" Mom asked.

"Oh, some shit about respect for the name of the Lord and blessin' this food and all that."

"I mean, what did he say to *you*."

"He looked pretty damned sheepish knowin' how I feel about— well, you know, about all that bein' born again crap. Once is bad enough." He snorted a soft laugh. "Anyway, Tots was on the back porch putting on his shoes. I guess bein' barefooted is some kind of sin too. I could hear 'em in the kitchen finishin' up sayin' a grace that must of been a mile long and a yard wide. I don't see that they got that much to be thankful for in the first place. Beulah was a'Amen-in' so loud you could hear her in Blue Eye. And that early in the mornin'. I don't know how they can stand it. What a asshole way to start the day. Why, I'd be a nervous wreck inside of a week."

"Might even turn you to drinking."

"Thought you'd never suggest it." Dad produced the bottle and handed it to Mom who opened it and handed it back to Dad. Dad's head did a little flip backward—not enough for him to take his eyes off the road for a second—gulped and held the bottle up for Mom to screw on the top. The bottle disappeared under Dad's seat. They laughed easily and intimately. This was so private and secret that I felt ashamed to be listening. But it didn't stop me. This was how they were when they were alone. When the times were good between them.

"So?"

"Where was I? Oh yeah. I stood there in the door and I guess I would still be standin' there if I hadn't finally said good mornin' myself. 'Good mornin' all,' I says. Very jolly, I was. Well, I said, 'All washed in the blood of the lamb last night, eh? And drinkin' the leftovers this mornin'?'"

Mom gasped. "Woody, you didn't . . . ."

He laughed. "Naw. Shit no, Milly. But I wanted to. I just wanted to make 'em feel as silly as they are."

Mom was giggling. "Come on, Woody, what *did* you say?"

"Oh, just somethin' about how good it had been to see 'em all—even if the reason wasn't the happiest one—and that we'as hittin' the road . . . you know, just makin' noise and sayin' goodbye. Then they all got up, hugs and kisses and shakin' hands and good lucks and . . . oh, you know, Milly, a lot of sad-eyed looks and all that shit. All I wanted to do was get Totsy and get the hell out of there." He handed Mom a packet of Spuds from his shirt pocket and she lighted a cigarette for him with a box of big kitchen matches, making her usual face of distaste and coughing slightly. I was now peeking at them through slitted eyelids. I hadn't been in on this part of the morning's events, I had gone straight to the car and got into my place in the backseat. Ronnie had followed me and stuck his head through the front window.

"Didn't I tell you he was a clod? I'm sorry, Tots . . . about a lot of things. But Ed didn't have to be so . . . *tacky*. About the shirt and everything. That was my fault . . ."

"It's OK, Ronnie." I wanted to make him smile, he was looking as downcast as if he were facing a prison term, but I couldn't think of anything to say. We heard the back screen door slam and saw Dad headed for the car with all the relatives standing on the back porch, waving and calling to us. I waved and smiled.

Ronnie's hand was on my shoulder, turning me to face him. "As soon as I can, Tots, I'll come and find you." He squeezed my shoulder and turned and ran toward the barn. Dad was in the car in one quick movement and we were in motion down the steep drive, turning into the main road practically on two wheels, roaring back through Oak Grove to pick up Junior and Mom.

"And I did," Dad continued with smoke curling around the words. "I hit the road with my blood still boilin'. You know I couldn't let it go. When I got out on the back porch, there by the milk separator, I could see Tots in the back of the car talking with Ronnie. He still didn't have a shirt on and what the hell difference did it make, I thought. Ed was standin' nearby and I pointed out to the car and Tots and said, 'Well, Ed, there he is. Just look at him. Little half-naked heathen. I don't know what the hell I'm goin' to do with him."

Mom was giggling, "You *didn't* . . ."

"I sure as hell *did*. I said . . ." He took a puff of the cigarette and blew the smoke out leisurely. "I said, 'Why, hell, Ed, that's why were goin' to California so I can get work to buy that poor little savage some clothes to hide his sinful nakedness. Get him sanitized, sanctified, san*fori*zed, or even circumcized if it'll lead him to the arms of the Lord . . ."

Mom was rolling around in her seat, trying to stifle her laughter, saying "Oh, Woody . . . you didn't *really* . . . that's too funny . . ."

I'd rolled over so that I could throw an arm over my face to hide my own giggles.

"That's exactly what I said, Milly. If I hadn't been so damned mad, I'd'a laughed myself. They're all such fuckin' hypocrites, Milly. Using the name of the Lord to cover up for their own mistakes and bad . . . well, *behavior* in the past . . . usin' praying and carryin' on to make their . . ." Dad paused for a split second and glanced at Mom, "*them*selves feel better. It don't have nothin' to do with the Christian spirit or livin' a good Christian life. You don't have to scream and make a damned fool of yourself in front of a lot of people who've just come to laugh at you mostly anyway. All you need to do is try to change your ways. Do it inside yourself." Mom was scrabbling around under the front seat and came up with the bottle. Dad grinned at her. "Now what the hell are you up to?"

"Nothing. Go on." She went about the business of opening the bottle slowly and deliberately.

"I mean, that wasn't no way to treat my kid. *Any* kid. Hell, Milly we got us two good boys. The best. They're goin' to amount to something. I'm going to see that they do, by God. Why, Junior's . . . He's *got* something, Milly. I know it. He's going to be somebody." I was holding my breath. "And so's Tots. He's different, but he's smart as a whip and he'll . . ." Yeah, I thought. He'll *what*? Just how *different* did he think I was? *Am*? I went on holding my breath. "He'll make it. He's small, but he's tough. You'll see. I keep thinkin' that we're doing the right thing for them . . . takin' them where they'll have opportunities that I . . . well, you, neither, really, didn't have . . ."

"I'm waiting," Mom said softly.

"Waiting?"

She nodded meaning for him to go on.

"I guess what I'm sayin' is . . . is . . . that I've been wrong. And I know it. Knowed when I was doin' it. Couldn't stop myself. He rolled the window down and threw his cigarette butt out. "But I'm goin' to try, Milly. I've got you and two fine boys. I can try . . ."

I couldn't see, but I guessed Mom touched him on the leg as she turned toward him and leaned over and kissed him on the cheek. "Halleluljah, brother," she said so quietly that I wasn't sure that was what she'd said.

"What?"

"I said, Halleluljah, Brother." She raised the bottle in the air. "You may not know it, but you've got religion."

Dad threw his head back and laughed. "Oh, shit! Is that what I got?"

"Same as."

"Well, I'll be goddamned."

"I'll drink to that," Mom said and took a slug from the bottle, something I'd never seen her do and I almost sat up in surprise.

We pulled into Ada just before sunup. There was a rosy glow in the sky and not a cat in the main road of this one-street town. Dad pulled into a firmly closed filling station, dropped his head back on the seat and promptly snored the rest of us awake. It was certainly his turn. He got in a good hour without moving before the front door of the service station was opened from the inside and a rumpled man in overalls came out, unlocked the gas pumps and started filling the big glass cylinders with the pink fuel that always reminded me of strawberry soda pop. His rhythmic movement on the handle didn't change pace until the liquid reached the line marked "O" at the top of each tank. Without looking at us, he turned and went back into the small room where we could see him fiddling with an ancient ornate cash register. Finally he looked out the window, seeing us for the first time and came back outside and up to Dad's window.

"Can I help you folks?" he asked.

"I don't know," Dad said. "You open for business yet?"

"Oh yes."

"Well, if you're sure you're ready, fill it up."

Once out of Ada—which we were by the time Dad was in high gear—the country was flat and dusty with cotton plants as far as the eye could see. It was about two or three feet tall—the first I'd ever seen—and covered with limp, straggly, off-white woolly growths that looked anything but fluffy.

"They ought to get that crop in," Dad said knowingly. "Get a good rain on that now and you'd lose half the crop."

We all watched in every direction, searching the flat landscape for signs of life. There were sheds dotted along the road, but no houses. At least what we'd have called houses. Postboxes appeared but the numbers danced about, following no pattern. Now and then we caught glimpses of straw-hatted heads moving slowly through the rows of cotton.

"Hey, Dad! Stop!' Junior cried. "That one was it. Didn't have a name on it. Look, that one just back there. I swear it had two-six-eight printed on it."

Dad backed up a few feet and turned into a rough dusty lane, leaving the car in low to keep the dust down. We bounced along for about a mile then the land sloped slightly revealing a little group of buildings that had been concealed from the road. I figured the one with the broken down porch was the house although the bigger building—a barn, I supposed—was in considerably better repair.

I wondered how the rickety boards of the front porch withstood the stampede of cousins that erupted out of the sagging screen door. Uncle Ralph and Mom hugged each other for a long time. He was Mom's older brother and she hadn't seen him since he headed for California years ago. Aunt Ada stood back shyly and then hugged Mom as they both rubbed tears off their cheeks. The cousins were mostly girls and considerably older than Junior and I. There were two male cousins, one grown-up, the other just older than Junior. The latter's open hostility to us was palpable. He kept his hands inside the bib of his overalls when we were introduced, spat an impressive arc out between his front teeth—there was plenty of room between them—and muttered, "Sissies. Still suckin' sugar-tits," dismissing us both.

Junior lifted his eyebrows and moved off after him determined to make friends. I stayed close to Dad's side, sensing that he was feeling as foreign here as I was.

We were fed a huge country breakfast, with Aunt Ada and the girls fussing over us while they chattered about family news and gossip. Eggs sizzled, bacon hissed, the smell of hot biscuits filled the one room that appeared to be the whole house. I didn't notice until after we'd eaten that the walls were papered in newspaper.

Junior came quietly into the room and slid into a chair beside me whispering conspiratorially, "Tots, we've got to pick cotton."

"What do you mean?"

"To get the sugar-tits out of our mouths." He gave me a knowing look and indicated the hostile cousin with a slight movement of his head. I understood.

We picked cotton for nine long hours under a sun that sat in the middle of the sky unmoving except to drop its full weight on our shoulders and drill into the small of our backs. The sharp points of the boils tore at our nails and cuticles until they were bloodied and numb. We only half filled the long canvas sacks that were slung over our shoulders and were paid at the end of the interminable day the staggering sum of thirty-six cents for our efforts. Junior earned twenty-one cents, I, fifteen. It was the longest day of my life.

"Lord," I said on the way home, "Can you imagine doing this every day of your life?"

"I guess that's what they all do. Marvin told me . . ."

"Marvin? I thought he was Melvin."

"*Marvin*. He told me that usually they were all out here—even the girls and Aunt Ada," Junior's eyes bugged. "Boy, this sure isn't what I'd call women's work. They're taking today off because we're here and they didn't want Mom to know."

"But we saw those really little kids get on the truck. Were they picking, too?"

"I guess so. That head man gave everybody a sack. Marvin calls it nigger work. He even said their house was a nigger shack."

"Did he *say* 'nigger'?" Mom said that only ignorant people used that word.

"Yeah. He says he hates them. They make the nig . . . the colored people work in different fields. That's why we didn't see any. They're doing the same work, but they have to be segregated."

"Like we were in Springfield?"

"Yeah. Only here it's the whites who put up the fences. Marvin says black oil and water don't mix."

"Marvin, Melvin or whatever, is about to grow up into an asshole."

"Oh, he's not so bad," Junior said. "He made me really laugh. Once. When we were on that old truck going to the cotton fields and could hardly see each other for the dust, he muttered under his breath, 'Dryer'n a popcorn fart.' I never heard that expression before."

"He'll replace Will Rogers on the stage some day."

It was on that first stop that I instigated the practice of Junior and me sleeping in the car. It was an inspired idea. Inspired by several things—mostly the cracks between the floorboards in the house. They were far enough apart in places to allow almost anything to crawl up in the night and join us in bed. Since I'd seen a vicious little fox terrier kill a snake at the barn where we'd picked cotton I assumed that under the rickety floors would be an ideal snake sanctuary. Marvin and his grown-up brother had given their bed to Mom and Dad. And if there was ever a cousin I didn't want to sleep with, Marvin was it. It was a toss-up between him and the snakes.

Arranging myself in the front seat for the night, I discovered if I left the gearshift in second, it was less likely to poke me. That first night I also discovered not to sleep with my head under the steering wheel. Strange night noises woke me and sitting up suddenly had left some knots on my head. Junior was getting so tall that he had to curl up in the backseat to make room for his legs. We both decided that it was much more comfortable than the floor. Particularly Uncle Ralph's floor.

"It's not very clean, either, is it?" That was the sort of observation that Junior didn't make often—he noticed people more than things.

"Marvin may hate colored people but not even in Springfield did I see anybody live in places like this."

"Well, this is Oklahoma."

"What's that got to do with it? Mom says people are people the world over."

"I know, but it's the times, too, don't forget. They're just poor, Tots. I mean really poor. I've never seen anything like it either. Not even the backwoods farms back home. They're stuck here and don't know how to get out. I guess it's like being in prison. Maybe Marvin hates the colored folks because he's doing the same work as they are. Their lives are exactly the same. He just hates his own life, I guess."

"I can understand that." I plumped the pillow and rolled down the window a bit more. "You sleepy?"

"My body's died and gone to heaven. But my mind's . . ."

"What'd you think? Wasn't it kind of funny when Uncle Ralph said they didn't need a calendar? Remember? He said he could just peel back the newspapers on the wall and figure out how many years they'd been here. The first one was 1932 he said—'Roosevelt Inauguration.' They used the *Kansas City Star* that first year then the Oklahoma City newspapers after that. He claims it's the best insulation in the world. Newspapers! 'Not a breath of wind comes in through them cracks,' he said, 'and wind here can blow the hide off a mule. No siree, not a breath of wind blows through them cracks in the walls. Now it just comes whistlin' up through the floorboards.'" I laughed but heard no sound from the backseat. "We all had a good laugh when he said that they'd had to sew rocks to the girls' skirts to keep them from blowing up around their necks. Those were good jokes, I thought."

"Yeah. But did you see Mom's face? All the time he was counting out the years and listing disasters. I don't mean world disasters, either. He *was* trying to be funny but Mom was doing anything but laughing. I don't think Mom had any idea that they were living like this."

"You remember when we were catching crawdads in Springfield? Down under that little bridge? You remember, when those little colored girls called us white trash?"

"Un-huh."

"Well. What do you think they meant by that? It always kind of bothered me."

"I don't know. Probably didn't mean anything. Just kids being nasty to other kids. They all do it."

I felt I shouldn't say what I was thinking, but I said it anyway. "I think they meant something like this. White trash would live like this."

There was a long silence. "I suppose they could have meant something like this."

Later in Arizona and California when I was called an Okie, the memory of this pathetic existence gave the insult an extra sting.

Our second stop was Albuquerque, New Mexico, where a second brother of Mom's would be our host along with his new wife, Doreen, whom we'd not met. From Ada—and we all wanted to be away from Ada—Albuquerque was over six-hundred miles as the crow flies. But since we weren't going by crow—our copilot's little joke—we decided to go flat out and try to break Dad's long-distance driving record.

The Model-A purred sweetly along the endless straight roads through the rest of Oklahoma and into Texas where the landscape was as relentlessly boring as it had been in Oklahoma. Cotton fields stretched as far as the eye could reach relieved only by the occasional patch of dried out cornstalks which looked like strange elongated skeletons of beasts who'd been picked clean by crows. Little towns popped up unannounced, treeless, all but empty of inhabitants in spite of population listings on the signs—Childress: 457, Silverton: 1,045, Tulia: 79, Dimmit: 574, Floydada: no listing (had they all gone west?)—and then would disappear as quickly as they'd appeared, swallowed up again in lakes of cotton.

We'd had the roads pretty much to ourselves until we were nearing the New Mexico border where we became aware of more traffic. It seemed to be filtering down from Amarillo—to the north—down to the more southern highways in order to avoid the front ranges of the Rocky Mountains. Cars and trucks and buses of all sorts started appearing along the way—some pulled over to the side of the high-way, some gathered with others in clearings, camping just off the roads. Like covered wagons forming circles to protect themselves from the Indians, Junior said. We stopped only to fill up our gas tank and the canvas water bag (and the eye-opener) and use the toilets. The latter more often than not a mistake when bushes beside the road offered at least clean virgin territory to squat down in. Even Mom was soon disappearing discreetly when we stopped to let the motor cool down enough for Junior to fill the radiator.

I'd taken a side trip into the cotton field and come back to the steaming car and said to Dad, using one of his favorite expressions. "If you want to know where I've been, well," I glanced around to make sure Mom wasn't in sight, "I've been shittin' in tall cotton."

Junior roared with laughter and spilled some water from the canvas bag causing him to mutter "shit" under his breath.

"Weeelll, now," Dad said, drawling it out as he cupped his hands around a match to light a Spud. "Ain't we gettin' to be the big boys?"

Junior blushed, "Sorry, Dad. It just slipped out."

"Aw hell, son, if you ain't old enough now to say shit—when it's the right time and place, you won't ever be." He let out a long cloud of smoke as he squinted following the direction Mom had taken. "As for you shittin' in tall cotton, boy, well there's more to that old ex-pression than just that."

"You mean like 'keep your gallouses clean' has more meanings?"

"'Xactly. It means—well, like you're tryin' to hide something. You know what you're doing. You're shittin'. But nobody can see you. In other words, you're doing something you don't want any-body to know about. Anything you do that you might be ashamed of, that you know is wrong, well, that's shittin' in tall cotton." He flicked the ash off his cigarette with his middle finger. "It can also mean just the opposite. Like cheatin' on your husband." He grinned sheepishly. "Or wife. You might think nobody knows what you're doin', but you're only kiddin' yourself. The whole town probably knows and you think you're foolin' everybody, but you're only foolin' yourself. That's also shittin' in tall cotton." He took a last deep drag and flicked the butt out into the middle of the road. He looked up and pointed. "Here comes your mom." He opened his door and we clambered into the backseat as Mom waved and hurried to the car.

That monologue sent chills all through me. I was going through my mind the amount of shitting in tall cotton I'd already done.

There was Bonnie Lou and Mary Ann and—but I wasn't even able to think about Ronnie yet. That was shitting in the tallest possible cotton. Or so I thought at the time. It's amazing how tall cotton can grow.

Albuquerque was as satisfying as Ada had been disappointing. Uncle Ernest and Aunt Doreen were living with her parents while they prepared for a California expedition of their own. Uncle Ernest was waiting delivery on a house-trailer—the latest model with all modern conveniences, he said proudly. We stayed with them for two days, soaking in hot baths and luxuriating in real beds—even Junior and I had one to ourselves, nobody was forced onto a pallet.

The haul to the next stop was one to try men's souls, as Mom said later. Almost from the moment we left Albuquerque things started going wrong. We never thought of car trouble. We all had perfect faith in the Model-A and in Dad's ability to fix anything short of a broken axle. We'd decided on the southern route down to Silver City and across the Arizona border at a small town called Paradise. It turned out to be anything else but.

Our first flat tire wasn't so catastrophic, it was the second and third that had our nerves twanging. We were a fairly expert team at changing wheels and tires, and fixing patches on inner tubes, but two blowouts happening almost on top of each other can have a pretty destructive effect on your morale. Not to mention your pocketbook. Having to buy two new tires and tubes caused Dad to have a blowout of his own that sent the rest of us fleeing into the desert. He was his father's own son as far as temper went. Remembering how Grandpa had killed his prize cow, I feared for the Model-A's life until his rage had subsided.

After that things went more or less smoothly all the way to Silver City. It was just after Silver City that we shot the rod. Somewhere between Paradise and Silver City—purgatory, Junior said. It took Dad about four hours to fix, flat on his back under the car with Junior under there with him half the time. At least they were in the only available shade. Junior explained to me in detail what a rod was, where it connected whatever and why it was so difficult to repair and what a genius Dad was since he was working with the minimum of tools and what looked like a great deal of bailing wire. I didn't understand a word of the mechanics of the thing and let his words drip off me along with the sweat.

"Paradise, my ass," Dad said after he'd been up and down both sides of the main street of this little border town finding nothing open. It was Sunday and there wasn't even a diner or a cafe where we could eat. That was problem enough, but Dad's bottle was as dry as mules' balls. With the hope that we'd find a roadside diner we headed out of Paradise into the Arizona desert.

If we thought we'd seen desert before we were sadly mistaken. Oklahoma, Texas, and New Mexico were the Black Forest compared to this. The road was straight as a die, cutting through rolling mounds of sandy red earth, with only a mesquite bush or tumbleweed hanging to the barren surface.

"A place here on the map looks like it might be big enough to have at least a Woody's Cafe," Junior said. "It's called C-o-c-h-i-s-e. However you pronounce it. We ought to be there soon."

"Isn't that an Indian tribe?" Mom asked.

"Wasn't it something to do with Custer's Last Stand?" I risked.

"This is *my* last stand," Dad said. "If I don't get something cold to drink pretty soon—a beer is frothin' in my mind—I'm going to stop and get out and drink that mirage." The road was so hot that the water effect created by the mirage was so convincing that it gave the illusion that we were driving through water. Once Dad mentioned it, I couldn't take my eyes off it and in some reverse order it made me feel cooler.

We ate in Cochise at a diner-filling station. Dad washed down his food with two cold Budweisers and was out having the car attended to while we finished. He seemed in a particularly good mood when we piled back into the car. Back on the road, he reached under his seat and pulled out his full bottle. "Whooeee, looky here what I got." He shook the bottle of a particularly dark liquid. "That ole boy back there claims this is the best moonshine in Arizona. Looks like molasses. I think it's made out of used sump oil and kerosene. Figured if I can't drink it, I'll just use it like smelling salts. One whiff and it'll curl your hair."

Junior and I studied the map—anything was more interesting than looking out the windows at the bleak moonscape—checking and rechecking the mileage to Tucson where we'd decided to spend the night. We'd finally be in a motor court and have a good night's rest and clean up for the last hundred and twenty miles to Phoenix and Aunt Dell. We couldn't arrive on her doorsteps looking like grubby hicks.

We stopped for gas and a cold drink in the mid-afternoon at a place that advertised modestly on a hand-painted sign: Reptile Farm. Adm. 5-cents. I was dying to go in, but didn't dare ask for the money.

The man pumping the gas saw us looking at the sign and called out, "Go on in. Hell, it ain't much. Ain't worth a nickel. Just a couple of rattlers and an old Gila Monster."

We followed the painted arrows to the back of the shed to a fence which enclosed a hole or pit in the ground. We were both cautious about getting close to the fence, but we sidled up and looked over. The man was right, there were two rattlesnakes, diamondbacks, looking more dead than alive coiled lazily around each other and at the other end of the pit was a yellow and black mottled lizard about two feet long that really did look dead.

"I guess he could be pretty scary if he was moving and coming at you," I said.

"He doesn't look like he'd ever move again." Junior shuddered.

"Rabbit run across your grave?"

"Sort of. I was thinking of Grandma. That hole. That big hole they dug for her. These poor things look pretty lost down there in their grave."

"Don't say a word about them snakes," Dad demanded when we were back on the road. He had a fear of snakes so violent that even stories about them would turn him pale. "Or that Geela Monster."

"The man pronounced it Heela, Dad. Did you hear him, Mom? It must be the Mexican pronunciation." He unfolded the map again. "Hey, Tots, here it is. I thought I'd seen it. It's all over down here— Gila Bend, the Gila River. And here, this whole area is the Gila Desert."

"Are we in it? This is sure a desert."

"No, we're still over this way—a bit to the east of it." He burst out laughing. "Here's Tombstone!"

"Tombstone?" I said. "I thought that was just a name they used in the movies."

"No. Look right here." He pointed it out for me. "Tombstone. And over here the Gila Desert." I thought he shuddered again as he folded the map up quickly and muttered under his breath, "What a place to be buried."

We were as fresh and clean as we could be when we arrived in Phoenix. We'd found clean cabins outside Tucson with big shower rooms and we all soaked, shampooed, slept and were shining with excitement about seeing Aunt Dell and Sister.

Just after a sign reading City Limits, we went over a long low bridge above a dry riverbed where I noticed a lot of people were camping out.

"Now, go slowly, Dad." Junior had a letter of directions in his hand. "Aunt Dell says right after the bridge there's a stop sign. Then we go two more blocks and turn left. That'll be her street. Tam . . . Tamar . . . I don't know quite how to say it. Tamarisk, I guess. Tamarisk Avenue."

It couldn't have been easier to find and there we were being hugged and kissed with tears being rubbed from cheek to cheek in front of a neat, little wooden house with a long screened porch across the front, very much like Grandpa's. The box with the lump of excelsior and chicken wire air-conditioners were hanging on two of the windows, stamping the known with something foreign. Houses, I was learning are like some plants—one is always surprised to find them cropping up, looking so familiar, in places thousands of miles from where you first knew them. We were home. Off the road. We all sighed and laughed. *Home.* At least Aunt Dell made us feel at home. For the time being.

It took no time for us to be brought up to date: Sister was working in a nightclub as a waitress, making eye-bugging amounts of money. Mavis had got a job in a lawyer's office as a file clerk. ("Have you had any experience in filing, Miss Slokum?" she'd been asked.)

("Only my nails, Mr. Griggs. And horses' hooves when they've just been shod. And sharpening a hoe. But I can read and the alphabet is no mystery to me.")

"That lawyer!" Aunt Dell roared, "is still in her lap." She nudged Dad in the ribs. "And she swears not in her pants."

I thought I'd understood but it wasn't until I looked at Junior's stunned eyes that I was sure I had.

"Anyway, Mavis'll be home about five. Sister's . . ." Aunt Dell cleared her throat. "Sister's out shoppin'. She ought to be back any minute. We didn't have any notion of just when you all'd be gettin' here." We soon learned that "out shopping" meant that Sister hadn't come home after work in the nightclub. When she did get home and I saw her for the first time in two years, I caught my breath. She was more beautiful than I'd ever imagined. I was glued to her side.

That nice-looking man standing shyly back by the front door was the new man in Aunt Dell's life. Roy Blake. A World War veteran, now a cattle inspector for the Arizona State Meat Board, an amateur broncobuster, ex-cowboy and now live-in . . . Well, it was never explained adequately since Aunt Dell made a big point that he had the room at the back of the garage and was just a boarder and lodger who'd become part of the family. "Well, Milly," Aunt Dell said. "How'd you start out? Roomin' and boardin' with us Slokums down on Indian Creek when you'as teachin' school there. Now look what it got you. Two big chips off that old block of Woods that you married." She hugged me and Junior. "And no way out." Then she hugged Mom. "We'll just see if we can't get Roy in here permanent." She rolled her eyes suggestively. "Into the family, that is."

"I've paid six-months' rent in advance," Roy said quietly. "If she throws me out, I'll sue." His light blue eyes were so steely I thought he was serious. But of course everybody laughed. He really looked like a cowboy—sort of like Gary Cooper—blondish with a craggily handsome face.

Within minutes of our arrival, Aunt Dell was at work preparing what she called a down-home Woods Pow-Wow. The food portion of this festive Pow-Wow was always hamburgers with every conceivable sauce from catsup to pickalilli, sliced onions, lettuce, Kraft cheese and toasted buns. She went at the job of creating the meat patties with the seriousness of a French chef. The liquid accompaniment of the Pow-Wow was already lined up on the kitchen table: bottles of bourbon and every sort of mix from Nehi to Seven-Up. "But not a Zest-O, you'll notice," she yelled above the din of voices—Sister's and Mavis's now added to the rest—all trying to fill the two-year gap at once—"and there's one hell of a story about good ole Zest-O that I'm dying to tell you if I ever get the chance."

Stories were coming hot and fast. Grandma's funeral, the general exodus from around Galena, Aunt Dell's adventures with Sister and Mavis hitchhiking across the country, how she'd met Roy (he'd had the good fortune to be the one to provide the purtiest hitchhikers in the world with their last ride—right into Phoenix city limits and hadn't been far from them since), the death of Woody's Cafe became a comic disaster story in Dad's hands. Also in Dad's hands the bourbon was fueling and feeding his storehouse of tall tales and he was enjoying himself enormously, having found an appreciative audience in Roy.

A new audience didn't produce new stories, necessarily, but Dad's set-pieces took on fresh paint, bright and colorful and almost sounded new to us. He was off and away and his stories would always last longer than the bourbon.

He was in tip-top form and kept us all laughing. When he launched into my favorite story that never failed to keep the idlers around the courthouse in Galena riveted, Roy had the same awestruck look they got when Dad mentioned Bonnie and Clyde's name with easy familiarity. According to Dad's eyewitness account, Bonnie and Clyde had just robbed a bank in Crane and he'd been in the sheriff's office when the call came in that the robbers were headed toward Galena. This, of course, had thrown Maude Stevens in the telephone office into a frenzy and everybody in town who had a phone had the news in seconds.

Clem Walters, Dad's friend and the recently elected sheriff, had Dad deputized by the time they hit the first landing of the courthouse. Dad had been deputized by Clem before and all it seemed to take was a wink and a nod. Being deputized couldn't have been very exclusive since almost every man in Galena swore he'd been in that famous posse. They probably were. As Dad explained it, Sheriff Walters didn't actually pin badges on anybody and on that great day, he just yelled, "It's Bonnie and Clyde! Let's *go!*" And all those who could, went. With Dad in the lead car with the sheriff.

The town had gone crazy. I've heard it claimed that some sheriffs would do everything but direct traffic to assure Bonnie and Clyde a safe getaway—they were heroes—but Clem Walters wanted to be famous. He wanted the extraordinary feather in his cocky Stetson that the capture of the notorious team would bring. People were running around like chickens with their heads cut off. Men had grabbed rifles and guns and were piling into cars, cranking them up and roaring around the town square following the sheriff's car with Dad and a bunch of other men packed in on top of him. Dad said Clem kept yellin', "For Christ's sake, sit down! I can't see out the fuckin' windshield!"

They headed out the road that led to the high school which was on the main highway from Crane. They'd wait there, the sheriff explained, trying to be very calm and cool, Dad said, but the fact that he was whispering like a kid playing hide and seek gave away the fact that he was scared shitless.

They must have looked plumb silly, Dad said, a whole line of cars—the number varied from fifty to over a hundred—bumper to bumper, backed up the hill across the railroad tracks and some at the tail end still back up in the town square. And there they sat, motors being gunned, guns being cocked and uncocked, hundreds of pairs of round excited eyes on the highway and not a sign of traffic. They sat there for over ten minutes, not a cat stirring on the road, dead silent, not daring to take their eyes off the road even to light a cigarette. "Shit!" was the only word Dad heard in the sheriff's car when somebody burned his fingers on a match until all of a sudden Clem opened his door and said, "God *damn!* I've got to piss."

"Pure nerves," Dad said. The minute the sheriff's stream was seen or heard, the whole damned bunch as far as the eye could see had jumped out of the cars and started creating a small flood flowing down the hill. "And right then, in mid-piss, somebody yelled, 'Jesus Christ, here they come!' And sure enough," here Dad really starting rolling with his story, "roundin' the nearest bend was a Ford V-8, spanking clean and gleamin' chrome, spare tires fitted into the front fenders—just like in the pictures. That was it all right. Well, every-body started scrambling back into their cars, half of them with their cocks still hanging out, others pissin' down their legs. Never seen anything so funny in all my life. Clem jumped back in the car, tryin' to get it in gear and his cock in his pants at the same time and I'll be damned if he didn't stall the fuckin' motor." Dad grinned. "He'd been better off to let his cock drive the car. I mean, there they was—Bonnie and Clyde, for Christ's sake!—barrelling down on us and the whole damned posse lined up with piss runnin' down their pants' legs and the sheriff stalled!

"I stuck my head out the window and yelled back to Wilbur Simms—he was behind us—'For Christ's sake, Will, give us a shove!' Will looked plumb disgusted and hauled off and rammed us so hard the two bumpers caught. I tell you I like to'a died. Stuck! Stuck like a couple of dogs fuckin' and by this time that V-8 was whizzin' past us so fast I couldn't hardly see who was in it. They got a good quarter-mile ahead of us by the time we got out on the main road, still stuck, with Will sort'a pushin' us and us sorta pullin' him. Then Clem said, 'I'll be goddamned if I'm gonna' miss the chance of a lifetime,' and he done the quickest maneuver I ever seen. He sort of double-clutched and gunned her and slammed on his brake all at the same time, causing something to snap loose and we took off like a big-assed bird. I mean, we was flyin'!

"I could hear something bangin' and clatterin' and I looked back and seen Will had lost his front bumper. I knew what we was draggin' then. But it sure as shit didn't hold us back. We started gainin' on that V-8 by the time it swerved left onto the bridge—you got to slow down on that corner or you're in the James River. I don't know who was drivin' that Ford, but he shore knew what he was doin'. They went around that corner on two wheels and how he ever pulled that vehicle back down on all fours is still a mystery to me. But Clem? What'd he go and do? I'll be goddamned if he didn't cut that corner too short. Not only that, but bashed in the left rear fender and we lost momentum and careened like a pig on ice. I figured for sure we'as goin' have to swim. We bounced off both sides of the bridge like a ballbearing in one of them pinball machines. By the time Clem straightened her out, that V-8 was all but out of sight. I knew it was useless to go on, they had us outclassed in every way and had gained on us by a country mile. But Clem floorboarded that old heap of his and kept tryin'. He ain't a piker, I'll give him that.

"But Bonnie and Clyde by then was headed toward Reedspring, going up that hill off the bridge like it was flat as a pancake. I don't think they even had to shift gears. Clem sure as hell had to. We went all the way down to low before we even started up that damned hill. I was sick. I just closed my eyes and groaned. We didn't have a chance in hell now of catchin' 'em. Several cars behind us started honkin' and tryin' to pass us. I thought Clem would bust a gut. It was pitiful. Clem was all hunched down, head workin' like a chicken's, bobbin' back and forth in the seat trying' to coax her up that hill. He was urgin', talkin' to that pore ole heap—'Come on, baby. Come on, goddammit!'

"Well, as I said, it was just plain pitiful. I didn't like to say nothin'. I knew Clem was heartbroke. I never felt so sorry for a man in my life. His big chance. It was *Bonnie and Clyde,* for Christ's sake!" Dad shook his head sadly. "You might say he pissed it away."

Dad played the whole story to Roy. I think he somehow judged people by the way they responded to his oft-told tales. Roy proved to be one of the most responsive listeners I'd ever seen. His laughter and attention were in perfect harmony with the narrative, as if he'd rehearsed his role. Perhaps he and Dad had something in common. At any rate, he was *in*. Dad was beaming with triumph like he had when we danced together in the Domino Cafe. Roy had been fascinated by the occupants of the car. He and Dad whispered lewdly about things too mysterious or improper for women and children's ears. I remember wondering at the time if they were talking about things that only men could do together. Whatever it was, it kept their heads together and their laughter low and suggestive of dark, devious goings-on.

"Let 'em talk dirty to theirselves," Aunt Dell said dismissively when she was certain that she wasn't going to be allowed to listen in. "We got better things to do, ain't we? Like choppin' some more ice. Junior, you're the strong one. Grab a pick—and that ain't spelled with no 'r'—if they can talk dirty, so can we. Oh yes. More ice. Never could stand hot bourbon."

"You might not be able to stand it," Dad teased, "but I never seen you turn it down. Except down your throat."

"Don't say that sort of thing in front of Roy," Aunt Dell yelled and ran laughing toward Dad with her hand raised ready to slap. "You still ain't too big or too smart for your old—er, *younger* sister to give you a right good 'un."

"Momma," Mavis called. "You're pretty feisty for somebody with a busted back."

Aunt Dell and Roy exchanged a look and Aunt Dell put her hand over her mouth and widened her eyes like a naughty child. "Oh Lord. I've been forgettin' to limp."

"Oh dear," Mom said. "Have you hurt yourself, Dell?"

"Well, I *did.*" She looked at Roy and they both laughed. "That's what I've been dyin' to tell you about."

Aunt Dell had been working at a soda pop bottling plant—Zest-O—feeding the caps into a machine that snapped the tops on, sitting on a high stool. One day she almost fell off her perch, and in an effort to catch herself, the stool slipped out from under her—"One of them damned little rubber ends was missin' on the stool's leg," she said then added with a roll of her eyes, "fortunately."

She had fallen, injuring her back. The company doctor had poked around and examined her and declared her only bruised but Aunt Dell's back didn't seem to get better. She went to other doctors and they couldn't find anything wrong in the X-rays, but would shake their heads and say, "You just can't tell with the back. A nerve can be pinched, a bone slightly chipped, a vertebrae knocked a bit out of line . . ." They couldn't say anything positive but Aunt Dell had kept her ears open and learned something positive. And invaluable. She learned that the back was territory that defied intensive investigation and she also learned that she could sue. She did. With the help of Mavis's employer, she sued Zest-O and won the case—doctor bills paid and a thousand dollar settlement which she split down the middle with the lawyer. "Smartest man I ever seen. He don't miss a trick. A real shyster."

Aunt Dell was in business. She fell in ladies' rooms in gas stations, in hotel lobbies, department stores, anywhere where a likely suit could be filed. She and Mavis's boss were a formidable pair—she was a born actress and he wasn't without histrionic talent himself. They had several cases going at once. Of course, doctors could never find anything wrong but she won at least seventy-five percent of her suits.

We all—except Dad—tried to take her accidents seriously but the scales dropped from my eyes the second day we were in Phoenix. I was with Aunt Dell downtown on Van Buren Boulevard and we went into the Goldwater Department Store. I was eating an ice-cream cone I hadn't asked for but when offered could hardly refuse. We stood just inside the doorway, Aunt Dell looking smart in a pretty summer dress and looking over the premises with a practiced eye. There was a perfectly flat, not highly polished wooden floor with no cracks to catch a heel, no sudden changes of level to trip over, not even a carpet to provide a trap for a toe. The staircase to the mezzanine was on the other side of this sea of perfectly safe flooring dotted only by islands of counters. She would never have risked doing herself real damage by falling through a glass-topped showcase. I recall she sighed rather sadly, having taken it all in and then turned abruptly, knocking the ice cream out of my hand and whispering to me as she did, "Scoot. Git back to the car. *Run!*"

I was too bewildered to do anything else. I ran but caught sight of her stepping deliberately into the ice cream and falling beautifully onto her bottom and following through onto her shoulder and arm showing just the right amount of a well-shaped leg. It was not unlike Junior sliding into home plate. Being a witness to her methods made me feel like an accomplice and I was careful in the future not to be alone with her in "falling down" territory.

Everybody contributed to the household expenses on Tamarisk Avenue—even Aunt Dell in her erratic and original way. It was imperative that we do the same. We were family, after all, not houseguests. School would start soon and Mom's Law decreed that school-terms were inviolable and we had to be settled in our own place as soon as possible. We had to get work.

Sister got Mom all tarted up (Roy's expression) to go to work as a waitress with her at The Ship. Sister was able to choose extra help for the weekends if she wanted to share the tables assigned to her. Mom had had experience as a waitress so it seemed a logical thing for her to do. I thought she looked very glamorous—her short hair had been put up in tight little curls all over her head, her eyes were heavily made up and she wore a skirt whose brevity gave Dad a shock although he tried to make a joke of it. Mom bravely pranced up and down the living room trying to get used to her new role, smirking and smiling in a clumsy imitation of a flirtatious vamp. "May I bring you a drink, sir?" she asked, bending down over Junior.

He looked embarrassed but played along. "Why, sure thang, honey-pie. Ah'll have a . . . a . . . Ah'll have a mint julep, please. But without the julep."

Everybody laughed and Mom suddenly looked stricken. "For Heaven's sake, Sister. I don't know the names of any of those fancy drinks. What'll I do?"

"Honey, just come to me if you have any trouble. There isn't a mixed drink that I haven't heard about."

"Or tried," Mavis said in a quiet, dry voice. Junior slipped out onto the front porch with me behind him while they all laughed.

He plunked himself down in one of our wicker chairs and squinted his eyes as though he were trying to see through the rusty screening into the night. A night pitch black with only a few lightning bugs snapping their lights off and on. A neighbor's house here and there had lights on, shining dimly out onto the crabgrass lawns but there were no streetlights and no cars to puncture the blackness. I crawled over his legs to where our pallets had been made up and started taking off my shoes.

"What're you looking at," I asked.

"Nothin'."

"Well, you're staring."

"Staring into space. Empty space."

"What're you seeing?"

"Nothin'."

"Then why stare?"

"Just trying to see." He leaned back into the chair and closed his eyes. He was quiet until I had my shoes off and stood up to take off my shirt. "Just trying to see what it's going to be like."

"What do you mean?"

"What it's going to be *like.*" He shrugged his shoulders and leaned over to untie his own shoes. "What we're going to have to do to make a living." He pitched a shoe at me which I caught and placed next to mine. "I mean, is Mom going to have to have her hair curled up like Little Orphan Annie and wiggle her bottom and serve a bunch of drunks so we can buy some food?" Another shoe hit my chest. Then a wad of damp socks. I lined them up with the others. "What sort of work will Dad have to do? Dig ditches?"

Junior was always the one to hear the plop of the paper being thrown onto the front yard early every morning during those first desperate days at Aunt Dell's. He ran with it around the house to the kitchen where Dad was already up, having made a huge pot of coffee for the grown-ups who'd come drifting into the kitchen one by one. Mavis had to be at the office by eight-thirty. Aunt Dell either had a doctor's appointment or one with Mavis's boss by no later than ten, or else was making plans to scout for new places to fall. Mom would sleep only until about eight no matter what time she'd got home from The Ship. Sister's room was a fortress—we never knew whether she was there or out shopping—until about noon. Roy's hours were so irregular that he couldn't be counted on. If a herd of cattle had come into the stockyard during the night, he'd have to be there by five to inspect them "on the hoof," which was his job before they went to slaughter. Sometimes he'd travel out of town to ranches to check on reports of hoof and mouth disease, which could mean that he'd be gone for several days at a time.

So Dad was there, waiting for the paper that Junior delivered and they'd divide it up, tiptoeing around, whispering, folding it with care so as not to make noise and then settling down to get the bad news of the day. Our bad news wasn't found on the front pages, but in the want ads. If there was something in the Male Wanted section that Dad could possibly fill—gas station attendant, short-order cook, delivery-truck driver—he'd light out immediately after he and Junior had found the address on a city map. Mom would go through the paper again more thoroughly when she got up. There would then be the long morning wait for Dad's telephone call or return. It was always the latter—the job had been filled yesterday; he hadn't enough experience as a chef (Woody's Cafe didn't seem to count for much); didn't have an Arizona State driver's license. Or something. Always something.

"We don't have any money *at all,*" Junior told me. "Absolutely none. We're still waiting for some money from the auction in Galena and that won't get here until God knows when. We can't go on living off Aunt Dell. All we have is what Mom makes in that . . . *nightclub.*" He spat out the words as though it were a whorehouse.

"But we only just got here . . ."

"Yeah. Have you looked at the want ads? There aren't *any* jobs, Totsy. I wish you'd pay a little more attention to the . . . *realities.*" He raised a hand to shut me up. "If you ask me what that means, I'll slap you winding . . ."

"But maybe Mom can . . ."

"She can't. She can't teach here. Oh, there are jobs listed for engineers for the copper mines down in places like A-joe or A-hoe or whatever it's called, but Dad is not an engineer. Mining or otherwise."

Junior's concern was reflected in Dad's face every day. And Mom's. Well, everybody was getting pretty depressed as that first week wore on.

Mom continued to work at The Ship with Sister, bringing home an apron-pocket of change that we'd all count out on the kitchen table. One night, $2.65, another $1.98, a $3.46, and her top of $5.75. When we realized that Sister was coming home with twice or three times that amount, Mom had to confess that she hated it about as much as we hated picking cotton.

Every morning was spent scouring the papers—the want ads were gone over by Dad and Mom, then by Aunt Dell, then by Roy, then by Junior and me. Possibilities were circled. Letters written and rewritten. Phone calls made. After the first week there simply seemed to be some sort of breakdown in communications. Not one answer from our letters had been received. Phone messages left were not returned. The list of jobs in the papers seemed to shrink daily. Mom investigated teaching possibilities. Letters to the State Board of Education had been sent in the hope that she would be eligible for an Arizona teaching credential. Even that seemed to have become snarled up in a tangle of red tape.

Junior came up with a good idea for us after we'd gone through the Sunday papers' ads. We'd go into business. We'd mow lawns. Well, he would and I'd rake. We cleaned and oiled the old lawn mower in the garage and started out. We were stymied by the "No Peddlers—No Soliciting" signs. How could we get to mow a lawn if we couldn't talk to anybody?

"Let's print a sign," I suggested. "I'll carry it on a stick like the strikers do, and the people can read from inside their houses. Then we don't have to ring doorbells or so . . . solicitize or whatever it is."

"Solicit, dummy." Junior grinned. "That ain't a dumb idea."

We found an old can of black paint in the garage, that had a crust about an inch thick and hard as cement on the top when we finally got the lid off. We managed to break through the crust with a hammer and chisel to find enough liquid to make our sign. We cut a square off the side of a cardboard box that had "Clabber Girl Baking Powder" printed on the outside, but the inside was perfect for "Lawns Cut (and raked): 25 cents. Any Size." I wanted to add "Within Reason," but Junior pointed out that the sign was the come-on and we'd be able to dicker about the price once we'd lured the residents out of their houses. While the paint dried, I decided to go to the big public swimming pool down at the end of Tamarisk Avenue. Sunday was the only day children under twelve were allowed in free. Junior didn't have the dime he'd have to pay and besides, he was going through the Sunday papers from front to back, "Boning up on Arizona," he explained.

I was halfway down the driveway, with my towel and swimming trunks under my arm when I heard him call from the screened porch, "Hey. Listen. Y'all shore that white trash don't have to pay?" I walked on with a back as straight as I could make it.

The changing room smelled of hot bodies, Clorox that Mom used for cleaning, and a bit like the men's room in the courthouse in Galena. I huddled on a bench and wormed out of my short pants and underwear and into the slightly too big, dark blue woolen trunks whose moth holes had been darned with regular thread making the repairs pucker like sores with the scabs just off.

Glimpses of heavy dangling cocks and balls spilling out of nests of curly hair—resembling the excelsior used in the air-conditioners—were not things of beauty. I'd never seen naked men before.

The water in the pool was like soup and smelled like the changing room. I felt lonely and bored. Even going down the slide was no fun without someone to watch you and wave to. I missed Junior. So much for solitary outings.

"He's a little upset," Mom said when I asked where Junior was. "I think he's out in the garage."

The garage doors were closed. He surely wouldn't be in there. I called anyway, to make sure. Nothing. I pushed on the side door but it wouldn't budge. "Hey, Junior, you in there?" Silence. "Then why is this door locked?" Still silence. "Come on. Mom says you're in there. What are you doing for Lord's sake?"

"Go away."

"What?"

He screamed. "I said go a-WAY."

I'd never heard him scream like that. I moved closer to the door and talked softly as though we were standing close together. "What's the matter? You mad at me? You said you didn't want to go to the pool."

"Oh, Tots, please, just go *a-way*. I don't want anybody to see me. Not even you."

"For heaven's sake!" I was alarmed. This was not like him. "Let me *in*. What in the world's the matter with you? Have you got another boil on your neck?" He'd had them before, a series of them one spring and the unsightliness of them bothered him more than the pain. "Looky here. I've seen them before. You know that doesn't bother me." I waited and listened. I heard him move toward the door and open it slightly.

"OK." He was hiding behind the door. "Come on in."

I poked my head around the door, not knowing what to expect. He was standing stooped over wearing a funny-looking knitted cap. He looked stricken as though he'd either been crying or was about to. "What in God's name are you wearing that thing for? It's boiling hot. Have you gone ker-flooie?" I moved forward and reached for the cap. He grabbed my hand in an iron grip.

"Don't," he said dangerously. "Don't touch that cap."

He *had* gone ker-flooie. "Well, at least pull it up from your ears. You'll have a heat stroke or something."

"I can't pull it up. That's the whole point. I've got to wear this . . ." My eyes widened, I was sure he was going to use Dad's word. And he did. ". . . *fucking* cap for the next month. At least."

"Did you hurt yourself?" That could be the only explanation.

"No. Aunt Dell did."

"Aunt Dell did *what*? For Lord's sake, you're driving me crazy. What are you talking about?"

He stood perfectly still for several seconds not looking at me so much as through me. Then he slowly lifted both his hands and pulled the hat all the way down over his face and then let out an awful cry of anguish as he ripped it off. "Just *look* what she's done," he wailed.

At first I couldn't figure out what was wrong. Then I saw and a great hoot of laughter burst from me before I could control it. His hair had been cut or rather butchered. It was what we all called the "bowl cut." It looked as though a bowl had been put on his head and every strand of hair hanging beneath its rim was cut and then the area shaved, leaving a circular crown of hair. It was awful.

"There, you see," he said accusingly. "Even you laugh at me."

"I'm sorry. Really I am. It just slipped out. How in the world did it happen?"

"Oh, you know Aunt Dell. She knows how to do everything. And we all thought she knew how to cut hair. She said it was pure robbery to pay twenty-five cents for a haircut. So."

"So?"

"So, she went at me with a pair of rusty clippers that I swear was used for shearing sheep. About a hundred years ago. I could feel her going up the back of my neck and then before I could open my mouth, I felt the clippers practically on top of my head. She'd cut a broad strip right up behind my ear." He turned his head sideways for me to see. "Just look at that. See? Right up to here. Then there was nothing to do but try to even it all out. Well, you see what happened. I'm a mess. I look like a worn out mop." He did, too. We looked at each other for a second and then we both laughed. He choked on his laughter and I thought he was going to cry.

"It'll grow. Your hair always grows faster than mine. Why in a week . . ."

"In a week, we're supposed to be starting school. Well, that is, that's when school starts here. I'll be laughed out of the schoolhouse . . ." He was deadly serious now and I realized what he was saying was true. It was going to be difficult enough getting adjusted to a new school filled with people we've never even seen and I'd already had enough comments on my accent to know that we were all going to have to battle some sort of prejudice for just being from out-of-state. New kids in school are always the ones to be ganged up on and looking like a worn out mop was not the best way to start out.

"Well, we can't do anything about it today. It's Sunday. I know Sister will loan me a quarter and we'll take you to a regular barber and he'll even it all up."

"He'll have to shave my head to even it all up."

Nothing I could say could make him leave the garage or take off that terrible cap. He'd decided that the heat generated by the airless room and the wool would perhaps stimulate the growth. I went back to the house promising to bring him something cold to drink.

I got sidetracked by considerable excitement in the kitchen. Mom had gone back over the Sunday ads and found something under "Couples Wanted" that didn't sound very good, but she'd called on the off chance and talked to a lady called Mrs. Jones who had, Mom said, a southern accent thicker than molasses and twice as sweet, who seemed eager to have an interview—the sooner the better. Mom had confessed that they were more than a couple—two young sons came with the package—but had been assured by Mrs. Jones that the "quarters" were adequate for a family.

"North Twelfth Street is fancy," Aunt Dell had pointed out. "That's on the other side of Van Buren, the *right* side of the tracks. Now way up there—what did you say the number was? 1548? Oh me, that's waaaay up there. By the new high school. Lincoln High. Couldn't be better. New grade school too. Best schools for the boys."

I was ordered into the bath with Dad's leftover water—there was always a water shortage in Phoenix—and told to make myself "shine." Mom and Dad kept moving back and forth into the bathroom, Dad turning purple in the face buttoning his shirt collar and sliding a pre-knotted tie under his chin. Mom fussed with her hair with a worried look.

"But what if they *are*, Woody?" Mom said, pushing him away from the mirror.

"Milly, a job's a job."

"I know, but would you work for . . ."

"People are people, Milly." Dad had the tie crookedly in place. "That's what you're always sayin'."

"Yes, well, I don't know." She grabbed at Dad's tie. "Hold still." She made a slight adjustment that didn't change a thing. "There." She patted his chest absentmindedly, noticing me in the bathtub as though for the first time. "Oh. Where's Junior?"

"In the garage."

"What in the world is he . . . Oh, dear. Is he still sulking?"

"Sweltering is more like it. He's in a heavy wool cap and he won't take it off until his hair grows back."

"Well. He'll just have to stay here then. You hurry up." She stared wide-eyed at herself in the mirror, rolling her lips together to spread the lipstick. She shook her head at her reflection and bustled out of the room.

We drove past the swimming pool, up to Van Buren, then down it to the "old" high school, Phoenix Union—soon learning to refer to it as old P.U. pronounced Pee-Yew, with a suggestion of clamping out smells with thumb and forefinger—where we turned left on Twelfth Street and went up and up and up. The numbers getting bigger as we went along past neat low houses set in ever-increasingly elaborate gardens. The houses got more and more substantial, some even two-storied, squelching the idea that I was beginning to get fixed about Phoenix that everything was built low and squashed out because the sun melted everything and prevented it from growing tall, rather like the crabgrass that covered everything by hugging the ground.

We almost missed 1548 North Twelfth Street because all we could see was a high beige-colored wall that extended for more than a city block to an arterial stop at what we saw was Missouri Avenue. "By God," Dad said, "we're back home."

"It's back there, Dad," I called. "I saw some big gates painted that same color as the walls. You could hardly see the numbers. Brass ones set into the wall. Small. Back up."

Dad had to wait for several cars to go past before he could reverse, then he expertly backed into a gravelled drive in front of the big gates. We all just sat for a moment. I twisted around in my seat and looked out the back window. "There's a bell right there beside the number."

Mom and Dad just sat looking straight ahead. Then they turned and looked at each other and suddenly burst out laughing. "Ready?" Dad asked.

"Ready," Mom answered and they opened the car doors at the exact same moment.

I clambered out on Mom's side and closed the door and adjusted the crease in my pants—an old pair of Junior's—and clasped my hands behind my back to hide a none too discreet patch before joining them. I saw Dad pushing the bell and looking up at the top of the huge gate. It was still daylight, but not bright enough for us to have noticed a small door so neatly cut into the big one that we all jumped back when it was opened by a young man.

Mom started to say something but the young man said unceremoniously, "Come in," and stepped aside to let Mom step over the high board at the bottom. I saw her catch her breath once she was on the other side. Dad stepped in briskly and I followed and caught my breath too.

We were in an exotic tropical garden shaded by a huge tree on the left that I learned later was a magnolia. Creepers with flowers that looked like orchids climbed up and across a long lattice trellis that covered the gravel drive. The tropical effect was made complete by a hair-raising squawk that made us all jump in surprise. It came from a huge parrot on a stand with a chain connected to one of its legs. It looked as ferocious as it sounded and I also learned later, was. The young man had disappeared after motioning us to a stone bench in a paved area off the drive surrounded by rosebushes all in full bloom of blazing colors. We none of us could speak. I watched the young man disappear up a slight ramp and through two dark swinging doors into what must be the house but it was so buried in vines and flowering bushes it was hard to tell. If it was the house, it was made from the same material as the exterior walls and painted the same pinkish beige.

A door next to the swinging doors onto the ramp opened silently revealing a tiny elegant woman whose hair really was Little Orphan Annie's—so blond it was almost white. She took a step toward us and stopped with a slight frown. "Mrs. Woods? We were expectin' a couple by the name of Woods." The voice was as Mom had described it but was now sounding sweetly confused.

"That's right, we're the Woods." Mom took a tentative step forward. "Mrs. Jones?"

"Yea-us, ah'm Mizzus Jones . . . but you see . . . Well, ex-*cuse* me, but ah'm just a bit taken aback . . . ah had the ah-dea when ah talked on the phone that you must be . . . Your accent . . ." I knew our accent was going to be a stumbling block.

Mom glanced over her shoulder at Dad who shrugged slightly. "I'm sorry, Mrs. Jones, if there's been some mistake . . ." She took a deep breath and started talking rather fast. Fast for Mom. "I must confess that I'm a bit confused, too. You . . . on the phone . . ." Mom laughed a bit nervously, "*your* accent, well I thought that you might be . . ."

A great booming laugh startled us and directed our eyes to the ramp. Poised on the top of it was a low flat bed with small wheels on which a man was stretched out who continued to laugh until he was wracked with a cough that left him breathless. His beautifully trimmed beard was the first one I'd seen outside the movies or on ancient farmers in Galena. His handsome head was propped up somehow and for a moment I thought it was the only part of the thin motionless body that could move but a hand came out from under the impeccable sheet with a huge handkerchief to dab at his mouth as his spasm of coughing died. The young man who'd let us in was at the head of the bed with a slightly glazed expression, paying no attention to what I assumed was his patient.

"That's the funniest scene I've ever witnessed," the man gasped, half laughing and half coughing. "Alice, you really must remember our old family motto: Don't Never Assume Nothin'."

Mrs. Jones laughed and blushed prettily and said, "Oh, Brad, don't embarrass me in front of these nice people . . ." She turned back to us with a limp wave toward the man, "this is Mr. Jones." She smiled charmingly and leaned toward us conspiratorily. "And don't pay any mind to *any*thang he says."

"Pure comedy of errors," the man roared. "Too funny! Just because Mrs. Woods has an accent different from yours, Alice, you figure she must be colored—or a *Nigra*, as you'd say—and since you have always sounded on the phone like my old black mammy, it's no wonder that she thought you *were* my old black mammy." Dad was the first of the Woods to join Mr. Jones in laughter. I was the last. People are people, Dad had said in the bathroom. Had they thought they were pursuing work for colored people? And Mrs. Jones thought *we* were colored? We'd come because a job was a matter of life or death, black or white. Where was the joke? Why were they all laughing at something deadly serious? Was there something hypocritical in their uneasy laughter and everybody's obvious nervous relief?

We made the laughter last a little longer than necessary to cover another coughing fit that threatened to strangle Mr. Jones.

"You've simply got to quit smokin'," Mrs. Jones said absently as though it were something she said hundreds of times a day.

"Well." Mr. Jones had his cough under control but the laughter stayed in his eyes. "If we niggers, negroes, *nigras,*" he winked playfully at his wife, "coloreds or whatever we are can still talk sense, let's get down to business." He grinned at Mom. "I gather Mrs. Woods that if an educated nigger such as yourself would answer an ad for house-keeper for what you must have thought was *rich* niggers," he nodded appreciatively at Dad's chuckle, "then you must be ready to work." Mom was grinning back at him in agreement. He turned to Dad. "And a great tall, handsome man like yourself is ready to spread horseshit on three acres of garden?"

"It's still on my shoes from home," Dad said. I'd never seen him look so pleased.

Saying horseshit made us know that there'd be no horseshit where Mr. Jones was concerned. He seemed pretty pleased with Dad, too. He looked up at him with shrewd eyes. "May I call you Woody?"

"Everybody does."

"That's it, then." He clasped his hands together. "If you'll put up with us, I know that I can't do without you." He looked at each of us in turn. "*All* of you." He turned to his wife, "Alice, show the Woods their new house and if they don't like our terms, *make* them like them." He waved a hand up behind his head. "This zombie is our son and heir. Bradford, Junior." He rolled his eyes. "He's not worth a damn." He laughed, didn't cough, and called out to him, "Home, James!" He was slowly pulled back up the ramp and in through the swinging doors, disappearing, rather as Grandma had into the hearse. Just before the doors closed we heard him call softly, "Bless you, Woods. Welcome."

We moved with almost unseemly haste into our new "quarters" (Mom had said that that had been the key word in her telephone conversation with Mrs. Jones—all she could think of was slave quarters) which were perfect—fully and beautifully furnished down to sheets and towels and kitchen equipment. Our one-hundred dollar a month salary on top of all this luxury made us wonder if the Joneses weren't more than just eccentric.

Our house was behind the main house and separated from it by a huge lawn. It was designed and built as a self-contained guest house—two bedrooms, living room with fireplace (something I couldn't imagine using until I'd spent a winter in Phoenix), beautifully installed kitchen and bath. It, like the main house and exterior walls, was built of adobe—Captain J had experimented and made his own bricks and then invented a sealer that gave the walls the unique natural pinkish beige look. On the flat roofs he'd had rigged up networks of piping under sheets of glass that heated our water by the sun. Having running hot water was novelty enough, but to have it straight from God was awe-inspiring.

Our new employer was Captain Bradford Jones, a flying hero from the Great War, totally paralyzed except from his arms up from an accident so hideous that the details were glossed over. He became a hero for Dad, too, and there was nothing he wouldn't do for him. "Just put yourself in his place," he'd say and shake his head sadly. They worked together planning the gardens with a mutual understanding and respect that was amazing. Captain J's infirmity seemed to stir his imagination. He loved watching any physical activity. Dad said he thought he just made up things for him to do so they could talk and he could watch Dad dig new irrigation ditches (Junior had been right about that), transplant trees or do grafting so delicate he felt as though he'd been performing brain surgery. Captain J was constantly designing, sketching, working out new planting methods or hybrids. He'd already produced some roses that dealers were begging to put on the market.

Junior's hair had been straightened out—if that's the right expression. It was *very* short, but actually looked nice. "Like those beautiful German boys in the Olympics," Uncle (as he was now called) Roy pointed out. I didn't know boys could be called beautiful.

Our trunk from Galena still hadn't arrived when school was about to start, and we needed school clothes. We'd been at the Joneses' for a little over a week and Mom said we couldn't possibly ask for an advance on our lavish salary, it was simply too shaming. The auction money had just arrived and been spent. All forty-eight dollars and fifty-cents of it, paying back Aunt Dell and stocking the new house with staples.

"There, you see, Tots?" Junior had said. "That's what we were worth. Forty-eight dollars and fifty-cents."

"What do you mean, 'what we were worth'? People can't be worth . . ."

"I mean, that all our worldly goods," he said with a quaver in his voice, like a hammy actor, "were only worth forty-eight dollars and fifty-cents. Doesn't that say anything to you?"

"No, not particularly. We didn't have very much anyway."

"Oh, God. I don't know whether you're dumb or just don't care."

I cared a lot about the pair of pants Aunt Dell bought for me from a jumble sale or secondhand store or God-knows-where. They were cream-colored cords and in very good condition and had only cost a quarter. Actually, a very good buy. The only thing wrong was that they were girls' slacks. No fly in the front. A zipper down the side, sort of hidden by the pocket.

"But these are for girls," I wailed.

"Just try 'em on, honey," Aunt Dell encouraged. "Pay no attention to that. Let's see if they fit first." They fit perfectly. "Look at that," she crowed. "What a eye I got! I picked 'em out of a whole pile. My hand went right to 'em. Totsy, I said to myself. Just his fit."

"But Aunt Dell," I repeated. "See, there's no fly. Boys' pants have openings in the front."

"Ya' kiddin'! Whatta you need a hole in front for?" She started dancing around the room, doing a comic imitation of a jitterbug. "This is Swing Time. Everybody's swingin' it! Why, honey, if Benny Goodman can swing it, so can you. Life don't mean a thing if you ain't got that swing!" She put her hands in front of her and made a graphic gesture. "Just swing it from the middle right over there to the left side . . ." Everybody bust a gut laughing.

"You can all laugh just like everybody else will laugh when they see me in girls' clothes." I ran from the room, close to tears of shame and embarrassment. I'd *have* to wear the damned things. I didn't have anything else. Just some short pants and I couldn't wear those to school. There are times when I felt in my bones just how poor we were and that was one of them. A new school and me in girls' pants. How'd I ever manage? I fell on our bed and wept tears of frustration and self-pity. I was ashamed of the self-pity—there were always others worse off than we, we were constantly reminded—but I couldn't help it.

"If you wear," it was Junior standing at the foot of our bed. "If you wear . . . hey, Tots, can you hear me? If you wear your shirt outside, maybe nobody'll see."

I heard the sympathy in his voice—he was putting himself in my place, knowing how much it mattered to me and would have mattered to him, too. His hair had turned out fine. Maybe if I did wear my shirt outside . . .

"But what'll I do when I have to pee?" I sat up on the bed.

"I don't know," Junior said and sat down beside me. He was in deep thought for a minute or so and then sat up very straight. "How long can you go without peeing?"

"I don't know. How could I know, for Lord's sake. I never tried."

"Maybe if you start now . . . I mean if you practiced . . . If you could hold it for four hours, say . . ."

"But I still have to take the . . ." If Junior could use Dad's word, so could I. ". . . the fucking things practically *off.*" I stood up and demonstrated. "See? I have to unbutton up here, unzip this . . . and this fucking thing *sticks* . . . oh, my God. Why do we let Aunt Dell do these things to us? OK. Now they have to come down over my hips and then . . . well, you see, the fucking things are hanging around under my ass, for Lord's sake . . ."

He couldn't hold it any longer, he burst out laughing and I joined in finally realizing how ridiculous it was. "At least," he said, with his arm around me, rocking us from side to side, "you won't have to worry about leaving your fly open."

Our laughter brought Mom to the door. "What in the world are you two up to in there?"

"Cutting a pee-hole in Totsy's new pants," Junior yelled back and we fell back on the bed and rolled around in hysterics.

Our school was grand in every sense of the word. It was brand new—only open for a couple of years before we came there (I guess a WPA project like all the others) and filled with children from the grand houses on the upper north side of town. It took Junior no time at all to establish himself in sports and I relied on some innate sense of self-preservation that enabled me to pick out the right friends and ingratiate myself to my teachers. "I swear," Junior said at one point, "if somebody called you a shithead you'd smile and say 'thank you.'" Whatever methods we used, we survived and if not exactly triumphed, we were absorbed, integrated, incorporated or whatever it is that every transplanted mid-westerner dreamed of— consciously or unconsciously—in the depressed thirties. We younger ones made it with only small scars that would disappear as we got older while some of the older ones simply couldn't find a slot that fitted them. I don't think Dad has ever been completely comfortable out here. Except perhaps while we were at the Joneses'. But that was because of Captain J.

In no time, our Model-A was up on blocks in the back of the big garage and Dad was in charge of the most beautiful vehicle I'd ever seen. It was the newest—not even unveiled yet in Detroit, Dad said—Chevrolet innovation, the 1938 Stationwagon. The body was fitted hardwood, in sections like the parquet floors of palaces in Europe, and varnished and waxed like a yacht. There were four doors—plus the two that opened up the back—and Captain J had redesigned the interior to take his little low bed which he'd designed also. He removed the back seat altogether and placed three small single seats along the left side behind the driver, leaving space on the right to hold his bed. There were little clamps that held the tubular legs in place and an ingenious fold-up ramp that fitted under the bed when not hooked over the rear end for the bed to be wheeled up or out. Dad was not only gardener, he was a very proud chauffeur and according to Captain J, the best driver he'd ever known. Except himself, of course, when he could drive.

We walked home from school along Missouri Avenue which seemed to be the boundary of Phoenix proper—the south side of the avenue was built up with houses on large plots like the Joneses', while the north side was groves of citrus trees. The old irrigation ditches still existed and worked, because Captain J and Dad had tapped into them at the northeast corner of the property and the ditches Dad dug watered the whole three acres. The main ditches in the groves not only worked, they were almost irresistible on hot afternoons but we were warned that the water was dirty and swimming strictly forbidden. It didn't seem forbidden to some children and was most definitely not irresistible to a group of Mexican kids that we saw and envied practically every day cavorting in the muddy water.

They'd yelled taunts at us often as we walked by, sweating and trying not to look at the cool fun they were having. I suppose they mistook our envy as stuck-uppishness. In response to their yells one particularly hot day, Junior whispered to me, "Yell *bese ma coula* at them."

An order being an order, I yelled at the top of my lungs, *"BESA MA COULA!"*

I didn't know such havoc could be created with just three words. Bodies scrambled out of the water with alarming speed. Two were naked and if not considerably older than we, considerably more physically mature. I didn't have time to investigate, we were running full out, as fast as we could. Fortunately a car coming down the avenue stopped the two naked ones by forcing them back in the water for decency's sake but flying glances over my shoulder told me others were still hot on our trail. We dashed to the corner of the property where the canal attached to the Joneses' smaller ditches and where there was a gate for trucks delivering manure or plants. We were halfway up that when I felt a stinging pain on my right shoulder and then heard stone hitting the gate as we clambered over it. Once inside we were fairly safe, but we kept on running until we were hidden by a tamarisk hedge.

"What . . . what . . ." I panted and gasped. "What in . . . the world? What did you have me *say?*"

Junior looked sheepish. "Kiss my ass. I mean, I think that's what it means."

"*Kiss . . . my . . . ass!*" I was stunned. And my shoulder hurt. And that gang chasing us had scared the daylights out of me. "You told me to scream *kiss my ass* at those kids . . ." I hauled off and hit him as hard as I could. "Trying to get us killed, for God's sake?"

"I'm sorry, Tots. It was pretty stupid . . ."

"*Stupid!* Well, you can just kiss *my* ass. In plain old English," I screamed and ran on home, tears running down my cheeks. Mostly of relief that we hadn't been more damaged considering the cause. It also meant that I wouldn't dare walk down Missouri Avenue for awhile and that meant an extra half-mile going the long way around the other end of the long, long block.

Chapter Eight

BRADFORD, THE JONESES' SON AND HEIR, fascinated Junior because he'd been to a military academy in Virginia. The best possible school, Mrs. Jones avowed, primarily because it was in Virginia, her home state. "Back home," she'd say (at least a hundred times a day, Mom claimed), "in *Virginia,* that is, we did thus and so . . . When they'd moved here almost ten years ago, Bradford was kept in school "back home" so that the southern tradition of family and manners and customs would be firmly instilled in him. The move to this "frontier town" was necessitated by Captain J's condition. Lung condition. It wasn't exactly T.B. but his doctor had recommended a dry climate for his delicate health generally and Mrs. Jones made no bones about pining for the old family plantation and "another, more gentle and *genteel* way of life."

Junior's open admiration for Bradford made them particular friends but we were both bothered by his slyness or deviousness. But the most disconcerting thing about him was a maddening inconsistency in his behavior. One day, friendly to the point of not wanting us out of his sight, other days, cold and unresponsive to the point of rudeness. One moment roaring with laughter, the next, sullen and closed-in. That glazed look that I'd noticed the first day was probably the most constant thing about him. It was always there, to a greater or lesser degree. We were all puzzled by it. So much in fact that one day Captain J slapped the side of his cot in irritation and said, "What

124

the hell's the matter with that boy, Woody? He's in a fucking daze half the time. If I didn't know better, I'd swear he was pissed."

"What?" Dad said. Captain J had spent time in England during the war and used expressions we didn't understand. "Did you say *pissed?*"

"Yes. Pissed. Swacked. Boozed up."

Dad laughed. "God knows I know enough about that to recognize it when I see it."

"Well, what do you think? Do you think he's hitting the bottle?" Dad knew that Captain J wanted the truth from him straight, no frills. "I have to say that it has occurred to me. I mean, there's something a bit . . ."

"I'll mark the bottles," he said decisively. "Wouldn't be at all surprised. All southerners are alcoholics. Alice's entire family is a bunch of drunks."

Although he was almost eighteen, Bradford wasn't much bigger than Junior at thirteen and Captain J and Dad enjoyed watching them compete in various sports—sparring with boxing gloves, playing table tennis, badminton, footraces down the long driveway (one of the competitions that could include me and at which I could hold my own), or wrestling. When the boxing gloves were brought out, I slipped out. I hated boxing almost as much as baseball but like baseball, when forced, I showed some aptitude. Perhaps aptitude is not right—I simply assailed my opponent with a whirlwind attack to get the encounter over with as quickly as possible. Captain J had been on the boxing team at Princeton University and coached Junior and Bradford very seriously and scientifically for some time and then encouraged a real free-for-all, becoming overexcited, calling out, "Keep your guard up, idiot," to Bradford and "Hit him, Woody-Two, hit him *hard.*"

These bouts sometimes ended with bloody noses but they always ended for the Captain in a coughing seizure so violent that Mrs. Jones would swear, ". . . no more! This is the last time. Y'all get too excited and besides, I think it's barbaric."

Captain J had initiated the "Woody-Two" for Junior on our first day at 1548, insisting that Junior wasn't a name, it was a designation and as for "Totsy," he shuddered when he heard it and steadfastly called me Carlton.

Dad of course was the undisputed baseball coach and he worked with both boys, well, all three of us, but you could tell that his eye was on Junior. When Dad coached Junior, it was with as much seriousness and professionalism that Captain J brought to boxing. Dad's eyes would shine with that special light—that name-up-in-lights light.

Any excuse for an outing was a good excuse as far as the Captain was concerned and the beautifully polished station wagon was often pulled up near the practice field at school where both men could watch Junior put into practice the coaching he'd been getting at home. And the coaching was paying off. The seventh and eighth graders had a team that was shaping up pretty well and Junior was making a name for himself already in just the practice games with a couple of other schools.

We finally got the notice from Railway Express that our trunk had arrived a week after school had started so that I could get out of the detested girls pants and into something with a fly. I told Junior that I was going to leave my fly unbuttoned all the time so kids would notice and point and giggle. At least they'd be giggling about boys' pants. I went with Dad in the station wagon to the depot and as always when we passed the Arizona State Mental Hospital, I had a delicious shiver looking up at the windows and wondering which one Winnie Ruth Judd might be looking out. She had been sent here after she was convicted of chopping up her lover and somebody else and had been in the headlines in the local papers almost constantly ever since. She had a talent for escape that was compared to Houdini's. Parents could keep their children off the streets after dark by simply saying, "Winnie Ruth's out again." She could be anywhere, behind that bush, that dark corner, that vacant lot, anywhere and everywhere. Most recently, she'd got out rolled up in a carpet that was being sent to the cleaners. She was one of Phoenix's most famous citizens and her lively escapades kept everybody amused. "She's escaped!" people would say with that same pride they'd used back home in referring to Bonnie and Clyde. "You think she's crazy? Anybody who can figure out how to get out of that nuthouse is *not* a nut." She was always caught again, but she managed to get out another day. Winnie Ruth—Watching was almost as great a sport in Phoenix as the annual rodeos.

"Now, when you go in with the notice," Dad said as we neared the depot, "don't let it out of your hand. It's our only receipt."

"Yeah. OK." He'd told me that four times already. We were all anxious about the trunk, me to the point of obsession. It somehow represented our identity. We weren't anybody without it.

In it were photos, certificates of marriage (perhaps a divorce?), births, even deaths, our books (not many), momentos that couldn't be parted with, school records, some clothes (fewer than I'd thought), Dad's riding boots, and three porcelain dinner plates that Mom hung up on a wall in every house we'd ever lived in. They'd belonged to a set her family had had and were the only remaining pieces. There were some odd bits of silver and . . . I guess that was about all. Not much. But it was us.

I jumped out of the car and was headed into the office when Dad called, "Don't get mixed up and get the wrong one, Tots. There's still one of Winnie Ruth's they haven't found yet."

I was through the door before I realized what he had said. Winnie Ruth had chopped up her lover and someone else, but what I'd forgotten was that she'd stuffed their bodies into trunks and sent them by Railway Express somewhere. Here? Could it have been *here?* She was locked up here. Here in Phoenix. This must have been where she'd been tried. Was it here that the victims had been found? Wherever it was, they'd given themselves away by the leaking blood and smell of rotting flesh. Supposing . . .

I was feeling a bit whoozy when a voice from behind the counter said, "What can I do for you, sonny?"

I showed the man the notice with a trembling hand. "A trunk. For Woods. From Galena. Missouri."

He glanced around and I saw our beat-up old trunk just behind him. The sight of the old familiar black tin case was such a relief that I almost jumped over the counter to help the man load it on a hand-truck. It wasn't oozing blood—I knew what was in it.

The plates went up on the wall in the living room so quickly that I realized Mom must have placed them in her mind when she first saw our house. Books were out and on shelves. Clothes tried on—I was pleased that I could still wear my things but secretly bothered for not having grown more. The riding boots were polished and Dad looked at them lovingly. "It looks like the closest I'll get to a horse here is the horseshit I'm fertilizing this whole place with," he said resignedly.

"Why don't we just hang the boots up on the wall too," Junior suggested dryly.

"Sure," I agreed. "And we can put some pots of ivy or geraniums in the top."

"Smart-alecks, both of you," Mom said.

Mom cooked two Thanksgiving dinners that year. She had to prepare the dinner for the Joneses and for us too. We were really celebrating. We were going to have Aunt Dell, Uncle Roy, Sister and Mavis to dinner—our first party in our new house.

Everybody was gay—Aunt Dell hadn't fallen down recently, so didn't have to limp or groan; Sister was a knockout in a pale-blue wool jersey dress that showed off her figure to a spine-tingling tee; Mavis

was flashing an engagement ring with a pretty good sized stone—
whether it was actually a diamond, nobody would hazard a guess;
Uncle Roy preened in new cowboy boots and western trousers cut as
tight as Levis and Mom's dinner was quite up to our smartly turned-
out guests. Sister had brought some wine and what with a few drinks
before, by the time the meal was over, we were twice as gay as before.

We were a bit reluctant to go outside on the lawn that separated
the main house from ours because we could see the Joneses all sitting
out on their covered porch (Mrs. Jones called it a "lanai" but Captain
J confided to Dad that if it were in Hawaii it might be a lanai, but
here in Phoenix it was a porch) that faced the lawn. Junior and I
broke the ice by having a bit of post-prandial roughhousing near our
own smaller porch. "Tell them all to come on out," the captain called
to us. "You've got to shake that good cooking of Miz Milly's down so
you can have some more." He'd called Mom Miz Milly from the first
day as some sort of private joke that only he seemed to understand.
Mom said she liked it because it reminded her of teaching since that
was what most of her pupils called her.

Mavis had been the only one to comment on the obvious (something Mom had always taught us not to do) when we first took the job
with the Joneses. "My God, Milly, I don't see how you can go from
being a teacher to being a *maid.*"

"Well, Mavis, if you think about it for a minute you'll see that it
isn't a very big step. One way or the other. Taking care of children or
taking care of grown-ups. Pretty much the same thing."

"I guess so," Mavis shrugged. "But you were *my* teacher."

"Oh," Mom laughed. "It's *you* I've let down, is it?"

One by one, we moved outside. We started a game of badminton
in which Bradford joined without his usual reticence. I soon thought
I knew why. Sister jumping in the air with a flash of tanned leg and
bouncing breasts had him mesmerized. I was also aware that Captain
J was his son's own father. He was fairly slathering. I heard him say to
Dad, "Woody, you are the luckiest devil. A niece like that! Well, both
of them for that matter and that's not mentioning your sister." He
poked Dad with an elbow and added, *"Or* Miz Milly." All our women
were on the lawn, shoes off, barefeet flying over the grass. "But that
one," nodding toward Sister, "that's for eating. I may be paralyzed,
but I'm not dead yet."

Dad blushed for some reason, something I'd rarely seen him do
and shot a quick glance at me. "Yes, well." He cleared his throat. "We
all have pretty good teeth. Runs in the family."

Captain J turned his head slowly toward Dad and looked up at him with a quizzical expression then roared like a lion from the depths of that emaciated body with choking laughter that was only stopped by Dad holding his glass to his mouth—bourbon and water, which was never far from his side.

Enthusiasm for badminton, even with enthusiasts, is limited and it was soon replaced by a most unathletic activity. We all sprawled out on the lawn in the late November desert light—soft and purple—listening to music from Captain J's phonograph which had been turned up by Bradford and filled the area between the two houses, bringing them together, the two houses and the people in them, our family and theirs, wrapping us all in melody, tying knots around us all in a sweet musical euphoria. I'd never known such happiness. I felt I could float up so that I could look down on 1548 with a bird's eye view like some maps I'd seen so that each corner of the place that I knew and loved and was beginning to feel so secure in—the whole square, the three acres themselves, cut out by streets and adobe walls as straight as dies, the houses all basically square, the flat roofs, the great rectangle of lawn now with us all on it, seen from above, languid, flowing bodies, all beautiful, smiling, happy and still—caught in a moment like a painting or a snapshot—forever in my head, bodies not touching, exactly, but relating to each other, forming patterns of infinite intimacy and beauty.

Soon bodies were touching. Couples formed and danced slowly on the grass, bare feet hardly moving, only the upper bodies touching, swaying to the music, more a suggestion of dancing than the real thing. The light had faded and turned paler and the moon's brightness didn't diminish the brilliance of the stars. I don't remember going to bed. Dad said he carried me in and he said I must have been having sweet dreams because I was smiling.

Bradford's fascination with Sister had him dogging our heels. He followed me and Junior practically to school, demanding more information, more stories, anything we could remember about her. He cursed not having money. He was determined to go to The Ship every night and see her. I wasn't sure how old you had to be to get in but we all three knew that it must cost a lot of money. We had no idea what sort of an allowance Bradford got, but he referred to it as adequate for a six-year-old. He'd be eighteen just after the first of the year and had completed his schooling at the academy and since his grades weren't satisfactory he was being tutored three hours a day in an effort to help him pass college entrance exams.

"Never get into Princeton," Captain J said. "Too damned dumb."

Bradford claimed that he didn't want to go to college. "Why should I bother? The old fart can't live forever and when he pops it, I'll sell this place so fast it'll make your head spin. And go back to Virginia and live like a human being."

To Bradford, living like a human being meant a southern mansion and about a hundred slaves. And to hear him tell it, he wanted the slaves primarily for beating. He told us stories about the military academy and most of them involved tricks of humiliation for the "darkies" who worked on the school grounds or as their batmen. Nothing to do with baseball, Junior assured me. How they'd sometimes tie them up and take turns beating them with long whips. We had difficulty understanding how students could have individual manservants but he said that only happened in the last year of school when you became an officer and had all sorts of privileges. Some of the privileges included cornholing the younger students, which apparently was not only great sport, but great fun. Junior refused to explain to me what "cornholing" was on the grounds that I was too young to know, but I don't think he understood what it was either. So I figured it had to do with some sort of torture of a particularly nasty kind.

We listened to his stories with fascination, but Junior always said not to believe half the things he said.

"He's making it up, I'll bet you. He gets a funny look in his eyes when he tells those stories."

"He gets a funny look in his eyes almost all the time," I pointed out.

"Dad told me to watch him and see if he drinks."

"Drinks what?"

"I swear to God!" He slapped his hands against his thighs with impatience. "What do you think he drinks?"

"Well, I saw him in the garage—over by the washtubs with a bottle of Clorox."

"He doesn't drink *Clorox*, for heaven's sake."

"I don't know. He says he gargles with it all the time. He showed me. He does gargle with it. Said that it made his breath smell fresh and since it was a bleach, it made his teeth whiter."

Junior looked at me for a minute. "You're making it up now."

"OK. I'm making it up. But just get a whiff of his breath some time. He smells like a washtub drain."

By Christmas vacation, the rains had hit. We'd never seen anything like it. The Salt River—that desert with a bridge across it near Aunt

Dell's—was full to overflowing. Uncle Roy checked it every morning and evening for over a week. They were afraid they'd be flooded. Parts of downtown Phoenix had flooded. Junior and I were in a movie house one Saturday afternoon when Dad came down the aisle looking for us and drove us home through streets like rivers. We learned later that people had to be evacuated from the movie house we'd been in. "I just had a funny feeling," Dad explained.

It wasn't nighttime when we got home, but it was dark enough for Dad to have the headlights on. Junior jumped out to unlock the big gates and was drenched by the time we'd pulled through. Dad and I ran from the garage in the pelting rain assuming that Junior had beaten us to the house. He wasn't there.

"He's probably having trouble with that catch at the bottom of the gate. Go help him, Totsy, or he'll be out there all night."

I grabbed an umbrella and ran. The gatelight wasn't on and I couldn't see whether the gates were open or closed until I was practically at the end of the driveway. They were closed and no sign of Junior. I looked around and called.

"Be right there, Tots," he called back. I thought I heard whispering. I was peering into the dark under the magnolia tree and wondered if Junior was talking to MacKenzie, the parrot, when he suddenly appeared, wet hair sticking to his forehead.

"Where's your coat?"

"Come on. I'll tell you in a minute." He grabbed my elbow as he ducked under the umbrella and propelled us both down the drive.

"Did somebody leave MacKenzie out in the rain?"

"No."

"Well, who were you talking to?"

"Brad."

"Brad? What in the world is he doing there." I stopped and looked over my shoulder.

Junior tugged at my elbow. "Come *on.* He doesn't want anybody to see him."

"Why not?"

"He's naked."

I stopped dead. *"Naked?"*

"Stop screeching."

"But what's he *doing?* I mean, *why* is he naked? In the *rain?"*

Junior pulled me under the garage roof overhang and started whispering, "Now listen, he doesn't want anybody to know about it . . . well, he said he thought it might be fun to, well . . ."

"Fun? In the rain?"

"Listen, for God's sake," he hissed. "Well, he thought it might be fun to sort of . . . well, he said he was just going to run around naked. It'd be fun . . ."

"He's nuts."

"He looked pretty nutty. He had that funny look again. You know . . . kind of like he doesn't quite see you. Anyway, he's naked. In the rain and he's cold so I gave him my coat."

"Why doesn't he just go back in the house?"

"I don't know. He was mumbling something about his folks finding him like that and he was afraid . . . Oh, I don't *know.* His teeth were chattering and he looked so silly. Pathetic, really . . ."

"Listen. Get Mom's keys. There's one of those French doors off the guest room and we could slip him back in that way."

"You go get them. I'll go get him. Meet you at the back of the house."

We flew apart. I opened our kitchen door carefully—the keyboard with hooks was just inside the door. I felt for the keys, rattling some as I counted the hooks to get the right ones, but Mom and Dad were in the living room listening to the radio. I grabbed the keys and closed the door with an inaudible click.

Brad was standing next to Junior at the French doors, shivering and trembling, his white bare legs sticking out the bottom of Junior's slicker. He certainly did look silly. I unlocked the door and he squeezed through the door without saying anything. Then he ripped off Junior's coat and shoved it through the narrow opening between the doors. I could see that he was fairly hairy, but he covered himself with one hand and I couldn't see anything else.

The new station wagon was Captain J's new toy but put to serious use. Almost every weekend found us discovering all the national parks and Indian reserves that could be reached in a day. Captain J refused to spend the night anywhere except in his own bed so we were limited to about a two-hundred mile radius but even so that kept us from repeating trips all through the fall and winter. The sights were superb and varied and apparently endless. Junior studied maps and books on archaeology and Indian history and lore.

Before the novelty of the station wagon wore off, we'd all crowd in—Dad always driving, Mrs. Jones beside him and Bradford beside her. In the single seats, Mom directly behind Dad, then me, and Junior in the end next to Captain J's head where he'd read to him about what we were going to see. Actually read to us all. By the New

Year, it was usually just the four of us, the captain, Dad, Junior and I. Then even I started bowing out as my interest in my Queen Isabella became obsessive. Mrs. Jones was the first to go. Then Bradford and then Mom. Mom with the legitimate excuse of being just plain tired. If no outing were planned, Captain J would think of something that would engage us all. It was obvious that he liked our company and Bradford's irritated him. The most enjoyable alternative to the trips was making ice cream. There was a big two gallon old fashioned freezer with the wooden bucket to hold the ice and we'd all take turns turning under the big arbor near the rose garden. It seemed to take forever to make—Captain J supervised every step, making sure we turned the handle at precisely the right speed, that the ice was packed properly and salted just enough to keep it from melting—but the results were always superb. The best was fresh peach. I can't even talk about it. I start drooling.

My birthday in March fell on a Saturday and a family get-together had been arranged at Aunt Dell's. It would be the first time we'd had dinner away from 1548 since we moved in the first of October. I think Mom and Dad had felt that they were on twenty-four-hour call because of Captain J's condition. Indeed, they had been called in several times during nights when he was having trouble with his breathing and needed to be lifted up and moved about.

I took the North Twelfth Street bus from the corner at Missouri Avenue and went down as far as Van Buren and then got out and walked to the Tucson Hotel where I had a date to meet Sister. We were going to have an "outing" she said. Sister was never on time but I was early by over half an hour. I strolled from in front of the hotel down to the corner looking in the shop windows, admiring the richness of the displays rather in the way one looks at things in a museum—they were as unattainable for me as if they were priceless and belonged to the state. A small window glittering with silver and turquoise jewelry did make my mouth water—the turquoise held me hypnotized, it was *like* water, the deepest pools that went to the center of the earth, bottomless but where you didn't drown but floated in a slow-motion dance of pure delight. I had to force my eyelids down and closed and then make myself turn away like a blind man and head back toward the hotel entrance before I opened them again.

There was a clock above a big door on a bank across the street. Still twenty minutes to go. I walked in the other direction, determined to avert my eyes if I passed another jewelry shop, particularly one with the Indian handmade silver and turquoise. I strolled, watched the people, counted out-of-state license plates on the cars pulled up at the stoplights, found myself crossing the street with some other pedestrians then turned back toward the hotel. The light had changed and I was standing on the curb when I saw Sister come out of the hotel. I started to call but she darted across the street right through the traffic which caused me to catch my breath in fear and disappeared behind the cars. I stretched up on tiptoe to look over the tops of the cars, but I'd lost her. I panicked. That clock must be wrong and she'd been looking for me and couldn't find me and probably gone to call Mom. Finally the lights changed and I ran down the street and stood on the long marble step that led into the hotel lobby, making myself as tall and visible as possible. All of a sudden I saw her crossing the street with other pedestrians at the corner. She saw me and waved, her white teeth flashing in her suntanned face. My chest filled with pride at being smiled at by so beautiful a creature and looked around me to see if anybody had noticed.

"Oh, honey," she called breathlessly when she got near me. "Am I late?" She glanced over her shoulder at the clock on the bank and then hugged me. "No. Not for me." We laughed. "You just get here?"

"No, I've been . . ."

"Oh, honey, you've been waiting, haven't you? Oooh, how I hate that bus. It takes forever. And Saturday traffic. Well, I finally just jumped off and ran. That's why I'm so out of breath." She took a deep breath and stood back and looked down at me. "And don't you look fresh and sweet." She grabbed me by the hand. "Come on, I want to show you off." She led me through the lobby door that she'd come out of a few minutes before.

"Why are we going in here? You were just . . ."

"I'm showing you off, honey, that's why," her spirits soared over the questions forming in my mind, sweeping them up and away.

She smiled radiantly at the doorman who winked and made a vague saluting gesture toward his cap. She seemed to know him. Maybe she was going to show me off to him. I smiled what Junior called my "cutest" smile.

"This way, honey," she led me across the wide, carpeted lobby at such speed that I could hardly take in its luxury. She went sailing through a pair of swinging doors marked "Saloon" into a dimly-lighted bar, unlike anything I'd ever seen. Not even in the movies. There were low, dark brown leather (real, I ran my hand across the back of one) couches placed around big, low square glass-topped tables in symmetrical groupings all over the room, separated now and again by potted plants that were more exotic than anything the captain produced in his greenhouses and I wondered how they could grow in the dark. We headed toward a long bar at the far end of the room in front of which were tall leather-topped stools. There was a man in a white jacket bending down at the far end of the bar with his back to us. He straightened and turned when Sister called a cheerful, "Howdy, Jim."

His face beamed and his bald head gleamed as he came toward us with arms outstretched in greeting, "Ah, my lovely. Oh, it's almost a sin. It's too much. The beauty of Ginny is blinding." He shaded his eyes from her brilliant smile and bubbled with nonsensical good humor. "How'd it go last night, baby," he said confidentially, doing a little dance with his head and eyes.

Sister's eyes widened and she seemed to stiffen in a sort of warning. "Fine. Good Friday crowd. We got a good band this week. The Duke. Ellington." She was talking as fast and as breathlessly as she had since we'd met in front of the hotel. "But that's *work* talk. I brought my *real* boyfriend in to show you." She put an arm around me and drew me to her. "This is Tot . . . ah, *Carlton* Woods. My baby." We were using our proper names—Virginia and Carlton—which always gave me a sense of lost identity. For both of us.

Jim leaned over the counter and stuck out his hand which I took and shook. "Well, hello down there, little feller. Didn't see you at first." He glanced from one of us to the other. "By golly, he's almost as pretty as you. Yours?"

"Sure, Jim. All of us hillbillies have babies by the time we're ten." We all laughed. Jim uproariously. "But he might as well be mine. "I've took care of him since he was born. Cousins."

"And now you're just takin' care of Ginny. Right?"

"Weeelll," she said, coyly rolling her eyes and easing her bottom insinuatingly onto the stool and opening her big handbag. She pulled an envelope from it and waved it teasingly in front of Jim's face. It had the name of the hotel stamped on its corner. "Sometimes I take care of you too, don't I?"

He clutched his hands to his heart and looked up at the ceiling. "I swear you're just too good for the likes of me."

"You take care of me," she said snapping her handbag shut with a metallic click, "and I'll take care of you. Buddies, right?"

"Right, my lovely, right." He bowed his head over her hand as though he were going to kiss it but lifted the envelope in his teeth and straightened up with his hands in the air. "Look, Ma, no hands!" he said with a comic leer through clenched teeth.

Sister laughed and turned to me. "Let's get out of here. This man is keer-aaa-zzy!" She was off the stool and halfway across the room with me at her heels when she called over her shoulder, "Bye, Jim. Thanks a lot. Call, y'hear?"

"Whenever I can catch a live one, my lovely. You know that." When I glanced back and waved, he was waving the envelope at us.

Heads turned when Sister walked by. She wore her beauty like a thoroughbred, not arrogantly, just with a sparkling pride. She walked tall, shoulders back, head up, with long confident strides. She knew where she was going. Her dark suntanned skin she let shine. And it did, with a healthy glow. "Powder just clogs the pores," she claimed and she wore no makeup but a touch of mascara and lipstick. She was only a year or two older than Bradford but of a totally different generation. I was proud and amazed by her. It amazed me how well she knew her way around the city—how she could walk into the elegant hotel as if she owned it and be on first-name basis with the bartender, how she handled the salesmen in the shops with just the right amount of flirtatiousness and sophistication. Her brilliant smile melted all obstacles. I wondered how she did it and wondered if I could learn. I was still puzzled about many things, but I knew she didn't want me to know that she'd come out of the hotel, and I respected her wishes.

She started to turn into Goldwater's Department Store but suddenly took my hand and said, "I guess not here," and we walked on a few paces before she looked down at me and smiled, "Want an ice-cream cone?" We got the giggles right in the middle of the sidewalk.

I managed to choke out, "No, but I'd love a milk shake. I've never had one."

She looked wide-eyed with disbelief. "You poor underprivileged child. Come on." We went into a chrome and glass ice-cream parlor and sat down at a table. She ordered me a chocolate milk shake and a coke for herself. The milk shake was like eating silk. It was a new experience that I wanted to last as long as possible. I sipped and played with it, wanting to get inside the tall glass like getting inside a turquoise. They had something in common.

"Come on, honey. Stop dawdling. It's your birthday, baby, and we're supposed to be home having a party. Oooohhh. Just look at the time. Your folks'll be there before we can get you in your new outfit."

I knew she'd got me Levis and a shirt but she'd made the purchases at J. C. Penney's with me outside after I'd had my waist and inseam measured. They were gift-wrapped and I had to open them in front of everybody and pretend I didn't know what they were. Well, I hadn't seen the shirt yet, but they'd all done the same thing for Junior's birthday in October and what one of us got, the other eventually got too. Sometimes by a hand-me-down.

Aunt Dell and Mavis oohed and aahed at my Levis as though they'd never seen a pair of them in their lives. The shirt *I* oohed and aahed over because it was turquoise blue (how could Sister know?), cut western style with a yoke in the back, tight fitting and little smiling pockets on the chest. It had white pearl-faced buttons that snapped. I was overjoyed.

"I've got something for you out here," Uncle Roy said. "Come on. I'll also give you the basic pointers on the wearin', carin' for, and feedin' of Levis. They are a special breed and have to be handled with the utmost consideration. You gotta' tame 'em just like you would a bronco."

In Roy's room behind the garage, I spread out my loot on his single bed while he kept up a running monologue, half to himself, muttering and humming—not songs but sounds—as he gave me instructions. "Yes, put them things down there. Uh-huh. That's right." He moved around the room with preoccupied concentration. "Yes. Well, you can't put on Levis over your other pants. Better get outta' them. And your shoes." He was pulling what looked like an old army trunk out from under the bed. "This ought to do the trick. Yeah, that's better. More room. Better height." He shoved the trunk around with his feet, pushing it back near the wall. He'd picked up my new shirt and was looking at it carefully as though he were checking the seams to see if it were well made. "Now, that's a dandy. Real dandy. Good color." He glanced at me and frowned. "You can't wear that undershirt with this. Ain't nothin' supposed to be wore under a shirt like this. See them tucks there? That's the real western cut. It all flows together in a line."

With my undershirt off, I was standing not too patiently in my socks and underpants. I was anxious to get into my new clothes. "You want me to help?"

"Nope." He was unsnapping the buttons. "Got 'er now." He bit his lower lip and looked around him. "Come on over here, Tots, and git up on this trunk." I looked at him questioningly. "You're too damn short to git at. Come on over here." I obeyed. "There we are." He held the shirt for me to slip on.

"The sleeves are just right," I said holding out my arms.

"Tailor made." He turned around and held my Levis up between us. "Them's the real McCoy. The little leather label and them brass brads. That's how you know." He shook them out. "This is the hard part." He chuckled. "They're really stiff, but that'll loosen up in the wash." He pushed his arm down the legs and shook out some of the stiffness. They crackled with a nice fresh new sound and smell. "You have to git them underpants off."

I wasn't sure I'd heard him correctly. "What?"

"Git them underpants off. You can't wear them knitted things under these pants. They'll bunch up and drive you crazy."

We'd always worn underpants. We'd been brought up to think it was . . . well, indecent not to. Mom never said so in so many words, but that was the feeling I got. "But, I've never *not* worn underpants."

"You ever had real Levis before?"

"No."

"Well, there you are. You don't know then, do you?"

"Don't know what?"

"How to wear them, that's what. I been wearing Levis purt' near all my life and I know. They ain't like regular pants. Like I told you, they are a special breed."

"How?"

"They're cowboy pants. Right?" I nodded. "Well, a cowboy has a special job to do, don't he? And these pants was designed for that special job." I nodded again. "Now listen, this can git a bit . . . well, *technical.* That's why I'm showing you all this. These is men's pants. *Real* men's pants. Now . . . ." He crossed his arms across his chest and then put one hand up on his cheek and sort of thumbed his fingers against the side of his face. "How to git this . . . Well, let's start at the beginning. We are men. We are made different than women." His eyes twinkled. "You followin' me so far?"

"Yea-up."

"OK." He reached over and slipped my underpants down before I knew what was happening. "Now just step outta' these useless things . . . ." I took hold of his shoulder for support as I did as I was told. "There." He stood back and looked at my naked lower body. I started to cover myself but he grabbed my wrists. "No need to do that. We're both men together." He stared at my crotch. "Well, we're *gittin'* there." He reached out and cupped my parts in his hand. "Yes, sir, we're gittin' there." He moved things around as he inspected me as impersonally as if he'd been a doctor. "The hair's so blond it don't show much, but it's comin' along. It's all comin' along." He held the

Levis open at trunk-top level. "OK. Now let's git into these." I slid a foot into one leg and he bunched the stiff material up the leg until my foot came through the bottom. Then the other one until the Levis caught at about my knees. "This is, as you can see, no easy chore. Everybody needs help that first time. Now, grab and *pull.*" I did and got them just up to my hips. "Uh-oh. 'Most forgot." He went over to a chest of drawers and took something out of the top drawer. He grinned and handed it to me. "From me," he said shyly, rubbing the back of his hand across his mouth. "My little birthday present."

I felt pretty silly opening a present with my pants half on and naked in the middle. It was a belt. A beautiful one. "Real Hand-Tooled Leather" it said on the little cardboard box with the cellophane opening showing what was called a "Real Silver-like Buckle." It would complete my western outfit. I was really going to be decked out. "Oh Lord, Uncle Roy, that's just . . . just perfect. Thank you." I smelled the real leather. "Just smell that . . ." I leaned over. "Oops, *sorry.*" My crotch was practically in his face. "Excuse me . . ."

He waved my apology aside. "Like the belt? It's got that double bit there that kinda' laps over the other. Real cowboy belt." He started fitting it through the loops around the top of the pants. "Just check the size . . . I wasn't too sure just what . . ." His arm was around my waist and the other one was reaching behind to pull the belt through on the other side. His cheek brushed against my exposed parts. He seemed to almost rub his cheek against me. His whiskers gave me a funny sensation and I pulled back.

"I'm sorry. I keep getting things in the way . . ."

"Now that's just what I wanted to talk to you about." He went on adjusting the belt, "as I said, these pants are made for a special . . . a specific job. When you're in a western saddle and you're roping steers or just plain riding along, well, this here," he cupped my privates again, "is goin' to rub against that front part of the saddle—there where the horn is. Right?" He was still holding on to me and I was beginning to feel something in his hand that wasn't so impersonal. "This part of you is goin to push up against that front part every step that horse takes . . . like that, see?" He pushed his big hand up against my crotch, pressing my parts up toward my body in a rhythmic motion. "And there . . . see what happens? You start to get a hard-on." I was. My knees were beginning to feel weak and I took hold of his broad shoulders for support. "Well. That's what any man would do. You git your cock rubbin' up against something warm like that and it's goin' to happen to any man." He kept the gentle rhythm going. "Now, if you're just ridin' along even, you don't want everybody to see your hard-on." He looked up into my glazed eyes and grinned as he took his hands away and spread them out to his sides. "There'd be a hard-on because you had on them damned underpants! Don't you see? They got you all bunched up like this," he demonstrated by cupping both his hands around me and exerting the gentle pressure again. I thought I was going to faint. "Whereas, if you have it all like this," he straightened me out and lay my cock gently along my thigh, "ain't nobody goin' to notice anything. See?" Mine felt so hard that I couldn't figure out where it could go if it couldn't go upright. "And everything is comfortable over to the side . . ." He was trying to hold me against my thigh but it hurt not being able to spring free. I took his hand off it and it flew up. "Well, that don't look like it's goin' to fit in them pants sideways, does it? We'd better fix that . . ." He leaned his head forward and took it in his mouth just as his hands touched my buttocks and pulled me slightly forward. I think I did faint.

I felt suspended in air. His hands on my backside supported me and moved me gently back and forth in his mouth. I was dead from my knees down. Suddenly the same tingling sensation Ronnie had created in me returned, starting in my fingertips at the back of my scalp, where his fingers kneaded my bottom, in my toes and feet that were useless except as conduits for this electric current carrying this storm that was gathering in my groin and was going to explode into the deep silky bottomless haven of milk shake, turquoise, and fresh peach ice cream that was Roy's mouth. I collapsed with a cry over his left shoulder, sobbing as I had with Ronnie, not knowing what had happened, but knowing that this was something as rare as those special things I thought about while it was happening.

I hung there limp, like a sack of flour over Roy's shoulder, shuddering and trembling. He soothed me with his mouth and hands, gently stroking me back to consciousness and as consciousness came, a deep black self-knowledge came with it—a knowledge I closed my mind to but my body had already accepted.

Roy eased me back on my feet and straightened me up as though stroking a piece of clay into a shape that would eventually stand balanced on its own. He was murmuring something I couldn't understand, just sweet soothing noises of encouragement and reassurance. I still held onto his shoulders, my elbows locked, my head thrown back, gasping for air.

"Sweet," I thought I heard him whisper. "Sweet. You can come. Funny. I'd have thought you were a bit young . . ."

"Huummm?" My head was still back.

"Was it the first time?" I forced myself to look down at him. I was terrified at what I'd see. My body couldn't have gone through that without us both changing. He looked the same. He hadn't changed. Perhaps I was the only one who had but I didn't want to see. I didn't know how I'd changed, but I was sure it would show somehow. "For you to come?" he said, slowly moving the back of his hand across his lips.

"I don't know . . ." I was stunned that I could speak and that my voice sounded all right. Or at least recognizable. "Maybe one other time like that."

He was suddenly all business. "Well, that ought to fit where it's supposed to go now." He eased my pants up and with great care put me into them, easing them into place with one hand while holding the fly away from my body. "There. That's where *that* goes. Put your shirt-tail in and let's get all this locked away." He patted and smoothed me until I felt I was going to get hard again. "Whoa, now, baby." He looked up at me and laughed as he buttoned my fly from the bottom, meeting my hands coming down from the top. He squeezed my hands and patted my cock once more. "Locked away." He looked up with a raised eyebrow, "Until next time?"

I looked away from him as I buckled the stiff new leather belt and patted it against my stomach. "Am I OK? A proper cowboy?"

"You got the makin's . . ."

Pure fake bronco-bustin' bravado got me through the evening. Everybody made so much noise and such a fuss over me that I don't think they noticed that I was in a state of shock, drowning in shame and guilt. If I'd done what Roy said—come—then my body had changed. And the change must show. Mom would be bound to notice it. Either she or Junior. I found myself sitting with my hands folded over my crotch, hiding it as though some strange essence might still be oozing from me.

"All you need now, Totsy," Aunt Dell bellowed, "is a pair a boots—like them of Roy's—and you'd be a real cowpuncher."

And look *really* tacky, I thought. That's what Ronnie would have said. "Hillbilly tacky. Cowboy tacky. Both the same." I could hear his voice. If my body had changed, something else had changed too. I suddenly looked down at the cowboy shirt with the smiling pockets that frowned from this angle and knew that it bordered on being tacky. Imitation anything was tacky. Boys got up to look like something they aren't or ever will be was basically silly. Like those men who leaned against the courthouse in Galena in railroad engineers caps when they'd probably never been on a train. Little girls done up in long dresses like their mothers, wearing lipstick before they wore bras, the boots and ten-gallon hats on men who drove convertibles and worked in offices, all fake and tacky. But how should I be dressed then, I wondered? Who was I? *What* was I? I was getting hair and I could come. OK. But where was I going?

After dinner, I danced, showing off something awful, but I knew it was expected of me. Dad and Mom danced around the room with everybody saying how Woody was the best dancer any of them had ever seen. Sister did her famous Charleston and Roy took off his shirt, flexing his muscles and did his sixty-five—count 'em—push-ups. The whiskey bottle on the table in the kitchen where we all sat around had only a bit left in the bottom and everybody's eyes were glittering except Mom's. Hers were clouded with concern.

"We'd better get back, Woody. We're not in our own car." It wasn't nagging, just a statement of fact.

Dad's eyes flashed dangerously and his voice was unnaturally hard, but low. "I think I got a pretty good idea of what kind of car I'm drivin', Milly." He reached for the bottle and drained it into his glass.

Junior headed for the door with me on his heels. "Where are you goin'?" Dad called with the same edge in his voice.

"Pee," Junior said without turning around.

I followed him to the back hedge where it was the darkest. We peed in silence. My cock felt different in my hand—bigger and slightly bruised. There was a strange stinging sensation. Maybe from rubbing against the rough Levi material. The buttons were difficult to close.

"They take time to loosen up," Junior said, noticing my efforts to close my fly.

"Yeah. How do you like my shirt?"

"It's nice."

"You don't think the pockets are kinda' tack . . ." For some reason using Ronnie's word seemed like a confession of sorts. Why was Ronnie on my mind this evening? Because of what he and Roy had done? I guessed that must be it. But had Roy done it to Junior too when he showed him how to wear his Levis? ". . . kinda' silly?"

"You put some pencils in them and they'll be smiling with teeth."

It was so dark I couldn't see his face, but I knew his brown eyes were sparkling with mischief. I punched him on the shoulder. "Come on. Be serious. Tell me for sure."

"It's fine. It's very nice. Really."

I tried to believe him. "Did . . . ah . . ." I wasn't sure I could bring up the subject. Then I blurted it out. "Did Roy . . . Uncle Roy show you how to wear Levis?"

"Tried to."

"What do you mean 'tried'?"

"Said I had to wear them without underwear."

"Well, what did you do?" I tried to keep my voice calm and low, but sometimes getting something out of Junior was like squeezing a stone.

"I just said I couldn't."

"Why?" My voice was getting out of control.

"Why?" He took my elbow and headed us back to the house. "To keep my underpants on."

"I meant," I said carefully, "why *couldn't* you. What did you mean when you said you couldn't? Couldn't take off your underpants, I mean."

"Oh. I said I had a heat rash down there and the new pants would irritate it."

"Well?" I stopped in exasperation. *"Did* you?"

"Did I what?"

"You know you're going to drive me crazy one day, don't you? You know that?" My voice sounded not unlike Dad's a few minutes ago. I took a deep breath. "Did . . . you . . . have . . . a . . . *rash,* for Lord's sake?"

He walked straight on toward the back door. "Of course not," he said.

Then why me, I kept wondering as I tossed and turned in our bed that night while Junior breathed deeply and evenly next to me. Sleeping the sleep of the innocent? What was there about me that allowed things like that to happen? First Ronnie and now Un . . . no, just Roy. The word "uncle" was a lie to begin with and now I simply choked on it when I thought of what he'd done. My hands slid down between my legs. I was hard. Junior's hands were both on top of the covers.

Chapter Nine

IT ISN'T HOARDING," Captain J explained rather defensively as we carried the endless cartons of canned goods up from the basement storeroom. "It's just part of my eccentricity." His eyes shone. "Oh, I admit it. I'm an eccentric. But of the best possible sort. I'm just thinking ahead. I was in the last war and I know what can happen. That crazy little shit in Germany. Hitler or *Hateler*, well, you just mark my words. He's going to raise one large amount of hell."

His wheeled bed had recently been rigged out with a little chrome arm that swung out from the side of the metal frame with a ring to hold his glass. He was seldom without the bourbon and water now. His nervous energy spawned project after project. He'd recently come up with a new method of fertilizing. A truckload of manure was dumped at the north gate and Dad simply shovelled it into the main irrigation ditch and the water would carry the floating fertilizer all through the property and all Dad had to do was lift it back out of the water when he wanted to spread it around. It was a brilliant time-saver—no hauling with wheelbarrows—and Captain J was fascinated by his innovation and ordered more and more horseshit.

Now the project was repainting the basement with a new product he'd ordered—a rubber-based paint that was designed for swimming pools that would be just the thing to keep the underground room dry and clean. Junior and I, free from school for Easter, were to be the painters along with Brad. The basement could double as a bomb shelter, the captain said. "The next war will be fought in the sky. You wait and see. And you won't have to wait long. They'll bomb the bee-Jesus out of everybody. Why anybody would bother to bomb Phoenix, I have no idea, but better safe than sorry."

There were strict rules about using the spray gun and working with the new paint. It was highly toxic and none of us was supposed to work down in the airless room for more than fifteen minutes and then only with an elaborate mask. There was a delicate filter in the mask that had to be changed after every hour's use. Bradford had been checked out on all the rules as we all were and was the first down in the cellar. He was back up in less than ten minutes complaining that it burned his eyes.

"I can breathe OK," he said, "but my eyes water so, I can hardly see."

"Is the filter properly seated?" the captain asked. He checked it carefully. "Seems all right. How about you, Woody-Two, are you feeling up to it?"

"Sure." Junior fitted on the mask and went down the stairs. I had to call him when his fifteen minutes was up. "It works fine. Boy, does it ever go fast. I got one wall almost done. The underneath part of the shelves is a bit difficult to see in the mask, but I just lay down on my back and shot the spray up at them. Great fun!"

The mask gave me claus . . . close . . . Well, that feeling you get when you're in tight places like under the floorboards of a house and you can't move front or back and you get the knotted feeling in the stomach of . . . I guess it's fear. Anyway the mask gave me that feeling but I wasn't going to let anybody know it. My fifteen minutes seemed endless. They were. They turned out to be over thirty. I finally staggered up feeling quite peculiar—light-headed and not so much dizzy as uncertain on my feet. I had difficulty getting out of the mask because my hands and arms didn't take orders very well. I almost fell over as I ripped the thing off my face. My balance was all off. I blinked to focus my eyes which brought Junior into view.

"It's almost time for my turn . . . Hey, Tots, what's the matter with you. You look funny." He grabbed me and seated me on a carton of wine. "You all right? You looked like you were going to faint."

"Faint . . ." I couldn't hear my own voice. The thought of fainting seemed nice.

"Where's Brad?" He picked up the mask. "Have you been down there all this time?" He was shaking me as though he were trying to wake me up—like he did sometimes in the morning—but I wasn't asleep, just floating. "Tots!" He was screaming and shaking me. "BRADFORD! Where are you? MOM. MOOOOOMMMM."

"What's the matter?" Dad's voice called. I could vaguely see him pushing the bed with the captain on it.

"It's Totsy," Junior called. "I think he's poisoned by the paint."

Everybody arrived at the same time. Brad sauntering lazily from inside the house. Captain J gave orders for somebody to bring the oxygen tank he kept for his coughing fits. Mom dashed into the house and was back lugging the cylinder in a flash. Another mask for the pure oxygen was fitted over my face and I was ordered to breathe deeply and evenly. "Just keep taking it all down. As far down as you can, Carlton," Captain J said quietly. "In, waaay in. Now let it out slowly. That's it."

I was stretched out on my back on the porch floor feeling perfectly all right. I sat up, looking dazed, Junior said later and he added that if I'd dared say, "Where am I?" he'd have slapped me. He was that scared.

He was nearly as scared as Bradford was when his father went at him. He called him every name in the book—many I didn't know. ". . . stupid little son-of-a-bitch," the captain screamed. "Do you understand what could have happened? Oh, Jesus, if you ever understood *anything*, it'd be the surprise of my life." He took a steadying breath of the oxygen himself. "That can cause brain damage, for one thing. Do you understand that? You ought to, you're one of the most severely brain-damaged people I've ever known. Or you could have killed the poor kid." Bradford stood, looking as dazed as I had earlier, not seeming to hear his father's tirade. "You're eighteen years old, for Christ's sake. When are you going to act like it? You practically killed this ten-year-old kid . . ."

"Eleven," I corrected.

"Well, you'll be lucky to see twelve if you have anything more to do with this silly shit."

Dad often thought the captain was a bit rough on Bradford and tried to ease it off now, "Well, Tots seems OK now. It was just an accident. He'll be all right."

"I gave you firm instructions. *Nobody* was to be down there more than fifteen minutes. You send this kid down there and just . . . just *disappear*. Where'd you go, for Christ's sake? Wanking off, again. If you'd learn to keep your hands off your cock . . ."

Bradford suddenly bolted. In one movement he had his father by the throat, screaming at the top of his lungs, "I'll kill you, you son-of-a-bitch! I'll kill what's left of you. You deserve to die. You're more dead than alive any . . ." Dad was on him from behind and had his arms locked behind him but he was kicking out at the bed and its occupant and still screaming hysterically. Junior moved in quickly to pull the bed out of range and help the captain get back straight on his pillow. He was choking and I grabbed the oxygen mask and put it over his nose and mouth and turned on the cylinder—reversing our recent roles, telling him to breathe deeply.

Mrs. Jones appeared at the door leading into the living room, looking calm and unruffled. "Let him go, Woody. He's all right now." Everybody was still. All I could hear was breathing, all of it heavy. Dad slowly released Bradford and took a cautious step back but still looking ready to spring. Nobody moved. We seemed frozen to our spots all looking toward Mrs. Jones. She put both her hands out toward Bradford, "Come, my darling. Come here." There was a long moment before he dropped his head and dragged his feet toward his mother's waiting arms. She held him to her breast for a moment, patting him soothingly on the back and then led him quietly into the house.

We all stood silently, not looking at each other—not knowing where to look I guess—when Captain J spoke so quietly that I wasn't certain that I'd heard correctly.

"He's mad, you know," and we turned toward him. He was looking down into his empty glass. He sighed heavily and lifted the glass to Mom. "Miz Milly . . . *dear* Miz Milly would you please do the honors?"

The incident was treated as a trifling—nothing more than a loss of temper, a momentary lapse of control. Just a silly family quarrel. Of course, the fact that I might actually have suffered brain damage was referred to frequently when I misbehaved or did something stupid.

I didn't need an overexposure to a toxic paint to behave stupidly. I'd been doing that unaided for months. I'd fallen helplessly in love with Queen Isabella. Well, she was Queen Isabella in a sketch I wrote, directed and starred in as Columbus in a Thanksgiving school program. I had chosen her—Rosalind Rawlings—as the queen because she was the prettiest and the smartest girl in the fifth grade and judging from the palatial house I passed every morning on my new route to school to avoid the Mexican Marauders, rich. Just which of these sterling qualities carried the most weight in my abject fawning devotion to her is difficult to say. Combined, they made me reel. I have to admit that when I put the girl and the Southern mansion-type house together, my adoration knew no bounds. I was besotted by this elegant little figure—not the cutesy Shirley Temple idol type of the time, but a slick pint-sized Katharine Hepburn—and made a complete ass of myself at every opportunity. I was a puppy dog, a panting, slathering slave to this haughty beauty who behaved in life as though she really were Queen Isabella. I was her knave and I prayed that nobody in the family—Junior, particularly—saw me in this embarrassing role of fool and toady. I was so far gone that I was hanging around Rosalind at school, on the way home from school, outside her house on the way *to* school. That is, until I learned that she was leaving home early. It never occurred to me that she was doing so to avoid me. I suppose what kept me going in the face of mountainous odds was the unconfirmed—not to mention shaky—conviction that I was basically irresistible.

God knows there were plenty of rivals. She was as popular at school as her beauty warranted. She made no bones about who my main rival was and there was nothing I could do to eliminate him short of poisoning his hay. Stormy, her pony, was the love of her life.

The Rawlings's property touched the Joneses' only at the southeasterly corner. Both lots were the same size, but were of different worlds. Instead of filling their three acres with greenhouses and irrigations ditches, they opted for a miniature Kentucky bluegrass stud farm—a manicured green oasis smack in the middle of the Arizona desert. Through the white-washed fences and under the legs of stunning horses, the line of stables and riding ring could be seen through trees and lawns filling what area was left over from the superb house. There was even a large bronze statue of a handsome stallion bolted to the top of their mailbox that matched the one on the radiator of Mr. Rawlings's Packard. Horses reigned supreme in Queen Isabella's realm. Even their discarded shoes were worshiped and were tacked or hung precariously over doors, gates, entrances and exits of all kinds causing me to flinch instinctively, half expecting a sharp metallic rap on the head from a falling "good-luck" token.

The emphasis on horses was a bit overwhelming but the whole place fascinated me and I was determined to learn everything I could about these superb animals—another species altogether from the mules and plow horses I'd known back home—from the ground up if necessary. And that's where I started, raking up the shit from the riding circle after Rosalind's workout. She claimed that she was sitting on a horse before she could walk. I have no reason to doubt her. Her singular devotion to that four-legged beast matched mine for her and I wouldn't have been surprised if she'd been born on one.

She didn't exactly think *she* was a horse—she knew perfectly well who she was; the prettiest girl in the fifth grade, heartbreaker of the highest order, rivaled for the highest marks in class only by one Carlton Woods, who, along with her proud parents and colored mammy, doted on her. She was also the proud possessor of a wall full of blue ribbons and trophies won in horse shows as far away as San Francisco and Chicago. Those were just for show-riding and jumping. On the *other* side of the room were the trophies won in rodeos and western-style shows and events. She was as comfortable in English saddle as Western, in jodhpurs as in Levis.

My devotion to her continued undiminished even when I realized there'd never be the remotest possibility of anything resembling the sweet puzzle games I'd shared with Mary Ann. I'd have to consider that kid stuff, something outgrown. Besides, if I had wanted to touch an intimate part of her body; the only way that could be managed would be to turn myself into a saddle. Or better yet, saddle blanket and then bore a hole up through the saddle so that when she posted up and down, up and down on my . . . Whooee, a fantasy so outrageous that it made me laugh thinking that not even Mary Ann could come up with something so bizarre.

The closest I got to that part of my beloved was the polishing and waxing the places where it spent most of its out-of-school time. I became an expert with saddle soap and wax, could make brass reflect in the dark, and the amount of horseshit I shovelled would have compared favorably with what Dad was floating on the irrigations ditches right over there. I actually heard his voice at the corner once, and thanked God for the high walls. If he'd seen me cleaning out the stables, he'd probably have suggested that charity begins at home.

My unstinting efforts were rewarded in one positive way—I was allowed to ride once in a while and was becoming familiar with the intricacies of the English saddle and bridle, posting with increasing ease and authority. Cleveland, the head groom and husband of Rosalind's mammy, allowed I was developing a good seat. He was a kind, gentle man and it was he would let me ride, saying it was the least he could do for all the work and time I put in helping him.

I'd been riding with Rosalind in the center circle with Cleveland calling out instructions in his quiet voice when she suddenly bent down and whispered something to Cleveland and galloped out of the ring, down the drive and out onto the main road. I started to follow her since we often gave the horses a good run along the nearby country roads, but Cleveland caught my horse's bridle and said softly, "You better git down, Lil' Carl." I could tell from his face that something was wrong. I swung my leg around and slid down to the ground.

"What's the matter?"

"Well, it's like this," he led the horse toward the stable and motioned with his head for me to accompany him. "Mr. Rawlings, he thinks you spending too much time over here. Taking up too much of my time." He chuckled. "I told him you was turning into a pretty good stable boy." He stopped and stroked the neck of the horse while I patted her and wondered what this was all about. "And . . . he says . . . Mr. Rawlings says . . . Well, they don't know your folks and they think you and Missy getting pretty thick . . . And well, they think it's maybe a good idea to well . . . separate you two for awhile. I mean, you see each other at school all the time and . . ."

"And they don't think I should come around here any more. Is that it?"

"Yes. I don't know why Missy make me tell you this."

"I don't under . . ." I couldn't believe what I was beginning to believe. "We live right over there, Cleveland. We're *neighbors*. We go to the same school . . ."

"I know, I know, Lil' Carl. But he says . . . Mr. Rawlings says . . . oouuaah," it was sort of a strange sighing noise, "so many new people comin' in . . . strangers . . . Okies and the like . . . and he . . ."

I didn't hear any more. I was running as fast as my legs could carry me. I made it to the road as fast as Rosalind had made it on the horse. If there'd been cars coming, even one, I could have been killed because I was blinded by the tears that were streaming down my face and I was in the middle of the road, running, running, running, choking on sobs until I was well out of sight of the Rawlings property and then I slowed down to a walk, a very slow walk, one foot slowly being put down and the other even more slowly being picked up. This would be the last time I'd ever walk on this road. That much I knew. I'd walk forty miles to school if I had to. I'd face those wild rock-throwing Mexicans and battle them until I was bloody but I wouldn't ever as long as I lived walk down that road again. I turned into North Twelfth Street. The beige adobe walls looked protective and warm. Home. I hit the wall with my fist and then my forehead with my fist. God! What a dummy!

"What's happened to the big romance," Junior asked when I suggested we take the old way down Missouri Avenue to school the next day. "The horse finally win out?"

"Yeah. Something like that." It was a bit soon to joke about. If I was ever going to be able to.

He looked at me closely. "You sad?"

"Kinda."

"Oh, don't worry," he said putting an arm around my shoulder. "You were just blinded by her unearthly beauty." He squeezed me to him. "And her earthly goods."

"Probably." Her house was really nice. But as I thought about it, I realized I'd only been inside once. To the room where the trophies were—a sort of playroom or family room, whatever they called it. I hadn't even seen all the inside. Okies weren't allowed in. "Well, anyway, I was learning how to ride. A bit."

"I was only joking. I mean, I was just teasing . . . What happened?"

"Aw, she's just a stuck-up snot."

"Wow! Never thought I'd hear you say *that*. About the sweet, sweet Rosalind."

"They're all stuck-up. Big house, horses, a whole bunch of cars. Live-in help."

Junior stopped. I stopped and turned to look at him. "So have the Joneses," he said evenly.

"But the Rawlings have Negroes . . . old family retainers, they call them."

"Live-in help comes in all colors, honey chile." Suddenly I understood it all. White-trash Okie servants.

I just stood there looking at him for a long minute. "Well. Ah'll be dawg-goned." We burst out laughing in the middle of Missouri Avenue. What better place. And what better place than with the Joneses'. We were living better than we ever had—servants or not. The only great loss was Mom's giving up teaching.

Facing Rosalind in school was a dread so intense that it cut off my breathing. I found that just the thought of seeing her on the playground or in the classroom, knowing what she and her parents thought of me cut some vital connection between my head and body. That I could have been so insensitive, so unaware of their real feelings about me while I polished their fucking brass and shovelled their horseshit, struck me as beyond idiocy. Dumb. Real dumb. When I thought about it, I don't think it was a blind rage that affected my eyesight, it was just a blindness about how to go about my daily life with others and still hold my head up.

I resolved it by deciding that I was going to be the best in my class. Best in everything. I would read and give more book reports than anybody else. I'd work on the multiplication tables until I could say them in my sleep—Junior swore I did. Whatever activity was being arranged, I'd head it and lead it. I'd instigate things—outings, class projects for geography, history, natural science—anything so long as I ran it. I even appointed Rosalind to committees on my projects more often than not. She was never to know that *I* knew for sure, no matter what Cleveland reported back to her. What I wanted her to know was that this white-trash-Okie servant was smarter than she was. It was not easy to prove.

I burned the midnight oil as long as Junior did. I was caught with my nose in a book as frequently as he. Mom was wide-eyed with delight. Dad just threw up his hands at the prospect of having two bookworms to contend with. I won on the battlefield I'd chosen—the classroom—but I was still not invited to her birthday party just before school was out in June. Reba Jean had been excluded by her classmates in Galena and now I had been. I really did know now how she must have felt. We had a common bond now, besides the secret of Clementine.

During spring baseball practice, the varnished station wagon was parked on the playing field several times a week. It was such a familiar sight that the kids had stopped staring at the flat still figure of the captain on the cot in the back. The bearded face straining up from the pillow was full of interest and the sharp eyes followed the play intently. The captain's interest was keen so long as his glass held fortification. Dad said without the bourbon to push things along, the heart couldn't possibly pump the blood through that immobile body. When Dad heard the clink of the empty glass dropping into its metal ring it meant it was time to go. The refill was more important than baseball even if Junior were up to bat or was pitching.

"Such are Dad's sacrifices," Junior intoned dramatically, "having to leave when I'm just about to slide into home."

"On your fat ass," I muttered and we'd roll around on the grass in a strenuous wrestling match. It was here that I really could hold my own. I was slippery as a snake and very rarely did Junior or any of the other boys pin me down and make me say "uncle." Perhaps choking on that word—thanks to "Uncle" Roy—inspired me to extraordinary feats of supple defense. Then, too, the positions in wrestling got awfully close to playing puzzles again and I found some were giving me those tingling sensations and superhuman efforts were often required to keep from getting a hard-on. Simple horsing around and wrestling couldn't be allowed to become a forbidden game.

I'd had enough forbidden games. I didn't need any more. Guilt had been applied with a trowel. In layers. I could feel it getting thicker, like a tree growing a new circle every year. I felt that if my core, that secret core somewhere there under the rib cage where the guilt stabs deepest and shame is stored, were dissected, a stratified cross-section would show those layers—some with names on them, others, nameless.

One of the forbidden games was swimming in the irrigation ditches. Not a terrible thing in itself, but forbidden is forbidden. And that was most definitely NOT ALLOWED. I tried to excuse it by saying it was a case of self-preservation. It was. Sort of. I was all but forced into it.

Since the after-school route home past Rosalind's place was *out* I was going to have to face the terrifying Mexicans on Missouri Avenue. And alone. Junior's after-school baseball practice saw to that. There was no choice.

The first afternoon I ran into absolutely nobody. And ran is the word. I flew past the main ditch so fast I didn't even notice it was dry. I was over the back gate, home-free earlier than I had been in months. The second and third days were the same. The long black ribbon of road with the few houses close to the school on the left and irrigated lemon and orange groves on the right was lonely, but safe. No marauders. I began to feel secure and carefree and paid less and less attention to the place where we'd first encountered the boys who were so violently opposed to the idea of *bese*-ing my *coula*. They were, we'd found out, the children of the poor Mexican itinerant fruit pickers who apparently didn't go to any school. They were called "wetbacks" with the same snarl that people used when spitting out "Okie." I thought at first they got the name by swimming in the irrigation ditches which was illegal—NO SWIMMING signs were posted at intervals—and were breaking the law.

They were breaking the law so quietly one afternoon that I didn't see them until one jumped out onto the road in front of me to head me off while I saw three others start to move around between the school and me, all slickly wet-backed and menacing. Fear and my week's practice at racing down this road gave me a bit of an advantage. I took off like a shot, dodging the boy in front of me somehow and headed for the gate, my feet barely touching the tarmac. I could hear the running bare feet behind me as I jumped from the road's shoulder down the slight incline to the big gate. I was up it, clinging to the top when my left foot was grabbed by two very strong hands pulling me down. I kicked furiously with my other foot before it too was grabbed and then I felt both shoes being pulled off. Was the attacker after my shoes? Having just one pair of school shoes can make you want to protect them. I let go of the top gate slat and dropped down. Straight on top of my attacker. I felt his body under me and I was elated. This was wrestling and once on top I knew he wasn't going to get me off. In a flash, I had my knees on his upper arms and his thick black hair in my hands. I was bent over him like a jockey on the final lap to keep his thrashing legs from locking around my upper body. My face was so close to his I couldn't focus. I could see my eye reflected in his big black one. I lifted his head slightly off the ground and banged it with considerable force into the gravel of our back entrance. His breath was in my face, hot and straining. I banged his head again. A bit harder. He cried out. I could hear the other three there on the road stop dead in their tracks.

"I'll beat his brains out if you come any closer," I called not even looking up. I kept my eyes on my opponent who I could now feel relaxing under my weight. "Tell . . . them . . . I'll . . . bash . . . your . . . brains . . . out . . . if . . . they . . . come . . . one . . . step . . . closer." I accented each word with a bump of his head on the ground like Dad had done with Coot Jenkins at the Domino Café His teeth were clenched and he was rolling his head from side to side as much as my grip on him would allow. *"Tell them!"* He screamed something I didn't understand as I put all my weight on his head and ground it into the gravel. Then his body went slack.

We stayed where we were, breathing into each other's faces, my grip on his hair a death grip, I was fighting for my life. I could feel nothing except my own shuddering breathing and my determination to hold my captive where he was until . . . until . . . hell freezes over is all I could think. The other three stayed frozen in their positions on the road. I glanced up at them at the sound of an approaching car. I tried to signal with my eyes that the car would bring me help. They suddenly turned and fled.

I looked back into the big black eyes that had softened and for a moment I thought they were filling with tears. But then the corners of his mouth twitched into a smile. I could see the shadow of a dark moustache beginning on his upper lip. He muttered something I couldn't hear. I bent down closer. *"Bueno,"* he whispered. I didn't understand. *"Usted. Bueno."*

My grip loosened on his hair and I felt the tingle of relaxed effort in them. I shook my head uncomprehendingly. Our positions hadn't changed, but we both breathed more normally now. "No understand."

He lifted his head a fraction and whispered again. *"Usted."* He was willing me to understand with his eyes. *"Usted, bueno."* He licked his lips and bit the lower one and frowned in concentration. "Goo . . . *Good,"* he finally burst out with a flashing display of perfect teeth.

"Me? Good?"

He nodded as best he could. *"Amigos. Yo. Usted. Good amigos."* Amigos I knew from cowboy films. The Lone Ranger and Tonto were amigos. I nodded and relaxed my grip a bit more. His dark eyes narrowed and he moved his body slightly underneath me. The gravel must be eating into his back. He was wearing only wet underwear which wouldn't give him much protection from the sharp stones. I eased one knee cautiously from his arm, releasing my hold on his hair and transferring my hand to his wrist and then did the same thing on the other side. I held his arms spread-eagled which drew our faces even closer together. How do you say "uncle" in Spanish? Or even "give up?" I tried to explain, speaking softly and clearly. "If I let you up, will you promise not to chase me or throw rocks?"

He watched my face intently, concentrating on what I was saying, even moving his lips to try to form the words I said. Then he shook his head and let it drop back. *"No comprendo."*

I grinned. *"I* no comprendo." We smiled at each other. That eased the tension. My grip on his wrists relaxed but then tightened with sudden apprehension. It could be a trick. I'd let him up and then the others would suddenly appear and I'd lose everything I'd gained. I was only the winner so long as I was where I was. We couldn't strike any bargain because of the language problem. I sighed and shook my head. I smiled into his eyes again and shrugged. How were we going to call a halt to this?

His eyes smiled back at mine and he shook his head and mimicked my shrug. He lifted his head again close to mine and whispered, *"Amigo,"* breathing his last syllable against my cheek. *"Amigo, amigo, amigo,"* the breath became a touch, his cheek on mine, the fuzz on our cheeks tickling, *"amigo, amigo, amigo,"* he chanted so softly that it wasn't so much heard as felt. That unfamiliar tingle was filling my body. I turned my head slightly and his lips brushed mine, still breathing the word. I felt myself going faint. All thought suspended as his lips brushed my cheeks and lips and then suddenly his tongue ran across my lips and set me on fire. I sat up and at the same time pushed my body back along his until my bottom hit an obstacle.

I rose on my knees and looked through them. He had a hard-on, straining at his damp shorts, looking big and vulnerable in the broad daylight. My God! Anybody could see us. I scooted back a bit further and dropped down on top of him to hide the hard-on which dug into my groin next to my own erection. Could we pretend to go on wrestling? I still had my clothes on but our groins were rubbing against each other as my hold on his wrists relaxed. He slowly lifted one arm and put it around my neck and held my head against his with our mouths pressed together. I doubt if anybody would have thought we were wrestling, but it didn't last very long. I came in my Levis. Roy hadn't explained what I was supposed to do about that.

I ran down Missouri Avenue every day after that but now for a different reason. I'd meet Miguel at a place where he had taken us that first time to wash off. It was where I had to prove myself to the others by stripping and swimming naked in the ditch. I was terrified of the muddy water—it looked thick and dangerous—but Miguel smiled encouragement and he seemed to be telling the others how strong I was, how I'd won our fight fair and square, how we'd now become friends. He put his arm around my shoulder and shook his fist at the others indicating that he'd fight anybody who bothered me.

I ran to provide an explanation for arriving home with dampish clothes, in addition to racing to the ditch to swim with Miguel. I could truthfully say that I'd run all the way home and was sweaty. I was in training—I swore—to become a long-distance runner. That thrilled Dad, two sports-minded sons instead of two bookworms—and as long as I needed an excuse, it worked. Unfortunately, I didn't need it very long.

Those forbidden games with Miguel are mortared in there on the guilt side, but they're not filed under "shame." We couldn't really talk to each other so we had to use our bodies. They spoke eloquently. We ker-plopped our come into the irrigation water with the same shamelessness as the Wilkins boy had. We touched each other all over— Miguel's wet silken skin was what I'd imagined a seal's would feel like. We were two young animals, making grunting noises to communicate when a touch failed or succeeded, cavorting like puppies nipping at each other, as natural and spontaneous as any other beasts. Caressing and kissing was only a part of our cavorting. It had no separate meaning. It was as integral a part of being together as our going swimming. We just liked touching each other. There was that dark corner in me that made me try not to like it too much, but his infectious laughter, flashing black eyes, open excitement and obvious delight in me were too magnetic and broke down any barrier that that voice inside me tried to erect by beating out a rhythm of; bad, bad, bad—sin, sin, sin—shame, shame, shame—punish, punish, punish. I listened to the voice and redirected its message to the serious guilt I felt at our public lawbreaking. Swimming in the ditches was against the law. That bothered me more than anything else. But what excited me and gave our secret meetings an extra thrill was that we two outcasts—white-trash Okie and brown-skinned wetback, had come together with such joy and tenderness after the classic battle. Equally rejected, our joyous games made a mockery of prejudice.

I'd had hardly three weeks' long-distance running sessions before I resigned from the next Olympics. Miguel was gone. From one day to the next. I searched the lemon groves thoroughly as far away from our house as I dared, but saw only a long low farmhouse with shacks around it that looked forbidding and deserted.

The migrant workers, somebody told me, moved every few weeks—when the strawberries up north were over, they moved on to other things, depending on the season. Down in the southwest corner near Yuma, just beyond the Gila Desert where the weather was particularly mild, the land was rich and produced several crops a year: peaches, pears, apples and apricots. Most of the vegetables sold year round in Phoenix came from around Yuma. God only knows where Miguel was now. I felt an aching loss deep inside, like the loss of Grandma, but different—there was another feeling mixed up in there. One I didn't quite recognize, but it hurt, sort of in the way Ronnie's voice had sounded full of hurt when he whispered, "I love you, Tots. I *mean* it."

But I'd been in love with Rosalind. *In* love. There was plenty of hurt there—prideful hurt. What was the difference? Had I really loved her? If I'd loved her would I have felt the way I now felt about losing Miguel? She'd hurt my pride. That was all. Besides, what did I know of love—any sort of love—at eleven. Oh, God! Was I still only *eleven?*

"Hey, wait a minute," Junior called after me one day after school when I'd started off down Missouri Avenue toward home.

I waited for him to catch up. "What's wrong with ball practice?"

"Coach is sick or something. Anyway called off." He hugged me. "And what about *your* training? I thought you ran this long stretch every day."

"I do," I said defensively. "Did."

"Did?"

"Well, I don't do it every day. You can overtrain, you know."

"Noooo," he teased. *"Over*-train? Where'd you get that?"

"I read it somewhere. Jesse Owens says you have to . . ." He was eyeing me skeptically. "But it's true. I read it . . ."

"Tots, you're a devil. I know what you were running for." He was grinning down at me. My heart stopped.

"What do you mean? My running . . . running for *what?*"

"To go swimming, dummy. Don't think you can fool me."

I was dumbfounded. If he knew that, how much more did he know? "Swimming?"

"Oh, for Lord's sake, Tots, I ran after you one day—I just wanted to clock your speed. Hey, and you know what, you sneaky little devil? You're *fast.* You really are. I paced you and you were really cutting loose."

"Yeah?" Pride bubbled up, but fear of how much he'd discovered about my swimming strangled it.

"Yeah! I mean it. If you really did work at it, why I'd bet you could become a champion."

"Do you really think . . ." We were passing the big irrigation ditch and my eyes were drawn in spite of myself to check once more for Miguel.

"What happened to your swimming buddy?" Junior asked. I shot him a wild look. "Don't look so surprised. It's not much fun swimming alone." His eyes twinkled. "Just how in the world did you tame those wild rock-throwing varmints, pardner?"

"Beat one of 'em up."

"You're kidding!" He let out a wild whoop. "Did you, Tots? Did you really?"

"Sure," I said calmly and then told him the story while his eyes got wider and wider with pride. "And the one, Miguel, took me over there and told the others that we were friends and if they ever tried to give us any trouble, they'd get it from him."

"You licked them, and then joined them! I'll be doggoned." He chuckled and hugged me again. "You just go on surprising the hell out of me."

I punched him and ran over to the gate and started to climb it. "I'm going to tell Mom you said 'hell.'"

"Go ahead. You do and I'll tell her you use Dad's word all the time."

"I do *not!* Only when it's absolutely necessary, like we agreed." I felt his hand on my bottom, boosting me over the gate as easily as if he were scoring with a basketball.

He also scored plenty with a baseball bat. He brought the Lincoln School baseball team into the city finals and then, just before school was out, managed to win the championship game almost single-handedly. It was in the last half of the ninth inning, and a score of two nothing in favor of South Phoenix with the bases loaded, that Junior knocked a home run. It became sort of a litany that Dad repeated and repeated and repeated, eventually supplanting his Bonnie and Clyde story: It was in the last half of the ninth . . . and so on. He was as proud as if he himself, had pitched a no-hit inning to Babe Ruth. Captain J shared the vicarious thrills. He and Dad had attended every game of the playoffs and it was his idea that Junior have all the team to 1548 for an ice-cream party the Sunday after the final victorious game.

We all flew around making plans for the party. There'd be about a dozen boys and the coach and his wife. That would mean two separate lots of ice cream. Once Mom had the mix ready, I started cranking. We'd take turns, Bradford, Junior and I.

"Let's just forget about him," Junior said after Brad had disappeared and let a lot of ice melt. "If we try to depend on him, we'll never be ready by the time the team gets here."

"What has the idiot done now?" The captain's voice came from behind us. Dad was pushing him silently across the lawn.

"It's OK, Captain," Junior said. "We just got a bit short on ice there for a minute. All's all right now."

"But where is he? Isn't he supposed to be helping with the ice cream?"

"I . . . ah . . . I think he went to the toilet," I ventured.

"He's got callouses on his ass from the toilet seat. If anybody is looking for him—a highly unlikely prospect—that's where you can usually find him. He'll either develop piles or wank until his cock falls off." He looked back up at Dad. "Or both." Dad nodded and smiled. The captain lifted up his empty glass. "This, Woody, is a glass full of air. I find it difficult enough to try to breathe the damned stuff, let along try to drink it. Let's displace some air with some liquid." Dad winked at us and guided the cot expertly onto the driveway toward the house.

The party was a huge success. Mrs. Jones was charming, Bradford's polished manners were on display, and the captain was in excellent form. He'd had Bradford set up a bar for the grown-ups on the edge of the lawn. The clink of ice in glasses mingled with the light laughter from the adult group and the distant yelling and screaming from the badminton court of the young baseball champions. The Joneses treated Mom and Dad as co-hosts—Dad manning the bar and Mom sharing trips to the kitchen for ice or more plates or napkins with Mrs. Jones. We were all one happy family.

The ice cream was declared the best anybody had ever eaten. Every melting drop had been scooped up by the red-faced sweaty boys. I'd managed to get "The Look" from Mom when I headed back for thirds and quickly put my plate down and plunked myself down on the lawn next to Bradford.

"Christ, what a bore," he muttered without moving his lips.

"We've run out of ice cream. They'll go soon."

"Can't be soon enough for me." As though they were rationed or from a well that might run dry, his beautiful manners weren't wasted on me or Junior. They were saved for special occasions, like best shoes.

"What's that you're drinking?" It looked refreshing and I was thirsty after all the sweet things.

"Gin."

"Gin? You mean the white whiskey?"

"Gin is gin. Whiskey is whiskey. God, you're ignorant."

"Ignorance is bliss," I said for want of something else. I started to get up.

"Here. Want a taste?"

"Sure." I took the glass he offered and tasted. "Gaayaack. That's strong. What's it mixed with?"

"Gin." He grinned rather stupidly.

"That's all gin? That whole big glass?" I glanced over my shoulder at the grown-ups. They all had glasses in their hands too. "I thought you always mixed things in drinks like that. Gin and . . . and . . . soda? Like whiskey and water. Or bourbon and water the way the captain drinks it."

"Look at the old fart. He's getting pissed." He took a big swallow of his drink. I wondered if he really had been hitting the bottle all this time. "Look at him. Waving his arms around," he grunted derisively, "the only things he can wave. Ah'm shore he is bein' ever so witty an' chaaahramin'." He sounded like his mother. He made little faces and mimicked the captain's gestures. He took another big swallow from his drink at the same time as the captain did. "If he can get pissed, so can I."

I didn't like his mood or the things he was saying. "Some of the boys are leaving. I'll go help Junior with the gate." The boys marched by and bowed stiffly to their hosts—the Joneses and the Woods—thanking them formally for the "very nice party." They all said exactly the same thing as though they'd been coached by the coach.

The coach and his wife left, the former a bit unsteady on his feet and booming that, ". . . we must all get together real soon." They were all gone.

"What delicious quiet!" the captain said. "Woody, it's deafening. Quickly, make some noise with ice in this glass." He held it up with a slightly unsteady hand. "And join me with one for a postmortem. That's always the most fun about any gathering. To be able to talk about people after they've gone."

Junior and I stood talking to the last guests before we could finally ease them out by slowly forcing the gate closed and making that final adjustment at the bottom so the lock clicked firmly.

"Whhheeeeuuuuweeee," Junior cried. "What a celebration! I've been clapped on the back so much my teeth are rattling. They're all talking about next year and how we'll go right on up to State Champions!" He was beaming with his success.

I grabbed him by the shoulders and went slack, hanging down looking up at him in mock adoration, "Ooooh, our heeeeroooo."

"Let go, you nut. We've got to go help clear up the mess. Come on." I was still clinging to him with my feet dragging as he moved. "Quit fooling around."

"Woody-Two," the captain called out and raised his glass. "That's quite a team! All good boys. *Nice* boys. I enjoyed your party very much." He tilted his head in a slight bow. "Thank you for allowing me to come. I deem it an honor, sir." He drank a toast after lifting his glass again to Junior. "Yes, all good, nice boys. And Woody-Two, you're the head of the class."

Junior was blushing right down the front of his open-necked shirt. "It's you we have to thank, Captain. All the guys said how nice it was . . ."

"My pleasure, my pleasure—whatever I had to do with it. A pleasure to see healthy young lads . . ." He looked over at Bradford sprawled out on the lawn. "Just look at that, would you. How about *that* for an example of a healthy young lad." He shook his head and looked at Dad. "Jesus, Woody, you *are* lucky. Not just with your women. You've done pretty damned well with your male member . . ." he stopped and his eyes bugged comically. "To hell with plurals. Let's just leave it at that." Dad choked on his drink and then they both laughed and clinked their glasses.

Junior and I moved to the big table and stacked up plates and spoons and each took a load and headed toward the kitchen, stepping around Bradford as we went. Dad and the captain went on talking quietly. Mom and Mrs. Jones were gossiping at the sink doing the dishes together. Junior smiled at me and hugged me to him as we moved back for more dishes and glasses. I knew what he was thinking and I was thinking the same thing—that this was just about the most perfect day we'd had since . . . oh Lord! since *when*?

". . . and there it is," the captain was saying to Dad as we passed by them, "the result of the most expensive private school in Virginia. Look at that! The son and heir. Passed out in the sun and a head full of air. Or perhaps the air had been displaced by some liquid? And I don't mean water on the brain." He looked at Dad questioningly.

"I think maybe there was some inroads on the gin bottle."

"Might have known. What did I tell you? They're all drunks." Suddenly from somewhere deep inside his emaciated body a huge ringing bass voice filled the air. "Sergeant JONES!" he bellowed. "See if he remembers any military terms at all," he said in a normal voice to Dad. "SERGEANT JONES! *'TENSHUN.'* Bradford lifted his head dazedly. "I didn't say roll over and play dead, Rover. I said, 'TENSHUN. ON YOUR FEET! ON THE DOUBLE" The captain's voice bounced off walls and echoed, leaving our ears ringing. Bradford jumped to his feet and almost went over backwards but righted himself, arms stiff at his sides, chest out, chin tucked in so far it disappeared. "Now, if you think you can make it, FOR'ARD . . . *MARCH!*" Bradford lifted his left foot and put it down as the captain said, "Hup, two, three, four." He was moving like a wind-up toy, headed straight for the captain. "Deeeee—TAIL . . . *HALT!* PARAAAAADE . . . *REST!* Bradford shot out one foot to the side and snapped his hands behind his back smartly. "By God! Not bad. Not bad."

Dad lifted his glass to Bradford like the captain had to Junior. "Pretty smart there, Sergeant Jones."

"OK. Take off the military hat, boy and put on your chauffeur's cap." The captain suddenly sounded weary. "Home, James. I think we both need a nap."

Bradford went around to the handles and turned the cot around and pushed it toward the ramp and the swinging doors. At the bottom of the ramp, in order to turn and pull the cot up backwards, Bradford swung the cot around so violently the captain had to grab onto the sides to keep from falling off.

"What the bloody . . ." The captain was holding on for dear life. *"Idiot.* Be careful!"

Bradford was running backwards up the ramp, glancing over his shoulder. He hit the swinging doors with a sharp thrust of his behind and the captain's cot disappeared through the doors in a flash followed by an anguished cry from the captain. The cry continued as the doors made one continuous movement—snapping closed from the inside and then opening out with a crash as the cot and occupant came hurtling through them and down the ramp as though it had been shot from a powerful catapult.

Dad was beside the overturned cot almost before it came to a standstill, picking up the stiff little body from the gravel of the drive. Junior and I ran, grabbing at the thin foam-rubber mattress that had somehow wrapped itself around the captain's shoulders. Righting the cot and replacing the mattress revealed hidden tubes that connected plastic bottles and bags to the captain somehow. It was as though his insides had been ripped open—the tubes a tangle of intestines, the bottles and bags vital organs of some sort. The lifeless limbs bared for the first time reminded me of Clementine and I wanted to look away but was held by what was an obscene invasion of privacy—this immaculate man, with his silk pajama tops, the gossamer handkerchiefs, the manicured hands, was shown for what it was: lifeless bones encased in unfeeling flesh that was slowly disintegrating or rather turning into something like leather.

"Are you hurt?" Dad asked urgently as we all tried to reassemble the various parts of him back on the bed.

"Hurt?" That same cry of anguish we'd heard from behind the doors came chillingly from that deep reservoir where his drill sergeant's voice had come from. It was a wail of despair, of futility, of heartbreaking sadness. "I *can't* HURT. I can't *feel,* for Christ's sake. Except . . ." he poked all ten fingers hard into his chest. "Except *here* . . . HERE," his fingernails bit into the material of his shirt leaving marks, "except here, here, *here. Here* where it can *really* hurt. Where it really matters and not a Goddamned thing can be done about it." He moaned and rolled his head back on Dad's arm which was still under his shoulders. "Oh God. Oh, my God." He lifted his head suddenly. "Woody, for Christ's sake! Go find the boy . . . go . . . get . . . Brad . . ." He was tugging at Dad's shoulder with hands like claws and choking for breath. "God . . . knows what . . . what . . . he'll . . . do . . . ."

Mrs. Jones was on the other side of the cot, squatting down, leaning her face into the captain's, murmuring and kissing and soothing and caressing. Mom came running down the ramp. Dad looked up at her and she motioned with her head toward the garage. They both ran off in that direction. The scene in front of us was so intimate that Junior and I took off after Mom and Dad.

"Junior! Wait!" Mrs. Jones's voice stopped us dead in our tracks. "Come back and take the captain inside. Hurry!" She put her cheek against her husband's and then started running toward the garage. Junior passed her heading back. I didn't know quite what to do until Mrs. Jones came up beside me, panting. "Come with me," she said without stopping.

She headed for the side door of the garage which was open and we could hear Bradford screaming and cursing and heard Dad's voice trying to calm him down. I couldn't see at first because the station wagon was in the way, but I scooted around the tail end toward the back where the Model-A was and the big double washtubs on the side wall. Dad was holding Bradford somehow from the back. Bradford's arms were locked in Dad's but he was kicking and screaming and butting back at Dad with his head and his bottom. Mom was standing by the tubs holding a broken bottle in one hand and covering her mouth with the other. There was broken glass all over the floor. Bradford's kicking feet sent shards flying in every direction.

"Stay back," Dad ordered in a calm voice. "There's an awful lot of glass." And blood. I could see it all over Brad and on Dad's shirtsleeves.

Bradford was like an animal in a trap, kicking, biting, spitting, rolling his head from side to side, banging it back against Dad's shoulders and chest, all the time growling and gasping and spewing out obscenities from a frothing mouth that looked like he was having his mouth washed out with soap.

Mrs. Jones moved along the wall toward Mom. I followed her. Mom held up the bottle. It was Clorox. "He was drinking this when we came in," she explained in a quiet voice. "Then he broke it when he saw Woody and . . ."

"We've got to make him throw it up," Mrs. Jones said quickly. "Carlton, get that glass over there. Milly, get the water warm and make some suds with that wash soap." She was in charge. We did as we were told.

"He's calmin' down," Dad said. Brad had gone limp in Dad's iron grip. His head hung forward and his attempts at freeing himself had dwindled down to mere tics now, a spastic jerking that seemed involuntary, his body slack, twitching occasionally as though invisible wires were being pulled.

Mrs. Jones grabbed the glass, dipped it into the suds Mom had created at the bottom of the washtub with the bar of yellow soap. It looked like a peculiar beer, opaque but with a nice head of foam. She turned toward the two men who were still locked together, with Dad holding both Brad's arms with one forearm through the crooks of his elbows, leaving his other arm free to help support him around the waist. Mrs. Jones approached cautiously, crooning sweetly, "It's all right, honey. Everything's going to be all right. Momma'll take care of everything. Just relax, darlin' . . ."

We all were holding our breath. Brad's head still was slumped forward but even his twitching seemed to have stopped. "Now, listen, honey," Mrs. Jones went on. "This isn't going to taste very good . . . it's nothin' bad, you know I wouldn't give you anything bad, my darlin', just take a good swallow . . ." She was standing in front of him, slightly to his side, cocking her head to one side in an effort to look up into his face. "It's me, honey, Momma . . ." She put her hand on his forehead and eased his head up gently. "Just one big sip, for Momma, honey." She lifted the glass to his mouth and started to tilt it for him to drink. His head suddenly snapped forward and then backwards with a crunch of broken glass. He'd bitten off a large hunk of the glass which dropped to the floor as his mother let out a little gasp and brought her hands up to her cheeks in surprise. "Hon . . ." The sound of teeth grinding glass drowned out all other sound for a second. Dad did some quick movement with his free hand, a sort of fist-stabbing into Brad's solar plexis and at the same time with the same movement, he slapped Brad so hard on the back with the flat of his hand that he was bent double. His breath caught as Dad knocked the air out of him and then out it came. He was throwing up. Glass, gin, Clorox and blood. Choking on an eruption of vile-smelling liquid that was splattering all over himself, Mrs. Jones, and Dad. Dad kept hitting him on the back then jabbing him in the middle like priming a pump to get the flow started only he was trying to keep the flow going.

"Go phone Dr. Larkin, Milly," Mrs. Jones was back in charge once more, holding Brad's head in both her hands, moving with him as he retched, wiping his mouth and chin with her bare fingers, using them like squeegees, flicking off the disgusting slime, wiping her hands on her skirt and reaching back to wipe off the endless stream that kept coming like things from a vegetable or meat grinder. Dad's pumping motion on Brad's middle was steady and tireless. Mom and I flew past them and out the door.

Junior was handing the captain a fresh drink as we burst into the living room. "I'm to call Dr. Larkin," Mom said, heading for the library.

"It's all right, Miz Milly." The captain was as calm as if nothing in the world mattered except to find out if Junior had put the right amount of bourbon in his drink. He sipped. "Ahhh, Woody-Two, you are really your father's own son." He inclined his head and raised his glass slightly. "Thank you."

"But, Captain . . ." Mom was anything but calm.

"It's *done*, Miz Milly. It's over and done with. I've called."

"Was Dr. Larkin . . . It's Sunday."

"The call, Miz Milly, has been made." He looked up at her over the rim of his glass. "Made. Done." He sighed heavily. "Settled." When Mom tried to speak again, he raised his hand to stop her. "You'll know soon enough. You'll *hear* soon enough. The ambulance. The siren. We should be hearing it any minute. It's not that far away." He cocked his head as though he were listening. We all held our breath again. "There . . . Isn't that it? Shhhh. Listen." We all strained, looking at each other wide-eyed. "Woody-Two, open the front door there. We can hear better. And, I guess you might as well go open the gate." He motioned to me. "Go help him, Carlton. They'll need to get in."

"The ambulance? Which . . ."

"The State Hospital, Miz Milly. Right down there on Van Buren." I stopped in my tracks near the door. Did he mean the *mental* hospital? Where Winnie Ruth Judd was? The captain and Mom looked at each other a long time. "He *is* mad, Miz Milly. You knew it, too, didn't you?"

She held his eyes for a second more and then crossed her arms across her breast the way she had and looked down at them. She nodded, "I think I'd guessed."

We heard the siren's eerie call just as we clicked the gate back open onto their metal stoppers. The quiet Sunday evening air was filled slowly with the wail like the sound of a mosquito spiraling around and zeroing in on your ear. But this woeful alarm was one you held your breath for, hoping it won't zero in on you, leaving that wonderful feeling of relief as it disappears down the street with its sound getting dimmer as it disappears leaving you whole and unaffected. For somebody else, you think. Thank God not for me.

But now, we knew this terrifying siren was for 1548 and it was deafening as the ambulance screeched to a halt just beyond the gate, shifted gears noisily and backed up with alarming speed into the drive in a spray of gravel causing me and Junior to jump back. Two men were immediately out and we pointed them to the garage. They were wearing white uniforms. One was carrying a little bag like a doctor's, the other a rolled up piece of canvas.

Mrs. Jones appeared at the side door of the garage looking composed and with a gentle, ladylike gesture motioned the men to her. She spoke to them quietly, indicating the inside of the garage with her head. The men hurried past her as she walked purposefully toward the house.

Junior and I were frozen to the spot, the action taking place before our stunned eyes seemed far away, and yet still clearly in focus like a drama being played out on a movie screen. A drama in which we were only spectators. A silent movie, but riveting in its tension and excitement. As that character, the little lady smeared with filth walked tall and straight into the kitchen door, four men came out of the side door of the garage. One man was wearing some sort of thick whiteish garment that covered him from his neck to below his hips, causing his arms to disappear as though the tight shirt was rubberized and could be slipped over his head like the rubber tubes that were slipped over finger-bandages to protect them. The man looked bandaged as though his entire body were bleeding. He looked wounded and it took great effort from the two men to move him along toward the waiting ambulance. The fourth man stood near the garage, his hands held out dangling away from his sides as though covered with something he couldn't name.

Suddenly, Brad and the two men stepped out of the screen. They were real, Brad's face the same color as the weird body bandage he was wearing as he slumped against one of the attendants while the other opened the rear doors of the big white vehicle. A chill of recognition hit me. Would they put him in feet first? A litter slid out silently and was put on the ground. Brad's knees gave way and he collapsed boneless onto its surface as the men straightened him out like a strand of cooked spaghetti. The men picked up the litter and slid it noiselessly into place on the same side of the ambulance as the captain's cot fitted into the station wagon. Familiar clamps snapped and held it in place.

One of the men sat beside the litter on a small seat that folded out of the wall on hinges as the other stepped back and started to close the door.

I heard the kitchen door slam and Mrs. Jones appeared looking smart in a fresh summer dress, carrying a handbag that matched her high heeled pumps. "Wait," she said. "I'll ride in the back." The man stepped aside, holding the door open for her as the other one inside produced another little seat out of the wall. The door was closed. The man walked around and got into the driver's seat. The motor started, the siren with it. We jumped back again, away from the ear-splitting sound as much as the flying gravel. We stood stricken, listening to the sound diminish but we didn't move until we heard Dad call softly, "Close the gate, boys."

After that the atmosphere at 1548 was heavy with dread and unasked questions. Junior and I dashed off to school gratefully each morning and even started putting off coming home in the afternoons by stopping off at the irrigation ditch for a little light law-breaking. This was the last week of school—of actual working school—then we'd go back for two or three half-days the following week to collect grade cards, have some class parties, turn in library books and generally wind up the school year. A hot Arizona summer then loomed in front of us. We could feel summer's loose ends beginning to grow and dangle from parts of our bodies in the gathering June heat.

Talk at home was naturally of Bradford. He'd been diagnosed as having something called dementia praecox—a form of schizophrenia or *was* schizophrenia with just touches of dementia praecox, I never did get it straight. He was having shock treatments, something described as relatively new, and when mentioned everybody made faces of sympathetic pain like you do when you look at somebody's cut finger or even a healed scar. It took me some time to understand that he wasn't being given soothing medicines to calm him after the shock he'd been through—that's what I imagined shock treatment to be—and learned that it meant severe electrical shock actually given *to* him. On purpose. An accidental shock from a loose plug or lightbulb was terrifying enough, but to force somebody to undergo pain for pain's sake seemed to me to be just the opposite of what a doctor ought to be doing for somebody who was sick.

Mrs. Jones spent almost all her time at the hospital—sometimes even sleeping over. She reported home two or three times a day by phone—often talking to Mom because the captain had commenced an unprecedented number of new projects. He spent practically all day outside with Dad. New loads of manure had been ordered, new plants, seedlings, seeds of a new grass for lawns that he claimed would revolutionize gardening. He kept Dad running and he called me and Junior in as extra hands. The captain was working feverishly, keeping one step ahead as Dad completed each new plan by having another new one at the ready. Dad had even rigged up some floodlights so that he could work outside at night. He was being worked ragged and looked it.

"He's doin' this to keep his mind off the boy," Dad said, "and I'll be goddamned if I'll let him down."

"It's the general loneliness, too," Mom said. "I'm going to suggest we all eat together. Either at the main house or right here. Maybe he'd prefer here. Just to be away from the familiar."

Mom served the captain and Dad beer and sandwiches for lunch wherever they happened to be outside. Dinner in our small kitchen was too cramped for the cot, so we started dining with the captain in the main house when Mrs. Jones wouldn't be home. As the days wore on, the frequency of the shock treatments increased even though Bradford's reaction to them stayed fairly negative.

Evenings with the captain were a joy—he talked about everything with knowledge and wit. He'd take Junior into the library after dinner and go over lists of colleges and explain which ones were the best and which offered the best athletic scholarships. He advised, instructed, encouraged, always taking into consideration our financial position but also always stressing our potentialities.

"You've got something really special, Woody-Two," he'd say. "You have the athlete's body but you have a searching mind. A poet's mind. My God! What a combination. Hey, Woody—*Big* Woody!" he'd call to Dad in the kitchen helping Mom. "Do you really know what you have here? You have a budding Babe Ruth—not the candy bar, Carlton, you nitwit—with the soul of . . . of . . . a Tennyson or . . . a Burns."

"Tenny-who?" Dad asked.

"Oh my God," the captain would roll his eyes in mock dismay. "Well, Woody, not Tennessee Ernie Ford or the bazooka blowing buffoon on radio. *Robert* Burns, not Bob Burns." He'd shake his head at Junior. "I trust your poor father's ignorance will not be too much of a hindrance in what is otherwise bound to be a brilliant career."

Other evenings, he'd devote his after-dinner attention to me. Talking about musical shows on the stage in New York. Things I'd only read about. I hadn't dared mention my dancing dreams, I just said they interested me. He'd tell me which records to play. "There, Carlton, on that shelf. The Cole Porters. Pick any of them. It doesn't matter which. Each one is better than the last." When I had them playing he'd say, "Now, *listen*. Listen to the lyrics. Listen to what he's saying—*how* he's saying it." And to Junior across the room with a book. "This won't do any budding poet any harm either. You listen too." Then after a few minutes. "Of course Larry Hart's better. Not better, just the best. But Cole, the queer son of a bitch—a Yalie, wouldn't you know—can still hold his own. But then, he does his own music."

"You said 'queer.' How's he queer?" I wanted to know exactly what a queer was. What did the word queer—usually sneered—really mean. Having asked the question, a premonitory chill made me wish I hadn't.

"*How's* he queer? They're both queer, Porter *and* Hart as far as that goes. Maybe it has something to do with being geniuses. Well, they're queer like all queers are queer. By being cocksuckers. You suck cock, you're queer."

There it was. Just what I'd feared and suspected deep down. Did that mean that Ronnie was a queer? Was Uncle Roy? Miguel? It seemed a simple formula: cocksucking equals queer. I was struck as rigid as Lot's wife.

"Shame really," the captain shrugged. "Just a paucity of language more than anything else. A lot of people like to have their cocks sucked but that's all right. But if you suck one, the only thing you're called is queer. Nothing nice seems to be said about cocksuckers." He thought a minute. "I suppose one could say he's a *good* cocksucker."

The Porter record was stuck in a groove and it took me some time to put it right with my fumbling hands.

Wednesday, the last half-day of school was over and we three Woodsmen, under the captain's supervision had worked all afternoon spreading manure over the entire property on the intricate network of irrigating channels and were just finishing up dinner in the main house when we heard a car pull up outside. Junior ran to open the door. It would be Mrs. Jones' taxi. She came in through the kitchen door followed by Junior and sat wearily down at the table. I'd never seen her look so sad and defeated.

"Well," she sighed and gave her head a little shake. "It's nice to come home to . . . to the family." She looked around at all of us and smiled, reaching out and patting the captain's arm.

"How's our son and heir." The joviality was forced and it jarred. He covered her hand with his. "Better?" he said more softly.

She bit her upper lip and shook her head and closed her eyes. I saw her throat working, swallowing hard. She put her elbow on the table and rested her forehead in the palm of her hand, sort of shading her eyes from the light. "It's just not working. The treatment. The treatments." She took a deep breath but didn't change her position. "They keep increasing them. I don't know how many they're giving now." She dropped her hand from her forehead. "What is this? Wednesday? Well, that's ten days. You'd think in ten days . . ." She put her head in both hands now. "I can't go watch any more. Those wires on his head . . . Then the rubber thing in his mouth for protection from the convul—" she swallowed hard several times, "—sions. The convulsions are so . . . You can't really look. I close my eyes but I can still see his body contort and twist and writhe. The pain . . . it must be . . . un*bearable.*"

"Alice, love, Alice," the captain said gently. "Don't talk. Go have a bath." He sent a message to Mom with his eyes. She was up quickly and gone. "Hungry? A bite of Miz Milly's lemon meringue . . ."

"No. No, thank you. Oh, I know how good it is . . ." a faint smile softened the anguish in her face. "But I think I'll take that bath. If y'all'll excuse me . . . ?" She stood and moved toward the door as we scrambled to our feet, nodding and murmuring, "Good night."

Dad drove her to the hospital early every morning. By the time he was back, the captain would be outside with Junior at the helm of the cot ready to start the day. His energy was unflagging and depended less and less on the fuel in the glassholder by his side. Hours would go by before he'd notice his "glass of air" and send one of us back to the house for fresheners.

Some mornings the captain spent inside on the telephone or at a sort of writing tray that slanted at just the right angle for him to be able to write. I noticed when mailing his letters that they were primarily to addresses in the east. Mom had brought accordian cardboard files from cupboards at his request and his bed was covered with official-looking papers for hours on end. She'd help him arrange them back in the files and put them away.

"Have to get everything in order." he'd mutter. "Just don't know where all this is leading."

Then one day when we were all waiting outside in the drive for Dad to return from taking Mrs. Jones to the hospital the captain suddenly turned to Mom and said, "What the hell is the matter with me? What am I trying to do? Kill us all?" He dropped his head back on the pillow and laughed. "Look at the boys, there. Both getting black from the sun working outside all day. And you, poor Miz Milly. How long has it been since you've had a day off?"

Mom laughed and shrugged, "It's been a time when we all . . ."

"Well," he waved an arm to cut her off. "It's been about a month since the son and heir went on vacation. We damned well need one too." He was all excited. "Here, Carlton, you and Woody-Two go help Miz Milly pack us menfolk a lunch. Get out the hamper and I want it filled up to *here* with everything that's bad for us. Then, fill up the ice chest with bottles of chablis—and I mean *past* up to here. That's good for us. We'll go off somewhere where it's cool and make Miz Milly go suffer in the heat getting her head baked." Mom looked puzzled. "Baked or burned or broiled or even toasted—whatever it is they do to torture you poor creatures in the beauty parlors—where I want you to have the works. Curls, waves, cuts, massages, facials, pedicures, manicures, the lot! We haven't been looking after our prized possession properly." He came as close to bouncing up and down on his cot as I'd ever seen him. "Come on! Get a move on. Woody'll be back before you know it and have us all shovelling horseshit before we can tell him we're going for a drive."

We dropped Mom at a beauty parlor and then headed east out toward Camel Back Mountain, past Superstition Mountain whose sheer walls reminded me of the cliffs on James River and where according to local legend, many gold prospectors had been lost. Whether they lost their way once inside the peculiar rock formation that rose out of the flat desert or were done away with by a secret tribe of Indians was never made clear. It was wonderfully spooky and one could believe anything about it.

We drove up into the mountains along the Verde River eventually finding a rock pool with some trees near it, the perfect picnic spot where even the swimming would be legal for a change. The captain's cot was rolled out under the trees and Junior had his bourbon and water ready for him almost before Dad had him properly situated in the shade with a view of the rock pool. Junior and I were in the clear cold water in our underwear in minutes.

"What's the matter with you. Woody? Don't you swim?"

"Don't like to swim in it any more'n I like to drink it," Dad said with a grin.

"Woody-Two!" the captain called out. "Get back here to the bar. You have another customer!"

"Naw," Dad shook his head. "I'd better not." He indicated the car.

"To hell with that, Woody. You'll have plenty of time to sober up on Miz Milly's lunch. Besides, it's not much fun drinking alone."

Dad's attempts at teetotaling were halfhearted at best. He and the captain had made quite a dent in the bottle of Jack Daniels by the time Junior and I flopped down on the picnic rug dripping wet and breathless from our splashing around in the shallow water.

"Get out of here," Dad yelled. "Both of you. Like a couple of wet hound dogs. Go dry off in the sun."

We ran about in the sun. We got out the wicker basket. We drank iced tea until I thought it was going to come out of my ears and still the captain and Dad went quietly and steadily on sipping bourbon and talking. Junior rolled his eyes at me and rubbed his belly. We were both dying of hunger. At last, the bartender gleefully announced as he handed the two men drinks, "Well, that's it. That's the last of the bottle."

"I happen to know," the captain said without looking at Junior, "that there's another one in the glove compartment." Junior's face fell. The captain laughed his cough or coughed his laugh. "But there is no law that says we have to drink it. You boys are starving. Let's eat."

We set to with joy. I fixed a plate for the captain while Junior uncorked the wine with a fancy corkscrew the captain said came from France. As the screw went into the cork, two little arms on the side went up and then when pressed down, the cork came out as if by magic. It fascinated Junior and he'd become an expert with it. "Pour yourself some, Woody-Two. And some for Carlton. Let's all celebrate."

I'd had the white wine before and had already decided that if I ever became a drunk it would be on wine. Junior called me a wino and couldn't understand my being able to gulp it down like water. Nor could the captain. "Take it easy, Carlton. That's wine, not a Nehi. Sip it, son. *Taste* it. Feel it go all the way down." He demonstrated by rolling a sip around in his mouth and letting it slide down his throat with exaggerated delight. "Aaaaahh. There. I can feel it right there." He pointed toward his middle with a finger. "Granted I can't feel anything on the outside, but the good Lord left me that one little pleasure."

We ate. We polished off three bottles of wine. I noticed the captain barely touched his plate, but his wineglass was kept brimming by our attentive bartender who began to frown when I held out my own glass. "Let him have it," Dad said. "It's time you both learn what happens when you overdo. Better do it with us than sneak it."

"There is only one solitary pleasure that I know of," the captain said thoughtfully. "Sadly denied me now. Masturbation." Dad guffawed, Junior blushed and I looked blank—I didn't know the word. "But that, like anything else, can be overdone. Just like your dad says." He became serious. "That was part of Bradford's problem. It became an obsession." I turned to Junior for an explanation. He rolled his eyes heavenward, then glanced at the two grown-ups to make sure they couldn't see and quickly made the gesture. Then I blushed. "I've been talking a lot to his doctor. They're all frankly stumped. He's not responding to the treatment. They can't get him to talk, so they have so little to go on . . . He held his glass out for more wine. "I have to confess that I never understood the boy. We've never been particularly close. Maybe it's partly my fault. I always expected more . . . well, he's not like you two, you both are bright . . ." He turned to Dad. "I've always told you how lucky you were, Woody. You believe me now?"

"It's beginnin' to come home to me," he said looking directly at Junior almost as if he were apologizing.

The captain lay his head back on his pillow and closed his eyes. We were all silent for so long I thought he might have fallen asleep. He'd had an awful lot to drink. We all stretched out, making ourselves comfortable on the rug. Dad was leaning up against the tree, but eased himself down until he was almost lying flat out. The wine was making me drowsy. We could hear the trickle of water in the river, the katydids were sawing away in the heat. I put my head on Junior's stomach for a pillow and his breathing was so even and deep that I thought he was sleeping. When I heard the captain's voice, I thought I was dreaming. He spoke softly as though to himself. "He isn't mine, you know."

Dad grunted, "Hunh?"

"Bradford. He's not mine." None of us moved. I could feel the tension of our straining to hear. "Oh, Alice is his mother, all right. I guess she knows who his father is. I don't. But that was part of the bargain." We all lay perfectly still, waiting. "After I crashed . . ." There was a long pause. "She's a healthy woman, Alice. Healthy appetites. Naturally she wanted a child. We decided we'd do everything possible to have a child the minute we knew the extent of the damage to my system. The system. Quite simply, the system was finished. Fini. Kaput. Done for." He let a hand flop limply and graphically from his wrist as he gestured toward his crotch. "I needed a stand-in." He made a rueful little grimace. "Alice had to get pregnant quickly if we expected our little game to be plausible."

Dad's voice was as quiet as the captain's. "I thought the ac . . . accident happened during the war. Over there . . . overseas someplace."

"Huh." It was a derisive sound. "I couldn't even get that right." Junior rolled over onto his side, propping up his head on an elbow, and at the same time lifting my head so that I was able to look at the captain. Dad was sitting up straighter, too. "Made it all through the war. Not a scratch. Big hero! My squadron shot down more Krauts than any other. Oh, no. All that was fine. I was watched by the gods. Two years away in England and France. Not even a nick shaving. Home. Discharged. Decorated. Dashed to the arms of my beautiful young wife in a rented plane. Hail the conquering hero! There he is now! Look up there! Look at him! Her whole family was standing out on the rolling lawns of the old family mansion waving flags—some Confederate—and yelling. I could see all of them. See their faces. Alice's shining up at me. I did a showoff loop-the-loop and crashed into a cotton field. Broke my fucking neck." The silence was deadly. "The end." He looked at each of us, in turn. "For Christ's sake, I didn't even kill one of their prize Nigras. You all look like I was dead or was about to be. I'm anything but. Hey, bartender! What the hell do you think you're doing flat on your ass. Hop to! Let's get that wine flowing before the tears start." We all straightened up, blinking and shaking our heads. Keeping up with the captain's moods meant keeping on your toes.

"Our story," he went on, "a palpable lie, of course, was that the paralysis was a delayed reaction of some sort. Sort of crept up from my toes, I guess. And before it got to the family jewels . . . well, we'd somehow managed to make a child together. That was the story and we've stuck to it. We even worked up some cock-and-bull story about the doctors taking the casts off too soon and then something snapped or something. Anyway, so stupid that it wouldn't have fooled a drunken child of three." He raised a finger and tilted his head, "And let it be remembered that in Alice's family they often began that young." He roared at his joke. "But the point is, Alice was with child. *Whose* is anybody's guess. She is discretion personified. If either of us was a bit more religious, we'd have attributed it to God—Immaculate Conception and all that shit." His eyes bugged and he looked at Dad. "Listen, Woody, if you think my language is getting too strong for the boys," his eyes flashed wickedly, 'just say so. I refer to conception, not shit."

"So far there's nothing they don't know or should know." Dad laughed and looked at me. "Except maybe masturbate. I don't think Tots . . ."

"Carlton," he emphasized my name pointedly, "might not know the *word,* but he *knows.* Just look at that cunning look. You're going to have to watch that one, Woody. He's sensual . . . physical. I might even go so far as say sexy. Just watch him when he dances. Sexy in the sense of . . . well, for example, Woody-Two is cerebral, *not* sensual.

Oh, totally physical in the sense of physical coordination . . . while that little one there . . ." He pointed a finger at me and looked deeply into my eyes. I held the look. "Ooo-oooh!" he shook his head. "You are going to have one hell of a time. And I mean a *good* time." He made it sound naughty. I felt he was looking straight through me.

"Well, any man who says he hasn't done it is a liar," Dad stated.

"Oh, lordy, if I only *could,*" the captain said rolling his head on his pillow. We all tried to laugh along with the captain, but it was painful. I noticed Junior blushing. I wondered if he . . . but no, he just *wouldn't.* "So, Immaculate Conception or no, along came our very own little Bradford Jones, Jr. Adorable he was. Perfect. Those dimpled little hands. That infinitely kissable, bite-able, chewable little body. The first time I held him—naked and fresh from his bath—up in front and above me so I could really look at him—I was enraptured. It didn't matter who the father was. He was Alice's. *And* mine. I had a son and heir." His arms were lifted up in the air and he smiled fondly at the memory. "And then he pissed in my face." Dad fell over and spilled his wine he was laughing so hard. "Perhaps I should have known then . . ."

Dad was standing, brushing the wine from his trousers. "While I'm up and since you mentioned it . . ." He headed off behind the car to pee.

"Woody-Two, how's the wine holding out?"

"We've finished four, sir."

"As a bartender, Woody-Two, you must learn one thing. Never . . . but *never* tell anybody what they've drunk, how *much* they've drunk, unless you're trying to collect the bill. Always tell them what's left. That avoids making people feel guilty and also fills them with determination to bloody well get on with the job. Understand?"

"Understood." Junior threw a napkin over his left arm and played his role. "There are two excellent bottles of Chablis," he looked carefully at the captain to make sure he'd pronounced it properly and received a nod of approval, "in the cooler, sir. And I would say they're chilled to perfection."

The captain let out his full-throated laugh. "By God, you don't miss a trick, do you?" Then, almost to himself, "Oh, how I shall miss you." He took a deep shuddering breath and called out, "Woody! get back here. We're about to pop another cork."

Glasses were refilled—not mine, I got "The Look" from Dad this time—and the captain went on. "And so our son and heir grew and flourished. If there was a room big enough to swing a cat, little Brad would swing a cat. And usually sail it out an open window. If the window wasn't open, that presented no great problem. The weight of a flying cat can break most glass, if not, it still has a tendency to do the cat some damage. The mortality rate for any living pet was about three days until Brad was about six when it became considerably less. Of course inanimate toys were disemboweled or reduced to rubble in seconds." He was obviously having a wonderful time recounting this family history and we listened attentively, knowing that he was exaggerating outrageously. "I don't suppose he set fire to his first house before he was . . . oh, I guess he must have been eight. The cave man discovering fire couldn't have been more delighted and fascinated with it than our boy. We didn't buy tickets to the fireman's ball, we *gave* it. Widows and orphans are still on my payroll." He took a long swallow of wine and stared into his glass. "This is all in highly questionable taste. Forgive me. I'm making fun of a sick boy. *My* boy. As much mine as I could make him at the time. Perhaps that's why . . . Maybe I always resented the fact that he wasn't *really* mine. I cursed my dead body through him . . . Poor kid. Maybe he didn't have a chance."

We three exchanged nervous glances as he eased back on his pillow and closed his eyes again. Dad cleared his throat. "Well, maybe there was just something wrong . . . something went wrong maybe right in the beginnin'. Maybe some little . . ."

"Flaw?" The captain didn't move his head. "Oh, no doubt. Some little flaw . . . a tiny chip, a microscopic fissure, like the famous San Andreas fault in California where the earthquakes will happen, like the one that happened before in Los Angeles. And San Francisco before that. It's there, but you don't really know it until it snaps, cracks open, separates. You can be born with it—that flaw—like the earth has its flaws."

"It's nobody's fault . . . I mean, nobody can be *"responsible* for things like that. You shouldn't think . . ."

"Oh, I don't blame myself completely. But I have to accept some blame. Look at me. What kind of a father is this?" He held his arms wide, making his poor body look even more vulnerable and insignificant. "If I only knew how his mind worked. What he was thinking, what his dreams are . . . I don't even know what he wants to do with his life. If anything."

"He said he wanted to go back to Virginia and live like a . . . well, he said like a human being," Junior said.

The captain lifted his head and he came alive. "Why didn't I talk to you boys before. Come on, tell me. What has he said to you? He'd maybe tell you things that he wouldn't mention to his mother or me. Tell me more . . . *Anything*. Anything at all that you remember. It might help the doctor if we could have some idea what was bothering him." His eyes were beseeching, begging, imploring us both. *"Try* to remember. Both of you . . ." He turned to me. "Carlton? *Something? Anything.*"

Junior looked at me and I shrugged. "Well . . ." he hesitated.

"Oh, for Christ's sake." The captain shook his head and looked at Dad. "You've got a fine pair there, Woody. God! That's marvelous. They won't tell because it would be giving away confidences. How about *that!* Innocent integrity. Long may it live! Hallelujah!" He rolled his head on the pillow in a wild display of delight. "Here these two are, protecting a poor sick boy whose grasp of right and wrong is tenuous at best. Oh, Woody. Tell them it's all right to tell me anything. Everything. No matter what Bradford said—and I'm sure he said plenty about me—can't hurt *me*. But it might help him. Whatever you know about him. No matter how distasteful it may seem. It's your *duty* to tell me now. If he weren't sick, I'd be the last person in the world to ask you to be . . . be tattletales."

Dad nodded to Junior and he told them the story of the rainy night when Brad was locked out of the house naked. The captain just nodded. "He has called you . . ." Junior shot a look at Dad who nodded again. "He has called you . . . an old fart." The captain noted it by inclining his head slightly. "He said he wished . . . wished . . . you were . . ."

"Dead?" the captain asked.

"Yes. And then he'd sell the place here and go back to Virginia."

"All that figures. Actually, it's fairly normal. Most young men wish their father were dead." He saw the look of horror on our faces. "You two may be the exceptions. So far." He looked at Dad with amusement. "Also, you're both very young. Maybe Woody hasn't had time to show you just what kind of a shit he can be."

"They've been pretty well primed," Dad said.

"Is that all? Carlton, you have anything to add?"

"Only some wild stories he told us about his school," I said. "I don't think they were really true, I think he was just trying to . . . to impress us—you know the way boys do. Try to make a bigger story than the last one."

"What sort of wild stories?"

"Well, he said they used to tie up the darkies—he called them that—and then whip them."

"Pure fantasy," the captain said. "Not a very pretty one, however."

"And then they'd—what was the word, Junior?—corn something. Corn*hole,* that's the word. They'd cornhole the younger boys in school."

Dad spewed wine all over his shirt and the captain fell back on his pillow and roared. Junior and I looked at each other helplessly. "Wasn't that the word?" I leaned over and asked him.

"I think so."

Suddenly Dad sat up straight and looked furious. "He never tried out anything like that with you, did he?" Dad was speaking and looking directly at Junior. "Not that I know of," Junior answered.

"Not . . . that . . . I . . . know . . ." the captain was having one of his coughing and choking attacks. Dad was beside him, lifting him slightly under the shoulder and arching his body, his chest up and head back so that he could breathe. Each time Dad started to ease him back on the cot, the spasms would start again. He was gasping for air and bit by bit, his shallow inhalations relieved the attack and I wondered why we hadn't brought along the oxygen tank. Finally, breathing normally and with a fresh glass of wine for both men, the captain was able to speak.

"Now. Let's go back calmly, ever so calmly—to cornhole." He was grinning broadly at Dad who was having difficulty keeping a straight face. "I gather from your answer to your father's question, Woody-Two, that you haven't a clue what cornhole means." Junior shook his head and so did I. "Woody, you have two abysmally ignorant sons. Are you going to let them grow up not knowing what cornhole means? It is one of the most important things to know about. Since they don't, Woody, I think we can safely assume that Bradford couldn't have had his degenerate way with them. Either one of them. Right?" I was totally lost but Junior nodded. The captain paused and then looked at Dad. "For Christ's sake, how do you explain this? They're your boys, you explain it."

"They learned it from your boy, *you* explain it." They were teasing each other while Junior and I sat in bewildered silence.

"Got it!" The captain snapped his fingers. "I'll tell you a little story. One of the oldest stories in the world. OK? Ready?" He looked at Dad and shrugged. "The scene is set back in the days when the Puritans first arrived in this country. And this story is about that old too. Now. There was one Indian whore . . . prostitute . . . in this whole area. Let's say the whole eastern seaboard. There weren't very many women—Indian or otherwise—so this Indian . . . *lady* had lots of customers." He looked at us to see if we were following so far. We were. "One day a customer arrived with a sack of corn and he asked this . . . er . . . lady for her services but explained he had no money. He'd have to pay with the produce from his farm." We were still following. "She agreed and lay down on her stomach." He looked at Dad who nodded. "The man asked her why she was lying on her stomach and she answered, pointing first to her . . . her front section, her crotch, 'This money hole.' Then she pointed to her backside, 'This corn hole.'"

Dad fell about. Junior exploded with a great hoot of laughter. It took me a minute or two to get the images straight in my mind and then I realized it was something I'd done to Miguel in the muddy water of the irrigation ditch—our slick bodies rubbing together but I remembered his backing up into my lap in a particularly exciting way, fitting us together like a cork in a bottle, just another aspect of our games, a throwback to the puzzles with Mary Lou only with Miguel it was the tightest fitting puzzle I'd known. I had no idea that there was a name for it. My God, I thought. I'd better laugh quickly. I did, rather hysterically.

"I'm not absolutely sure," the captain said with eyes that bored into me, "that Carlton hasn't heard that story before."

My laughter was sounding very false to my own ears. "No, I never did . . ."

Dad's eyes were back on Junior. "You're sure Bradford didn't try any funny stuff?"

"Woody, for God's sake. Unless Bradford finally did wank his cock off to a nub, I'm sure Woody-Two would have been aware if an invasion were attempted. No matter how subtly. Or minor the equipment."

We all laughed, the tension gone. Nobody was paying any attention to me. I'd actually done it but Dad was in a state just thinking that Junior might have been touched. Contaminated? Junior contaminated? Never! But I'd touched and been touched. I'd participated in acts that had now been given names. Dirty names. Names to sneer at. Dad didn't seem to care what I'd done. It was only Junior's virtue (virginity?) that he cared about. Perhaps there wasn't all that much reason for me to feel guilty. As far as Dad was concerned, what I did couldn't possibly matter very much. So, why worry? What was it the captain had said I was? Sensu—something. I'd better look it up.

That outing had been a revelation from several points of view but the most bothersome point to me was one that was never fully made. The captain's muttered, "Oh, how I shall miss you." It echoed in my ears. Dad hadn't heard, he'd gone to pee and Junior was busy with the corkscrew. I was the only one who'd heard it and it made the ground shake under my feet. What had he meant?

Chapter Ten

IT WAS A PAINFUL waiting time for the Joneses. June's heat became July's with a great leap up as though an oven setting had been increased automatically. Mrs. Jones's vigil at the hospital was as unvarying as the temperature and Bradford's condition as steady as the thermometer. He neither got worse nor better. Everything that could be done was being done but to no avail. Everything was static. Life at 1548 moved on oiled hushed wheels. Everyone was particularly sensitive to the others' moods. We tended to give each other a lot of space—physical contact was kept to a minimum either because of the heat or the almost audible buzz of tightened nerves that we were all giving off.

Mrs. Jones was the most visibly altered. She'd lost a great deal of weight and what little color she had was applied. She'd become almost as removed and remote as they reported Brad to be. The captain's active imagination still spawned new projects. Dad worked harder than ever. Mom was kept hopping taking care of the captain's complicated needs. Now as much secretary-nurse as housekeeper-cook. The hours on the telephone gave way to visits from lawyers or specialists for Brad brought out from the east coast. All this added more work for Mom and I helped as much in the house as I could while Junior worked along with Dad. Every time I saw the captain, I could hear the echo of his saying, "Oh, how I shall miss you . . ."

It was almost a relief when it all fell apart. At least we knew where we stood. We stood right back on the road in the Model-A. It came down off the blocks, Dad and Junior ground the valves and over-hauled the motor, new tires were bought and installed and Mom and I recovered the seats with a bright blue rough-textured cotton.

The captain broke the news to us all one night at the beginning of August after dinner in the main house. They were going to have to sell 1548. That's all I heard for some time or at least that's what registered like a bolt of zigzagging lightning through my body. The rest, the reasons, soaked into my consciousness in bits and pieces; the place was a folly . . . a hobby that was pure selfishness on his part . . . Alice deserved something more for her patience in letting him indulge his ideas and schemes . . . And there was Brad. It was fairly conclusive that if he got better at all it wouldn't be for years. It was possible that his condition would never improve—an un-happy thought but it had to be considered. Alice missed her family and . . . and . . . and . . . "As it turns out, I didn't have to die to make Brad's wishes come true. I'm selling the place and we're moving back to Virginia just as he said he'd do. Now I wonder if he'll even know where he is." The captain sighed. "We've already contacted a private place to take care of him—it costs the earth. The idea of a state hospital galls Alice. I mean he's in there with Winnie Ruth Judd! We know what she did, but do we know her background? What kind of a family does she come from? We must take care who our son and heir associates . . ." He dropped his chin on his chest. When he spoke again, his voice was barely audible. "That was not funny. I apologize." He was quiet for some time and when he spoke again, he didn't look at us but kept his chin on his chest. "I don't have to tell you . . . I hope I've made you feel it but I've . . . I've loved . . . I have loved you all. *Love* you all. From that first minute . . ." He took a deep breath. ". . . that first minute when I saw you standing in the drive . . . your wonderful faces . . ." he swallowed hard, ". . . faces shining with eagerness and honesty. Ready to work . . . to do anything to make an honest living for your two fine boys . . ." He lifted his head and looked at Mom. "But it couldn't last. I think I knew that from the first minute. You're not cut out for this . . . this sort of work, Miz Milly. You're . . . special." He looked around at each of us. "You're *all* special . . . and we've been priv . . . privileged and . . . and oh, I'm going to miss you so." There it was fi-nally. That phrase in its full context. "I don't . . ." He choked and hit the side of his cot with his fist and said, "Oh, SHIT!" The word hung in the air. Then he muttered. "For Christ's sake, Woody, get me out of here . . ."

We were out of there and on the road to Yuma by the beginning of September. We'd stayed on to help the packers, although they made us feel more in the way than anything else. The captain had been more than generous with his "golden handshake" which made it doubly difficult for us to make the final break, and 1548 had been sold to one of the doctors who'd fallen in love with it when he'd come to discuss Brad's case.

"It's a relief to think that it won't be turned into a chicken farm," the captain said. "He's not much of a doctor, but he does have some feeling for the place."

Mrs. Jones had flown with Brad a few weeks earlier and got him installed in the private institution and come back to escort the captain. Dad offered to drive them to Virginia in the station wagon and the possibility was seriously considered until it was decided that accommodations along the way for the captain would be too unpredictable and risky. They'd have the car driven out by an agency.

The Model-A was packed—everything fitting in as before. Our trunk was left at Aunt Dell's along with another large case of a year's accumulation of things. There were no big farewells there—Aunt Dell, temporarily out of sueable parties in Phoenix took this moment to go back to Galena and sue Jesse for divorce and her portion of their joint property. She'd stay with Grandpa and Uncle Ed would drive her to the Galena Court House for the trial. There was talk of Uncle Roy being transfered away from Phoenix by the State Meat Board. Sister was heavily involved with a handsome young bartender and Mavis was busy being pregnant with her shyster's son and heir. Everybody's life was going its own direction. Our direction was to continue on west.

We headed toward Buckeye which was the first town outside Phoenix and then it was, "Gila, Gila, Gila!" Junior said. "There's the Gila River, the Gila Desert just over there to the left, Gila Bend, Gila this, Gila that. That Gila monster is going to dominate our lives. We follow the Gee, hee, hee-la River all the way to Yuma."

"That's the rich farming country," I remembered. Where the Mexican migrant workers headed when they first sneaked across the endless straight border into Arizona from Mexico. Here their backs could only be wet from sweat—there wasn't a stream between Yuma and the Santa Cruz River over two hundred miles away to the east. I searched the fields and orchards for Miguel, but most workers were hatted and too far away to be recognized.

Not all migrant workers were Mexican. We were barely outside the Phoenix city limits before we became aware of cars and trucks filled with people and belongings all headed southwest as we were. The battered license plates listed the disaster areas: The largest disaster area seemed to be Oklahoma, then Texas, Missouri, Arkansas, Tennessee, with the more rare Ohio, Indiana, Kansas, but a vast section of the middle of the U.S.A. was represented right here, on a steaming hot highway leading toward the California border at Yuma, Arizona. The traffic flowed steadily. The space made by a vehicle pulling off the road because of a flat tire or a motor boiling over was soon filled. Few cars overtook others. It seemed futile to rush. We were all going the same way, to the same place for the same reason. Might as well settle back and move with the tide. The Gila River bounced over boulders and around steep cliffs in a much more erratic playful way than our implacable river of cars. We honked our horn and waved when we saw a Missouri car but the response was seldom joyous.

"Maybe," Junior said, "our fellow-Missourians aren't very friendly because we have Arizona plates now."

Dad smacked his forehead. "Oh, for Christ's sake."

"We've changed nationality, Woody," Mom said.

Around Yuma the orchards and acres of irrigated land spread out on both sides of the road. Signs began to sprout and grow as though they'd been fertilized and irrigated: "No Pickers," "No Workers," "No Help Wanted," "Season Over. Beware of Dog." We saw cars laden down, bumping as though on their last legs down the lanes toward the farms in spite of the signs. I wondered what kind of reception they'd receive from the people who warned about their dog.

Yuma is not exactly on the border with California—it's some five or six miles inside Arizona—but we were forced to come to a halt before we were out of the city limits. The cars and trucks were lined up as far ahead of us as we could see.

"All the way to the border," the man driving the truck in front of us told Dad. "Border inspection. They're bastards. They tear everything to pieces. You'd think they're prospectin' for gold in these here pore old beat-up vehicles."

"How long will we have to wait?"

"Aw, Lord. Cain't never tell. They git some pore sonumbitch in there with a whole truckload of stuff and they'll make him take ever damn bit of it off. And reload it, piece by piece. Oh, I tell you, they'as bastards of a kind you don't know nothin' about."

We'd move a few feet and then stop. We all took turns looking for tall cotton. It was awfully public. Everybody else had the same idea. The fields were alive with figures walking along and then suddenly ducking down out of sight. Mom said she'd wait until dark. That wasn't much of a wait.

"Hey," Dad called to the man in front. "Do they keep things open at night? I mean, will they go on lettin' people through after dark?"

"That depends. I know the border station on '66 there at Needles'll just close up whenever they want. Meanest sonsumbitches I ever seen in my life. No respect for women nor children. Hateful, all of 'em."

This curious train we'd become linked up with—and it was behind us as far as we could see—crept like a misshapen caterpillar toward the golden state. Junior and I were awakened by a flashlight in our faces sometime in the middle of the night. We didn't seem to be near any building and the same truck was in front of us. "Just the four of you?" the flashlight barked.

"That's right," Dad said into the night. "Just left Phoenix this mornin'."

"Git out," the rough voice said. "All of you." When the light was out of my eyes, I could see that the man was wearing a tan uniform, a tan cap like a policeman's and a gun in a holster on his belt. Mom was out on her side and Junior followed her. I was out with Dad. The officer flashed the light around inside the car. "Got any fruit? Any food of any kind? Fresh food?"

"Nope," Dad said.

"You said Phoenix. You got Arizona plates. What you doin' in with this pack of Okies and Arkies?"

"We're just on a trip to see my brother," Mom piped up. "Near Los Angeles."

He stuck a little piece of paper onto the windshield. "Well, they ain't no need of you being held up. It's a pleasure from time to time not to have to go through people's private things. But, that's the job. You folks get back in. I'll guide you around these trucks—Lordy, look at all that stuff. They'll have to unload it. Feel sorry for 'em." We were back in the car in a split second, nodding and smiling our thank-yous. "OK?" He flashed his light down the road. "Just go on down on this left lane here. Stop at the gate house and show 'em that sticker and then you're on your way."

We couldn't believe our good luck. We'd only been in the line for about five hours and now we were free. And in California! Dad let out a whoop after we'd passed through the last official-looking barriers. "Well, if that man's a sonumbitch, then give me a sonumbitch any time."

Dad drove straight on up the coast to Long Beach to the Seaview Trailer Court where Uncle Ernest and Aunt Doreen were temporarily installed. We were awed by our first sight of the great Pacific Ocean—our first sight of any ocean—the power of those pounding breakers was terrifying and hypnotizing.

One nice thing about the Seaview Trailer Court was that it was near the sea. As a matter of fact, that was the only nice thing about it. There were about three-hundred trailers parked haphazardly just off the main highway—the deserted beach was on the *other* side of the busy road—on a flat stretch of sand without a tree in sight. What shade there was was created by bits of cloth or awnings spread from the trailers to poles stuck into the sand at odd drunken angles. The core of the place was a cement-block building that turned out to be the toilets and shower rooms—men on one side, women on the other—and washrooms with the manager's office squeezed in one corner. The manager himself looked squeezed. A most disagreeable man who pointed out immediately that if we'd come to visit the Billingses, our car had better not be there the next day.

"Here in Seaview," he growled, "We rent space. *Space*. Space for trailers. You come in here, you take up space. We ain't making any money on the space your car is taking up. Cars that don't have trailers just ain't . . ."

"Welcome?" Dad said.

"That's the idea."

"Well, we're not the sort of folks to stay where we ain't welcome, so I don't think you'd better get into too much of a tizzy about where we park the car." Dad's voice was getting that dangerous edge.

Mom leaned over and smiled out Dad's window at the man. "We have just dropped by to see my brother. He's Ernest Billings. Can you tell us where he's . . . er . . . parked? Situated?"

"Billings. Billings," he muttered. "Oh yeah. New Mexico? That blue trailer. Third one back from that one." He pointed "New one. Good looking job it is. Sleeps four, got gas stove—even a gas icebox. All aluminum. Slick as she can be . . ."

"We ain't intendin' to buy it," Dad said. "Just to know where it is."

It was slick. It did have a gas stove and icebox. It did sleep four only there were already five living in it. Aunt Doreen's two sisters, one married with husband in tow, were there and installed. They'd arrived for a day or two some three weeks ago and were still looking for work. Here we were, another quartet who'd planned on using the trailer as headquarters. Nine people in a four-people place. But, curiously, it worked.

I never have quite figured out how Aunt Doreen did it but she was an organizer of infinite imagination. The various beds inside the trailer either slid out, folded down, popped out of walls, covered up tables or contracted or expanded in such a way as to fit all the grown-ups in. Junior and I were the problem.

"Wall to wall bed," Aunt Doreen had declared. The problems of who went to bed first were worked out carefully, because once in, you couldn't get out. I think Aunt Doreen and Uncle Ernest were the last ones in and God help anybody who had to get up in the night.

Since our car wasn't allowed to be parked there, it evolved that Junior and I would sleep in it on the public beach across the road. Mom was in a state, but Dad said that he could see the car from the trailer.

"I know," Mom said, "but once we get into bed you won't be able to get out if something goes wrong."

"What could go wrong with a car parked beside the road?"

"Some hobo could come along and try to steal . . ."

"What? The Chinese checkerboard?"

"I mean, Woody, is it safe for the boys to be over there by themselves?"

It was decided we'd be all right. That is, the grown-ups decided we would be. I was frankly terrified but I'd die before I'd let Junior know. It wasn't that I was afraid of the dark. I never had been. For example, I'd never had any fear at all going to the outhouses back home at night. I'd walk out perfectly calmly and fearlessly, do what I had to do, close the door and run like lightning back to the house. For some reason, it was the coming *back* that always scared the life out of me. It has always struck me that the return journey is the dangerous one. Going is easy, it's on the way home that accidents happen. Just when you can almost see the open, welcoming arms and feel the warmth and security of the known destination that disaster is most apt to strike.

Uncle Ernest had learned a trade in the Navy—he was a qualified steam and pipe fitter and was waiting for a job to come through with a big construction company. The company had several government contracts, but the most important was a dam on the San Joaquin River near Fresno, California, which was already well started and construction slated to last several years. If we could just hold on for the next few months, while Uncle Ernest got his toe in the door with the company, he could then get Dad work on the dam as an apprentice fitter. He gave Dad a set of manuals of the trade to study.

Dad and Mom were back at the familiar task of following up leads in the want ads, finally winding up under Domestic Help Wanted—Couples, which offered the most opportunities. They took a job as live-in maid and chauffeur in Hollywood while Junior and I continued to live in the Model-A on the beach. The experience they'd had in Phoenix and the glowing recommendation Captain J had written made them most desirable. I was thrilled. A movie star? No, something to do with production.

The job was doomed from the start what with Dad ridiculously clad in white jacket trying to remember to serve from the left and remove plates from the right. When he was ordered to wear his hat and heavy wool uniform driving the car in blistering heat, he didn't say "I don't have to take that kind of shit from nobody," he simply pulled up at a stoplight on Sunset Boulevard, yanked on the Cadillac's handbrake, got out and walked away leaving his boss stranded in the backseat. "That's all she wrote," he said. "Besides I heard that silly son-of-a-bitch say on the phone that it ought to have been amusing to have a hillbilly as a butler but it had turned out to be a fucking bore."

That ended our Hollywood career. Dad had heard that there might be work—ranch work, outdoor work, dealing with horses, farming, livestock, things he understood and was comfortable with—north of Los Angeles around Santa Barbara. A lot of rich Easterners had bought up huge ranches—three, four, six thousand acres of mostly virgin land. It was time we got settled somewhere for several reasons but mainly because school was about to start and Mom's law of keeping us in school was unbreakable. Also, Junior said he was developing curvature of the spine sleeping in the car and my jumping at every sound in the night was beginning to take its toll. We'd begun to bicker and argue. Junior had developed a persistent cold brought on no doubt from the dampness in the night air next to the sea. He didn't cough but he sniffled with maddening regularity and it drove me crazy in the tight confines of our wheeled bedroom.

We got as far north as Oxnard, about fifty miles along the coast toward Santa Barbara, and decided we'd spend a day or so and check the possibilities. It was farming country and looked promising only we couldn't find any place to stay. We turned from the want ads in the local paper to the Rooms To Let section. The rooms listed, we soon discovered, were either taken or in houses so seedy that we'd really rather sleep in the car, curvature of the spine or no.

It was getting dark when we tried the last house on the list of ads. Dad was standing on the porch of a reasonably respectable frame house, ringing the doorbell and we were all holding our breath, praying that this would be it, we were all tired, cross and cranky.

The door opened and a gray-haired lady stuck her head around it. "Yes?"

"We seen your ad here in the paper, ma'am," Dad said, "and wondered if the room was still available."

"Why yes, it is," the lady opened the door further and peered up at Dad. "How long would you be taking it for?"

"We had in mind two, three days. Depending on how things work out."

She squinted toward the car. "That'd be your wife?"

"It's better be," Dad said dead earnestly.

She squinted up at him. "Oh, I see," she made an attempt at a laugh. "You're making a joke." She said it as though she'd never heard anybody make one before.

"Well, I mean she was my wife the last time I looked," Dad expanded on the theme.

"Yes. Well, then there's just the two of you?"

"And our two boys. Two heads there in the backseat if you look real close. And each head's got a body to go with it." Dad was enjoying himself. "We ain't no traveling freak show."

"Oh dear!" the lady clutched her breast and took a step back. "Oh dear me, no. Oh no. We can't have that." She shook her head and continued her retreat back into the house. "Oh no. No children. We don't take children. That just won't do."

"Well," Dad seemed to be pondering possible courses of action. "We sure do need a place . . ." He snapped his fingers as if he'd just come up with a solution. "Why that's what we'll do, by God. We'll just kill the kids." He turned on his heel and headed down the cement walk with a determined stride. We were trying not to laugh.

"Oh dear," the little lady called after him. "I wouldn't go and do *that* . . ."

We laughed all the way to Ventura, a bigger town about ten miles on farther where we found an auto court and paid the exorbitant dollar-twenty-five for a double room and slept like babies.

We moved from the expensive motor court to another one on the other side of town called Sleepy-Time, but quickly rechristened Sleazy-Time. The only beneficiaries of the move were our pocketbook and me. Sleazy-Time was next door to my new school, the Luther Burbank Grammar School, but its proximity was lost since I ran all the way around the block to arrive at school from the other direction, successfully denying its existence. Junior's new school was something new they called Junior High School so he was right at home.

We were in school and Dad was out of work. I knew that the captain had given Dad three month's salary as severance pay, but that huge three-hundred dollar bankroll was being chewed away at, not nibbled, daily.

Every newspaper and magazine—weekly, daily, monthly, yearly— no matter how specialized like *The Citrus Growers Almanac, Horse Breeders Stud News, Daily Diary, Veterinarians' Vigils, Auto Mechanics, The Hobbyists' Hobby* or *Dental Care Monthly*—was gone over by each of us. The only job offer we got was from the man at the drugstore who, noticing our all-consuming interest in the printed word, talked me and Junior into selling subscriptions to *Liberty* and *The Saturday Evening Post* magazines. Canvas bags with *Liberty* and *Post* printed on them were slung over our shoulders, an order pad thrust in our hands and off we went every day after school. Around every corner we found somebody else with the same canvas bag over their shoulders. There was an army out selling those magazines. No wonder the signs we knew from Phoenix—No Peddlers—No Soliciting—were as prevalent here as there.

When the canvas bag over our shoulders became so common that the casual observer might have decided it was some sort of mutation endemic to all boys in the area between the ages of ten and fourteen, we decided to resign from the army. Needless to say, we hadn't sold one subscription. Our commanding officer was reluctant to let us go.

"Just look at them satchels," the druggist said. "Filthy! And the magazines. What the hell you been doing with them? Sleeping on them? What good are they going to be now? I can't sell them."

"Neither could we," Junior pointed out.

"But you were responsible for this property. You'll have to pay for the damages. You signed this paper when you checked this stuff out. Here's your signature."

"Where?" Junior asked. The man slapped the paper down in front of us. "Oh yes. I see. And my brother's?" The man riffled through some sheets of paper and slapped a similar one down beside the first. "That's what we signed?"

"Yes. And it states that you had received in your custody so many copies . . . and that they would be returned in the same condition . . . If not, charges for destruction of property will be paid to . . ."

Junior snatched the papers off the desk and quickly tore them into little bits. "Those mean nothing, and you know it. You've got a whole bunch of kids tramping the streets doing your work for you—so many kids that not one would ever be able to make a sale. Besides, there's a Depression on, in case you hadn't heard. *Nobody's* got any money." He threw the bits of paper up into the air. "Sue us!" he said, his face so red with rage I thought he was going to cry. "Kids of a certain age aren't supposed to be working anyway. I think I'll sue *you.*" He was his Aunt Dell's own nephew and I cheered him on. "You're taking advantage of us kids . . . we don't have anything . . . nobody has, except people like you, and then you try to get money out of us after we've worn out our shoes dragging those things around." He took a deep breath and swallowed. "I think . . . sir, you are an . . . asshole!" We both turned and ran toward the door. "Worse than Fagin," he yelled over his shoulder. I had the door open for him as he shouted out one last thing, "But I doubt if assholes read Dickens." We flew and didn't stop running until we were at our favorite spot on the pier, down some side steps where we couldn't be seen. When we'd caught our breath, he said, "I'm sorry about that. I shouldn't have said it."

"Well, I won't tell," I said. "Besides he is one."

"I mean saying he's worse than Fagin. Fagin was a Jew. It could have sounded like I was making fun of Jews." I was lost and apparently looked it. "Dickens made him awful . . . Fagin, a wicked man using little boys to steal and you know . . . You know the book. And he was Jewish which was supposed to make him even worse. I mean, I think that's why Dickens did it that way."

"I thought you were sorry you called him an . . . well, what you did."

"Oh that," he stood up and dusted off his bottom. "That doesn't worry me." He headed up the steps. "I said 'sir' first."

Junior found the lifesaving ad in one of the big Los Angeles Sunday papers after a static week in Ventura. It's still a mystery to us how he did it. And how it all worked out. In the first place, the ad was in

the Engineers Wanted column—we'd already discussed the useless-
ness of that sort of listing, but Junior had got into the habit of reading the want ads from start to finish so that's how he found it. The
mystery was how he'd figured it out because it read, "Engineer in Hydrodynamics." Now that would have been a listing that my eye would
have flown past as apparently Mom's and Dad's had. Engineer in Hydrodynamics was what Dad was and he got the job.

It was on a big property about ten miles inland from Ventura
called Alligator Ranch. Hydrodynamics, Junior quickly found out by
checking his dictionary, was nothing more than the simple science of
moving water. In this case, irrigating an avocado grove. Acres and
acres of avocados and Dad, with his impressive letter from the captain, convinced the owner of the ranch that he could keep the trees
as sopping as he wanted them. There was the water, there the
ditches, there the little locks or gates to regulate the flow.

"Engineer, my ass," Dad said. "Anybody could do it." It seems that
the owner of the ranch was aware of that too, but was clever enough
to couch the ad in such a way as to eliminate the dullards.

"Mr. Woods," he'd said, "if you're smart enough to know what hydrodynamics is, then you're the man I want. And incidentally, you're
the only one who answered the ad." He beamed at his own cleverness.

It was a job. And one didn't look a job in its nomenclature, as it
were. The salary was twenty-five cents an hour for a ten-hour day and
a nice four-roomed house was provided for the family set right in the
middle of a grove of every sort of tree imaginable. We could pick oranges out the kitchen window without leaning out, lemons and limes
pecked at the panes of the living room windows while only a bit of a
stretch was needed to reach the avocados from the bedroom window.
The outside was perfect. It was the inside that offered the problem.
It was empty. Not a stick of furniture. That meant spending a large
hunk of whatever was left of the captain's golden handshake on fur-
nishing the place.

I'd spotted a secondhand furniture store in Ventura and we were
able to get the barest necessities with a minimum down payment
once we mentioned Alligator Ranch and Dad's new boss, Mr. Logan.
Mom and I did the choosing of the things and we both seemed
slightly surprised when we picked out the same things.

"Tacky," I'd say and she'd nod.

We picked out a round dining table that made Dad shake his head
in disgust but after we'd sanded it and waxed it, he always acted like
it was an old family heirloom. It looked as though it could have been.

The only really new things were the mattresses. They weren't Super-Slumber innersprings, but they were clean. The settee for the living room was a sort of daybed we covered with green corduroy and stacked with cushions. Two ladder-back rockers completed the living room with an occasional table. There was no electricity—a beat-up icebox for two dollars served more as a food cupboard than anything else. Dad swore that there was some secret heating device inside that caused the ice he brought every other day from our nearest town—El Centro—to melt faster than if we left it out on the porch in the sun. The coal-oil cookstove had an oven, but even by trimming the wicks in the burners with surgical precision, there was always a faint taste of kerosene in everything that had been baked. But we had a place to live and Dad had a job.

Junior was bused back to Ventura to the Junior High School, while I was forced to transfer to a two-room country school about a mile from our new house.

Mom registered me with the principal, Mr. Harris, who was also the teacher of the fourth, fifth and sixth grades, just before Thanksgiving vacation.

I had been there less than three days when we broke on Wednesday afternoon for Thanksgiving vacation but I'd got my classmates straight in my head. The Oklahoma girls were sisters. Nola and Noreen Whittaker. The silent Mexican beauty was Louisa Fernando and the painfully shy one, Rosa Torres. The good-natured boy was Boyd Beavens. The brooder, whom I still distrusted wasn't Mexican, but Italian, Victor Scrittorale. Distrust is perhaps not the right word. Fear, quite honestly, is what I felt. He looked like one of those bullies who would get you cornered and insult you to the point where you *had* to fight.

With holiday homework under my arm, I took off up that lonely mile stretch toward home with nothing on either side of me but acres of burgeoning lima beans. The little black ribbon of road was like all the others—dead straight, following the squared off farmland boundaries. I seemed to be the only one who took this road—the others all spread out in different directions, mostly headed over on the other side of the railroad tracks. Being so close to the tracks and painted yellow, the schoolhouse looked like a small wayside train station and it was always surprising to find there was no waiting room with a big potbellied stove or a little man behind a ticket window in a green eyeshade.

I'd gone only about a hundred yards when I heard an earsplitting whistle and looked over my shoulder. The whole schoolhouse area was deserted as though a train had carried everybody away. Except for one figure. Victor. He was standing at the corner where a road crossed the one I was on with the little finger of each hand in the corners of his mouth. He created the shrill whistle again and motioned for me to come back. I hesitated. If he wanted to fight, he'd have to run after me. There didn't seem to be anybody around and traffic was rare on these roads. I couldn't dash off into the lima bean patch and hide. The plants were only about knee-high. I walked back, trying to figure out an avenue of escape if there was going to be trouble. Junior said I was fast, so if necessary, I'd just let him swallow my dust if I had to make a break for it. Nobody was there to report my cowardly running away.

He just stood there, legs apart, his arms folded across his chest, looking much bigger and more aggressive from a distance than he did when I got nearer.

"Where you goin'?" he called.

"Home."

"Why that way? It's hot as hell. I know where you live. On Alligator Ranch, right?" I nodded. "Well, we're just up behind you." He pointed over my head and to the right. "Just above that slope. See? Where all them small trees is planted?" I wasn't quite sure but I nodded anyway. "Well, that's our place. Papa's growin' citrus fruit—oranges, lemons. Four hundred acres."

He was so matter-of-fact that I wasn't sure whether I was supposed to be impressed or feel sorry for him. "Good," I nodded. "Nice."

"Yeah." He pushed his thick dark hair back from his forehead. "Let's go." He turned and headed back along the road in front of the schoolhouse. "See up there? Them trees? At the end of the bean patch? Well, there's a path through there. Shady. Nice. Comes out just below our place. You'll have to double back a bit to get to your house, but it's better'n that old bare road." He led us on for about a quarter of a mile and turned to the left under some big evergreen trees. "Cypresses. Like they got in Italy. Papa says they're the best windbreaks in the world. He's trying to buy this land here just because the cypresses are here, I think." He smiled for the first time. "My papa is real Italian. He's trying to make a little Italy here." He waved his arm in a wide gesture taking in the whole area. We walked along in silence for some time, then he turned and looked at me. "You don't like baseball, do you?"

"Ooh, I can play . . ."

"But, you don't *like* it. I've watched you at recess."

I laughed. "My secret is out. It's unAmerican, but I don't."

Now he laughed. "Blessed Virgin," he made a funny little gesture in the air in front of himself. "You're the first one I ever saw who says so."

"Do you?"

"I'm *supposed* to. Papa may be making a little Italy, but we boys have got to be as American as we can. We have to go to school. We have to study. We have to do everything American. All of us."

"*All* of you?"

"We're five brothers but Momma's making more." He held his arms out in front of him making a big ball of a stomach. "Two older than me—Gino and Umberto—and two younger. The two older ones go to school in Ventura on the bus."

"So does my brother."

"We'll all be together next year. On the bus." His face clouded. "If I pass. My readin' ain't so good."

"I can help you maybe. If you want me to."

"Sure. That'd be swell. I can't get my brothers to help me and Papa says if I don't pass he'll beat my ass off."

"If you work hard, I don't see that there'd be any problem."

"Hey, you can come to my house and we can go off and read and have lots of fun."

"Study isn't all that much fun."

"I'll see to it that it is." He grinned at me slyly. He stopped and took me by the hand and led us off the path up behind one of the trees. "Let's see each other first." He was undoing his belt and unbuttoning his pants. I stood frozen to the spot. He stopped at the last button. "What's the matter?"

"Well, I . . . I don't know what . . ."

"It's just to look. We can fuck later."

"*Fuck?*" I hadn't heard the word used that way since Crane and Mary Ann.

"Sure. Don't you do it? You have a brother. You said so."

"Yes, I have a brother, but we don't f . . . We don't do anything like that . . ."

"Why not? What's the matter with you? Here, let me see." He reached over and had my fly open before I could protest. Which I realized was the last thing in my mind. As he felt around in my underwear for my cock, my hand automatically went to his open fly and reached into his underwear and we released each other into the bright daylight at the same time. "There. You see. We're both hard."

We certainly were and our heads were leaning together touching as we looked down at ourselves. He was bigger than I, long, dark, and velvet and I stroked it, feeling soft hair at the base as though I were caressing a silken little animal. We were both making little purring animal sounds. He lifted his face to mine, "Can you come yet? I only started a few months ago, myself. But it makes a difference . . . OOooops!" He felt my body begin to contract and dropped to his knees and took me into his mouth. My knees sagged as I had that fainting feeling.

I was holding onto him for support as he raised his head and looked at me, smiling. "No need getting that all over your pants. Besides it shouldn't go to waste. Come on down here," he said. I dropped weakly down on my knees in front of him.

"*Come* on down here?" he laughed. "You sure can. Ooh, do you taste good. Not like Gino. Gino tastes bitter—you're sweet." He still had his hand on me, caressing me, pulling on my cock rather like Grandpa taught me to strip a cow after she was milked, watching for the few drops of fluid that came out which he rubbed into my cock like a lotion. His other hand was on himself, stroking gently and I reached over and put my hand on his. We moved our hands back and forth on his velvety cock with his hand dictating the speed and pressure. I could feel that he was increasing the pressure and was stricken with horror. Did he expect me to do the same thing for him with my mouth?

My hand came away from his cock as if it had been burned. "Ah, Vic . . . I, uh . . . ah, I can't do . . ."

"Can't what?" He stretched up on his knees, hips thrust forward, "Just watch! Look how far I can shoot. Hey, look out! Here she comes!" His hand was working wildly on himself, his chest curved in, hips out, and then a great jet of fluid spurted from him as he let out a whoop of joy. "Just look at that, Carl. Ain't that something?" I applauded his performance which made him roar with laughter. "Should I go on the stage?" I admitted to myself that it was a more impressive performance than the Wilkins boy's. He fell forward and leaned his face on my neck at my shoulder, breathing hard and laughing. "Well, thank God I can do it. It was starting to be a family problem. Gino had been playing with me for years. So had Umberto. They worked on me every way they could think of and they just couldn't make me come. Then, oh, when was it? I guess just before school started—Gino had been sucking on my cock for what seemed like hours and Umberto was fucking him and then they both came and I was still hard. And dry. Gino said, 'I give up. You try, Bert. I mean how am I going to have enough come if I don't get any? I mean, you gotta' take it in to have any to come out.' Well, Bert is sixteen. He says he needs as much come as he can get because he's going to start fucking girls and if he doesn't get a regular supply, then he won't be able to get a hard-on and fuck a girl. He's got a girl now and he says she's just about ready to give in. And he didn't feel that he was going to get enough from Gino and I was going to be needed."

"You mean that's where it comes from? Come? You have to swallow it?"

"Sure. Didn't you know that? That's what makes you a man." He made a gesture with a clenched fist and held up his forearm. "Strong. Like that. And big. So you can make babies and . . ."

"You mean you can't make babies if you don't . . . if you don't do what you just did?"

"Well, I don't know for sure." He paused and thought for a minute. "Momma's making a baby now. Right this minute. I don't know where Papa gets *his* come. He's always working in the fields. I don't see how he'd have time . . ."

"Maybe after a certain age, it starts growing by itself, inside you, like growing a beard or hair . . ." I wanted to look at Vic's body naked to see how much hair he had on his body.

"Maybe that's it. Maybe you just have to lay on a certain amount at the beginning and then it can develop on its own. Like Momma puts a bit of bread dough that's ready to bake into the new fresh batch that's just been mixed before it rises. She says that's what makes it rise. Maybe that's what makes our cocks rise. We take a bit of come from each other and that starts the other thing working . . . you know, like the yeast."

I didn't understand a word he was saying. But if that was his excuse for sucking my cock, I wasn't going to tell him he wasn't making any sense. "Yeah, that must be it."

"Anyway, Bert took over from Gino and he starts working on me. He's been at it longer and he really knows how. He could take me *all* in his mouth. This," he held onto his balls, "this too."

That struck a familiar bell and I knew how good that could feel. "Yeah, I know."

"You do? Boy, that's something, isn't it?" His hand on himself was beginning to caress again. I moved over just slightly, pretending I was making myself more comfortable, but getting my cock within his reach in case. "We never kissed much, Bert says that's sissy, but for some reason Gino started kissing me on the neck and Bert is determined to make me come and bit by bit, I feel Bert's hand moving up to my ass. Well, I haven't been fucked yet. Gino tried, but he's too big. It hurt too much and he's not even as big as Bert, so he never did try. Gino likes to be fucked so there was no need for me to get in on that. But what Bert did to my ass with his hands and fingers didn't hurt at all. I mean it seemed to add something . . . a different feeling that went all through my body. I began to sort of understand why Gino likes to be fucked. But still, fucking wastes the come."

I was in a daze of incomprehension. I was doing our puzzle games in my mind and I simply couldn't come up with any reasonable image of what Vic was describing. "No, if it makes you manly, you shouldn't waste it."

"Let's face it, I was the center of attraction. I have to admit I kinda liked that. Up to now, I was just the younger one, fitting in wherever there seemed to be space or a reason. You know, wherever I was needed. Now there I was getting the works. I had Gino's cock in one hand, and Bert had moved so I could hold onto his." He reached over and took hold of mine. "I was jerking on them both." He proceeded to do it now with the cocks available, "when Gino all of a sudden started nibbling and kissing me across the chest and belly and then up to my mouth and kissed me with his mouth open and his tongue fiddling around in my mouth! Wow! I tell you, Carl, I went off like a volcano! Papa always talks about seeing Vesuvius or one of them mountains in Italy erupt with hot smoldering rocks and lava and shooting fire for miles up into the sky . . . Well, that's the way it felt. I'd have screamed my head off if Gino hadn't had his mouth on mine." He was stroking us both now with a purposeful rhythm. There was a faraway look in his eye, a sweet little smile on his lips, "Oh boy! That first time. There's nothing like it." He leaned forward to me and smiled directly into my eyes. "Was it like that with you, Carl?"

"Something like that . . ." I reached for his hand to slow down the motion, but he dropped forward and took me into his mouth again. I came in gasping spurts and he swallowed me at the same moment that I could tell he'd come too, into his hand. I hadn't been taking any in, but I certainly seemed to be able to keep up a running supply. Could there be something lacking in his knowledge of biology or body chemistry or whatever it's called? Just bodily functions, I guess you'd call it. Or was I made differently? All I was absolutely sure of was that no matter how it was made, it was much more fun to have somebody else extract it for you.

I met all the Scrittorales—Momma so big and fat you couldn't tell she was pregnant unless you'd known her before; Papa, also big but not fat, shy about not speaking English very well even though he'd been here since 1920. He had the biggest hands I'd ever seen and they were so gnarled and calloused that it was always a surprise to see them bend and move, especially with the delicacy with which he handled the seedlings for his grove. Gino and Umberto were big and muscular and worked so hard along with their papa both before school and after that I decided Vic's stories about what they all did together were fantasies. When would they have the time or energy?

The two youngest boys, Enzio and Luigi, were eight and almost six. "Your momma seemed to have skipped one in there between you and Enzio," I joked one day. "Sixteen, fourteen, twelve, and then nothing until eight. Did she go on strike?"

"Naw. Lost it. Born dead. A little girl." He shrugged. "I was too young to know anything about it but I sure do remember Luigi's arrival." He laughed. "Momma almost didn't get back to the house before—pow! Out he came."

"What do you mean 'back to the house'? Didn't she go to the hospital?"

"Hospital? We'as all born right here. Papa knows what to do. But Luigi was a surprise. Momma always says he didn't knock on the door. She was out in the vegetable garden weeding—I was there helping—when she all of a sudden lets out this scream. Scared the daylights out of me. 'Momma mia!' she yelled. 'Get Papa!' She went running toward the house and I ran hollering my head off for Papa. We heard Luigi screaming bloody murder before we got back to the house. Momma says he was the noisiest baby she ever had. She figures since he'd been so quiet about letting her know he was coming, he must have been saving all his energy to scream after he got here."

Could babies just arrive like that? "Does she know when this next one is going to get here?"

"She thinks about Christmas so that makes names easy. Maria, if a girl and Christo for a boy."

They seemed to have everything worked out so well. They had their own house, hundreds of acres and once all the trees were producing would be rich. Again, I was struck with envy but tried to squelch those sinful thoughts. I did help him with his reading and he did improve in spite of the fact that our concentration was mostly on our cocks.

Our families didn't socialize in the sense of going to each other's houses for dinner or tea or that sort of thing, but we were all very friendly through us boys. Gino and Junior practiced baseball endlessly. Endlessly on Sundays which was the only day the boys didn't work on the ranch. They'd all pile into an old beat-up pickup truck and drive to El Centro to early mass and then the rest of the day was theirs. And often spent with us.

Little Maria arrived just after New Year's. Mom went up to help and she said she'd never felt so useless in her life. "It was remarkable," she said. "I don't think she actually went into labor—not like I remember with you two. She winced a couple of times, but didn't cry out. And there was this perfect little creature—as though she appeared from nowhere. I'd have screamed my head off. I've never known such pain. Both times." Then she hugged us. "But it was worth it. But never again."

We'd had some Christmas cards. The Joneses, ". . . Brad seems to be improving . . . Bradford joins me in wishing . . ." Aunt Ed, ". . . Grandpa Woods keeping the local widows happy (ha ha) . . . Ronald enjoying high school in Blue Eye (and scrawled on top was 'Like heck I am. Hiya, Tots—Ronnie') . . . our prayer meetings here at the house are filled to overflowing . . . The Lord is truly working his miracles. We pray for you daily."

"Shit," said Dad.

A letter from Aunt Dell saying she'd write more later. That made the holiday season for us all. "She's been fallin' down so often, she's knocking her marbles loose," Dad laughed. "And they never was packed in all that solid."

Mavis's card had The Griggs printed on the bottom. Nothing else. The card unsullied by pen and ink. "Tacky," murmured Mom.

Somehow I pulled Vic through the midterm tests in February with a "C" average. His parents were overjoyed and kept sending us fresh vegetables, cakes, fruit by the basket.

Aunt Dell did write later. Much later. A week or so before Easter. She said everything was "Totsy-turvy" (ha ha) because Roy was going to be transferred down somewhere south of Phoenix and they wanted to get out of their rented house when the rent was due and so she thought it was a good time for her to send the trunk and the suitcase and she'd just come along with them (ha ha). Of course, she didn't say when.

"I suppose she'll wire," Mom said with a worried look.

"Well, you'd better write right back and make sure she knows we don't have a phone so she can't just arrive out of the blue and find us. The fourth orange tree on the left past the avocado grove on the right . . ." Dad shook his head. "Spell it all out plain for her. Tell her to come to Ventura, but for Christ's sake let us know whether she's coming on the bus, the train, or on roller skates. And *when*. She could get here and wander around for a month and we wouldn't know it. And while you're at it, you could write Ed and Edweeeeena and tell them to pray that she stays upright. On her own two feet."

We still hadn't heard from Aunt Dell when I was invited to spend the night before Easter at the Scrit's and go with them to early mass the next morning. I'd never been in a Catholic church and I kept making Vic repeat to me just what I was supposed to do. "I don't want to embarrass your whole family," I said anxiously.

"Don't worry. Stay close by me and do what I do. It's simple."

"Show me how to cross myself again." He went through it patiently with me. "I can *do* it, if I only knew *when* to do it."

We had a huge supper—steaming thick soup and lasagna, roast veal and vegetables, and a special cake called zabaglioni. They couldn't eat again until after mass tomorrow morning. Nothing apparently, not even a glass of water till they'd had communion.

After supper, we four older boys went out to what they called their bunkhouse. That was something else I envied. It was private, had its own shower and toilet, was spartan, but neat and clean. It was where Vic and I did our homework at a long table along one side of the room, long enough for each of the boys to have their own work area, then bunk beds at one end and another larger bed, almost double on the wall opposite the table desk.

Vic's stories of the sex they had together had me worried, anxious, frightened and eager all at the same time. What would it be like doing what we did with the other older brothers? I was so nervous, I went to pee twice while the boys got undressed and chatted quietly together. They all hung their clothes up neatly on wooden pegs on the wall and moved about easily with each other completely naked. Junior was never completely naked with me.

As it turned out, I needn't have worried. Aside from some jokes about sex, mostly about giving it up for Lent, nothing happened as far as I could see to confirm Vic's wild tales of the sexual goings-on. I might as well have been at home with my own brother. Gino did drape a towel over his morning erection—not a concession to modesty, but to make a joke I didn't quite understand about his cock having taken the veil. Perhaps they *had* given up everything for Lent.

The mass was a revelation. It was like going to a show. I loved the pageantry, the costumes, all the highly decorated plaster statues, gilded and gleaming with fresh paint. They weren't quite as carefully painted as they might have been, as though the painters had been in a hurry. There were little globs of gilt that had run away from the bumps and ridges in the plaster where they belonged. The faces on the little dolls in plaster were almost a caricature of what a face should be. Eyebrows were slightly askew, eyes little daubs of color, not quite matching. One little angel was wonderfully cross-eyed. On either side of the big front altar were two identical ladies holding identical babies—the Madonna and child—where the painters had really expressed themselves. The ladies' faces were as garishly painted as if they were made up for the stage or some other more lurid profession. Their robes were of a blue so electric I'm sure they would give off shocks. There were golden stars painted in the background of the niche that held her, and their halos were a tiny circle of real electric lights. Beautiful things, but as I looked from one to the other, I could make out that one was serenely innocent while the other had a definitely salacious smirk on her face.

I tried to keep my eyes on the ladies or the priest and his two young assistants and away from the crucifix in the center of the big altar. It bothered me. It was blindingly white so that the great glistening wound in Jesus' side gushed a brilliant glossy red so intense in the flickering light it seemed to be moving, actually oozing down his middle and on down his legs. I kept glancing up at his pathetic pinioned feet convinced I saw the blood dripping off the end of his toes. It was terrifying.

The feeling of being in a theater was further enhanced by the mystery of the service. I didn't understand anything that was going on. My Latin was not quite fluent enough to follow it all, I told Junior very grandly later. What I did understand, the announcements the priest made from the beautifully carved wooden lectern, wasn't very interesting. A lot of emphasis was on money—the donation hadn't been up to par—in other words, the same things all preachers say.

"Did I do all right?" I asked Vic when it was over.

"You're a born Catholic," he assured me.

Momma Scrit said something to Gino in Italian and then laughed behind her hand, hiding her many gold teeth. "She wants me to tell you her favorite joke," Gino said to me. He put his arms around her and hugged her to him. "She thinks this is the funniest story she ever heard, but she always gets it mixed up in English." She laughed and made a gesture for him to go on and tell me. She watched and listened as though she were hearing it for the first time. It was about a non-Catholic man with a Catholic wife who finally went reluctantly to church with her for the first time. All through the service she was whispering, Sit down. Stand up. Make the sign of the cross. Kneel. Read this section. Do this and do that. Then all of a sudden she looks down at his fly and hisses, Is your fly open? By this time he's disgusted with the whole thing and says, I don't know. *Should* it be?

We all laughed, but Momma roared and slapped her thigh. She really did love it.

The theatrical season begun by my visit to the gentle little church in El Centro was continued the next day with the announcement by Western Union that a road show of sorts—anything but gentle—was on its way. Aunt Dell was on a Greyhound bus somewhere between Phoenix and the west coast and was due in Ventura late Monday afternoon. And now here she was, talking and waving her hands through the window of the bus—the closed window of the bus before it had come to a stop. Mom hadn't come with us so there'd be enough room for the trunk and suitcase in the back if I sat on Junior's lap and Aunt Dell could ride in front.

I just knew she'd slip down the tall steps of the bus or slide in some heavy motor oil that spotted the floor of the dirty bus terminal but she didn't. She managed to get to the car and in it without mishap. Dad reached across in front of her and gave the door an extra pull to make sure it was solidly shut. By the time we got her home, she'd covered her trip back to Missouri and Arkansas, her divorce from Jesse, the battle over the property, everybody's health generally and her own in vivid detail.

She went back over all the stories for Mom aided by a bottle of whiskey she and Dad shared: The divorce was a cinch—no longer a Slokum ("Too damned close to Yokum—that Cal Happ or whatever his name is has ruint that name for any poor fool unlucky enough to have it—Ma Yokum, Ma Slokum. Same thing. As far as that goes, he's give all hillbillies a bad name."), but she couldn't do anything about division-of-property. All she got was a paper saying that if Jesse tried to sell, she'd get her share. Ed and Edwina were so deep into prayer meetings that drowning was the only logical next step. Ronnie was running with a pretty fast crowd there in Blue Eye and Oak Grove—Junior Dodgen, Dorothy Hale, the Humbard bunch—drinkin' quite a bit but he's a good boy—"Oh, Tots!" she called to me in the kitchen where I'd gone for more ice water for their drinks. "Ronnie said special—'Tell Tots I'll see him before he knows it.'" For some reason my legs felt weak. Ronnie. He was the first one I'd—I even had difficulty saying it in my head—had sex with. I wondered what he'd think of me now. Would he approve of what Vic and I were doing? Of what Roy did? I knew he'd think that was tacky.

"I ought to get dinner ready," Mom said and stood up.

"No, Milly, don't go yet," Aunt Dell was all but bouncing up and down on the daybed where she'd be sleeping. "I've saved the best part for last. You've *got* to listen to this. This is a real killer." She patted the place next to her. "Come on. Tots! Get a glass for Milly. We'll each have one more little swig—well, that's about all they is left." She blinked comically. "Where'd that all go to, Woody? You really been knockin' it back."

"Me?" Dad said incredulously. "You haven't had your hand off that bottle long enough to allow me to have more'n a smell of the stuff."

I got Mom a glass and she barely covered the bottom of it with whiskey and then filled it to the brim with water.

"Well." Aunt Dell's eyes were glittering with excitement and mischief. "You ain't going to believe this, but I swear it on a stack of Bibles. Well, I don't even have to do that. It's all over the county and Papa ain't denyin' it." She stopped and looked at each of us over the rim of her glass to make sure she had our attention. We were riveted. It seems Grandpa had been "callin' on" a widow that lived on the Green Forest road at the old Atchley place about four miles from Grandpa's farm. He would cross the field there behind the Garner's and cut off almost a mile of the walk, which he did every afternoon early, making sure he'd get home before dark and still have his little visit with Mrs. Youngblood. Of course he'd been takin' a lot of teasing about this, but he'd just smile and agree with whatever anybody said. The Garners said they got so's they could set their clock by that tall figure in his dark suit coat, big brimmed black hat, walking straight and steady toward the old Atchley place.

"But this last time," Aunt Dell continued, "somethin' seemed to go wrong," She leered. "Or maybe it went too *right.*" She laughed like a child saying something naughty.

"For Christ's sake, Dell, what happened?" Dad exploded. "So far, you've not made a lick of sense."

"What happened?" Aunt Dell was looking wide-eyed. "Well, the old girl popped off, that's what happened." There was a stunned silence.

"You mean while Mr. Woods was there?" Mom asked.

"While he was *right* there," Aunt Dell said, spilling a bit of her drink as she took a swallow. "Right there where it counts."

The corners of Dad's mouth were starting to twitch and his eyes started to twinkle as he leaned forward in the new rocker toward Aunt Dell, "You mean to sit there and tell me that she . . . that Papa was . . ." He started a slow laugh that built to a roar as he flung himself back in the chair with such force I thought it was going to topple over backward.

"But, Dell . . ." Mom was glancing anxiously from me to Junior and back to Aunt Dell.

"Yep," Aunt Dell declared, slapping her leg. "Heart attack. Kicked the bucket right then and there. Dead as a doornail and naked as a jaybird." She and Dad hooted in unison. "And I guess Papa in his long johns runnin' around like a chicken with his head chopped off. Cain't you . . . just see? Imagine him . . . Oh Lordy, I like to'a died when I first heard . . ." She was reduced to uncontrollable laughter, tears streaming down her face.

"Why was she naked?" I asked when the roaring subsided.

"*Why?*" Aunt Dell let out a screech and collapsed backward onto the cushions.

"Were they having sex?" If you learn a new expression, you should use it, I thought.

Dad's eyes widened with a where-did-you-pick-that-up look that included Mom in the question. "That's one way of putting it."

"The polite way," Aunt Dell choked out.

There was a slight pause. "How old is Grandpa?" Junior asked quietly.

"Ooohh, God. Let me see," Dad closed his eyes and concentrated. "I'm thirty-six, Dell's . . ."

"Hush your mouth, Woody!" Aunt Dell screamed.

". . . Daisy'd be fifty-something. Dad's well over seventy."

"Then I guess he's old enough to know what he's doing," Junior said, standing up and heading for the kitchen.

"I can only hope that I'm my daddy's own boy," Dad said with a chuckle. "Still gettin' it up at seventy . . ."

"Gettin' it up is one thing," Aunt Dell's words were getting a bit slurred. "It's the actual *gettin'* it that counts."

"Totsy," Mom said, standing up decisively. "Get the sack and go get some fresh limas."

"Oh, Mom. Do I have to?" I whined.

"You're over twelve years old now. When I tell you to do something I mean for you to do it. And one thing I am *not* going to stand from you or anybody else is whining. It puts my teeth on edge." She was out-of-sorts and she was taking it out on me. It was Mom's opinion that Aunt Dell's recent emancipation—from the soil, from Jesse, from the Ozarks—had gone a bit to her head and she sometimes lost sight of that fine line between being . . . well, vulgar and tacky and knowing when not to use certain words and phrases. Dad said she just had a good-ole-boy complex and sometimes went off the mark in her effort to appear modern and up-to-date.

I hated picking those lima beans. I always felt like a thief. Even though that bean patch I used to walk beside going to school belonged to the Alligator Ranch and we had permission to pick what we wanted, I couldn't help feeling conspicuous out there in a sea of knee-high beans picking the young succulent pods. If there'd been a whole bunch of people like there was when they harvested, it would have been OK. But one lone figure, bending over could only be taken for one thing; somebody stealing beans.

I'd roll up the brown paper poke into a tight little wad and walk with straight-backed purpose into the field, trying to appear as though I were just taking a shortcut from one side to the other. Once in a good spot, I'd dart looks in all directions to make sure no cars were coming or nobody could see me and I'd suddenly drop to the ground as though I'd fallen into a deep hole or trap. Then, crawling along on my stomach, I'd pick the beans, wriggling along like a snake—and often wondered what I'd do if I came face to face with one or rather eye to eye with one at that level—until I'd filled the bag. Then, ever so carefully, I'd peek up over the tops of the plants and when the coast was clear, jump up as though shot up in the air by a spring and walk with that same straight-backed determined gait until I was out of the field and then I'd run as fast as I could up the lane through the fruit trees, with almost that same feeling of fear in my chest that I got at night returning from outhouses—that somebody or something might be chasing me. In this case, I imagined a policeman arresting me for stealing lima beans.

Aunt Dell was decidedly shaky in the morning and laced her coffee generously with whiskey from a new bottle. I began to wonder if her whole suitcase was filled with bottles since she was wearing the same clothes she'd worn yesterday, but she explained that by saying, "Couldn't make the effort even to decide what to put on. Easier to just put on these dirty old things than have some sort of nervous breakdown makin' decisions." She refused any breakfast, even toast, becoming her sprightly self after her second cup of . . . well, the first one was coffee laced with whiskey, the second was whiskey laced with coffee.

Dad had taken the day off to visit with Aunt Dell and we'd made elaborate plans to fill the day. Junior and I would go see "Franken-stein's Monster" at a special kiddie's morning show in Ventura while Dad drove Aunt Dell and Mom around local sights, mostly consisting of the Pacific Ocean.

We had to wait ten minutes to get into the noisiest place I've ever been in my life. I think Junior, at fourteen, was the oldest member of the audience—he was certainly the biggest—and the rest were hyster-ical children who were working up to being terrified by the monster by screaming and trying to scare each other before the film started. When the film finally started the storm noises over the scary castle could scarcely be heard above the din coming from the theater.

We didn't hear Dad when he leaned over and called to us, it was only when he put a hand on each of our heads and tugged our hair—thereby causing me to add a fairly bloodcurdling scream to the general bedlam—that we knew we were being hauled out of the movies. Would we ever be able to watch a film all the way through?

We followed him up the aisle and knew by the set of his shoulders that something serious had happened. He was walking so fast we both had to take little skipping steps to keep up with him. When we got to the lobby and could hear ourselves think, Junior tugged on Dad's arm and said, "What's the matter? What's wrong?"

"Your Aunt Dell," he said through clenched teeth. *"Fell."* He hit the word with a note of disgust in his voice which implied "wouldn't you just know it?"

"Fell?" Junior asked as though he'd never heard of her falling in her life. *"Where?"* That was what I was wondering. Who was she going to sue now?

"Where?" Dad repeated. We were out on the sidewalk. "Where do you think? Fell out of the fuckin' car! *Our* car!"

"Sort of slipped on the running board?" Junior was trying to get the story. Dad was not helping much.

"Slipped?" He shot a look at Junior. He was in a rage. "Slipped, he says." He lifted both hands helplessly from his sides and let them drop limply. "Shit, no. Slip? Do something as simple as slip? Sheee-it! She flew out that door like she was takin' off for a flight across the Pa-cific." He shook his head. "Naw siree. Her and Amelia Ear . . . nose

and throat or whatever her name was. I mean she was flyin'." He was enjoying himself now, the edge of his anger dulled by his story- telling. "I went around a corner, the door snapped open and away she went, arms flappin', legs kickin', skirt up over her head and then landed like a big sack of potatoes—ka-*flub*—and was a-rollin' around in the sand like a hog-tied steer."

"But, *where*, Dad?" Junior insisted.

"Right down there at the beach. You know, over there next to the pier. Down that road where you park. There's where she started her flyin career."

"Is she hurt? Bad?" I asked.

"Shit, how can you tell? She's always pissin' and moanin' with some pain or other but she did land in soft sand. And she was so drunk she couldn't possibly a-hurt herself bad. Limp as a noodle. She's over to the doctor's now. Her and Milly. Come on." He was going around to the driver's side of the car and Junior and I piled into the front seat next to him. "For Christ's sake see that fuckin' door's closed proper."

"That's public property there, isn't it Dad?" I asked. "I mean the beach is the town's?"

He chuckled. "You wonderin' who she's goin' to sue?" He looked at me and grinned. I grinned back. "Lord only knows. She might even sue *me.*" He laughed. "That'll be the old blood from a turnip story."

Mom was supporting Aunt Dell by holding onto her elbow when they came out of the doctor's office. Aunt Dell was giving one of her more convincing performances. It was a shame she had such a small audience—just the four of us. The street was deserted. Her head rolled weakly as though she were going to faint, her knees were obvi- ously unable to support her more than a few steps. Junior was out of the car and had her by the other arm as I ran up to her making inad- equate gestures of helping maneuver her to the car. She was moan- ing quietly but most effectively.

"Oh my God, Milly," she mumbled. "I think I might just a done it this time." She tried to straighten her back and her face was a mask of pain.

"Just take it easy, Dell, the doctor couldn't find anything wrong. There's nothing broken."

"There's always the insides, Milly. Internal injuries." She said it pa- thetically, but there was a gleam of hope and even optimism in her eyes.

Mom crowded in next to Aunt Dell in the front seat as Dad started the motor. "For Christ's sake, Milly," Dad said, only half joking. "Don't *you* take up flying."

"I'm holding on for dear life, Woody," Mom said.

"It's that damned door," Aunt Dell declared. "It don't close tight."

"Now, I suppose you're going' to sue me," Dad said drily.

Aunt Dell shot him a quick look. "Are you insured?"

"Relax. Down, Rover," Dad teased her. "You know we don't have . . ."

"Well, everybody *ought* to have insurance."

"I'll write F.D.R."

There was some sort of shot the doctor had given her—to calm her after her jolt, Mom said—and after taking some pills and resting during the afternoon, she was to return at five-thirty with a urine specimen. I never did understand why, but Junior said it was probably to see if any damage had been done to her kidneys—she had landed on the flat of her back and if pain continued, it could be kidneys.

We unfolded the daybed and put her to bed where Mom gave her the pills and then we all tiptoed around for the rest of our ruined afternoon.

"I could have clocked up four or five hours' work this afternoon anyway," Dad said, "if we didn't have to take her back to the doctor."

"Woody, I'm worried," Mom glanced at me reading in the corner and leaned across the table toward Dad. I heard her whisper, "Dell wants me to do the specimen.

"Do *what?*"

"Ssssh." She glanced at me again. "She says she's been drinking too much and she thinks it'll show up in her urine."

"It's probably pure bourbon."

"Then, if she *has* hurt herself, they'd—whoever *they* are—would just dismiss it on the grounds that she was drunk . . . intoxicated— under the influence or something."

"Who the hell does she think she can sue? The hoboes livin' down there under the pier?" Dad had always been embarrassed by his sister's blatant and transparent racket although not even he had come right out and accused her of fraud. "She probably just wants to get this doctor's report that she hurt herself or that she had some injury from such-and-such a date and then claim she fell down the stairs in the Greyhound bus station or some such nonsense."

"Well, do you think I should?"

"Do the specimen? I don't know. It won't do you any harm and it might save her some embarrassment. Do whatever you think's best."

Aunt Dell was merry as a grig the next day. She was outside pick-ing oranges for our breakfast at seven in the morning. Our vacation was over—back to school for us and work for Dad. "Look at her," Dad said over his coffee. "Swingin' through them trees like a goddam monkey. If she falls down here and tries to sue Logan and Alligator Ranch, I'll kill her."

"Then she'd probably hand St. Peter a subpoena at the Pearly Gates against you, Dad," Junior said.

"And then trip over the entrance and sue St. Peter," I added. "And that is just about enough of *that*," Mom said. "A little more respect for your elders, please."

Junior picked up the results of the urinalysis during his lunch hour and brought it home on the school bus. Junior was always the last one home so we were all there when Aunt Dell opened the envelope, read it, turned the color of the paper and swooned onto the daybed.

"Oh, Christ," Dad said. "What's the matter now?"

"Oh, my God!" she said faintly, the back of one hand resting dra-matically on her forehead. "That's all I need." All of a sudden she sat bolt upright, eyes round with fright, her hand on her cheek and mouth open. "I'm not even married, for God's sake. What'll the girls say? Mavis'll *die.*"

"I give up," Dad said. "*All* the marbles are gone now."

"Dell," Mom sat beside her and put an arm around her shoulders. "What in the world are you talking about?"

"I'm pregnant," she said as though she were announcing cancer.

"But *can* you be?" Mom asked. "You're over forty-five . . ."

"Not only can be. *Am.*" She shook the paper in Mom's face.

Mom grabbed it and read. Then *she* slumped back onto the cush-ions. "Well, I'll be damned . . ." She looked up at Dad and burst into laughter. "Well, Woody, are you ready for the good news?" Dad looked puzzled for a minute and then the corners of his mouth began to twitch. Mom nodded her head. "Un-huh. I was beginning to wonder . . ."

"Goddamnit," Dad was laughing, "whose piss *was* it?"

"Mine," Mom fairly shrieked.

"Oh, thank God," Aunt Dell murmured. "I'd forgotten."

"You have all, each and every one of you, gone stark raving mad," Junior said in what he thought was an English accent. "Come on, Tots, let's vamoose from this nuthouse."

Aunt Dell threw her arms around Mom's neck. "Oh, thank God it's you and not me."

"I'm not so sure I'm all that delighted." Mom was looking up at Dad with a questioning look. "What do you think, Woody?"

Dad's eyes twinkled and he grinned, "Shit, we can't afford to feed the mouths we got. Why not have another one to starve along with us."

Mom jumped up and threw her arms around Dad's neck. She kissed him on the cheek and whispered, "It's your fault, you know."

He drew back. "I sure as hell hope so!"

Junior cleared his throat to get attention and continued in his silly voice, "As I understand it, this lady flew out of a speeding car, falling into some soft sand and doing herself no great damage but in the course of events too strange for me to remotely comprehend, her trip to the doctor has made *this* lady," pointing at Mom, "pregnant. My knowledge of the science of reproduction of . . . of the *human* species is . . . well, limited, but somehow or other I had the impression that it was more or less impossible for ladies to make each other pregnant."

"Oh, for heaven's sake," Mom was choking with laughter. "Will you please just stop."

"I'll have you know," Dad was imitating Junior's prissy manner, "that as *this* lady's husband, I can say he didn't need any help whatsoever in . . . well, making . . ."

"He's his papa's own boy," Aunt Dell bounced up and hugged both Mom and Dad. "Like Papa, like son."

"Were Grandpa and Mrs. Youngblood making a baby?" I piped up.

"Oh dear, Woody," Mom said, mock-serious. "It's birds-and-bees time. You've got to do it." She beamed with happiness and clutched her tummy. "I've got enough on my *mind.*"

Dad discussed the birds-and-bees in roughly the same manner he discussed the combustion engine and curiously enough, they were not dissimilar—by that I mean, he knew the names of the parts and their inter-reaction but he couldn't make me completely understand it. Junior seemed to understand fully while I grasped only basic working principles; that valve pumped oil into that cavity, keeping it lubricated while this piston moved to create a friction which ignited that mechanism, causing a fusion which in turn . . . What it really boiled down to was what the silly Wilkins boy had said—only the names were more genteel, as Mrs. Jones might say. Seeds were mentioned a great deal—sexual intercourse was the same as *having* sex. Come was also called semen or the seed and so forth. After a private session with Junior, I really did think I understood. It all seemed remarkably simple. If you could come, you could make a baby. It was that seed, that diabolical little seed, that could get in there and cause all the trouble. That's why men wore rubbers.

"Can you come?" I asked Junior, taking the bull by the horns and this God-given opportunity to get that burning question answered.

"That's a very private and personal thing."

"But Dad said that anybody who said they hadn't masturbated was a liar."

"You asked me if I could come, you didn't ask me if I masturbated."

"Well, how can you come if you don't?"

"You don't *have* to do anything," he shrugged. "It can just happen."

"Just *happen?* You mean without *doing* anything?"

"Sure. Wet dreams."

This was really new. "Wet *dreams?* That sounds like wetting the bed."

"In a way it is. It just happens when you're asleep. When you don't know it."

"What causes it?"

"It's just in the body, I guess. And when there gets too much well . . . I guess it just comes out."

So much for Gino's theory that you had to swallow some to make more. "Are you sure?" If I told Vic this would he stop sucking my cock?

"Sure, I'm sure." I just stared at him. "What's the matter?" he asked. "What are you thinking?"

"Thinking it doesn't sound like much fun."

"You mean like you and Mary Lou?"

Mary Lou? Talk about kid stuff. I was thinking of Vic, Ronnie and, not necessarily wanting to, Uncle Roy. "Yeah," I nodded. "Like me and Mary Lou."

We all but put Aunt Dell on the bus on a stretcher. Not because she had really hurt herself, but to keep her from having another chance to hurt herself. Junior told me that he thought it best since she was so accident prone to be always near her lawyer. Not her doctor. And since he was Mavis's husband, there was no difficulty.

By the time school was out in June, Mom was beginning to show a bit. Until then, I'd almost forgotten that we were expecting a baby in the house. Now that I could actually see it, the idea fascinated me. Mom would let us put our hands on her bulging middle and we

could feel movement! It was spooky and marvelous. There was a little brother or sister growing in there. I couldn't take my eyes off her
belly. Mom and the baby became my special concern. I'd grab chairs
for her to sit down. I didn't moan about doing all the dishwashing. I
scrubbed the house, made beds, washed the woodwork (a special
mania of Mom's—she could spot a finger mark through a solid wall)
until the paint started to come off. I took over the family laundry—
the sight of Mom leaning over the washboard trying to keep her middle from bumping against the tub was more than I could bear. I'd
heat up the big black pot out in the backyard under the biggest avocado tree and have the white things boiling before she'd finished her
morning coffee. I'd have her chair placed just so, away from the
smoke of the fire under the big pot and she'd sit and talk while I
poked the boiling sheets and towels with a fat stick that was bleached
as white as the clothes. She'd tell me stories of her family, how she
and her sisters would do the laundry on the weekend when she came
home after a week's work of teaching, boarding out with some family
or other. It was her favorite time, she'd say, her momma was there,
running the country store, her papa running the sawmill and the
blacksmith's shop. She'd get misty-eyed and sometimes tears would
come into her eyes when she talked of her momma. How she'd loved
her. And her papa! He was quite simply a god.

Mom taught me how to lift the clothes out of the pot and into the
tub so they wouldn't lose the heat or the water and how to keep the
article being scrubbed submerged all the time for the same reason.
No picking the towel up and holding it in the air, that just cooled off
the water and didn't do any good except for you to admire your
work. You had to bunch it up with your fingers, one hand-length at a
time, rubbing it on the board about three times to each bunch until
the whole thing was bunched painfully in your hands. My hands were
small but doing that laundry every week had made them strong and
I was beginning to notice I had to lean farther over to reach into the
bottom of the tub. I was growing taller too! Maybe I'd begin to look
my age—'way over twelve. Practically a teenager.

Then something happened—an insignificant incident in itself—
that took my joy at watching the new little Woods growing and replaced it with a premonitory fear that threatened to drive me crazy.

The Scrits stopped by one Sunday morning on the way back from
mass—an always welcome invasion—for a visit and strong hot coffee
Mom had brewing every Sunday just in case. Gino and Junior
promptly started throwing balls around. Bert was, in Gino's words,

chasing skirt in El Centro. Vic was holding little Maria who promptly came to me. She and I had a special relationship—I adored her and she seemed to recognize the adoration and knew she could do anything she wanted with me. I'd watched her since she was born and hoped for a little sister just like her.

The insignificant incident that changed my life happened in a flash and is there in my mind like a familiar photo: The Scrits were at the table with Dad under the big avocado tree, the two youngest boys were up it, Vic had joined Junior and Gino. Mom walked over to where I was seated with Maria on my lap, bouncing on my knees, holding onto her hands, laughing into her dancing eyes when she suddenly threw her head back with terrific force, hitting Mom squarely in her bloated belly. Baby bashes baby. Mom let out a choked cry and bent over double. At this point, the picture becomes jagged and jerky as though it were running through a projector at the wrong speed.

Somehow the Scrits were gone, Mom was stretched out on the bed and I was putting cold cloths on her brow.

"It's all right, it's all right," she kept mumbling. "It'll be fine. It was just such a shock. And painful!" She attempted a laugh. "My goodness that child has a head like a cannon ball."

"Should I go get the doctor?" Dad asked from the foot of the bed.

"Good heavens, no. It'll all pass in a bit. Don't make a fuss about it."

It did pass in a bit as far as Mom was concerned but it didn't for me. From that moment on I was obsessed. I was haunted by fears of what *might* happen to the baby—or to Mom. Pathetic nineteen year old Clementine's withered little body was fixed in my head, overlaying everything I looked at with the image of her boneless legs and arms. She'd been *born* like that. Nobody's fault, they said, it just happened. And poor Brad with his flaw—born with a flaw, the captain had said. And then Mrs. Scrit had had one baby born dead! All the things that could possibly go wrong became possibilities—almost certainties—in my mind. How could I have been so dumb and complacent about something so serious. It isn't just a simple, normal everyday thing, I told myself. What about the cripples, the maimed and twisted—all born that way. Only recently there was a big story in *Life* about a little girl born with no arms. She ate, wrote, cut out paperdolls with her toes. I'd turned away from the smiling pictures of the distorted little creature. And there, right there, inside Mom could be some sort of monster or a cripple or . . . I was tormented. Every waking moment, every nightmare night was filled with horrors. I was convinced that even if everything had been all right at the beginning, the blow of Maria's head would leave some bruise, some little wound, perhaps undetectable at birth, but would come out later, as Brad's flaw finally cracked open into madness.

I wasn't just obsessed, I was possessed. There was no one to talk to. I didn't dare voice my fears to Junior—he'd just say I was being silly. I actually hoped I was being silly—that my wild anxieties would just go away, but they didn't. Weeks went by, I went on doing more and more for Mom. I watched her like a mother hen.

"You'd think it was Tots who was having the baby," Dad joked.

It was no joke to me. I did feel responsible. If I could only *do* something, anything to make sure that the baby would be all right. I prayed with a fervor that would have put Aunt and Uncle Ed to shame. I begged, pleaded and bargained with God. I made every sacrifice I could think of. I even quarrelled with Vic—on purpose—cutting off that physical pleasure. I made a sort of sacred oath or vow like Bert and Gino had done for Lent. I forswore anything to do with sex. I told God that I wouldn't touch myself except to pee and then only absolutely minimally if he'd see to it that all went well with the baby. I was doing all I *could* do.

The baby was due in either October or November. In September, we were back on the road. September was working out to be moving time. Always the question of getting us into school. We'd had word from Mom's brother, Ernest, that work for Dad on Friant Dam was *almost* assured—he was safely employed himself—but he wouldn't know for sure until about October or November. Babies and jobs both due at the same time. Both, please God, safe, sound and secure.

Uncle Ernest and Aunt Doreen were living in a town near Fresno called Clovis and there we headed. It wasn't a long trip, but it was hot, the car kept overheating on the San Luis Obispo mountain roads as we headed inland toward Bakersfield and up through the San Joaquin Valley to Clovis. Mom was frequently carsick which had me hysterical with concern. We were, as usual, saving money on motor courts and made the two-hundred miles or so in one nerve-wracking haul. When we arrived on our relatives' front porch at midnight, we looked like the sort of relatives that relatives are reluctant to claim.

We were back in comfort—always somebody else's—for a few days. A refrigerator! Gas cooking stove! Bathroom taps that actually produced what they advertised. The floodwaters of the Nile filled, foamed and flushed the toilet. A separate dining room with a real heirloom table and chairs. Velvet—*not* cut—covered furniture in a softly lighted living room. Right out of *Ladies' Home Journal.*

So we shouldn't possibly get spoiled by all that luxury, Dad found a stopgap job—Friant Dam was there, but Dad had to wait for it—on a farm just outside town. The job provided housing of sorts and a minimal wage for taking care of several acres of grapevines. Wine grapes.

Our housing was in or rather part of the house of Dad's new bosses, B. V. Hollings and Son and consisted of a kitchen on the slanting floor of a screened-in front porch, the living room (just big enough for Mom and Dad's double bed, a table and some chairs), and a closet-like room deemed a bedroom simply by calling it one which Junior and I shared. Alligator Ranch had been a mansion by comparison.

I was enrolled in the seventh grade of Clovis Grammar School, one block from Uncle Ernest's house which I tried not to look at from the school yard, and Junior was a freshman at the local high school several blocks away. Here the Junior High school system didn't apply, it was a standard four-year school. School started almost as soon as we were settled in at B. V. Hollings and Son (Ranch). Ranch was added like that in parenthesis, as an afterthought on the mailbox in front of the cluster of dilapidated buildings. One of which was our outdoor toilet, a fly-blown horror that spelled instant constipation until Mom and I whitewashed it inside and out and covered the offending contents with many layers of ashes.

B. V. Hollings turned out to be a woman. Well, she said she was. Her only concession to femininity was to wear dresses. Her son was definitely her son and she was as proud of him as if he'd been normal. He was a casebook moron, but had the good grace to be mute and didn't make any pathetic, drooling, moronic sounds. This was a mixed blessing because he was sly and cunning and was always where you'd least expect to find him. Within days we were all tiptoeing around, peeking behind doors, around corners, even under beds to make sure Syl wasn't there. I thought at first Syl was short for Silly, but it turned out to be Sylvester.

"That's right," Mrs. Hollings cackled, "Sylvester Reginald Hollings. Used to be Hollings-*head* but we was decapitated." She screeched with manic laughter. "Old family joke. Old English name." She winked and nudged Mom with an elbow dangerously close to her mountainous middle. Since she came up just below Mom's shoulder, it was difficult for her to make any gesture without inflicting grievous bodily harm. She was as awkward as Sylvester was stealthy and I was constantly insinuating myself between her and the new baby Woods. "Hey, you didn't start out with that old English name, Woodcock, and have your cock cut off, did you?" she asked Dad innocently.

"As far as I know," Dad said, trying to keep a straight face, "it was just plain Woods. We never had a cock."

"Don't know why people change their names. It was that crazy husband of mine. Ought to a chopped his own head off. That'd been a right smart better." She screeched again. "It's *my* family that had the names. I've got one that there ain't nobody can guess. Can you? Can you guess what B. V. stands for?" Her little eyes became slits as she glanced from one to the other of us. "Hah! Thought not! Won't tell you, neither. Won't tell nobody. Put an ad in the paper once—the *Fresno Bee*—said I'd pay anybody a hundert dollars if they could guess my name. Whoooeee, you shoulda' seen what I got in the mail! I mean, letters by the *thousands,* didn't I, Syl?" she poked him on the shoulder which caused his eyelids to droop lower, "and the things they wrote! Why things you couldn't even find in the dictionary. Some was outright nasty. You wouldn't believe what people'll do." She nudged Syl, "Come on, son, let's get them geese and ducks in."

"Looney as a birddog," Dad said, shaking his head. "But she knows how to grow grapes. She's got quite a harvest out there."

Chapter Eleven

DISCOVERING YET ANOTHER BIRTH DEFECT—the moron (the mere idea of having a Sylvester in the family was more than I could cope with)—sent me straight into the arms of the nearest Baptist Church. I needed more spiritual strength than I could muster up on my own to carry this new load of worry about the baby.

Once involved, I became a very active member of the First Baptist Church. I'd stuck firmly to my sacred vow with God and thought if I was in the house of God as much as possible, He might take a bit more notice of me and keep His side of the bargain. Time was drawing near. Mom said toward the end of October or mid-November at the latest and Halloween had come and gone and no baby. Mom didn't walk now so much as waddle. She'd sit with her legs wide apart and lean back in her chair holding onto her enormous stomach and sigh, "Oooh, dear. If I could just get a good deep breath." All this to make us laugh. "And I swear I've carried this child for a year. If the stork doesn't come soon, I'm going to send him an urgent telegram."

I did feel closer to God in the church. Each time the preacher said, "Let us pray," I'd start in a monologue on that same obsessive subject—we'd long ago dropped that "thee" and "thou" routine, or at least I had and I talked directly to Him as the only friend I could discuss this problem with, as indeed He was. "I'm still keeping my promise to you, but you know that (you're watching all the time—I wouldn't *dare),* and don't know what else I can do to make further sacrifices, but I *would* . . . I haven't had a bite of candy in . . . oh, heavens, I don't know how long. I've not fussed with Junior. I've even learned not to let his sniffling in bed at night bother me. Well, not too much. Anyway, I don't *say* anything to him. I've been doing his share of the dishes every night—have you noticed?—and without grumbling so's he can get at the extra homework from high school. All those other chores I keep right on doing—the laundry and all that, so I don't know what else I *can* do, but I have to ask one more thing of you.

"It just seems there's no end to what can happen . . . can go wrong . . . well, when a baby's born. I mentioned—well, you know—like what happened to Clementine and Bradford and being like Mrs. Scrit's little girl, being just plain dead on arrival and I've asked you to please, with all your power to see that those things don't happen. Now then, I've just met somebody called Sylvester Reginald Hollings. Mom says he's a moron. A casebook example—which I figure must mean the very best possible example—and well, it's . . . it's just pathetic. I know you wouldn't want to feel responsible for bringing somebody else into the world like that, so I'm asking just this one thing more . . . if I can sort of sneak it on the list with all the others? I hope I'm not asking too much, but things . . . things keep cropping up. Oh dear God! *Please,* please, please . . ."

I'd been singing lead soprano in the choir right up through the big Thanksgiving service. Actually right up through half of it. Then my voice broke. Cracked on my solo chorus in "Peace Be Still." It didn't crack in an up and down line—you know like some boys' voices do—it broke right across the middle. One second I was holding a nice high note, then there was some sort of momentary stoppage in my throat and the note dropped down about a mile. Well, more than an octave. And there my voice has stayed, sort of comfortably down there just by my navel. I was mortified on the one hand— having it happen in performance—but delighted on the other. All my bodily changes were happening right on time and I took it as a good omen. Almost as a sign from God that everything else would be all right. With the baby, I mean. When we were getting out of our choir robes in the vestry, I heard one of the boys from my class in school call me a "pious prick"—I must have been looking awfully smug. In my enlightened state, I took it as a compliment.

Mom had been taken to the county hospital by Dad while I was in church. He didn't get home until about three in the morning. I was sitting up waiting for him, having kept up the running monologue with God for hours but finished abruptly when I heard the car pull up the dirt lane with, "OK. It's up to you, now. I've simply done all I can . . ."

The door flew open, Dad was, as they say back home, loop-legged drunk. "She's fine . . . *both* shes is fine. She *and* she. Her and *her.* " He was hugging me and tears were running down both our faces. "Junior!" Dad called unnecessarily—he was already there hugging us. "You've all got a baby sister." He giggled stupidly and repeated, "She and she. Milly and . . . and . . ." he slumped in a chair and put his face in his hands and mumbled, "and I've got another mouth to feed . . ." I thought he was crying, but after a few seconds' silence, he lifted his face from his hands and grinned. "And *I've* got a baby daughter," he sat up proudly. "She's . . . she's . . ."

"Rebecca," I said softly, reminding him of the name Junior had chosen and we'd all agreed on.

The minute I was convinced—after an after-school visit to the hospital and a view of a little red-wrinkled squalling infant that Junior said had a face like a catcher's mitt—that all was perfect with Mom and baby, I was ready to toss my halo to the winds. God and I had kept our vows. It wasn't that I wanted to dash to the nearest secluded spot and masturbate, it was just that I felt free and exhilarated. But before I happily let my halo disintegrate into dust, I went into the Catholic church I passed every morning on my way to school. I had three pennies—how I'd amassed such a fortune eludes me—and I dropped them into a slotted box and lighted a long, slim, amber candle the way Mrs. Scrit had taught me. "That's for Rebecca, God, and for Mom. Thank you." I couldn't think of anything else to say but, "You're a gent. You kept your bargain."

I suppose I might have overdone the announcement at school a bit. I naturally told my teacher first—she seemed thrilled and said she'd come see my mother when she got home from hospital. My terror that she'd see where we lived put the first damper on my excitement, but I told her I'd let her know when Mom was ready to have visitors.

The second damper came from the bully from church who had called me a pious prick. He overheard me telling other classmates and he said, "That ought to be your name, suction. Rebecca. Rebecca of Sunnybrook Farm," he minced girlishly. He got the laugh he wanted from the others and God got one more request from me. "Please, God, I'm going to have to fight that asshole one of these days. Stay on my side once more, please, And *help.* "

No longer held by vows, I was open for all comers. That doesn't sound all that nice, but I guess it's near enough the truth. Masturbation wasn't even a consideration, Mrs. Hollings took care of the problem. That sounds even less nice. I mean she took care of the problem by hiring another family—the Strouds—to help with the grape harvest and they moved into what could only with the utmost kindness be called a shack. The Stroud family was made up of females—except for the skinny, drained-out father—of all ages, sizes and descriptions. A sort of take-your-pick. I was ready and I did. Mine was called Naomi and she was quite simply Mary Ann six years on. In age *and* experience.

Naomi could twirl a baton and she was going to teach me how. She was going to be the champion baton-twirler of the world. At the 1939 World's Fair in San Francisco there'd be a contest and she was going to enter and win it. And I believed her. She was that good. She had a real baton, silver colored with a large rubber ball at one end and a rubber stopper on the other. When she twirled it, you saw nothing but the blur of flashing silver. She could twirl it around her head, around her neck, around her waist, around both legs, around one leg at a time, she could toss it so high that it faded out of sight and she'd catch it each time without letting the speed of the twirling diminish by a second. She was a magician with a magic wand.

"You see, if you slow down enough for the eye to make out the ball on the end, then, poo, you're disqualified. That means you've got to keep up the same rhythm and speed or . . . well, poo, you just ain't in the runnin'." They were from Oklahoma, all blue-eyed, with matted blond hair and filthy dirty. "I say 'poo' a lot to break myself from saying 'shit.' Paw said I was sayin' shit so much I was beginnin' to smell like it." I was mad about her.

Naomi was an excellent teacher—both in baton-twirling and what she called "shaggin'." In both activities she was firmly in charge. She arranged the choreography for her baton-twirling presentation and worked out all the movements and positions when we shagged in a manner that suited her best. What suited her best was straddling over on top of me. It suited me just fine too.

"Ooo-ooh, *no*. You ain't goin' to get me in that position. That down-on-my-back position. I'm goin' to be right up here where I can see what's goin' on. That old flat-out business don't give a girl a chanct to run, jump or dodge." She never giggled, but laughed deep in her throat, husky and I found it sexy. "That's what happened to Patty May. She told me. When she was just fourteen. That little'un,

Bobbie June? Well, she ain't my baby sister, she's Patty May's baby. I'm her Aunt Naomi." Her laughter bubbled. "Auntie Naomi at thirteen. Besides, Momma'd be dead if she'd had us all. That's why I'm goin' to do it *my way.*"

And she did. I was putty in her hands. She'd stretch me out on my back on the big worktable in the barn and when she got me hard would squat down over me, guiding me into what she called her "cooze" while I lay back with my hands behind my head watching spellbound as this puzzle fitted so beautifully together. Squatting there, watching herself through her legs with her head bent over, she'd sometimes stroke herself at the top of her cooze while she'd spin around on me and her eyes'd get glazed and her head would drop back while she made a gurgling sound deep in her throat with her husky voice.

"What's that lump you play with," I asked on one of our first sessions.

"That's the little man in the boat. He's a girl's best friend. Feel. It gets hard like you do."

I did and it did. She'd move herself around on me in the strangest ways, in little circles, slightly up and down—rather the way Mary Ann had done on my finger that first time in the Valentine Post Office, but having my thing inside her instead of a finger was a considerable improvement. Being inside her cooze was as warm and moist as Vic's mouth. Then she'd put all her weight down on my groin and grind her buttocks into me so hard that it'd hurt. But the minute she felt me responding too much, she'd do a sharp little flipping movement with her behind that dislodged us and she'd drop down flat on me, so we were stomach to stomach and then she'd do delicious rippling movements with her tummy that made me come. There were variations on that theme, but only at her instigation.

As I became more adept at twirling the baton—and I could soon do all the tricks she did—I elaborated on her basic patterns and worked out more complicated combinations. I used an old broom handle for practice and had it with me most of the time. It all took a great deal of practice and I didn't have all that much free time what with school and taking care of Becky. She was my baby. Nobody seemed to question the fact when I just took her over. After Mom's breasts became too painful to feed her, I prepared her formula, boiling the bottles and nipples and warming the milk to exactly the right temperature, feeding her, burping her, bathing her and finally washing her diapers.

"I'll gladly do the dishes every night," Junior said, "so long as I don't have to even see those filthy things." The covered bucket in which the diapers soaked was kept discreetly under the sink in the kitchen. With no indoor toilet to dump the waste into, the water did turn a rather sickly yellow.

"Oh, don't be so fussy. It's just milk. That's all she eats now."

"Maybe it started out milk," he said pedantically, "but it has been through her entire system and it is now shit."

So I scrubbed the diapers as directed by Mom—soaked, rinsed, boiled, rubbed on the board in hot soapy water, then four—count them carefully—*four* clear water rinses or she'll get a rash. "I've got dishpan hands, and you've got diaper-digits," Junior said comparing our rough and reddened hands.

Christmas was as gay as we could make it. That is make it with no money. Mrs. Hollings brought us a huge tree from a ranch she said she had down near Visalia and insisted on helping us decorate it. Junior and I made much the same decorations we'd done that last year at Grandpa and Grandma Woods'.

"Ain't it lovely havin' a tree!" Mrs. Hollings cackled. She bore a rather alarming resemblance to a parrot and her watchful beady little eyes were pure MacKenzie. "It was Syl's idea. No good havin' one for us now. Both too old." She hit Syl on the shoulder and shouted—she always shouted at him as though that would make him comprehend and perhaps it did, but nothing we said to him ever seemed to register—"Go get the ladder and the angel." He slithered away into their part of the house. "Well, have you guessed yet?" MacKenzie's eyes flicked around at us all. We knew what she meant. She asked that question every time we saw her. "What the B. V. stands for in my name? Not yet? Well, keep workin' on it. You might git it one day. *And* the hundert dollars." Her look was of triumph, knowing we'd never guess. She scrambled up the ladder Syl had placed next to the tree with surprising agility, looking now like a cross between a bird and a monkey.

"Hold the ladder, Tots," Mom said. "It looks wobbly."

I stood holding the ladder while Mrs. Hollings placed a tattered little doll precariously on the top. It looked as though Syl had been chewing on the ornament and it gave our ratty tree the final comically tacky touch.

Junior and I had discussed it and decided that we'd get nothing for Christmas. No matter how much care Mom and Dad took in not letting us know our financial situation, it was apparent that we were at just about the lowest ebb we'd ever been. Mom's hospital and doctor bills took the last of what we may have arrived with in Clovis—it turned out that Dad wasn't even getting twenty-five cents an hour from Mrs. Hollings. She may have been as looney as a birddog, but she was a hard and cagey bargainer. Everybody worked by the piece or by the grape, as Dad said. "She's Mrs. Simon Legree. Not Hollings or head. Why, she's paying old Stroud less than what the wetbacks get for picking grapes. And she's chargin' him rent on that chicken coop."

But we, Junior and I, did get a present. One between us. A clarinet. A clarinet is not the easiest thing to divide up, though it does come apart in pieces—three, to be exact—but one is no good without the other. For example, I couldn't practice the lower scale with the bottom half of the instrument while Junior practiced the upper register with the top because there is only one mouthpiece and it fits only on the very top. Junior was thrilled. It was what he wanted. I was thrilled for him and figured that a real silver twirling baton *and* tap shoes was asking too much of our poverty-stricken Santa Claus in the first place. It was greedy and there was something basically tacky about the idea of working up a routine of tap dancing and twirling the baton at the same time. I could see Ronnie's shrug and hear his voice say, "I don't know, Tots. Tap dance, yes. Twirl a baton? Well, yes . . . sort of. But together?" He'd be pursing his lips and shaking his head, *"Tacky."* Well, maybe I could be a drum major and lead the high school band.

So I feigned inordinate interest in the clarinet and when Junior had learned the rudiments of the fingering, having joined the high school band, he passed his knowledge along to me. The squawks and squeaks were intermingled with our squabbling—"Let me try now, it's my turn." "You just bit the reed." "Well, you get it too wet and soft." "That's not the right fingering." "Can't you *count?*" "It's a delicate musical instrument, dummy, not a crackerjack toy." And so on until Mom would threaten to take it back to Santa Claus. Santa Claus being the Columbia Music Emporium downtown next to the movie house where we'd seen this secondhand instrument in the first place. We also knew that it was being paid off at so much a month and that knowledge curtailed our quarrels. Knowing the sacrifice Mom and Dad were making for us shamed us into serious practice and Junior made extraordinary progress and I even got to the point where I could squeak, squawk, and squeal my way through a vaguely recognizable rendition of "Home Sweet Home."

Junior became a full-fledged member of the high school band in no time at all. We were all terribly proud and decided he'd be the next Artie Shaw, even though he was barely through the first exercise book. "If you must know the truth, Tots," he confided, "they had forty-nine instruments and there was this hole in the rear right corner of the marching formation that had to be filled. I'm the plug." He grinned. "And I can't play all those trills and fast stuff yet, but the band director says fake it. I'm not quite sure how I'm going to do that."

"Just run your fingers up and down the stops and keys. Nobody'll know you're not blowing air into it. Just puff out your cheeks." I poked him on the shoulder. "But for heaven's sake don't get carried away and be playing along like crazy when everybody else has stopped."

"It's a cheat, but they need me for the big county fair parade in Fresno. I don't know whether you actually have to have a fifty-piece band to qualify or it's just because they have fifty uniforms."

Once the grape season was over, Dad was only doing odd jobs around the place to pay for our rent. But if we were broke and in debt, the poor Strouds were all but starving. Naomi's dream of being a champion baton-twirler was the only thing that kept her from sinking into the dull torpor that the rest of her family had allowed to creep over them as hope faded. Hope faded at about the same rate that shoes wore out, that dirt became imbedded into skin and scalp, that runny noses gave way to deep chest coughs, croup, and the constant gnawing hunger was a condition of life. Her dream was kept alive by her baton and the chewed-up, scruffy remains of her cheap majorette boots.

Thirteen is not an unlucky number. At least I've decided that it isn't. I turned thirteen—finally a real teenager—in March 1940 and the world turned upside-down. Up the *right* way for a change. The dam burst. Friant Dam burst through with a job for Dad. Uncle Ernest's promise was fulfilled. Dad went to work on April Fool's Day which also became a good omen for us. Within a month, Dad had passed his apprentice-status tests and was a full-fledged pipe-steam fitter. Celebration followed celebration followed celebration.

Another celebration when Junior was the first Clovis High School freshman to make the varsity team. Mrs. Hollings's house fairly rocked with the music and dancing—music via radio, dancing by all of us. Things were looking *straight* up and we all agreed that the only thing we needed to make us totally content was a decent house to live in. Even that little need was soon to be filled beyond all possible dreams.

Uncle Ernest was promoted to head foreman on another construction job and we could now take over the lease on his house. All that luxury. Ours. Mom burst into tears, Junior beamed and hugged me. Dad tossed Becky in the air making her gurgle with delight. I put a whole nickel into the slotted box at the Catholic church when I lighted that second candle. God had outdone himself.

We hadn't lost our knack for packing the Ford. In our eagerness to see the last of the B. V. Hollings (Ranch), we speeded up our routine jobs so we resembled characters in a silent movie played at the wrong speed. It was a silent and swift packing-up. We seemed to be afraid to speak for fear of breaking the magic spell of good luck.

The only one who seemed upset was Mrs. Hollings.

"I can't find that boy of mine," she called as we were settling into the car. "Is he in there with you?"

That was a thought that struck terror in our hearts and we all darted nervous looks around us.

"Well," she went on, moving closer to the car, "he can't hardly stand it that you're movin'. He just loves you folks." She stuck her head in the window, causing Dad to flinch and turn his head away. "And well, so do I," she said violently as if it were something shameful. Dad gunned the motor impatiently and Mrs. Hollings jumped clear of the car. We all waved merrily, callously untouched by her declaration, feeling no shame at our joy of leaving as Dad roared out the drive and onto the road into Clovis town.

We all tended to tiptoe around for the first few weeks. The silence of carpeted floors after the clatter of feet on cracked linoleum all our lives bordered on the spooky. Junior and I opted for the big screened-in back porch as our room. A curtain divided it from a little breakfast corner at the other end. The front bedroom was called the "guest room" and although it wasn't mentioned, I rather gathered Mom hoped for a paying guest. The rent was high and we'd be able to save a bit of Dad's new wages if we had a lodger.

By the time school was out and we'd been in the new house over a month, we felt like real city folks. Clovis was hardly a metropolis, but it was the biggest community we'd ever lived in and we were anxious to become a part of it. Dad surprised us all by joining the Masons. He'd always referred to clubs and lodges as "Amos and Andy" crap. He sported an odd-shaped ring on his finger and talked importantly about secret handshakes and greetings. It all sounded childish to me but I was pleased that Dad was making an effort to "belong." I couldn't help but wonder if the Saturday night poker games he organized with his new friendly lodge brothers hadn't been one of the Mason's chief attractions.

Junior not only joined the Boy Scouts of America, he embraced the movement with the fervor of a religious convert. The Boy Scout handbook became as sacrosanct as his dictionary and all his trousers were stretched out of shape with the two books perpetually shoved in his hip pockets.

We even had our first bank account. Not to squirrel away our family fortune, I soon realized, but simply as a clearinghouse so that checks could be sent back to Galena and Crane and Oak Grove to pay off long-standing debts. Frugality was still the key word at home. Even in this new house where I wasn't ashamed to have my teacher come visit.

"You used to never bring any friends home," I pointed out to Junior one day.

"To the pee-stained house? Going through the Scott's front door to get upstairs to our three rooms? Those two tiny rooms in Crane?" His eyes bugged comically. "Or how about the motor court in Ventura? Wouldn't you love to have had a class party in that one room?"

"Alligator Ranch wasn't too bad," realizing as I said it that the few pieces of secondhand furniture were pretty tacky and we'd only had the Scrits to visit out in the yard. "Well, nothing could have been worse than Mrs. Hollings'."

"Grandpa Woods' smokehouse had more style."

I was puzzled. "I didn't think that sort of thing . . . you know, houses and decoration and that sort of thing . . . Well, I just thought they didn't interest you all that much."

"I'm not blind, you idiot," he said poking me on the shoulder. "It's just that if you can't help it . . . help where you live and you're not particularly proud of it, well, you just don't have to let everybody know, that's all." He was quiet for a bit. "I've been in a lot of kids' houses that were worse than anything we ever lived in—look at the poor Strouds in that shack on the Hollings place, *pitiful*—and I always felt sorry for them. I didn't want anybody feeling sorry for me. So, I just didn't ask anybody back to those places."

"But the Jones's in Phoenix—that was a lovely place. The gardens . . ."

"Yes, honey-chile, but remember we'as just pore live-in help there."

With the missionary zeal of the true believer, Junior convinced me to join the Boy Scouts too. We went to weekly meetings at the VFW Hall—the recreation room downstairs—that were pretty boring except for the games period at the end of the evening. All the knot-tying, presentation of badges for various accomplishments, first-aid demonstrations—since the war in Europe was heating up daily, this activity became particularly important—had a tendency to put me to sleep.

I caused myself considerable embarrassment one evening when the scoutmaster, Mr. Watson, one of Junior's high school teachers, demonstrated artificial respiration with me as the drowned one. He had me flat on the floor on my belly, straddling me from above and the moment he put his hands near my ribs, my old problem about being tickled came back. I got hysterical and wiggled and screamed until Junior had to tell Mr. Watson that I was an impossible "victim" because of my affliction. My ticklishness. This seemed to amuse Mr. Watson and he started at me in the same way Ronnie used to, just to watch me giggle and wriggle away from his reach practically every-time he saw me.

The recreation period after the "serious" part of the meeting was usually a rough and tumble game called "Hunt and Capture." We'd choose up sides, clear the slick hardwood floor of furniture, take off our shoes and then turn out the lights. It was pitch dark and the object of the game was to sneak across the floor and "capture" as many of the other team as possible by dragging them back to your side of the room. It was great fun and I loved it. Sometimes you'd get one of your own team members but wouldn't know it because of the dark and of course if you spoke, your voice could give you away. There was a lot of giggling and grunting and rolling around in the dark. Junior allowed as how it could get pretty silly. This was one game Mr. Watson always participated in and I'd hover in a corner to make sure he didn't get his hands on me. I knew he'd try to tickle me and my screams would give away my whereabouts and I'd be dragged off to the opponents' side of the room, thus helping my side to lose the game, and ending the game for me.

I have to confess that there were one or two boys with whom it was sort of understood that we'd grope around a bit in the crotch area and I'd even been hard with one or two of them briefly during the game and the only thing that kept us from exploring further was the thought that the light would go on at any moment. That was the fun. There was a referee-lightkeeper and when he wanted to count the captives, to keep score, he'd turn on the lights and you could be caught in very compromising positions. But I soon learned that it was one boy in particular who enjoyed exploring my body and we soon became good friends both in the scouts and outside.

His parents were Dutch and ran the local bakery. He was Artur Von Leer and was one grade behind me at school but bigger and the same age. All his family worked very hard, getting up at dawn to get the bread baked and the hard work had given him extraordinary muscles.

"Just feel *that*," he was always saying, flexing his biceps. "I can lift hundred pound sacks of flour from the truck with one arm."

We nicknamed him Justfeelthat and he took it with sweet good humor. But it wasn't just his biceps he wanted me to feel, nor was he remotely interested in my less developed arms. We'd meet in our garage when we could and make each other hard and compare those particular muscles. In that department we were on a more equal footing. His cock may have been a bit larger than mine, but I had the advantage in that I could come and he couldn't manage it yet. We both worked as diligently as possible, but it just didn't happen. He was very discouraged, but from my lofty mature position I calmed his fears explaining that it would just happen one day and everything would be all right. In the meantime, just keep trying. I even suggested that if he could find somebody to suck it for him—that had certainly helped *me*—it might facilitate matters, but good friends or no, I resolutely refused to help him to that degree.

Mom was having her hair done and I was feeding Becky one afternoon when I heard Artur calling me from the back door. "Come on in," I answered. "I'm feeding the baby."

The screen door on the back porch opened and slammed. Artur came bounding into the living room where I was sitting rocking Becky who was almost asleep with the nipple of the bottle just resting in her slack pink mouth. "I can do it, Carl!" he was all but screaming.

"Ssssh! for God's sake. The baby was almost asleep. Now look what you've done." I rocked her a little more vigorously as she rolled her eyes up to Artur and smiled at him from around her nipple.

"Oh. Sorry." He stood impatiently while I encouraged Becky to take her bottle and made soothing sounds to get her to go back to sleep. "But, Carl, I can do it," he whispered.

"Do what?" My attention was on Becky.

"Come! I can come!"

"Well," I looked up at him and grinned. "Today he is a man. Thank God. We don't have to worry about you any more."

"You want to see?"

"Sure." I was wiggling the bottle slightly and watching Becky's eyes dropping. She was almost off. Then I was aware of movement in front of me and the baby. I lifted my eyes only slightly and there it was, Artur's cock out, hard, and his hand pounding away on it practically in Becky's face. "For God's sake, Art, not *now!* Not in front of the *baby!* Are you crazy? She's a little *girl,* for Lord's sake!" I picked her up and ran out of the room protecting her gaze from what Artur was doing. This could mark her for life. I put her in her crib, propped the bottle on a pillow and smoothed the silken hair back from her brow. What an idiot Art was. What in the world was he thinking of?

"Carl! Carl!" he was screaming from the other room. "You're going to miss it! Hurry!" I walked back toward the living room hearing Art groan with pleasure before I got there. Oh God, now he's probably come all over the carpet! I ran the last few paces. "Oh Carl, look. You missed it. Oh *darn.*"

"*Where'd* you do it?" I was searching the carpet all around him for spots.

"Here. Here in this hankie. See? I caught it. You've got to see it so you'll know I'm not lying."

There was a damp spot on his handkerchief. "You say it's come, it's come. Could be spit, you know."

"Oh, Carl," he looked stricken. "I wanted you to be the first to know. Now you're kidding me."

"I'm sorry, Art. Just put your thing away. Give it a rest for awhile and when Mom gets back, we'll go to the garage and do a proper celebrating job. OK?"

"Oh God, yes," he sounded worn out. "I can lift dozens of sacks of flour, but I tell you, making myself come is the hardest work I've ever done."

"OK. I'll help next time." After all, what's a friend for?

The only thing left at the end of summer for most of the scouts to qualify for their tenderfoot badges was the required fourteen-mile hike. The plans had been made for weeks. There was an official Boy Scout camping site on the San Joaquin River out of town beyond Friant Dam. The property had been donated to the Boy Scouts of America by a rich rancher and was used by scout troops from all over the country. We'd get the hike under our belts and also fulfil other requirements for badges like campsite cooking, building fires, putting up tents, swimming, lifesaving, canoeing (there was a caretaker and plenty of equipment), tracking animals and map-reading.

I don't remember how I was chosen—eenie, meenie, minee, moe or by drawing straws, but I was. I won the envied opportunity to be credited for the fourteen-mile hike without having to walk it. All I had to do was to be driven to the site by one of the fathers along with all the heaviest equipment and guard it—from what, I wondered— until the hikers arrived. I was hooted and jeered at by the hikers. as I drove off seated grandly next to my chauffeur. As it turned out, I'd rather have done the hike on all fours. It wasn't that the pickup truck broke down every five minutes or we had flat tire after flat tire, it was just that my chauffeur got—in the words of the captain—pissed as a coot. We'd hardly got out of town before he stopped in front of a bar, hopped out with "I'll only be a minute" and left me sitting for forty-five minutes according to the clock in a Miller's High Life Beer sign in the window.

After the second or third bar stop, I fell asleep. When I woke up, we were joggling along a rutted lane heading down an incline with a wide muddy river just ahead of us. He stopped the car and got out.

"Well, here we are," he called to me. "Let's get this stuff unloaded."

We were about a hundred yards from the riverbank and the rutted lane had just petered out into low scrub with no clearing or buildings. It didn't look right. "Are you sure this is the place?" I asked as I took the pack he handed me off the back of the truck.

"Dead sure. This right here's the Boy Scout Camp. They told me so back up there. And this here's *it.*" He shoved a pack off the end of the truck with his foot. That seemed to please him. "Heh, heh, that's a helluva lot easier'n liftin' them fuckin' things." He kicked off another.

He had the truckbed empty in no time. He stood, weaving slightly and grinning with self-satisfaction. "There. Done my duty. Done my duty to the Boy Scouts of America! And to Eleanor Roosevelt!" He jumped over the side of the truck and was back in the driver's seat in a flash. "And now, to get the hell outta here!" He disappeared in a cloud of dust.

By the time I'd arranged the packs in a neater pile, it was getting late and chilly. The sun was in my eyes and getting lower in the west.

I walked back up the rutted track to where we'd turned off a country dirt road. To the right I saw a cluster of buildings. A farm. I took off, walking fast, watching the sun sink rapidly.

Just before I got to the house, there was a big wooden gate set into the barbed wire fence on two huge posts. The whole place looked deserted except for the sudden appearance of a ferocious snarling dog that looked the size of a pony streaking toward me with fangs bared. I was up the gate in one leap and with another quick adjustment was sitting on the gatepost with my feet pulled up and under me as the wild beast jumped up the post growling, snapping and drooling like a maniac.

He stalked the post, pacing around and around, growling deep back in his throat, glancing up at me with crazed golden eyes that showed bloodshot fiery red when he rolled them in a fury of frustration at my inaccessibility. I felt like a treed 'coon.

After what seemed hours I heard a car. It was Mr. Watson. He tamed the beast with a quick word and helped me off the post. My bones felt frozen in a crouched position putting me eye to red-eye with what was now a cuddly puppy. I wanted to bite him. I did manage a quick kick at him as I got into the pickup truck.

"What in the world happened to you?" Mr. Watson asked as we drove back to the unattended packs. "We've been worried sick."

I told him the story as he loaded the packs onto the truck. A numbing chill was fogging up from the river. I got a sweater out of our pack and at Mr. Watson's urging, stretched out on the seat while he secured the packs.

I was vaguely aware of my head being lifted onto something soft and the motor starting before I was dead asleep. The motion of wheels under me had its usual effect until I was slowly awakened by a different motion or movement. There was something burning my cheek, moving along from my chin up to my forehead, hot, like a fever, only hard and moving slowly against my face. I felt a hand holding the other side of my face, pressing the opposite side of my face against the hot object. Out of the corner of my eye I saw white flesh rubbing slowly, so close to my eye that it filled all my vision. The velvet smoothness was familiar. Oh, for God's sake! I jerked my head up and away. with a crash against the steering wheel. That, too, was familiar. I let out a yell, rolling forward over a leg and ducked around under the steering shaft to avoid the gearshift and covered my face with my hands muttering, ". . . been asleep . . . Oh, God. Banged my head." I kept my face covered because I didn't want to see what had been next to my face. "Wow! I can feel a goose egg. Oouuuweee . . . does that hurt!"

"Oh, sorry, Carl . . ." I could feel him putting himself away, straightening to zip up his pants and talking fast to cover his actions, ". . . you sleeping . . . I know what a day you had . . . you must be dead. I thought it best just to let you . . . Ah, it's right up there. The camp.

See? What an ass Mr. Larson is to have left you down there . . . How's
the head? Not hurt too bad?" He reached over and took one of my
hands down from my forehead where it had been rubbing what was a
sizeable knot.

"No." I didn't look at him. "It's all right. Just a bump." I wasn't
going to talk about it, it made me too sick. What in God's name was
he trying to do? My body remembered something in the way he'd
touched it when he tickled me. He was like Uncle Roy. And he made
me feel dirty in just the same way Unc . . . *Roy* had. Not only dirty, but
ashamed. Defiled in some way. Why should I feel such shame when it
was him—*he*, dammit. (Miss Widmer is always with me)—a grown
man, a *school* teacher—who'd been using my . . . using me . . . my *face*,
for God's sake. He'd been fucking the side of my face!

I was hailed as a hero by the troop when they were told how I'd
been lost, my life threatened by a starving hound, and how I'd stuck
by my responsibility. I made it sound just a simple mistake on the father's part so the boy wouldn't feel bad. The story of being treed by
the bloodthirsty beast I tried to make as funny as possible. I wanted
everybody to laugh a lot. I wanted everybody to like me. I wanted to
forget . . . I wanted to pretend that I was just like all the rest of them.
Why was *I* the one singled out for these obscene acts? What I'd felt
up till now had been more or less natural and normal. But the fun
with Miguel, Vic and Artur was taking on new dimensions. Was it
really just innocent fun? I didn't consider the thing with Ronnie
along with the others. That had been special. It was the first time and
had been tinged with . . . With what? It was Ronnie who'd used the
word "love." Where was the line to be drawn? So far, it had just been
games. With boys *and* girls. Games with people my own age. Grown
men weren't supposed to play kids' games.

The camp in the bright morning light proved anything but primitive. There were clean toilets and a shower room in a big central
building. A boathouse held half-a-dozen boats of different sorts,
there was a swimming platform with a ladder down to the water and
a diving board. This was hardly roughing it. Even the tent sites were
numbered and had cement paving with permanent metal rings to tie
down the support ropes. The tents spread out in all directions, on
different levels, making it like a little village.

Junior and I were preparing our breakfast over a roaring camp-
fire—started with everything but a flint stone—when we heard a low,
long, attention-getting yawn, an exaggerated series of vowel sounds

associated with morning stretching and flexing. We heard various boys call, "Mornin', Mr. Watson." Looking up we saw him outside his tent, stark naked, stretching elaborately, scratching his hairy chest and stomach, eyes squinting into the light as though he'd just found himself there in that spot unexpectedly and was just waking up. It was a palpably fake performance. He was so obviously showing off his nakedness that I averted my eyes in embarrassment for him but not before I caught a message to me in his eyes and an almost imperceptible command to "come here" with his head. Junior had caught it too and when our eyes met, Junior's told me to ignore the message from the scoutmaster.

I went on cooking with my heart pounding and wondering how much Junior knew or suspected about Mr. Watson. Had he ever tried the sort of thing with Junior that he tried with me? Juniors's eyes had told me to steer clear of Mr. Watson so he must suspect something. Or was he just embarrassed by the blatant display of his naked body as we all were? Did all men become hairy? I glanced down at my own bare leg. There was no question about it, the hair was getting darker and thicker. Oh God.

The day's schedule was so full that it wasn't difficult to avoid Mr. Watson, but it wasn't so easy to ignore the pleading look in Art's eyes.

"Hey, Carl," he said finally, "what's the matter? You haven't hardly spoken to me. I thought we were friends."

How could I tell him that the idea of touching myself, let alone him, filled me with such shame that I didn't even want to think about it. There it was. That was what had happened. A light dawned. Mr. Watson had poisoned our games. He'd turned them into something nasty. "I mean, somebody might tell the scoutmaster. You know, if they saw us . . ."

"They all do it," he said reasonably.

"Well, maybe. But if Mr. Watson . . ." How could I feel him out on the subject. "Hey, did you see him this morning? Mr. Watson? Naked up by his tent?"

"Everybody did. He acted like he wanted us all to see him." Art hadn't been fooled by the performance either.

"Well, what do you think? Do you think he does . . . oh, you know, masturbates or anything with the older boys?"

"Men don't do that," he said with authority. "Just boys. Just good friends. Not men. Not unless they're queers."

"Queers? What's that?" I wanted to know what Art knew about queers.

Art looked confused. "I'm not sure. My brother said he met one at the movies. He said the queer was trying to play with his thing."

"Your brother's thing?" Maybe we were getting somewhere.

"Yeah. I guess so." He looked thoughtful for a moment and then brightened. "I know. Cocksuckers are queers." Captain J had already pointed out that fact to me.

Where did it all leave me? At least I wasn't the only one men tried funny things with. Art's brother had had an experience.

Junior kept everybody entertained later in the afternoon by repeatedly turning over in a kayak. He'd take about four strokes with the double-ended oar and then lose his balance and over he'd go. He'd keep coming back up, spluttering and spewing water, but laughing and trying it again and again until I started getting worried. He was staying under too long. I called to him, making some excuse for him to come in. I knew he wouldn't on his own until he'd conquered the unwieldy craft. By dinnertime, his nose was running as fast as the river. He was blowing it every few minutes and sniffling constantly. The old trouble again.

"You OK?" I asked, trying not to let the sniffling get on my nerves.

"Yeah, sure. Just a bit of a headache. Stayed in the water too long, I guess."

"Did you bring those nose drops?"

"Naw. It'll be OK." He went on sniffling, but he also went on doing everything on the schedule with full energy and enthusiasm.

School started the week after our camping trip. I'd managed to get the fourteen-mile hike credit, plus a map-reading badge, a cooking badge, a huge blister on my heel from the walk back and a new set of guilts, thanks to Mr. Watson. The blister healed before school started, but the guilts festered and spread like a cancer. I slowly eased myself out of the Boy Scouts of America movement and blamed a heavy workload of eighth-grade homework for not seeing much of Art. My own necessities in that direction I took care of furtively in the locked bathroom, getting it over as quickly as possible, not caressing and watching but causing orgasm roughly, almost painfully so that the feelings of guilt afterward might perhaps fade more quickly. They didn't.

I threw myself at schoolwork determined to be the valedictorian of my graduating class, a thing Junior missed by going to a junior high school in Ventura. We certainly weren't in competition in chalking up honors, but I wanted as much recognition as I could get—God knows Junior was getting plenty. He was now playing shortstop—a much more important position than center field, the varsity baseball team. He was also trying out for the basketball team, he was still in the band of course, and was voted president of the sophomore class almost on his birthday in October. At sixteen, he was a big gun, but didn't seem to know it. The coach had come up to Dad after a game and shook his hand proudly.

"It's good to know the father of such a fine boy, Mr. Woods," the coach beamed and pumped Dad's hand. "He's one of the finest athletes I've ever had the privilege of coaching. He's a born one. They don't come along very often. I watched him last year and I knew then. That boy's got it."

"I'm proud to hear it," Dad said, beaming even more than the coach.

"I can tell you right here, Mr. Woods, that if that boy works the way I know he will, why, they'll all be up here after him in another year— Berkeley, UCLA, USC—all of 'em. Word gets around, you know, and when there's real talent, those college coaches are out sniffing around. He'll have scholarships dangling under his nose by the dozen." He chuckled. "Don't let him know I told you all that, Mr. Woods. Don't want him to get a big head. But then, he's not like that. He won't get a big head. He's just . . ." he stopped and thought. "He's just *well-rounded*. All-around good boy. What more can you say than that?" He grinned and slapped Dad on the shoulder and walked away, bouncing self-satisfiedly on his heels. Dad did some bouncing too after that little conversation. That look was rekindled in his eyes again. Not that it had been extinguished, just banked, and was now glowing. My boy's a star! He was more sure of it now than ever.

Becky had her first birthday party on November twenty-second. It was just family, but Mom had hired a photographer to come take her picture with her cake and one candle. She was round, sweet and the apple of everybody's eye, but continued to be my special property. I posed her for the pictures and then the photographer suggested one of all of us. He'd already taken the four Mom had contracted for, another would cost extra. We all looked foolish and shy but Mom said, "Come on. Let's do it. Lord knows when we'll have a chance to be together and all clean at the same time." The flashbulb caught us grouped around the dining table with the one candle in the cake relighted to make it look festive. It's the only picture we have of the five of us.

Money continued to be a very scarce item, but our Christmas was considerably more festive than the last one if only because of the surroundings. Our tree was tiny, no giant from B. V. Hollings and Son's ranch in Visalia, and had one string of electric lights that twinkled through our living room window out onto the front porch and looked just like the others along the street. More and more, we were fitting in. We'd been in the same house for almost a year. A record. What's more, a nice house, one none of us was ashamed of. Clovis, California, had become home, even though all the end-of-year cards and letters we got were from what we continued to call "back home." Our lives were here now. We were settled down and in. Work on Friant Dam was assured for at least another five years and Mom had been in contact with the California State Department of Education in Sacramento to see what she'd have to do to qualify for a teaching position here. I'd never felt so secure. Not even at the Joneses. The Depression was still firmly with us but Roosevelt's New Deal was finally showing results.

"Back home's" biggest news was that Grandpa Woods had remarried—for the third time—a widow who had a house in Oak Grove. One of the more stalwart of the Population 30. A Mrs. Gardiner and their Christmas card was signed "Grandpa and Aunt Lilly." Aunt Ed wrote to say that the lady was one of the most respected women in the county, and if not well-off, at least owned her house into which Grandpa immediately moved, having sold the place where Aunt Idy had died and had then sewn the money into his long johns, according to Dad, never to be seen again.

"He's the tightest man alive. That poor widow won't see a penny of that money. He'll be living off her, you can mark my words." He laughed fondly and shook his head. "And, she'll be cuttin' the wood for Mr. Woods' stove in the winter, you can bet your bottom dollar on that, too."

Aunt Ed's letter went on to say that Ronnie was doing very well in school—graduating this spring and it was hoped he'd enroll in the Theological Seminary in Springfield.

I snorted with laughter and Mom said, "There's about as much likelihood of Ronnie's becoming a preacher as there is in my becoming a nun."

"Why in hell do folks try to live their lives through their kids, anyway?" Dad asked. I turned slowly toward him, expecting to see a twinkle in his eye. There wasn't one. He wasn't joking.

Aunt Dell's letter was briefer than usual: I'm Mrs. Roy Blake. Legal. We in the A-hole of anywhere. Ajo, Arizona. Ah-ho-hole, Ari-hon-a. Ha ha. Love, Mr. and Mrs.

"That place sounds familiar," Junior said. "We passed a sign outside Phoenix . . . Oh, yes. I remember now. On the map there's even an Ajo Desert. Smaller than the Gila Desert. On the map it looked pretty bleak."

"Well," I said, "Aunt Dell sure doesn't seem to like it."

"That's because an asshole ain't big enough for Dell to fall down in," Dad said.

"Really, Woody," Mom said and giggled.

March came and a few days before it left, I became fourteen. I found it an extraordinary experience, like nothing that had happened before. It wasn't even a happening, nothing had happened. Yet. It was just the simple accumulation of years. I'd racked up fourteen! In four more years I'd be eighteen and graduating from high school like Ronnie would be doing in Missouri in May, a month before I'd graduate from grade school here. Then in two more years, I'd be twenty and then twenty-one. A *man*. All of a sudden I could feel my future inside me. It was there, ready to unroll like a carpet down which I could walk. Or perhaps even run. It was an exhilarating prospect. Dreams of dancing were still in there someplace, but slightly out of focus.

Junior was forced to cut down on his sports activities. He dropped out of basketball practice and spent more time on his music and poetry. He was sophomore editor of the yearbook and that took time away from the sports he loved but was finding more difficult to cope with. What we called a chronic cold continued accompanied by serious headaches. He seldom complained but when Mom asked him, he'd have to admit, that, yes, his head *ached*. Visits to the doctor were inconclusive—a touch of sinus, perhaps, but basically a strong healthy specimen. Baseball remained his great love and he worked doubly hard on that. He confessed to me that basketball was fun and he liked it, but all the running up and down the court somehow loosened up everything in his head and made breathing difficult.

"Well, as long as you've got baseball, the rest don't matter all that much," Dad said, not quite convincingly. We knew he looked forward to Junior adding football to his other sports in his third year of high school, making him a real triple-threat. The light in his eye glowed a little less brightly.

Mom had heard that she'd have to take a few education courses and a crash course in California history in order to get a teaching credential and she was already enrolled in Fresno State College for the summer semester which would begin in June when the current semester was over. All our futures were set.

About a month before school was out, Miss Widmer, my teacher, let me know in no uncertain terms that I'd better pull my socks up in the mathematics department if I expected to have the grades to be valedictorian. She was a great joker and I hoped she was joking when she said that, but I could see she wasn't. She was rooting for me, she made that clear, but there was a real kiss-ass in class—Jerry Papas— who was so studious it made you sick. He played the piano, he played the organ at church and he was playing hell with my chances at the prize I sought. I'd tried to be friendly with him when he arrived at midterm, but there was a streak of cunning in him that I found re- pellant, and I secretly gloated when our class bully zeroed in on him as he had on me in the seventh grade. I know I should have felt pity and understanding for his plight, but his skin was so thick, his self- assurance so complete that he didn't need anybody's help. He was formidable competition.

Junior helped me with my work as much as he could, but that seed of doubt Miss Widmer planted made me very unsure of myself. I kept trying to reassure myself that if I didn't get valedictorian, I'd natu- rally be salutatorian, but that's second best. It even looks and sounds second best. I wanted to be first.

It is undoubtedly unfair to blame my poor showing—I came in third—in the final exams on the telegram we got during that last week of school but it had—*has,* still has—a profound effect on me: Ronnie had been killed in a car accident. That was all the wire said and it left me stunned. Literally stunned. I bumped into things, I didn't hear people when they spoke to me, my concentration had huge holes in it—I found that I couldn't remember what I was doing or why I had moved from one room to another. I was in a trance of loss. I didn't know what grief was, as such, I just felt that something vital to my life in the future had been ripped away from me. That car- pet that was unrolling wasn't meant to be an empty one—there were supposed to be people, things, places on it and one of the people I saw there clearly, vividly alive, had been Ronnie.

Miss Widmer knew something was wrong—she took me aside after the first day's series of finals. "All right, Woods," she said jauntily. "What's the matter with you? You look as though you've been hit be- tween the eyes with a blunt instrument."

She could always make me laugh and did then. "Just terrified, I guess."

"Well, *stop* being." She jabbed me on the shoulder with her fist. The second day of tests she suddenly blurted out as we were all bent over our papers, "Hey, Woods! Do you know your eyebrows go straight up? You look like Fu Manchu bent over your desk." The class laughed, squirmed around in their seats and shuffled papers. She'd done that to snap my concentration back but she'd also broken the tension of the room. We were all trying too hard, or as in my case, not hard enough. She was a legend in the school. She was a superb teacher and I'd never felt I'd learned so much from anybody as I did from her. She was gruff, tough seeming, but acute to the point of reading minds. There was a big yellowish spot on one wall of the room that she pointed out with pride on the first day of school saying, "That is where one of the biggest navel oranges I've ever seen— or thrown—hit and splattered." She watched the bug-eyed class look up at the spot and then back at her. She grinned secretly to herself and I could swear that even that first day she sent me a sly wink. "It is probably best that I don't explain just why I threw that orange." She paused to great theatrical effect, "Or at whom." I fell in love with her everlastingly.

On the last day of tests, she roamed up and down the aisles like a lioness taking care of her cubs, willing us all to do well, sending out silent messages by just pausing over our shoulders and glancing down at our work. She snapped her fingers in a nervous rhythm when she got near my desk. It worked. I'd get the papers back in focus. Then, it would go. I didn't know to what extent she was watching me until a felt blackboard eraser hit me on the side of the head. I'd glazed over again.

"Woods!" she called. "Wake up!" She created a scene again to pull me up and relax the class. I looked up at her. She was sending me such waves of encouragement, egging me on, pleading to me with her eyes to work harder, harder, harder, telling me she knew I was better than I was being. There was an earnestness and unguarded concern for me in her eyes, an open look full of worry and consternation that bordered on love and reminded me so of Ronnie that I burst into silent tears and dropped my head on my desk, a collapse that was mercifully covered by the loud ringing of the end-of-class bell.

Chapter Twelve

THERE WAS A GATHERING STORM AT HOME that had been gaining strength without my being aware of it so that when it hit, the devastation was so great, the reverberations so far-reaching, that I became even more the sleepwalking victim of shock. It's amazing the destructive power of a sentence containing less than a dozen words. They weren't even screamed. They were spoken in a voice icy with rage and indignation and they shattered our nice little world. "I don't have to take that kinda' shit off nobody." We'd certainly heard it before, but it hadn't quite the ramifications or finality as this time around. With just another declaration of I-don't-have-to-take-that-kinda'-shit-off-nobody, Dad destroyed everything. Everything that even he himself had worked so hard to create. That we'd all worked and longed for. He crushed it. Left it in rubble and ashes. Willfully and defiantly as though this small—this *great*—step forward we'd made in our lives was nothing. I never quite understood what Brad had meant when he said he wanted to go back to Virginia and live like a human being, but as far as I was concerned, this was the first time we'd lived like human beings. For one year. Out of fourteen. Sixteen, for Junior.

Now it was back on the road. Back to bib overalls and backwoods tackiness. Ronnie had died trying to get out. Why were we going back? I knew we'd not saved any money. Dad's job had been safe and secure—until he decided to throw it away. We'd go back to Grandpa in Oak Grove said the man of the house. It had taken us four years to get a decent life started and now we were going back to square one. It didn't make sense.

"What's the matter with him?" I whispered to Junior in bed after the numbing news.

"I don't know. I just plain don't know. It doesn't figure. What have we been doing all this time? Why didn't we just stay in Oak Grove?" He was as bewildered as I.

"But Grandpa isn't even in his own house now. He's moved in with his new wife. We can't all just . . . Well, it's *her* house. We don't even know her. Where will we live?" We could hear Dad's raised voice coming from the living room. We lay and listened, not making out the words but chilled to the bone by the tone.

Dad went at the Model-A with a fury—ripping at its innards, flinging parts all over the garage as though the car were responsible for the rage we knew was against himself. Junior helped after school and by the time my graduation exercises were over the car had its valves ground, new spark plugs, gaskets replaced, oil changed, a thorough grease job and two new tires. We could have it packed in less than an hour. We hadn't been settled long enough to forget how things fitted in.

It was parked in the front, in the driveway being packed when a beatup pickup clattered to a skidding halt in front of the house and Mrs. Hollings jumped out. Mom went out on the porch to greet her. I stood just inside the front door.

"I've come to say goodbye, Mrs. Woods. Heard you folks was aleavin' us. Can that be right?" She looked around her confusedly.

"I'm afraid so, Mrs. Hollings," Mom said and I heard the sadness in her voice. "You are very nice to come see us. Come in . . ."

"Oh Lord, no!" she cackled. "Much too messy to go into a nice house like that." She looked down at her dirty old men's workshoes and the stained cotton dress. Her statement made me blink with recognition—Mrs. Hollings was echoing what Naomi had said some time ago when she'd stopped by to say goodbye—they were "movin on"—and had refused to come in.

"Can't shag in *there*," she'd gurgled huskily in her throat, waved jauntily and disappeared down the dark street, the streetlight picking up her blond, matted and stringy hair, making it look like a white fright-wig. Mrs. Hollings was also pretty frightful in broad daylight.

"No," Mrs. Hollings went on. "Just wanted to tell you how much we thought of you. Of you all. Not like them Strouds." Had our thoughts crossed? "Filthy folks. Left owin' rent, can you beat it?" She caught

sight of me at the door and I stepped out. "Oh, there you are Carl."
She rummaged around in a string bag she was carrying and pulled
out a flat package wrapped in brown paper. "Could this be for you? It
come . . . Oh, Lord, can't call it now. Some time ago anyway and I
couldn't hardly make out the name so I just flung it on a pile of stuff
on my desk and when I heard you'as goin' it started naggin' at me
. . ." I'd walked down the steps and took the package. "I had to get Syl
to try to find my glasses and then when I could *see,* I guessed it said
Woods on it. But the first part . . ."

"It's a joke, Mrs. Hollings. Just a joke. Thank you for bringing it."

"Mrs. Woods." There was great urgency in Mrs. Hollings's voice as
she took a step or two closer to Mom. "Come down here a bit. I've
just got to tell you." She looked around furtively as Mom moved cautiously down the three front steps. Mrs. Hollings suddenly leaned forward right in Mom's face, causing her to tuck her chin in and flinch
slightly. I thought Mrs. Hollings was going to kiss her but she hissed,
"I don't think I can go on without somebody knowin'. The game's
over. It ain't much fun anymore. Suppose I die and don't nobody
know?" She looked intently in Mom's face. "The B. V., Mrs. Woods.
The *B. V.* Somebody has *got* to know my name. I thought you'd be the
best one. You'll be leavin' so you won't tell anybody else here." She
moved in closer yet and I could tell that Mom was holding her
breath. "It's Boshahwa Victoria. That's the B. V. Ain't that somethin'?
Can you believe it?" She cackled with manic glee and relief. "Bosh-
ah-wa. Ever heard *that* before? Heh, heh. My daddy was a corker.
Bosh-ah-wa Vic-tor-ia." She grinned up at Mom. "That's *me.*" She
turned and sort of skipped back to her truck, calling over her shoulder, "Don't tell anybody! You hear? Not a soul. You're the only one
that'll know. Heh, heh." She started the motor and with her head
barely higher than the steering wheel careened away from our curb
and wove drunkenly down to the next corner and with horn blasting
took a wheel-squealing right turn.

Mom and I were both shaking our heads in disbelief. "As your father said, she's looney as a bird dog. Boshahwa Victoria. Really!" She
joined me on the porch. "Knowing her biggest secret may be too
heavy a burden for me to bear." She pointed at the package, "What
was that?"

"Oh, I only looked at the front. Somebody has written . . ." I
looked at the package more carefully. "Oh, *shit!*" I'd never said that
before in front of Mom. I turned and ran into the house, screaming
"Sorry" over my shoulder. On our bed on the back porch I looked at

the package addressed to "Major" Totsy Woods and knew who it was from. I couldn't figure out why he'd used that address until I remembered I'd sent a Christmas card from the Hollings Ranch saying that I wasn't becoming a tap dancer but was learning how to be a drum major.

I ripped open the frayed twine with which it was tied. It felt like cardboard stuck down in a brown paper poke. I pulled it out. It was a color photograph of Ronnie, all dressed up in a suit and tie—his graduation picture—hideously tinted except they'd got the blueness of his eyes right. He'd turned into a handsome grown-up man. I dropped it on my chest and closed my eyes. Those dark blue eyes filled my mind and I could hear the words in my head of Aunt Ed's follow-up letter to the wire: ". . . we don't know where they were going or what they were doing . . . Dorothy Hale said they told her they were going to California . . . Ronald was driving but it wasn't his car—that belonged to the other boy who wasn't badly hurt . . ." I picked up the cheap cardboard picture frame that had been treated to look like leather but looked exactly like what it was. On the back was scrawled, "How about this for tacky, Tots? But ignore it. You'll soon see the real thing. Am on my way!"

I don't know how long I lay there before I was able to get up, open my packed suitcase, find the shoebox and slip the picture into it. Not at the top. I didn't want to see him smiling up at me everytime I opened the lid. I put him at the bottom. Buried him at the bottom, put everything back in place and continued with the chore of packing the car. I, myself, could have been packed with cotton or plaster of Paris or sand or . . . or . . . well, *anything* that fills up empty spaces. There was nothing inside me. I was as hollow as a birch bark canoe. It occurred to me to wonder just how much jolting the body can take before it stops functioning, before that emptiness becomes so great that there's nothing inside to support the body. The expression, "Beat the stuffing out of somebody" came to mind. I understood that expression.

Nobody was very talkative as we left Clovis. I was aware that Junior kept folding and unfolding a road map and kept his eyes down on his lap, not looking out. I stared out my side, but saw nothing. Our first stop was to be Bakersfield. Mom's brother, Uncle Ralph, and family with whom we'd stayed in Oklahoma had finally made it to California. We found them after considerable searching, living in a suburb of Bakersfield in a cotton patch, having brought their style of living with them.

"Dryer'n a popcorn fart," Junior mumbled to me as we got out of the car to greet our uncle and aunt and cousins, all spilling out onto a dilapidated porch identical to the one they'd left in Oklahoma. Four years later and a couple of thousand miles to the west and what did they have? Just what they'd left behind. Or perhaps they'd brought it with them. It seemed inconceivable to me that they'd be content with so little progress. But then, look at us. What were we doing? We had flushed our progress down the only indoor toilet we had ever been able to call our own and were heading back to the same old uncertainties. Which was better? Bringing your poverty, the lowest possible living standard with you, or going back to it of your own free will. It was a toss-up.

"The only way I can sleep—if I can sleep—in this car now," Junior said as we both squirmed around trying to get comfortable for this endless night in what Junior had dubbed Calihoma, "is just sit up. But even sitting up, I can't straighten my legs out on this back-seat."

"That's what you get for growing so tall. Ouch! I seem to have done some growing myself. You'll be interested to learn that I'm being—darn, what's that word? Brad's word?—oh, yeah, *cornholed* by the gearshift."

This didn't get the expected laugh. As a matter of fact, he was silent so long I pulled myself up and looked over into the back. He was sprawled out, one leg stretched out on my side of the back with the other foot on the seat and the knee bent. He was leaning against his knee with his elbow. He looked into my eyes a long time before he spoke. "Do you know why I didn't want you to go to Mr. Watson's tent that time? You know, when he motioned with his head for you to come over?" I nodded and thanked God for the dark that covered my blush and the inadvertent dip and dart that my eyes did. "Well . . . it sounds kind of silly now. It seems years ago now, doesn't it?" He chuckled. "*Years.* Wasn't even a year. But already I feel that Clovis never existed. Know what I mean?"

"Oh Lord . . ."

"Anyway, that night at scout meeting—you were playing a drowned or drowning victim or something. Anyhow, he was giving you artificial respiration? Remember?" I nodded. "Well, for some reason, I don't know what it was . . . some way he had when he was straddling you . . . it wasn't something *actual,* it just gave me a creepy feeling, that's all." He moved around on the seat, switching positions before he went on. "I guess we know what cornholing is. God knows the guys at high school joke about it enough. But he—Mr. Watson—looked like he was doing it to you."

"Doing it?"

"Cornholing you. I know that's the position you have to get into for artificial respiration and all that, but there was just something about the way he looked down at you and then when he touched you . . . Oh, damn. I don't know. It just gave me the creeps, that's all."

Junior had noticed. It wasn't just my imagination. He'd been there protecting me. I made a noise in my throat and kept looking at him with my chin propped on the back of the front seat.

"I've heard that some people are like that . . . you know, men who like boys or . . . or even other men. I guess it's just something they can't help. Something went or goes wrong—maybe you can be born that way, I don't know. I don't think anybody *wants* to be like that. Would *choose* it. Would you? I mean, would you . . . could you imagine? Well, *doing* something with a man?" I was riveted, bug-eyed, staring at him. He was finally talking to me. Really talking and about *sex*. *Having* sex. I couldn't have interrupted even if I could have thought of something to say. I just shook my head dazedly. "Me either. It's just not natural. But then, it's not natural to lose your . . . to get sick like Brad. It wasn't his fault. He wasn't to blame." He snorted a rueful laugh. "Well, hell, it's not natural for me to have sinus or asthma or whatever. It's just a sickness like any other. Like maybe men liking boys is a sickness. Not anybody's fault. And say, well, just for argument that you'd—that when you got older, I mean when you got grown up and maybe you'd like men or boys . . ." I sat up straight with a great gasping intake of breath. "Hold it! I'm just saying that anything's a possibility—anybody can have a sickness, that's all I'm saying. Look at me, sniffling all the time. I know it drives you nuts. Me too, but I can't help it. Any more than Brad could help it. Or you, if it turns out that you . . . What I'm trying to say is that my sniffling doesn't make you hate *me*, you just hate the sniffling. I can't *hate* Brad because he turned out like he did. I couldn't hate you—I couldn't possibly hate you, no matter what you did. Or how you turn out." He threw his head back and laughed. "For God's sake, Tots, you were doing *something* pretty hot-diggedy-dang with Mary Ann when you were only six years old! God only knows what you've been up to since then. After all, Captain J recognized you as a sensual type—and don't think I didn't look that word up quick as a flash. I was even jealous that I wasn't sensual and sexy. He said you were sexy. I guess you are. Maybe you just can't help doing it when you get the chance."

"Haven't you ever done it?" I guess I'd spend my life trying to find out something about his private life.

"That's a personal and private thing." He laughed as he used his old self-protective line.

"I mean, you're sixteen. Surely you've had . . ."

"When I do," he said in the measured way we used when we recited, "God plants the seed . . ." "You'll be the first to know. I'll send you a telegram."

That meant the conversation was over. Deader'n a doornail. I buried my head in my pillow but sleep seemed far away after this talk. Lying quiet, hardly breathing, I tried to figure out exactly what Junior had said, was trying to say or intimate. Was it all some kind of warning? Did he have some suspicion about my future? Or was he just telling me that he was on my side, behind me and ready to understand me? That's all he meant, I'm sure. What more could I ask? Or need?

When I'd been still for some time, Junior spoke my name softly. "Tots?" I grunted. "I know that Ronnie was—well, he was somebody special. Special, particularly for you. I know that." He, too, was still for a long moment. "You were something very special to him. He told me. He loved you in a special way. Maybe even a . . . *strange* way, who knows? He told me he wished you were his brother."

"I'm glad he's not."

"Why do you say that?"

"I kinda' like the one I got."

"Thanks, pard." He laughed.

"Besides, who wants a dead brother?" I lifted myself up quickly. "I wasn't trying to be funny. What I meant was that if he was my brother well, he'd be . . ." I dropped my head back on my pillow. "It's bad enough, just having a half-cousin. A dead half . . . well, a dead *anything.*" I choked but swallowed it. Was Ron's love for me "special"? *Strange?* Something he couldn't help. He'd said he was sorry and he couldn't help what he'd done with me. Was that the sort of thing Junior was talking about?

"I know. I understood what you meant. Don't forget, I know you pretty well. And understand you better than . . . well, better than you think. Anyway, he loved you." He chuckled again. "He always said, 'Totsy's crazy, but he makes me laugh and I love him.' I guess he didn't have very many people to love. He was always lonely, I felt."

I knew Junior was making an effort to tell me a lot of things—that he loved me too—most of which I understood. At least I understood enough to make a vow not to do anything he'd be ashamed of. That I'd be ashamed to talk to him about. If he was going to be willing to understand everything about me, the least I could do was to make all my actions understandable. And acceptable.

After a pause, I said, "He was on his way to see us. I think he was running away from home. He didn't much like being a hillbilly." I sighed. "I'm not sure I'm going to like it much myself."

He leaned over the seat and put his hand on my hair and sort of patted it. "I'm sorry, Tots. Sorry about poor Ronnie. It doesn't seem fair. It makes me sad. I liked him too, you know." He took a fistful of hair and squeezed it lightly. "But I know that . . . I know that the accident really knocked you for a . . . loop." He squeezed my hair again. "I'm sorry, Tots."

The Mojave Desert outside Bakersfield was an inferno in mid-June. By August you'd have to scrape your melted car off the black-top with a spatula. But not even the oven-dry air dried up Junior's draining sinuses. He tried everything, leaning out the window, letting the air blow directly in his face, or leaning his head back on the seat so the air could penetrate his nostrils, but everything seemed to cause him more discomfort.

"If the air comes in too fast," he explained, "it just seems to go right up here—right behind my eyes—and gets a firm grip on that steel band that goes around here," he'd gesture around his entire head, "and tighten it until it feels as though my head'll crack open."

"Do you want some more aspirin?" Mom said.

"No. No thanks. They don't seem to help all that much. It'll be all right."

Having Becky in the backseat with us didn't help the heat situation. She was bright red from the heat, cranky, cross and decidedly unlovely. Even to me. Mom and I kept shuttling her from the front seat to the back. It cooled off a bit in the San Bernardino Hills, but not much. By the time we got to Needles and the Arizona border in dark early evening, we were able to breathe but were limp with fatigue and heat. The car had hummed along beautifully, not even over-heating. You had to hand it to Dad, he could grind a mean valve.

Over the border into Arizona we spent the night in a motor inn because of Becky. Her misery was contagious and we all wanted a bath and a comfortable sleep. We got to Phoenix the next day.

"Back in mud-dauber land," Junior said, pointing out the familiar air-conditioners. "But some are getting pretty fancy. Look at that one. And that." They were sleekly designed metal boxes that fitted into the lower part of the windows, not disfiguring the houses like the makeshift ones do.

We skirted downtown Phoenix and were headed south toward Gila Bend back on the familiar main road we'd taken to California. How long ago? Almost three years? We'd made a full circle, a three-year circle—picking up a baby sister along the way—and were purring down the same road as if we were going to do it all over again. We were in roughly the same position we'd been in the last time—jobless, all but penniless, uprooted, unsure of our future beyond the stay-over with the next relative. This time it was Aunt Dell we were headed for and—I'd better get used to it—*Uncle* Roy just after this next turnoff toward Ajo at Gila Bend, down through the Ajo Desert.

It was really desert, reddish sandy earth supporting only the occasional cactus plant with odd rocky formations jutting up out of the flat terrain, creating lovely patterns of color and shapes. As we got nearer the town, we could see off to the right a huge hole cut into the side of a hill, miles wide at the mouth with roads or levels circling down into the earth like a giant corkscrew where the copper was being strip-mined. Hundreds of caterpillar earth movers far enough away to look like toys were scraping away at the red earth and then lifting it into dump trucks, which formed a constant moving line like a train curling back up the corkscrewed opening in the earth, filling the sky with dust and dirt.

"Can't leave well enough alone, can they?" Junior murmured. "Got to ruin everything. Maybe Aunt Dell was right. Ajo's just a big asshole."

The town was a few miles on from the mine and laid out on a flat plateau cut into perfect sections as though it was a plate of fudge. Straight lines intersected straight lines in which almost identical houses were set, all shaded by dusty palms, tamarisks or eucalyptus. We followed Aunt Dell's written instructions and found one of the main streets fairly easily—Caliente Road—but after that it was a lesson in frustration. The unpronounceable Mexican names had Dad swearing and cussing, doing U-turns where they were most definitely not allowed, backing up to trap some poor pedestrian who inevitably was deaf, dumb, blind and had just that minute arrived from Mexico and spoke no word of any known language. Fuming with frustration he ordered Junior out of the car with Aunt Dell's letter and orders not to come back until he could direct us to her street without a hitch. Dad's moods were unpredictable at best, but this display of impatience and anger had us all looking down at our hands with embarrassment. Even Becky seemed to understand the tension and sat quietly watching Junior go from one shop to another, stop people in the street, listen to gesticulated directions, nod vaguely and move on. He was obviously not going to risk coming back to the car until he was absolutely sure that he understood the way.

He was smiling broadly when he did come back. "It's just around the next corner," he said laughing, trying to lighten the mood, "then the second on the left." He gave me a I-hope-to-God-I'm-right look. He was. And we spilled out of the car to a loud and loving welcome from Aunt Dell who came running down the slanting cement walkway to the car.

"For Christ's sake, Dell," Dad called, all good humor restored, "don't fall down on your own property. That won't do you a damn bit of good."

"Only rented, you knucklehead," she screamed as she threw her arms around Mom. "And I can't wait to soak this damned landlord. God knows he's soakin' us enough for the rent."

Laughter, hugs, greetings, baby Becky the center of attention as we moved up the sloping walk, not noticing Uncle Roy standing on the porch until we neared the steps that led up to it. He was grinning down at us, pale blue eyes twinkling with pleasure—he was family now, welcoming family. I was eyeing him warily when behind him the screen door flew open and out flew Sister. We were all dumbfounded—she was supposedly in Phoenix working. I let out a whoop of joy. We were all wrapped up in each others' arms and talking at once.

"Let's git inside," Aunt Dell yelled above the din, "before the neighbors know for sure that this house is occupied by a bunch of nuts. I know they've been suspicious ever since we moved in."

By the time Junior and I unpacked the car, Aunt Dell had the down-home Woods Pow-Wow in full cry. As usual, that meant everybody bunched together in the kitchen screaming and laughing. Dad and Roy at the table with whiskey and mix bottles arranged in front of them, beer opened for Aunt Dell, cokes for me and Junior, and Sister sipping what she called a Scotch-on-the-rocks. Mom was feeding Becky her pablum and some Gerber's goop while we caught up on Sister's news first.

She was more beautiful than ever and known all over Phoenix now as Dolores Del Ozarkio. "Totsy," she laughed, "you remember that crazy bartender at the Tucson Hotel? Jim? Well, you can imagine it was him who gave me the name." She pretended to make a joke of the reference to her resemblance to the magnificent Dolores Del Rio but she did everything she could to accentuate the similarity. She wore her dark hair pulled back in what she tried to describe as a chignon but after mangling the pronunciation a couple of times, smiled and patted her "bun." In the evening, she often wore exotic Spanish combs, carved and bejewelled, not so much to secure the bun as ensure long appreciative glances from men. She didn't really need the combs for that. She'd also decided that black or white suited her dramatic looks best and rarely wore colors. She'd changed jobs—The Ship had sunk in a sea of financial troubles—and was now working in that bar at the Tucson Hotel with the crazy bartender. She was the only cocktail waitress. "I all but run the place."

"She was runnin' it around the clock when we'as there," Aunt Dell yelled over her shoulder from the stove where she was frying up hamburger patties, "and I figure she must be the cleanin'-up woman too since we never saw her for days on end."

Sister rolled her eyes. "Momma, like I've told you, there's rooms up on the top floor for the staff and when the bar has a good lively bunch that don't leave till . . . oh, sometimes till four or five in the mornin', well, you can bet your life I'm so dead on my feet that I'd have to call an ambulance to get me home."

And Mavis? "Aaaahhh, my God!" Aunt Dell really screamed this time. "She done it! Mean-hearted girl. She went and made me a *grand*mother. And just when I'as gettin' married! Made me feel kinda wicked standing there sayin' 'I do' knowin' I was a grandmother. Indecent is what it was."

"Oh, was it now?" Uncle Roy winked at Dad.

"Weeeelll," she actually blushed. "You know what I mean." She flipped a patty over. "Anyway her and George's doing real well. Hell, they got them a place out there where you was. Out North Twelfth Street. It's a new development. For young couples on the go. And that George is so much on the go, he's almost gone!"

Junior's phenomenal size at sixteen was discussed at length along with his sports' career. He and Roy stood back-to-back to check heights, and Junior looked a smidge taller.

"And Roy's got on cowboy boots. With *heels,*" Sister pointed out. "Listen Big Boy," she said running a finger along Junior's still relatively beardless cheek, "you can have a free drink in my bar any ole time." Junior blushed. "But Totsy," Sister frowned and smiled at me at the same time. "Just look at that one. He's filling out pretty good, but not gettin' all that much taller."

"Might be goin' to root," Aunt Dell called and laughed her most raucous. I seemed to be the only one who hadn't got the joke.

Mom went into the living room where she and Dad and Becky were to sleep. The couch let down into a double bed, hard as sleeping on the floor, but Mom said she could sleep anywhere after the days on the road.

By the time Mom got back to the kitchen, having got Becky tucked in, we were all stuffing ourselves on hamburgers with all the trimmings. The booze bottles had been replaced with the familiar mustard, Hellman's Mayonnaise, pickalilli, sliced onions, lettuce, tomatoes and slices of Kraft cheese and a contest was on to see who could make the tallest sandwich. The construction wasn't the main point; you had to be able to get it into your mouth and take a neat bite. We were anything but neat. We were all covered with meat juice, sauces, tomatoes, all running down our arms, messier than a Fourth of July picnic.

"I think I'd better go jump into the bathtub," Junior said, holding his arms up in front of him like a doctor who'd just performed a rather bloody operation. "I'm beyond napkins." He excused himself and went to the door. "Tots, come here and open the door. I don't dare touch anything."

"Real pigs, both of 'em," Aunt Dell said proudly.

At the door Junior whispered, "Come up with me," in an urgent voice. I opened the door and flung an "Excuse me, too" over my shoulder. I followed Junior up the stairs to the bathroom and opened the door for him. He headed for the sink and put his hands into it and I went up beside him and turned on the water. I glanced up at us in the mirror and he was as white as a sheet.

"Good heavens! What's the matter with you? You going to be sick?"

He closed his eyes and swallowed hard. "I don't know. I just feel funny all over." He reeled slightly and had to support himself on the edge of the sink. I took hold of his waist, thinking he might need to be steadied if he were going to throw up. He took a deep breath and straightened up and opened his eyes. "Wow! I never felt like *that* before. I thought I was going to faint there for a minute."

"Are you all right now?"

"I guess so. Mostly it's my damned head." He rubbed his temples and shut his eyes again. "Back up in here. Behind my eyes. It hurts so much I think I'm going to keel over."

"Should I call Mom?"

"Lord no. I may be just a bit tired. If I could just lie down."

"Look. You clean up. I'll get your peejays out of your suitcase and bring 'em to you. Get ready for bed and then just . . . well, *go* to bed. Our pallet is in the dining room there across the hall from where Mom and Dad's sleeping. I'll be right back." I flew down the stairs and into the dining room that looked as though it were used more for an office than a place to eat. Aunt Dell had an old mattress on the floor up against one wall, neatly made up with clean sheets for us. I found the peejays and dashed back up the stairs to the bathroom. Junior was standing up in the tub, drying himself, with his back to me. He'd have to be dying before he'd face me naked. "Here, put these on. I'll just tell them that you were feeling funny and thought you'd better lie down. Just tiptoe down the stairs and go in there. Nobody'll really know. Least of all Dad and Roy—*Uncle* Roy—they seem to be getting quite a buzz on."

"Yeah, I noticed. Aunt Dell isn't doing too badly, and that's not just beer in her glass. The Pow-Wow's heating up." He tried to laugh, but a flash of pain creased his face. "OK. I've got my stuff bundled up. Let's go."

He crawled into the pallet and eased himself back with a sigh. "Do you want me to turn off the light? Or are you going to read?"

"Nah," he said frowning up into the single light hanging down over the table with an old-fashioned fluted glass shade which diffused the light around the room. "Turn it off, I guess. It's right for reading only if you're sitting at the table."

"OK. 'Night." He just wasn't himself. Well, nobody had made much sense for the last couple of weeks. Dad erratic. Mom stoic. Junior feeling rotten and looking it, but giving into it wasn't like him.

Where the hell ya' been, Tots," Dad roared when I got back to the kitchen. The food had been removed from the table and the bottles were back in place and from the looks of it, a good drinking session was in the works.

"Putting my baby brother to bed. He says to excuse him, but if he didn't lay down, he'd fall down." Noises of commiseration came from all directions but Mom came up to my side.

"Is he all right?" She looked worried. "Is it the headache again?" I nodded.

"Tots," Dad called again roughly. "Get your ass over here and go get us some mix. We run out of 7-Up and ginger ale." He was scrabbling around in his pockets and brought out a wadded dollar bill which he tossed onto the table. "There's that little store Junior went in, remember. Just down there around that corner."

"Oh, Tots, if you're going out . . ." Mom turned away from me. "Dell, where's a drugstore? I want to get some more aspirin for Junior. Is there one close by? He's getting that awful headache again."

Uncle Roy was on his feet gathering up the empty bottles in his arms. "Come on, Tots. I'll take you." I glanced around the room frantically. I hadn't been alone with him since the lecture on the care and feeding of Levis. Didn't anybody know that I didn't want to go anywhere with him? Junior would've got my message and come with us. "That little store, Woody, won't be open now. Tots don't know the way. I'll show him where the drugstore is, Milly."

"Oh, thank you, Roy."

"Here, Tots, get your finger outta your butt . . . take some of them bottles there and help Roy." Dad's head of steam was more apparent than anybody else's. I glanced toward Sister for help, but she just flashed her magnificent smile encouragingly leaving me to fill my arms with bottles and follow Roy out the back door.

Backing the car down the sloping drive took all Roy's concentration and once out onto the street in front of the house, he turned in the opposite direction we'd come on arrival. I had the feeling that the town was back in the other direction. I scooted over near the door and sat forward on the seat, peering out with exaggerated interest at the passing houses.

"They's a little store down here, just on the outskirts that's open pert' near all the time," Roy said in his even voice.

"Oh. I thought town was back the other way."

"Yep. It is." Within five or six blocks, the houses dwindled into vacant lots, the street lamps became farther and farther apart until there weren't any. I glanced at Roy. "Just down here to the end—it's a dead end—then we cut over to the right to Caliente Road going out of town in the other way than you all come in on. He came to the dead end and turned left, pulled over to the dark curb and stopped the car. He sat back and sighed and looked at me with a slight grin. "Well, have you?"

My heart was pounding. "Have I what?"

"Gone to root?" He saw the confused look on my face. "Here," he said, putting his hand on my crotch. It was so sudden and unexpected that I could do nothing but bend over slightly to protect myself. "Relax," he chuckled. "I just want to see if Dell was right. See how much your root has grown . . ."

"Oh, I see. That's what the joke . . ."

"'Go to root' means when all your growth goes . . . well," he squeezed the lump under his hand which was getting hard in spite of itself, "here. Like a turnip, say, that ain't growing very much greens, but once the root is pulled out, well, you got the best part." He was expertly unearthing my turnip. His left hand was still on the steering wheel, the fingers of his right hand worked faster than Grandma Idy's when she was crocheting. In seconds I was exposed and he was feeling the length of it. I was still bent over glancing around to see if we were being watched. The streets were deserted. His hand eased up to the top of my cock and continued up my belly where it exerted pressure to ease me back in the seat. Not much pressure was needed, I was feeling faint in the way he'd made me feel the first time. Because there had been a first time apparently gave him free access to my body. I leaned back as I felt his left hand take over the task of undoing my belt and top button and then lifting out my balls as I raised my bottom to make it easier for him. As I pushed my hips forward, I heard a little groan of pleasure in his throat as he leaned over gently and took me in his mouth. I think I did faint. This hadn't happened since Victor. My God, how long ago was that? But this mouth was expert. I hadn't felt anything like it since . . . well, since Roy. The little noises of purring pleasure continued in his throat but not for long. I came with a shudder that started into my groin from my toes and I bit my fist to keep from shouting as his devouring mouth worked on me with experienced facility.

I lay limp, drained and tingling deliciously and he slowly licked me clean and put me back into my shorts and trousers, murmuring like a child finishing off an ice-cream cone. "Yeah-up," he whispered. "That's been growin' just about right.

Uuuummm-mmuuummm. You are turnin' into *some*thin' . . ." he muttered under his breath.

My hand was shaking as I handed Mom the aspirin after I'd almost dropped several bottles I'd carried into the kitchen from the car. "We had a little trouble finding an open drugstore."

"Just never know in this town." Roy was taking over again as host, opening bottles, offering drinks and pouring them. "They's two or three drugstores, but they take turns stayin' open after eight. Never know which one it's goin' to be." He got the ice pick and hacked away at the block of ice in the top of the icebox. "Who needs more ice? Milly? What are you having?"

Everything back to normal. Roy hadn't sucked my cock in the car. I apparently hadn't changed enough physically since this last knee-melting experience for anybody to take particular notice. My certainty that it showed all over me was just imagination fired by guilt. Why was there always so much guilt. I hadn't done anything but have an orgasm. Just another biological function. The only problem was that I hadn't precipitated it. That was the problem. God knows there's enough guilt attached to a simple lonely hand-job but the guilt with Roy weighed on me too heavily. It was all out of proportion. After all, coming was coming, wasn't it? No matter how? The truth was beginning to penetrate; the guilt was magnified in direct proportion to the amount of enjoyment I'd had. The guilt, consequently, was overwhelming.

I'd known deep down from that first time with Ronnie that it was wrong. Wrong and sinful. As Junior said, unnatural and sick. Was *considered* wrong. By everybody. Particularly wrong for a man and a boy. And sin, as we all know, is always punished. Somehow, sometime. Would I eventually be punished? If so how?

A thought suddenly struck me that sent a shiver so powerful through me that my whole body reverberated like the taut wire twanged on a bow when an arrow has been shot: Had Ronnie been punished? By *death*? For sucking my cock? I glanced around at the members of the Woods' Pow-Wow with alarm. Had anybody noticed my shivering convulsive movement? I could have sworn the chair danced under me. There were some whose eyes were so bleary they wouldn't have noticed any movement short of a cartwheel. Why was I so sure that Roy was so experienced at it? Just because he was so good at it? If he'd been doing this for—how old was he? forty-five? fifty?—several years, surely he'd have been punished some way or another by now. After all, he was a grown man, he knew what he was doing. Ronnie had been an accident. Ronnie and I together had been an accident. He'd said he was sorry. He apologized with all his heart. We were just two boys who love each other—*loved* each other—surely God didn't think that was punishable. Even if He did, it wouldn't, couldn't deserve a death penalty.

The conversation at the table ranged over all the well-known subjects. Grandpa's marriage, Dell's marriage, Mavis's *successful* marriage to her *successful* lawyer who was handling a case this very minute for Sister. When questioned, Sister pooh-poohed it as some silly technicality about a permit or license for working in a bar. Then hard times, harder times and hardest times were gone into in-depth. By the time it was going full circle for the third time I caught Mom's eye and she nodded, wishing me a silent good night.

I had a bath and got into the bed with Junior. It was an inferno. *He* was an inferno, giving off enough heat to burn. I felt his forehead and his cheeks as I had with Becky when we thought she might have a temperature. This was more than a temperature, this was red-hot burning flesh. I was afraid to turn on the light for fear I'd see him covered with blisters. He was moaning softly and gasping for breath as though he were being choked. I ran down the hall and eased the kitchen door open a crack. Mom was facing the door. My wriggling fingers caught her attention and she got up quickly and came to the door and out into the hall, closing the door behind her.

"It's Junior," I whispered. "He's on *fire*. He's so hot . . ." Mom was running down the hall and was in the room and on her knees on the mattress beside him before I came through the door.

"Oh God, oh God," she murmured, feeling him all over, holding his hands in hers and rubbing them and then she put her hand on his heart and snapped it back as though that were the central hot point, where the fire in his body was coming from. "Doctor. We've got to get a doctor . . ."

She was out in the hall again headed for the kitchen. When she opened the door I heard Dad saying for the umpteenth time, ". . . that kinda' shit from nobody . . ."

I stayed just inside the door of our room, not wanting to leave Junior and yet feeling that I ought to do something. Aunt Dell flashed past me down the hall on the run and out the front door. I could see her in the light from the front porch, running across the street, surprisingly sure on her feet. Mom came back into the room, brushing past me with a glass of water and a pan of water with a cloth in it. She was back on her knees on the mattress, speaking softly to Junior, "It's me, son, Mom." She had her arm under his shoulders trying to lift him up. I ran over and jumped across him to the other side and fell on my knees and pulled him up into a semi-sitting position. "There," Mom said. "Better. Can you hear me?"

"I . . . can't . . . get any . . . air . . ." he let the last word out with a gasp.

"Here, honey. Take a sip of this." She held the glass to his mouth and he drank thirstily. "Good. Good. Now . . . just wait a minute. Take it easy. Breathe deeply."

His eyes fluttered open and he pulled himself upright and put both hands on his head. "Whoooeee!" He shook his head slightly and looked around him. "Wow! Is this house on fire? I've never been so hot in . . ."

"Here, take these." She held up her hand with two aspirins on her palm. "It's just a temperature. These'll knock it out." He took them and put them on his tongue and tilted his head back as she put the glass to his mouth again. "Drink. Drink it all down. There. Totsy, are all the windows open?" She glanced around her at the draperies that covered the three windows that created the bay. I ran to them and jerked at the curtains. The windows were open a bit, but I pushed them up further. As I did, I saw Aunt Dell coming back across the street with a man in a dressing gown carrying a little black bag following her. She was talking animatedly at him over her shoulder.

"Here comes Aunt Dell," I told Mom. "She's got somebody with her."

"She said there was a doctor across the street." She stood up and opened the door fully and made little gestures of straightening her hair and her dress as the front door banged against the wall and Aunt Dell ushered in the doctor.

". . . in here, Dr. Hillsbury . . . my nephew . . . they all just come down from California today . . . and then . . . oh, this is his mother, Milly Woods. Milly, Dr. Hillsbury . . . We don't know what it could be . . ."

"Excuse me, Mrs. Woods," the doctor said. "He's in here?"

Mom backed away from the door as the doctor entered. She shot me a look and I left the room and closed the door on the three of them, bringing myself face to face with Aunt Dell. She grabbed me by the shoulder and we walked back down the hall to the kitchen.

"Where'n hell'd everybody go . . ." Dad was as drunk as I'd ever seen him. "We'as all just a-sittin' here and . . ."

"*Shush,* Woody," Aunt Dell ordered. "Lower your voice. The doctor's here."

"Doctor?" he tried to stand up, but got his leg tangled up with his chair and dropped back into it. "Did you say doctor? What the fuck . . . who needs a doctor, for Christ's sake . . ."

"*Woody,* for God's sake." Aunt Dell was in total command and seemed totally sober. Roy was looking bleary, but not quite as out of control as Dad. Sister was nowhere to be seen. "Junior's *sick.* Got a ragin' fever. I jest been acrost the street . . . Dr. Hillsbury. Nice man. I don't know how good a doctor he is . . ." she was whispering now and looking over her shoulder at the door. "But he's good enough for a fever . . ."

"What the hell do you mean? Junior ain't sick." Dad was having trouble focusing his eyes. "He's the healthiest goddamned kid in

California . . . his coach says so. Why he's goin' to be the biggest god-damned baseball player . . ."

"Woody, will you hush up, dammit." Dell slapped the table with the flat of her hand. Dad pulled back in his chair. "Now just hush up. I'm goin' to make some coffee . . ." She turned toward the stove. "Tots, would you help . . ."

Hot coffee was steaming on the table where the glasses and bottles had been. All was tidy and neat. Dad looked stunned—stunned or shocked into silence. We all kept watching the door. They'd been in there for ages. I risked tiptoeing out into the hall on the pretext of checking on Becky. I listened at our door and could only make out a soft rumble of a male's voice and occasionally Mom's with short concise sentences. Her voice didn't sound right. I went back to the kitchen.

By the wind-up alarm clock near the icebox, I saw that it was after twelve. The doctor had come at eleven. We heard Mom's voice out in the hall. I ran to the door and opened it in time to hear Mom saying, ". . . so sorry to have disturbed you this late, Doctor. We certainly appreciate everything you've done. Thank you again. We can settle all this . . ."

"Oh, my dear Mrs. Woods . . ." he made a deprecatory noise, half laugh, half cough. "I'll drop back in the morning."

"I'm sure he'll be better. Why don't we just leave it for the time being? We'll let you know."

"Fine, Mrs. Woods. He's a fine boy. He'll be all right. Good night."

"Good night to you, sir. Should we have somebody go along with you?"

"Oh, dear me no." He chuckled down the stairs. "I at least know my way home."

Mom stood at the door, watching him go, her back stiff and straight. When he'd got to the sidewalk, she closed the door with a slight slam. "Stupid man!" she muttered as she turned and walked toward the kitchen where all of us waited for news. "A quack!" she said when she got into the kitchen. She noticed a frown on Aunt Dell's face and put an arm around her shoulder. "Oh Dell, it's not your fault that he made me nervous. I'd just like to get somebody else's opinion. Who's the best doctor in town?"

"There's two new young'uns at the new hospital. Just opened a couple of months ago. Most modern equipment. Everything." She sounded as though she could hardly wait to be in it.

"We'll take Junior up there tomorrow morning . . ."

"Now, just a minute," Dad was on his feet. "What was wrong with . . . whatever his name was? You don't know him. How come you up and call him a quack? Dell's been here long enough . . ."

"I called him a quack, because he is," Mom snapped. I'd never seen her eyes blaze like this before. The brown had turned black and glittered. "For one thing he said Junior had a heart condition. The most idiotic thing I ever heard."

"You know better'n a doctor?"

"*I know my own kids, Woody,*" she was blazing with fury. "There's nothing wrong with Junior's heart. But there's something wrong. The temperature and the racing pulse . . ." she stopped and shook her head. "Must be some sort of infection."

"Dr. Milly . . ." Dad started sarcastically.

"You bet your ass I'm Dr. Milly." She spat out each word through clenched teeth. "Where my kids are concerned *I'm* in charge. I used that stupid expression so that perhaps even you'd understand. It's the only language you seem to be able to speak." She turned and left the room trembling with rage and went into the room with Junior. I followed her. I stood just outside the door and saw her slump down to the mattress on her knees again and then slowly she leaned her head over into her lap and her shoulders shook with silent sobs that seemed to be fighting each other for release. I waited for what seemed hours at the door for her to calm down, but she continued to be racked with a bottomless well of sorrow. Her curved, silently heaving back was the saddest thing I'd ever seen. I couldn't stand it. She looked broken, defeated. No, she looked *crushed*. Crushed by a weight at once invisible but real, resting on her bent and trembling shoulders. I was horrified at the spectacle of her iron control deserting her. I turned and closed my eyes and realized that tears were streaming down my cheeks. I could hear Aunt Dell trying to calm Dad who'd finally realized that his wife had given him a taste of his own medicine. He was not taking it well. I doubt if he'd taken her sharp words well even if he'd been sober. His unimpeachable position as head of house had been questioned—she was perfectly capable of taking care of her family without him and he knew it. That was what hurt the most. Perhaps it was time he got hurt. He'd been inflicting the pain long enough.

I darted out the front door onto the front porch, turning off the light as I did so. I heard Aunt Dell guiding Dad across the hall into the living room where Becky was sleeping. I only hoped his drunken roaring wouldn't wake her. I knew Mom wanted to be alone with

Junior and her sorrow. I went to the porch swing and got as comfortable as I could and was asleep in seconds.

The desert sun, a red ball of fire at dawn burned through my eyelids, leaving sharp blue flashes like echoes of acetylene torches glanced at without a protective mask. I turned my back, falling into a second deeper sleep.

Becky woke me the next time, standing beside the couch in the living room pulling on my nose and hair and gurgling with delight. I vaguely remember being carried down the hall and deposited on the opened-out couch. By who? *Whom.* Miss Widmer's voice was one thing from Clovis that I'd have with me always.

I remembered now. It had been Dad, smelling of shaving soap mingled with stale whiskey, who had picked me up from the porch swing. I sat up quickly and hugged Becky to me. Uuuggh! Her diaper was a study in what diapers were for—in full technicolor. I pushed her back from me and she grinned beguilingly "Becky," she pointed to herself and wrinkled her nose, *"phew . . ."*

"I'll say 'phew.' More than that, little lady. You *stink*. Come on." I grabbed her under the arms and swung her up the stairs in front of me to the bathroom. I kicked the door open and let out a cry of surprise. Roy was standing there naked at the sink shaving. "Oh, sorry . . . I'll get her out. I didn't know there was anybody . . . I just woke up." I was back in the hall, thankful that he hadn't turned around. I couldn't go on subjecting Becky to naked men. And he was one naked man I most certainly didn't want to see myself.

"It's all right," he called. "I'll only be a minute."

I bent down in front of Becky and started unpinning the revolting diaper—folding it over on its contents with practiced hands, as I wiped her with the small uncontaminated corners. I still wasn't awake. The events of last night filled my mind and I found myself calling out to Roy even though I'd vowed not to talk to him unless absolutely necessary. "Where is everybody? The house is so quiet."

"Dell's gone off with Woody and Milly to take Junior up to the new hospital. They left almost at daylight." He appeared in the doorway with a towel wrapped around his waist. "Looks like Junior's havin' trouble. Milly said he'd had a bad night."

"Bad night? How bad?" I kept my eyes on Becky.

"Seems she couldn't break the fever. She'as up with him all night."

"Oh God. Well, I hope it's just a . . . If I could get in. Becky's got to be cleaned up."

"Go right ahead. All yours." He did a sort of little dance step and bow as he motioned us into the steamy room.

"Thanks." I lifted Becky into the old tub, high up on clawed feet and turned the water on, drowning out further conversation. I busied myself with dumping out the diaper into the toilet and rinsing it in the sink before putting it into the covered bucket with the others.

Becky was a picture out of a Johnson Baby Powder ad when we got down to the kitchen. So pink, adorable and sparkling that the idea of a dirty diaper was unthinkable.

"Look at that dream!" Sister exclaimed. "She's almost as pretty as you were. Here. Give her to me, Tots. Isn't she something?"

"You should have seen her a little while ago. A dream was the last thing she was." I headed for the icebox to get her milk. "Ah, er . . . Uncle Roy says they've all gone off to the hospital with Junior. Did they say anything to you?"

"No. I wasn't up yet. Don't forget, honey, I'm a night girl. Except last night I conked out early. Being up before eight is not my usual habit."

"Well, you have no idea when they'll be back? Or what they thought was wrong with Junior?"

"Roy just told me that they were going up to the hospital where they could have tests and things done if they needed them and that's all I know." She was bouncing Becky on her knees. "But don't worry, honey. It can't be anything very bad. Junior is a real hunk of man. He'll be all right."

"I guess so." I fixed Becky's goop and took her from Sister and started feeding her.

"We'd all know a bit more about what's going on if Momma only had a phone here," Sister said, pouring herself more coffee. "I'm going out of my mind—why, when I was coming down here, there was no way to let them know. I just jumped on a bus and come . . . came. Couldn't even let Momma know." She studied her coffee cup intently. "It was a quick decision." She let out a hoot of laughter. "That sounds like I was run out of town."

"We were surprised to find you here. Thrilled, but Aunt Dell's last letter said you were working in Phoenix and we didn't expect to get to see you."

"Oh, you know how plans change. Or get changed for you. Soon as I get this little problem straightened out . . ." Her voice was vague. "Look at yours. Your plans. What come over Woody? Wasn't everything going good up there in . . . in . . ."

"Clovis."

"Yeah. Clovis. He had a good job."

"You've known Dad longer than I have." I gave her a knowing look and we both laughed. "You know how he is. Blows up and that's that."

"That's my Uncle Woody, all right. I'm surprised that Milly kept him tamed for this long."

"I'm not so sure it was Mom who tamed him." That just popped out and I looked up quickly at Sister to see if she'd found it a strange thing to say. She was stirring her coffee with a faraway look in her eye. It was a strange thought—a new thought that wasn't all that new somehow. It had been lurking around in my head for a long time. It was just something that hadn't been spoken, been brought out in the open. Sister wasn't paying any attention, nor why should she? She couldn't be aware of what Dad had been doing the past few years—what he was dreaming—what his hopes were for Junior. And now Junior was sick. Proving that dreams are pretty fragile things—particularly if you're depending on somebody else to realize them for you. But if he were banking on Junior being that star, the international name in sports, that rocket that would soar and make *Dad* somebody, why had he pulled the rug out from under himself? From under his own dreams? Perhaps it's better not to dream. Then disappointment won't demolish you. Was being able to say "I'm not taking that kinda shit" worth shattering all your hopes? Surely in life you can take just a tiny weeny bit of shit without losing your manhood or your self-respect. How healthy is your self-respect if you give in to every whim, every flash of temper, just drifting with the wind with no thought of your future or anybody else's? Was it manly to give up the struggles for a better life and sneak back home with your tail between your legs to the known, the sure thing, the cronies at the courthouse in Galena. Those ne'er-do-wells were constant. You could depend on them. They'd be there, feet up on the ledge of the big brick building, telling each other the same made-up tired stories until they dropped dead of boredom never having had a dream worth a fart. That light I'd seen shining in Dad's eyes had gone out. The stardust he hoped would sprinkle on him from his son's—no, dammit, *sons'*—success and fame wasn't worth waiting for. Why risk defeat? Why not accept it right off the bat and go home to the good ole boy horseshit and bury yourself in it? What gave Dad the right to decide our lives? He'd managed to ruin his own young life and was now dead set on ruining ours and what remained of his own. If he chose to disown his dreams, who said he could wrench ours from us?

"Watch it, honey!" Sister said and grabbed at Becky's dish which was about to slip to the floor. "Where'd you go off to?"

I shook my head. "Don't know. Daydreaming, I guess." I sat up straight and finished feeding my charge.

"Well, I can't daydream. I've got to get dressed and do my daily phoning. How can people live without a phone? I ask you. I have to do it early to catch George at home. If I don't, the secretary listens in and I don't want that." I wasn't following what she was saying. "Don't look so dumb, dummy. George. George Griggs. That up and comin' young lawyer. My brother-in-law. Your very own cousin. Married to my ever-lovin' sister Mavis."

"I know, I know," I laughed as she ruffled my hair. "But where do you go?"

"To place the call? The Del Rey Hotel. Right there on the main square." She headed for the door. "I'm in like that with the bartender there," she said grinning and crossing her index finger over the next one. She obviously had an affinity for bartenders. "It's the only lively place in this one-horse town."

"But how come you have to call every day . . ." I called after her as I heard her footsteps going up the stairs.

"Long story," she called back. "Tell you all about it later."

After I'd done the dishes, made the beds—Aunt Dell's and Roy's was neatly pulled together, thank God, I didn't want to go into their room—I dressed Becky in a sunsuit and took her outside for a walk. She was getting steadier on her feet all the time. She'd dart ahead of me and I'd have to dash up behind her and place her back on the sidewalk as she started heading for the street as though pulled by a magnet.

We made our erratic way down the street, around the corner and down the next four or five blocks that led to the pretty little square we'd passed when we arrived yesterday. Yesterday? Only yesterday? Here Becky and I were, walking along as though we'd known this little town all our lives. There was a small park in the center of the square with carefully clipped shrubbery and freshly mown lawn around an ornately carved stone fountain as its centerpiece. The water trickling from tier to tier sounded cool. Becky ran round and round the fountain, splashing her hands in the water, squealing with joy. I had to pick her up kicking and screaming when workmen appeared to string up lights around the fountain and up through the palm trees that formed a border around the edges of the square. I found out that the lights were in preparation for a three-day fiesta to begin that evening, commemorating St. Augustine's Day. St. Augustine was the first city founded by the Spanish in the New World in 1565 and was celebrated wherever descendants of the Spanish lived. There'd be music, dancing, stalls of Mexican food, games of chance, penny-pitches, and everything like a carnival—"But only a little one," the electrician told me.

I carried Becky across the busy street along the square and found myself in front of the Del Rey Hotel. It looked a bit dusty and run down, not like the glitteringly elegant Hotel Tucson in Phoenix, but then the whole square had a dusty, dog-eared look. All the buildings were run-down except the two churches facing each other at opposite ends of the square. One the Catholic cathedral, the other more modest, the Episcopalian. They stood staring at each other across the park but there didn't seem to be any competition or hostility between them. They lived in harmony. The Catholic one was decidedly more ornate and freshly whitewashed for St. Augustine's Day, but the Episcopalian one was impressive in its simpler solid architecture.

We walked up and down in front of the hotel just in case Sister might come out, but after several minutes on the hotel sidewalk, we gave up and headed back down our own street for Aunt Dell's house.

The Model-A was just pulling up to the curb as we turned the corner. I called and waved, snatched up Becky and ran toward the car noticing immediately that there were only three people in it. Junior wasn't with them.

Mom answered my question before I had time to ask it. "They're keeping him there for some tests," she said, reaching automatically for Becky's outstretched arms and calls of "Mama, mama, mama."

"Get us a beer open, Tots," Dad said unceremoniously.

"Oooh, lawsey, yes, honey!" Aunt Dell crooned. "Hurry. I don't know how a body can get so thirsty. We was puttin' away enough liquid last night to last a week. I guess it's like Chinese food. Don't stick to the ribs." She winked and shoved me ahead of her up the walkway.

Over sandwiches and salad it was explained that Mom had been right. There was nothing wrong with Junior's heart. Organically, that is. But something was causing it to work doubly hard. The temperature remained up but not alarmingly. The headaches had been eased with painkillers. He was not even assigned a room. He was stretched out on a table in the consulting room waiting for the results from the urine, blood, and mucus (from his inflamed nasal passages) tests which were being done now right there in the hospital. It was the most up-to-date medical center this side of Phoenix and Aunt Dell kept repeating the fact as though it's newness would make everything right.

They all went back at two o'clock, Aunt Dell insisting that she wanted to be with them and had nothing else to do. Sister returned just as they were getting in the car. She'd had lunch with the bartender at the Del Rey and hadn't been able to get through to George. She'd have to go back to the hotel and try George again in the afternoon. She had talked to Mavis who sent us all her love and hoped that there was nothing seriously wrong with Junior.

Becky was asleep, Sister back at the Del Rey, and I was soaking in the tub taking advantage of the empty house and empty hours. I was on my hands and knees, head under the taps lathering in shampoo from an elegant little bottle I'd found on the edge of the tub and couldn't resist trying. I seemed to have overdone it somehow. I'd created enough foam to put out a burning airplane and no amount of rinsing could make the shampoo disappear. I was manufacturing suds. I turned both taps up full and stuck my head under the water. Perhaps I'd misread the label and it was some sort of shaving lather or bubble bath. I could feel that I was spraying suds all over the room at the same time I felt a hand on my bottom. I gave a shriek and bumped my head against the spigot and let out another shriek. I rinsed enough soap out of my eyes to see Roy grinning at me, stroking my buttocks from a position on his knees beside the tub. I rubbed my head where I'd banged it—another good-sized bump. Just why in hell did people do this sort of thing to me? I was going to get killed one day by some idiot grabbing me unexpectedly when my head was in a dangerous position. And just why in the hell did people think they could take these liberties with my body in the first place?

"I think my head is bleeding."

There was a plastic basin on the floor which Roy picked up and dipped into the full tub and poured water over my head, rinsing all the foam off in one huge cascade. "There. Got the soap out of your eyes?" He splashed my face with water from the taps and turned them off.

"You scared me. I was . . . I thought I was alone." His hand was still moving between my legs, tickling me gently and giving me a hard-on. How old did you have to be to tell a grown-up no? When did your body become your own? Respect your elders . . . Should be seen and not heard . . . Do as I say . . . Your father knows best. I wasn't so sure of that last one. All that Dad knew was that Roy was a bronco-bustin', steer-ropin' son of a gun and a real he-man. A man's man. Sixty-five push-ups. There. See? Count 'em. A real man's man. Not a man for boys. Put his hand on a kid's ass? Are you nuts? Suck cock? Why Dad would beat the shit out of anybody who even hinted at such a possibility. Why, hell, Roy was his brother (in-law, same thing) and don't forget it. What do you think this family is, buster, some kinda' traveling freak show?

So there you are. No matter how you slice it, the grown-ups had power over us. Dad had total and absolute power over his family. Whether it was deserved is beside the point. Roy had power over me. Over my body. And power corrupts. Corrupts young boys in this case. How far was I to be corrupted?

"Oh, you never know when ole Roy's goin' to pop up." He did. He lifted himself up onto his knees in one quick movement bringing his hard cock up past the rim of the bathtub. I'd never seen a grown man's cock hard. The scoutmaster's I never actually saw. Roy's looked enormous and dangerous somehow. Muscular as though it too might have been doing sixty-five push-ups every day. I gasped. "Well, old Roy has really popped up." He looked down at himself and then at my stricken face. "Don't be scared. It won't bite."

He had both hands on my buttocks now, lifting me around to face him as though I weighed nothing. His elbows were locked on the inside of the tub and as he leaned his head forward, he brought my crotch to his face as though he were lifting a long barbell—doing curls I think Junior calls it. He brought me to his mouth, took me inside it and then did the weight-lifting curls gently, sliding me in and out of his mouth by bending his elbows slightly. He wasn't even moving his head, I was being moved into him. His fingers, cupped under my cheeks played along between them and up under my balls. Talk about being transported. I was suspended in midair in his hands, a weightless object, flying through space on wings, my whole being a mass of jangling, mind-boggling sensations. The body has its own demands, its own needs that have power over you, too. Particularly when aroused. I was aroused now and was overpowered by superior forces from every direction. I couldn't have fought it if I'd wanted to. I was becoming a slave to Roy's mouth. I surrendered but loathed those superior forces for making the surrender so abject. If I was being corrupted, it seemed to be a fairly complete job.

Somehow he managed to spread my legs so that they stretched out and up over his shoulders, with the small of my back resting on the edge of the bathtub while I supported myself with locked elbows and an iron grip on the far edge of the tub. I really was flying—my head back, back arched, my legs my wings, spread wide, upper thighs resting on his shoulders, supporting my weight while his mouth provided fuel and propulsion for my flight. This wasn't boys playing with each other, this was pure sex, pure pleasure. This wasn't experimenting—certainly not on Roy's part—this was the real thing, this was experience speaking, serious experience speaking loud and clear.

He knew what he was doing and I was loving it. *It*, not him. The sensations, not who was producing them. Stumbling attempts with other boys had been exciting, but we didn't know what we were doing, we'd just been trying it out. We hadn't been trained. We hadn't been exposed to experts like Roy who could render us incapable of thought. Or speech. I couldn't have said no now if my life depended on it. Roy's sheer professionalism paralyzed the mind to everything except the body's enjoyment.

He didn't have to ask me if I were in his power, he knew I was. He not only knew it by the way my body was reacting, but also he knew his . . . Well, his business. I snapped my head forward and looked down at him for the first time. Something about his loose-lipped avidity and total concentration on his task told me that he wasn't using all his knowledge and experience just to please me—he was being transported too. This wasn't a one-way street. Somehow I'd figured that so long as he was just giving me pleasure, it would lessen the inherent vileness in the act. The act between a man and an almost fifteen-year-old boy. He wasn't making love to my body with his mouth and hands for my benefit only. He was doing it for himself. He was using my body for his own pleasure and anything I got out of it was incidental. He was using his tricks with practiced ease and timing—knowing what he was doing to me, the inexperienced one—introducing me to sinful practices and making me like them. For the inexperienced one, how far were these practices supposed to go? Were they just a one-time thing? Then over? Something to forget about? Or was the sensation to be so intense and satisfying that search for repeats would be inevitable? That was where the real danger lay. Surely it would be difficult not to search for a repeat of the kind of orgasm he was bringing me to now. He must have known that it was like nothing I'd ever known. Would there be others tomorrow? Would it wind up with me seeking him out?

I slid off the edge of the tub onto his chest while his hands took a firmer grip on my bottom and his mouth worked its miracles. I came in such a thunderous thrashing way that I couldn't understand why he didn't choke. My body was so alive with new and overwhelming sensations that I wasn't even aware of bumping my head again. This time on the edge of the tub. It occurred to me later that if guilt didn't prevent me from indulging in these practices, grievous bodily injury might.

Sister's "Yoo-hoo" from the front door sent Roy scurrying silently to his room. I jumped back into the tub and took a quick rinse, letting the running cold water ease my aching cock and be my excuse for not hearing Sister until she knocked on the bathroom door. "Tots? You in there?"

"Yeah. Be right out. Washed my head."

"Well, don't dawdle. Becky's roamin' around downstairs like a caged bear." I heard her steps heading toward her room. Then she called, "The folks back from the hospital yet?"

"Nope."

I dried quickly, wrapped the towel around myself after wiping up the suds and water from the floors and walls and was downstairs dressed, slickly combed and innocent in a matter of minutes. A quick washup for Becky at the kitchen sink and a graham cracker and milk calmed the stalking bear. I was sitting with her when I heard our car pull up out front. I dashed down the hall and out onto the porch. I smiled broadly and prayed for good news as I walked to the front steps. I couldn't think of anything to say to cheer their tired sad faces, so decided to let the smile do whatever it could.

"Howdy, son," Aunt Dell sighed.

Mom managed to force the corners of her generous mouth up for a split second and a hand lifted almost imperceptibly in greeting.

Dad got out on the street side and slammed the door with a little more force than was necessary. They started walking up the steep walkway, heads down, watching their footing, which made it impossible to see their faces, but the way they moved—slackly and wearily—told me the news wasn't good.

Becky's pushing open the screen door screaming "Momma" brought a smile—however fleeting—to all their faces. Mom increased her pace up the last incline and looked up at me on the porch. "My, don't you look clean as a pin." She smiled then.

"How's . . ."

"Don't ask. It's all a big muddle. One doctor says this, the other says that. Nobody seems to know anything." She pecked me on the cheek and moved toward Becky and picked her up.

"The only thing that fine new hospital ain't got is a bar." Aunt Dell's laughter was halfhearted. "But, surely, Tots, there's a cold beer in there somewhere."

"If there ain't, go get some," Dad said, hardly looking at me as he handed me a dollar. "Go get some anyway. Need it sooner or later." His voice had that hard edge of command that meant *now*, not in a few minutes.

I went to the little store on the corner we'd passed on the way to the town square. No beer. Nearer the square there was a liquor store. I bought the beer and when I came out of the store I could see that traffic had already been cut off from the square and flimsy booths were being set up right in the middle of the street for the carnival or fiesta or whatever they called the celebration beginning tonight. It was looking pretty tawdry now in the late afternoon light but I still hoped to be able to watch the festivities later this evening. Maybe Sister would come with me.

Food that evening was second—a very long way down the list second—to drink for everybody but Mom, me, and Becky. Although the latter had a passion for beer and was constantly taking sips from whatever glass she could get her chubby little hands on.

"Well, she's her Daddy's own girl," Aunt Dell observed, her spirits revived on three beers and were now further enhanced by a second bourbon and 7-Up.

I helped Mom fix some canned vegetable soup and some cold-cuts and salad. Everybody agreed that the heat and the waiting around the hospital left them with little if any appetite. Dad, Roy, and Dell drank with such diligence and sense of purpose that I'm sure if we'd put the soup in a glass, they'd have tossed it back and not noticed the difference. It was having a glass in the hand that seemed the important thing. Sister stuck to her elegant Scotch-on-the-rocks which she sipped slowly.

"What the fuck is this?" Dad bellowed when I put the bowl of soup in front of him. I knew we should have put it in a glass. Everybody glanced at Mom and when she didn't say anything, nobody else did. I continued passing around the soup. Roy held up about a dozen big soda crackers above his bowl and crumbled them as though he were demonstrating how he could tear a telephone book in half. He looked at me and winked. I didn't respond.

Sister drank and I ate soup and talked to her in undertones. "Could we go down to the fiesta? It might be sort of fun."

"Oh, I don't know, honey. It's so hot and there'll be a big crowd. You seen one, you seen 'em all."

"I've never seen one."

"Well, we'll see."

Mom was sharing her soup with Becky and devoting all her attention to the task. She'd divorced herself from the group as completely as if she'd left the room. She talked quietly to the baby, making her giggle and her big eyes roll and glisten. Her little legs were swinging out from Mom's lap and thumping back against her thighs with indescribable pleasure.

Dad and Roy drank steadily—drink for drink—their heads together in deep conversation with only the occasional expostulation to keep the arguments going. Aunt Dell, humming quietly to herself, cleared the table and I helped her at the sink with the dishes. "You ain't havin' the time of your life down here, are you, son?"

"Well, Junior isn't either."

She patted my shoulder with a soapy hand. "Aw, now . . . That's goin' to be all right. Just as soon as they know . . ."

"What kind of shit is that, Roy?" Dad exploded. "Are you nuts? War over here? You don't know what the fuck you're talking about."

"Well, Woody, I didn't say war right here," Roy went on evenly. "But we've got to help England. Roosevelt says . . ."

"Roosevelt's an asshole . . ."

Mom rose from the table with Becky and moved toward the door without looking back over her shoulder. She could smell the storm. "Wave nighty-night, Becky. That's a good girl." She clearly wasn't going to witness any more scenes. I followed her out the door and over to the sitting room to help her make up the couch bed. How I missed Junior. I could see his eyes sparkling at me murmuring, "He's not batting a thousand tonight."

I got the sheets from under the folding couch where they were kept during the day and unhitched the hooks that held it in an upright position. I spread out the first sheet and began putting it into place. "Aunt Dell says everything is going to be all right. Just as soon as the doctors . . ."

"Oh, they're doing everything they can. I have faith in those two. Very young they are, they hardly seem older than Junior . . ."

"When can I go see him?"

"Oh, sweetheart," she stopped undressing Becky and stood up and faced me. "I just can't say. He's not in isolation, or anything like that, but they feel that until they actually know . . . They're just being care-

ful. And they're right. I know that. It could be something contagious." She bent down to Becky again, lifted her and headed up the
stairs toward the bathroom. I finished up the bed and turned the fan
to low and straightened Becky's little pallet. Mom and Becky came
back in the room just as I was leaving.

"Mom," I began to stutter, "There's a . . . well, sort of, I don't know
what it is called. Fiesta? Well, I'd . . . could I . . ."

"Ask your father." She said it automatically. That's what she always
said. Now she looked up at me and nodded to herself. "Wait a
minute." She put Becky on the little mattress and found her purse on
the end table. "Here. That's all I have. But take it. Have a good time."
It was a quarter. She tried to make a joke of it with, "Don't spend it all
in one place," but her heart didn't seem to be in it.

I hugged her and pecked her on the cheek. "Thanks, Mom."

"Don't be late."

I could hear the music the minute I turned the corner at the little
store and even the lights were visible blinking invitingly five blocks
further on. I hurried along, passing strolling couples and families
smelling of bath soap and wearing their cleanest clothes, all smiling
and nodding good evening. I was at the corner of the square before I
realized that this was the first time I'd ever been to this sort of thing
without Junior. I'd never been out alone like this. I glanced around
me. People were arm-in-arm or holding hands, laughing together,
whispering, sharing secrets or plans, calling out to each other, ex-
changing greetings with friends. I wasn't only alone, I was a stranger.
I'd take one look around and then go on back home. This didn't
look like much fun.

The loudest music came from a squeakily amplified band up on a
raised platform in front of the fountain. They were wearing huge
Mexican hats, big collared shirts with yards of garish satin in the
great full sleeves and cummerbunds knotted around their ample
middles. Each musician seemed to have an extra set of teeth as
though they too were part of the exaggerated costumes. I stood
around for a while wondering if somehow the teeth were going to
be used as percussion instruments or something—perhaps little
hammers pinged against them in a novelty number. Clacking instead of castanets? The same lachrymose wails continued, accompanied by whining guitars accentuated by maracas and tambourines
with half-hearted "olés" and "carambas" thrown in here and there. I
was obviously not in the mood for the fiesta. Or was this fiesta a
fiasco?

I moved away from the big band and went out to the stalls set up in the streets. Penny-pitches, raggedy dolls to be knocked down by thrown baseballs (Junior always won Kewpie dolls at those games), wheels of fortune, strange souvenirs for sale, toy Mexican hats, maracas painted every color in the rainbow only brighter, little devil dolls from Puerto Veragua which purportedly brought good luck. Spanish shawls in sleazy satin ("Tack at its tackiest—" I could hear Ronnie say) with skimpy fringe, little bullfighter dolls dressed in capes and sequins—not very many sequins—but each with a realistic little bulge in the crotch of its tight satin trousers, all of it sleazy, tacky, cheap but mostly just sad. My mood fitted the atmosphere. You can't manufacture fun on your own. I knew that if Junior were here with me, we'd be having the time of our lives. We'd invent fun together.

Having completed the circle, I decided to go back around one more time. Just as I got near the Del Rey Hotel, there was a small band of strolling singers and musicians. Band is hardly the word. There were only three: a guitar player, and two boys singing and dancing, one with maracas the other with a tambourine. They were all young—sixteen or eighteen—and seemed to be having more fun than all the rest of the people at the fiesta put together. Their smiles were real and blinding—superb white teeth flashing with joy and not for effect. The guitar player was playing a different sort of rhythm and sound—one not all that familiar to me—and the boy with the tambourine was doing intricate dance steps, close to the pavement, beating a complicated staccato rhythm with the high heels of his boots. I was fascinated and stopped to watch. The dancer flashed teeth and eyes at me from under his wide-brimmed flat hat. His skin-tight costume coveted a body lithe and graceful that was propelled toward me on feet moving so fast they were blurred. I unconsciously felt my feet twitching trying to imitate the movements. In an instant, with sound theatrical instinct, they surrounded me, urging me to join them in the dance, thus creating an instant crowd around all four of us. The dancer took my hand and started showing me the steps. I followed as best I could. It turned out that I followed pretty well. He squeezed my hand and winked at me. Within minutes, the crowd around us was clapping with the music, calling out to us, urging me on as the dancer pounded his bottom with the tambourine and led me through intricate turns and steps that seemed to be coming more naturally and easily to me. I was in heaven! I was dancing! I hadn't danced like this since Galena and the Domino Cafe, only now I had this handsome dark partner instead of doing the double-shuffle with Dad. The music gathered speed, the boy's feet beat a wild tattoo as he let go my hand and we were both on our own. I improvised and copied what he was doing with complete abandon. He was a thrilling and inspiring partner—his eyes sent me messages of encouragement as his movements became wilder and more complex and with a wild flourish of beating heels, turns, and twirls, he ended down on one knee with the tambourine held high up in the air, his hips thrust forward, his back arched and his head thrown back beaming with triumph as the small crowd around us applauded and cried "Olé" and "Arriba!" He stood up and we fell against each other, laughing and breathless while the crowd roared and whistled. He bowed elegantly and then bowed to me and applauded me. I tried to mimic his elegant bow and lost my balance, catching myself by grabbing him by the waist with one hand which got a good laugh. We fell against each other again and my hand moved down over his sleek bottom inadvertently, giving me such a thrill that I jerked my hand away. Somebody in the crowd threw some money onto the pavement and then more coins rained down on us. Everybody was laughing and I was relishing my small contribution to the performance. It was like being on a stage. Would Junior have condoned this sort of dancing in the streets? Perhaps it was just as well I was alone.

The boy with the maracas started picking up the money and putting it into his hat, doing a comic turn like Groucho Marx of wriggling his eyebrows and stalking around bent over to pick up the coins and making funny faces at the same time. My partner put a hand under my elbow and led me aside. "You very good. Good dancer. I could teach you in a—" he snapped his fingers smartly. "And *muy guapo,* also." He eyed me up and down and then squeezed me to him with his arm and threw his head back and let out a deep throated uninhibited laugh. "Aii-*yii,* amigo, *muy muy guapo.*" I looked puzzled. He put his cheek next to mine and whispered hoarsely in my ear, *"Handsome.* I say you much, much handsome." He roared with laughter again. "Come." He was fanning himself with his big hat. "Too hot. We take rest now. This way." He guided me expertly through the crowds down a side street. It had stalls of food and drink. He bought us tacos and cokes. We talked, me asking all the questions. His name was Juan, he worked in an office here in Ajo but had studied dancing with top Flamenco teachers in Mexico. He was going to be a professional. He couldn't wait to get out of this dead town and work his way to New York and Europe. He said that I had a natural talent. He said a great many things that pleased me very much. He said it was good business to have a blond boy come out of the crowd and dance with them—dance as well as I—and we could become an act, at least for these three nights.

I ended up promising to meet him tomorrow night, even though I didn't think I would. He fascinated me—perhaps too much. He also bothered me. There was something in the way Juan looked at me that made me wonder if he were only interested in my dancing. There was a sly knowingness about the way he rubbed up against me as we talked and in the way he touched me. I admitted to myself that I wanted to touch him since that electrifying contact with his bottom during our bows. But it all reminded me of the scene in the bathroom this afternoon and that was still too fresh in my mind.

Walking down the dark streets home I found myself wondering what it would be like to participate in sex—actually become an active partner. Could I with Juan? I'd only participated—and then only manually—with Victor and Art. I was never really sure of what went on with Miguel under the muddy canal water—I couldn't see. Even shagging with Naomi, she had been the instigator, the creator, she used me how she wanted to. What would it be like to respond? Could I? I knew I could never do what Roy did to me. But were there other things? Was I willing to learn? Juan was the first person to make me wonder about a sexual role. I was attracted to him and I sensed danger in the attraction. It was a sexual attraction—pure and simple— that hadn't developed naturally out of friendship, a logical progression of comradeship and mutual interest. Having recognized it for what it was, it scared the hell out of me. I was getting out of my depth. Had Roy succeeded in corrupting me?

Of course, everybody knew what their life was supposed to be like. You'd date, fall in love, get married and live worthwhile lives. We had been brought up to respect all girls like our mothers and sisters. If respect faltered, locked around our crotches as tightly as chastity belts was the fear of disease. Birds-and-bees talks began and ended with the big V. D. Sex with girls would happen when you were old enough—whenever that was—until then, little or nothing was said about sex between boys. Perhaps I hadn't been listening. The word "queer" had to do with men, not what boys did together. Granted what happened between boys could cause its share of guilt but I couldn't imagine burning in everlasting fire in hell for jerking off with a good friend. Was I beginning to slough off the Baptist concept of sin or was I trying, like Dad, to justify unjustifiable behavior?

I started off with Sister the next morning toward the hotel for her daily telephone call to George. I took Becky with me. "I haven't quite understood why you have to call Phoenix every day, Sis," I said as I panted along beside her carrying my charge.

"Listen, honey, you'll have a heart attack trying to run with that load. You'll just have to wait for me to call when we get there anyway. Why don't you put Becky down and let her walk and I'll scoot along and meet you by the fountain in the square when I get done. OK?" She was off, spike heels clicking on the sidewalk, a faint echo of Juan as she rushed on ahead.

It was a relief to settle Becky on her own feet and we sauntered along at her pace, a drunken, tottering pace, more one step forward, two sideways and an oops! reeling backwards. Even so, we waited for about twenty minutes for Sister by the fountain before she joined us with a look of consternation clouding her usual sunny expression. "Damn," she said under her breath as she joined us on the bench. "Damn, damn, damn." She was rummaging around in her purse distractedly and finally snapped it shut and slapped it down beside her on the bench with a long sigh.

"Not such good news, I guess?"

"Not so's you'd notice," she said in a flat voice. "George has a couple of calls to make and then he'll call back. I have to wait again down here. The thing that bothers me is that I might get blackballed."

"Blackballed?" I'd never heard the expression.

"You know, they could fix it someway so's I couldn't work. Not work in Phoenix, anyway. Or even Arizona." She sat a long moment and then suddenly slapped me on the thigh. "You poor baby," she laughed. "You haven't got the faintest notion of what I'm talking about, have you?"

"Not muckin' fuch."

She hooted. "I haven't heard that since I was your age. People still say that?"

"Not too muckin' fuch." We both laughed. She was recovering her good humor after whatever bad news she'd received. I automatically checked on Becky—she was sitting on the grass, determinedly pulling it up by the handsful and tossing it into her hair. She was fine.

"OK. Here's what happened. Step by step." She clasped her hands in her lap, her beautiful long fingers with the perfectly manicured nails digging slightly into the skin on the backs of her hands. "First.

To be able to work in a place that serves food and drink you have to have a doctor's certificate . . . a certificate that says you don't have some disease . . . er . . . oh, T.B. or something like that. See? Well, if you don't have that certificate, you don't work. And that certificate—more like a permit, really—can be re . . . re . . ."

"Revoked?"

"That's it. And mine has been."

"Are you sick?"

"Heavens, no, honey. Fit as a fiddle." She opened her arms wide as if to show that she was whole and healthy. "It was all a big mistake. All a joke. Just a silly joke." She stood up and crossed her arms across her chest. "A damned stupid joke. Only I sure ain't the one laughin'." I sat waiting for her to go on. She took a pace or two toward Becky who clapped her hands and called, "Sissy, sissy, sissy," as Sister waved and smiled at her. She came back and plopped herself down beside me again and took a deep breath. "Listen, honey, you're old enough to know these things and I care too much about you not to tell the truth. But I'd just as soon you'd soft-peddle the facts when you talk about it with Aunt Milly. She's one person in this world I've been try-ing to impress—and be as good as—ever since she was my first-grade teacher." She put her arm over the back of the bench and hugged me. "And you're next." She pulled me in close to her and lowered her voice. "Well, as you can imagine, working in a bar where every-body's drinkin' and having a good time, well, there's bound to be some pretty rough talk. You know . . . oh, some guy'll get a load on and start making passes. You know."

"Looking like you, you'd have to carry a club."

"On some Saturday nights, I've wished I had one." She leaned her head against mine and talked softly. "So. Last week . . . no, more'n that now. Lawsey, goin' on *two* weeks. I've got to get back to work, for heaven's sake and George just sits on his duff." She straightened up and sighed. "Back to what happened. We'd had a big night. Lot of people. I had my pockets so full of tips I was walkin' bowlegged. There was one table that stayed on and on and on. I'd cleared all the others, polished them a dozen times. Subtle-like, you know. All but saying, 'Yoo-hoo, y'all. Time to go beddy-bye', but they just set. The bartender—you remember Jim. Well, he's still a card. He'd done everything he could think of to get rid of them. He'd even made up some silly jokes like 'well, folks, almost time to open up the bar for to-morrow' and stuff like that. They just set on. They was two men and a pretty good lookin' young woman."

"Aren't there regular hours? When you have to close up?"

"Not in hotels. Not like the Tucson. You see, there's all night room service, course that doesn't have anything to do with us in the bar, but if the folks are staying there, we can't hardly kick 'em out. Anyway, I had to go to the little girls' room and when I was there washin' my hands and straighten' my hair, the girl comes in . . . from the table. She's friendly—we'd been talking back and forth all evening naturally when I'd bring drinks and clear up ashtrays and things—and she didn't head for a booth, she was just sort of primping in front of the mirror and as I was leavin' she said, 'Ginny—that's what you said your name was, didn't you? Ginny? Well, listen, honey, one of the guys—you know the one, he's been oglin' you all night, the dark one?—well, he's really got the hots for you. He said he'd give a crisp new twenty dollar bill for an hour or so with you."

"What'd he mean by that?"

Sister pulled back in disbelief. "I thought you were old enough to hear this story. Now I wonder."

"Oh, now I see. He was offering money to have a date with you."

"A date?" Sister rolled her eyes. "Yeah. That's close enough. Anyway, I just smiled at her as I opened the door and said, 'Honey, I'm so tired I wouldn't spend an hour with anybody for under a crisp new hundred.' And went on back to the bar. I told Jim what she'd said and we had a good laugh. Maybe we overdid the laughin' a bit, because they was watchin' us and all of a sudden just got up, paid in a kinda' surly way and left. I guess they knew we'as laughin' at them. Anyway, I cleared up that last table in a flash, grabbed my purse and was outside in front of the hotel in a matter of minutes."

"Why were they surly to you?"

"Too much to drink for one thing and the fact that I'd refused his . . . his . . . *request*, shall we say, for a date?" She laughed at some joke I didn't understand. "Oh, and Tots! I forgot to tell you. I got a car. It's a tin lizzie from the word go—when it goes. Makes your Model-A look like a Packard. Anyway, I was scramblin' around in my purse for the keys to the old jalopy—parked just up behind the hotel—when I bumped into him."

"To who . . . *whom?*"

"The dark guy at the table. The one who wanted a date. Blam! Right into him. Right in the middle of the sidewalk. I stepped back and he was holding something in his hand. Leather, looked like a wallet or something and then he said, "You're under arrest." He flipped the leather thing open and there was a badge—looked bigger'n a headlight. 'O'Neil,' he says, real tough. 'City Police. Vice Squad. You're under arrest for offering yourself for one hundred dollars. This lady here's the witness. Soliciting in a public place.'" She sat back, her forehead glistening with sweat, the hand that reached up to wipe it trembled.

"Vice Squad? What in the world is that?" I was lost. "Arrested? *You?* Soliciting . . ." That word was a Phoenix word. I'd first heard it there. When? It was way back when Junior and I were trying to start a lawn-mowing business. All those signs on the houses saying "No Soliciting." Then Junior explained that soliciting was like prostitution. Was Sister saying she'd been arrested for *prostitution?* That was the same as being a whore. I must have misunderstood. "You said it had been just a joke."

"Jokes can backfire." She looked drained and pale. She'd been booked on charges of soliciting. Her name was down on official ledgers. She was going to have to appear in court unless George could have the charges proved false. But in the meantime she couldn't work and the idea of appearing before a judge for any charge turned her to jelly. "It's a right old mess, Tots." I reached over and took her by the hand. "If the charge sticks, that means goodbye Phoenix. I won't be able to work there ever again." She squeezed my hand so hard it hurt. "And just because . . . some *bastard* with a badge decides he wants to make trouble. You got the badge, you got all the rights." I'd never seen her look so dejected. "If I'd only been staying at the hotel that night. But the next day was my night off and . . ." Something of her old gaiety came back when she laughed, "As my papa—your *ex*-uncle Jesse—used to say, 'That's hindsight and hindsight ain't nothin' finally but lookin' up your own behind and that's just a dark hole that won't tell you nothin'.'" We laughed again.

"But what does George say when you talk to him?"

"Oh, you know. 'We're doing everything we can.' 'I've got a friend at the courthouse that'll . . .' 'I know the judge.' Or, '*If* I knew the judge . . .' In other words, *nada, nada, nada.* Just the big run-around."

"But surely the girl with the officers will say that it was all a joke."

"Oh, honey, honey, honey. Don't you see? She's in it with them. They probably got something on her so she has to do what they say. That's how those guys work. She's probably on the game herself. She's not going to do anything to get in trouble with those bastards . . . they're all kooky anyway. They probably wanted us two girls to be together. Everybody says the Vice Squad's all screwed up—most of 'em queers probably."

"Queers?"

"Sure. Queers. Don't like woman anyway. Want to cause us poor workin' girls as much trouble as possible. Queer, goin' in for nutty sex."

"Like Roy?"

"Like *who?*" Her head swung so violently around toward me, one of her combs came out. I reached down on the ground to pick it up.

"Like Roy. I mean like he . . ." I handed her the comb as I looked into her horrified eyes. Oh God! I'd said the wrong thing. I thought we were supposed to be able to say anything to each other. She'd said so when she'd started her story. What made me mention Roy? And why was she so . . . *scandalized?*

"You mean like he does *what?*" Her voice was hard and demanding. Her eyes so searching and questioning that I had to look away. And just as well. Becky was not only covered in grass, she was covered in what was unmistakably shit. Just whose, was anybody's guess. I jumped up and ran for her.

"Oh good God! Look at her! I think she's eating dog turds!" I was brushing the disgusting stuff off her hands and cheeks. She seemed covered in it and was distinctly delighted with herself. "I've got to get her home." I looked over my shoulder. Sister was standing right behind me, still looking pale and trembly but now with an overlay of confusion and disbelief.

"But, wait, Tots. Tell me. What did you mean? Has he ever . . . Roy? *Queer?* Don't go yet!" I had Becky in my arms and was starting to run across the lawn toward home. "Wait! I don't understand . . ."

"I'll explain later. Got to get this demon cleaned up. She could get sick." I was off and glad to be. That had just slipped out. I was only trying to understand her story. After all, Roy was part of the family now. I thought Sister and I could talk about anything but apparently there were things you couldn't talk to anybody about. I should have known that. That was the secret part. I couldn't confide even to Sister. She'd been as shocked as if I'd suggested Roy had done something worse than murder. Was it really *that* bad? I'd been ashamed, and frightened at what we'd done, but to see those same feelings reflected in Sister's eyes magnified them to unimaginable proportions. She could talk to me about being booked as a whore, but say queer and Roy in the same breath and she's horrified. I'd heard that whores do whatever you pay them to do. Would they suck cocks? If they did, wouldn't that make them queer? Everybody says that cocksuckers are queers.

As I bounced along with my filthy charge, one thing was coming clear; sexual terrain generally was just too vast, it covered too many possibilities. It had too many hidden pitfalls, boundaries and barriers that I didn't comprehend. This subject was out of bounds, while that one was OK—up to a point, but no further. That you could laugh at, the other deplore. I knew it was idiotic of me to try to understand it. It was clearly uncharted territory. You had to sort of work out your own rules to suit yourself. It was a jungle—this sexual country—with no real signs, no paths clearly marked. Not even the taboos were listed someplace where you could read them. The permissible activities seemed to carry all sorts of qualifiers—you can "if"; according to; with jurisdiction and permits from; with age, sex, marital and social status of the partners considered, calculated, collated, correlated before anything could be taken into account. Mostly it seemed to me to boil down to: Do it but don't get caught. Above all, don't talk about it.

When the Model-A pulled up in front of the house at lunch time, Mom's little darling was smelling and looking like a rose. She tottered down the steep walkway to be grabbed up by Mom with me close behind her.

"He seems a bit better today," Mom said. "They've got the temperature under control—well, they understand its pattern—and they know what it *isn't*. The old process of elimination. We can thank our lucky stars that it isn't polio. Not meningitis. Diphtheria. Or . . . oh, I can't keep track of them all, but anyway they keep testing him for everything so at least they're doing that much."

"But can't they give you any positive idea?"

"That's just it," she said wearily. "They're lost. They don't *know.*"

I could feel Mom's attitude changing hour by hour. She was pulling back, deeply into a shell. Even when she held Becky—as she was doing now—she held her like a warrior holding a shield. She was fending off the enemy—unnamed, but everywhere—with Becky's tiny body. She seemed to be pulling her suffering in on top of herself, trying to hide it by swallowing it. The swallowed suffering offered no sustenance so that she wound up eating herself from the inside. As the doctors became more vague and unspecific, she did too.

Neither Roy nor Sister came home for lunch—Aunt Dell said she thought Roy had inspection jobs at a couple of ranches and had no idea when he would be back. Sis was probably lunching with her new friends at the Del Rey.

Being Saturday, visiting hours at the hospital were more relaxed so Mom took advantage of the later hours by lying down with Becky for a much needed rest. Dad relaxed nervously by washing the car out behind the house and barking orders at me to fetch and carry and then complaining about my performance. I was making a particular effort to be efficient but he didn't seem to notice. Dad was having his own form of pulling back, of withdrawal, at least as it concerned me. I was aware that he hadn't really looked at me in some time. Not just today. It was something that had been sneaking up on me—the realization, I mean—that along with ignoring me he spoke to me unnecessarily harshly. His rough manner and toughness were all a part of his personality, but lately the way he spoke to me bordered on the rude and offensive. Like the other night when he'd told me to get mixes and another time, the beer. He hadn't bothered to look at me then and his tone was insultingly off-hand. I'd put it down to booze, but now, sober, he was brusque and continued to avoid my eye. Something in his manner reminded me of Mrs. Webster. She'd made no bones about not liking me. Could a father actively dislike his own son? Dad's behavior toward me made me realize that it was certainly a possibility. With that thought firmly lodged, it occurred to me that it wouldn't take much for the feeling to be reciprocated.

Another awareness was scratching its way to the surface. I didn't belong here with him and the car. This was something he and Junior did together. I was in the wrong place. It should be Junior here and me up there in the hospital. That's the way it should have been. Ought to be. A new guilt struck me squarely between the eyes; the guilt of being healthy. I was an affront to Dad—scrawny, small for my age, dancing and singing and interested in anything but sports was shamelessly thriving while Junior, the great athlete, the prize physical specimen was laid low. Mysteriously and infuriatingly low, dragging all Dad's dreams down with him. The immensity of the unfairness of it as it must appear to Dad hit me like a blow. That must be what was the matter. That must be the explanation for his manner to me, that was why he found it difficult to even look at me. Things had gone wildly haywire. The wrong one had been struck down.

Dad ought to relax and quit worrying. Junior would be all right. If Dad basically disliked me, we'd just have to adjust to the fact. Where Dad had gone really wrong was to let his pride—and his pride was his shame, his flaw, his stubborn ignorant pride—cause him to make the unforgivable error of leaving California. He was probably just furious with himself and taking it out on me. After all, baseball players were known to come trotting out of the Ozark mountains fully uniformed and cleated. Maybe the dream was still alive. As soon as Junior was well, the light would come back to Dad's eyes.

"Shit," he muttered, patting his shirt pockets with no light at all in his eyes. "Out of cigarettes." He rattled change around in his pants pocket. He flipped a quarter in my direction without actually watching where it went and said, "Get a coupla packs a Wings," then turned on his heel and headed toward the kitchen door.

I trotted down the drive, careful not to slip on the wet incline and continued to trot to the corner store. Coming out of the shop, I stopped to pocket the change when a car came to a screeching stop in front of me at the curb, causing me to jump back startled. It was Roy, leaning across the seat, opening the door.

"Git in," he said in a tone not unlike the tone Dad had been using to me.

"I've got to get the cigarettes back up to . . ."

"*Git in!* Goddamnit."

I obeyed. He cut the wheel hard to the left and sped away from the store in the opposite direction from the house. Roaring down the street, like a hot-rod driver, he made a left turn at the second street practically on two wheels, just missing a red light at the corner of Caliente where he made another two-wheeled turn, this time to the right and headed out this main road north toward Phoenix. He was driving like a madman, but a madman in total control. His steely eyes were reptilian slits, darting in all directions from rear-view mirror to side mirror to the left and to the right. It was like being in a getaway car—it had that same feel of danger about it. Roy himself epitomized danger. He was as taut and knotted as if he had just pulled off a heist or had kidnapped me. The latter not far from the truth.

His jaw was set in such a hard line that it would have gone through a thick plank of wood or a brick wall like cartoon characters in the movies could do. The muscles in his cheeks were working so visibly that I expected to hear his rear teeth crack and crumble.

"Uh . . ." I cleared my throat. "Ah, Roy . . ."

The back of a fist, faster than lightning caught me in the solar plexus, knocking the breath out of me and doubling me over. The blow accented the first word he'd said since he'd driven off at this breakneck speed, *"Uncle* Roy, sonny boy, and don't you forget it."

I stayed doubled over. I felt safer that way. I didn't want to watch the road at this speed. All the stories I'd ever heard about Roy raced through my mind: He'd been an orphan, had joined the army when he was barely fifteen, had killed a man when he was a cowboy back in the twenties. He was tough, feared, physically fearless and capable of almost anything when riled. He was riled. And I was terrified. What in God's name was the matter with him? Could Sister have told him what I'd said? Did she have some suspicions of her own? About me? About Roy? Had she repeated my blunder to Aunt Dell? And then she . . . ? Oh, surely not. Sister wouldn't. *Couldn't*. But she'd looked so stunned, so . . . what was it I'd thought at the time? *Scandalized*. Scandal. Had I inadvertently caused a scandal? Something pretty serious had happened to turn Roy into this seething monster.

I felt the car take another heart-stopping turn to the right, hit some rough road, slow down a bit, but continue to move too fast over uneven ground—I could almost feel the rims of the wheels being jabbed at by rough rocks through the tires. Then another skidding turn and a halt. The handbrake scrunched into place and the key turned off. The car was filled with dust. I stayed bent over.

I felt an arm move across my back and open my door. Then the door on the driver's side opened and I heard footsteps going behind the car, opening first one back door and then the other one, just behind me. I could feel his presence standing beside me, but I couldn't hear him breathing. I waited.

"Git in the back," he ordered. I didn't move. "I said *git in the back*, goddamnit and I *mean* it." He grabbed me by both shoulders and lifted me out of the front seat, still doubled over and tossed me into the backseat as though I were a bundle of dirty laundry. "You and me's goin' to have a little talk." I huddled in the corner where I'd landed, a heap, now hugging my knees and burying my head in them to keep from facing whatever was going to happen. I hadn't a clue where we were, but we couldn't be far out of town. The trip had not only been fast, it had been short.

I still couldn't hear him, I could only feel him standing there, close, as clearly as if I'd been looking at him. I could feel, literally *feel* him. Him and his power. Pure physical power that seemed to be electrified, plugged into some greater power source to allow the giving off of a buzzing sound. His fury was palpable, alive and directed at me. I still wasn't sure why. I felt as though I were being burned, blistered by the effort he was making not to . . . to . . . what? *Beat* me? I had the feeling that if he touched me he'd lose control and rip me limb from limb. I was numbed by an overwhelming sensation of murderous intent. The electrical buzzing of power and strength deafened me and I wasn't aware that he was speaking—speaking barely audibly above the awesome sounds his body seemed to be giving off or was it only the sound of my own terror?

His voice was finally breaking through my fear. ". . . for the first time in my life. I'm goin' on forty-six and my life is just beginning . . . *was* just beginnin'. And I ain't about to let no cock-teasin' little nance ruin it for me." He paused and I slowly started to uncoil and risked peeking out the corner of my eye at him. I didn't understand all the words he used, but he was talking about me. There was no mistake about that.

"Yeah, I think you'd better set up and take notice. You got a ear-ful comin' and I don't want you to miss a word of it." He put his foot up on the running board and leaned down closer to me, his head inside the car with his arms crossed and resting on his raised knee. He stared deep into my eyes as I slowly raised my head, but at the same time, I inched myself further into the corner away from him. "Just what the fuck did you say to Sister?" That *was* it. "I think that's the logical place to start. Just what was goin' on in that . . . that . . . well, I can't call it a brain, an idiot's got more thinkin' power than you seem to have." He held my eyes with his burning blue ones and didn't move a muscle although he was still poised like a snake, every sinew alert and stretched ready to spring. I held his look as long as I could before my eyes dropped. What could I say? Say, OK, I blundered? I misread the degree of intimacy Sister and I had created which led me to indiscretion. I had in fact been an idiot but I was only now beginning to know to what extent.

"I thought I was dealing with a reasonable human bein', but I was wrong. My mistake. I admit it." Roy's voice had changed, softened. "I just had give you credit for more sense than you got." He shook his head slightly. "I had the idea that I was dealin' with a man—somebody growed up enough to know how to take a good blow-job for what it was worth and not shoot his mouth off." Another expression for it. Was there no end? "But, no, like some silly dumb-assed girl, you got to run and tell Sister." A hand shot out and the front of my shirt was in a grip of steel and I was being eased up closer to Roy's face until it melted out of focus. He shook me slightly and spat the words in my face, *"Why did you tell Sister I was queer?"*

I was paralyzed with terror. I tried to answer but no sound came from my throat. The sounds I heard next came from two sharp slaps across my face, leaving my cheeks stinging. *"What do you think a queer is, anyway?"* Tears were running down my cheeks, hot and burning when they reached where I could still feel the imprint of his hand.

"Am I queer just because I sucked your cock? Is that what you think?" He shook me roughly. "What *is* a queer?" Speech was beyond me. "Answer me, goddamnit," he raised his voice for the first time. He was losing control now and when he slapped me this time my ears rang and one of my teeth cut my lip. This is what I feared the most. I felt that once he let his anger off the tight rein he'd be capable of anything.

"I don't—know—what—it—means . . ." I finally blurted out.

"Then why did you tell Sister? What kind of a shit-stirring little prick are you anyway?"

"I didn't *mean* to tell."

"But you *did.*" He still held my shirt in the iron grip. I could hear him breathing now. "WHY?" He slapped me again. I reeled with the blow. "What in God's name were you thinking of? If you'd a stopped and thought you'd see what you done." He pulled my face in closer to his and he hissed, "You—have—placed—you have *planted* a seed. (*I* plant a seed? It's *God* who plants seeds . . . and . . . Oh God, where are You now?) A—seed—of—*doubt* in Sister's mind. Now, she'll be watchin' me—watchin' us *both*—like a hawk. Don't you see? Couldn't you have figured that out on your own?" I could barely shake my head. I was too petrified to figure anything out, not the least of which was how I was going to get out of this nightmare. "Now, I'm goin' to tell you what you are going to do. What you are going to do is *this.* You—are—goin'—to have 'ta UNplant—that seed." He shook me slightly. "Do—you—understand?" He was speaking to me as though I were deaf, blind and dumb. I *was* mute. But I managed an idiotic nod. I hadn't a clue what he was talking about.

"I don't have no idea *how* you're goin' to unplant that seed—you know what you said to her, I don't. I mean, *exactly* what you said. And *how.* I just know she was trying to make it sound like a joke when she come by the office, but she wasn't jokin'. She was smilin' that beautiful smile, but she was already watchin' my every move— watchin' how I acted, how I looked, surprised or whatever . . . You've put an idea in her head and you are goin'ta have to git it *out.*" He paused a minute and his jaw worked and his eyes got blue, that blue on a gas burner, that hot blue, so hot that I could almost feel the heat from them. When he spoke again, his voice was quiet and as blue hot as his eyes. "You got enough imagination to see what can happen. Sister gets sore at me about . . . oh, hell, it don't matter what. She'd go to her momma and tell her what you said. Just to get even with me. You see? Then *Dell* would have the seed planted. And my life wouldn't be worth a damn. You can't live with suspicion. I've waited for over forty years to have a home and family—you were . . . well, *are* part of that family. And I ain't about to let some snotty-nosed kid fuck it up for me. Family member or not." He glanced out the windshield and took a deep breath and turned his rock-hard face back to mine. "If you don't get this straightened out with Sister . . . *today* . . ." He paused and his jaw and neck muscles tightened. "I don't know what you'll have to say, call yourself a silly little prick for a start, because that's the way you been behavin', anything, but if this gets back to Dell . . ." He swallowed hard. "If this gets back to Dell . . ." his head moved ever so slightly from side to side, loose and easy on his tightly wound-up body, "and anything happens to our life together . . . I'll kill you, you little son-of-a-bitch." I never believed anything so completely in my life. His eyes held mine—I was as immobilized as if he were pointing a gun at me right then and there. "Let's get back to the question. Why? Why were you two talking about queers in the first place?"

"She was saying . . ." I could finally choke out some words. "That man in Phoenix. Something about Vice Squad . . . she said they were queer . . . and everybody says queers suck . . ."

He threw me away from him as though the dirty laundry had become a bag of garbage. "Hah! I thought so." I fell back in the corner of the seat and let the tears flow. "Everybody says cocksuckers are queers," he was muttering to himself. "That's what they all say. What *shit*. Some of the biggest queers I've ever knowed ain't cocksuckers. They'd do things that ain't even in the book, but they wouldn't suck a cock. If everybody who sucked a cock was a real queer, this old world would really be in a sorry state." He was inside the car now busy moving about on the seat beside me, ripping and tearing at his clothing. "Sucking cock don't mean queer—queer is mostly in the mind anyway." Fortunately tears blinded me. I didn't want to see what he was doing. "I was just giving you a little pleasure—if you were just pretendin' you liked it, you're one hell of a actor—and got pleasure myself. I'll admit that. When you get old enough to be able to admit things that might be painful—or even *shameful,* that's when you start growin' up. That's when you get to be a man. Man*ly*. It ain't unmanly to show somebody you care for them. And that's one way. Just one of many, but . . . in my experience—in that fuckin' orphanage, in them stinkin' trenches, or out on a lonely prairie—that little sign of, well, caring, that warmth really means something. Something important. Its the same as sayin' I love you."

I could see that he had his pants down around his ankles and I pulled back and started to let myself slide out the side of the car—I'd looked around us and we were in sight of town. I could make a run for it . . . Just the split second before I could make my move, his huge hands had me by the shoulders, lifting me up again as if I weighed nothing and plunked me down on the floorboards on my knees between his legs. His cock and balls were resting on the edge of the seat, looking exaggeratedly big as though enlarged like a filthy drawing or swollen by some hideous disease. My face was only inches from the distended horror. I clenched my eyes shut and snapped my head away to the side, tucking my chin into my shoulder. "Don't . . . *please*, dear God. Don't . . . make . . ."

"It ain't goin' to hurt you none." He reached over and took my face in both his big hands and turned my head to face him, handling me with a surprising gentleness. "This is just a necessary little lesson. If I'm queer, then you'll just have to be queer with me." He eased my head closer to his crotch. I could smell an unfamiliar odor—musky and foreign. My eyes were still tightly shut. He was talking quietly, like a doctor who's about to give you a shot that he knows is going to be unpleasant, but necessary. My mouth and teeth were as firmly closed as my eyes. He took one hand from my cheek and slid the other around to the back of my neck and pulled my head forward until my lips were touching flesh. He kept pulling my head forward, rubbing my lips against the flesh until it started getting firm. He made encouraging soft sounds, "Come on, now. Open up." From a doctor to a dentist. The flesh being rubbed back and forth along my lips was not quite hard. I'd seen it once in the bathroom and I knew what it looked like and became more resolute. "You might as well get it over with, Tots," his voice was even and reasonable. "It won't take hardly a minute. You're goin' to do this because you *have* to do it, whether you like it or not. It'll make you stop and think twice before you go around calling people queers." His hand went up the back of my neck and grabbed a handful of hair. He pulled my head back sharply, which caused my eyes to snap open and my chin to drop slightly. With a slight but coordinated move, he brought my head back down on his cock, easing it in my mouth, its powerful hardness like a crowbar. It filled my mouth, muffling my scream. I was helpless, totally invaded.

"There. Relax. Don't do nothing. Just let it rest there a bit so's you get used to it." Used to it! I gagged, I choked, my nose began to run or it might have been tears pouring down my cheeks that I sucked up into my nose trying to breathe. I was being suffocated. "Just breathe natural. Relax. Take a deep breath and swallow." Doctor, dentist and now an anesthetist. If only I could be knocked out and have this horror over with.

I sagged limply hoping the pain in my jaws and mouth would be relieved. He slowly moved his hips so that the huge thing rolled around in my mouth like an outsized all-day sucker. I tried to imagine that was what it was. My mind had stopped working. It had gone as limp and numb as the rest of me. My mouth was stretched to the breaking point. I was thankful for the numbness. Perhaps I was anesthetized. I was sure the corners of my lips must be splitting but they didn't hurt. Time was suspended. My mind was a blank, refusing to accept what was taking place. After an eternity, Roy's movements became more agitated. He worked my head by pulling my head back and forth with the grip he had on my hair. I don't know how long it'd been since I breathed. My chest ached with need of air. I was going to pass out—I was dizzy and blinded—but a final jerking plunge from Roy deep into my throat brought me back. There was a dangerous churning in my stomach as a sickening fluid filled what little space was left around the hard object lodged in my mouth. I choked and gagged. The fluid oozed stingingly from my nostrils, making room for more to pour in endlessly. I choked on an intake of air and threw up with a gush so powerful that the hard cock was forced out, flushed out like a bung in the bottom of a full barrel. Roy pulled back instinctively, letting go of my hair and I averted my eyes from the messy crotch and leaned over his right knee and got my head out the door as far as I could and retched and vomited until I thought my insides were coming up with the unmentionable fluid Roy had filled my body with. I vomited until I was dry, but it still went on, my heaving body, contracting, pushing, forcing everything inside me up and out. I was aware that a hand was holding my forehead and another was stroking my hair back from my forehead. A deep voice, full of shocked contrition, was murmuring, "Oh, oh, oh. Oh Tots . . . I was only tryin' . . . Sorry . . ."

We washed as best we could with the water from the car's canvas bag. We didn't speak until he dropped me in front of the store where he'd picked me up. The two packs of Wings in my pocket looked a bit the worse for wear. I opened the door and started to get out. "Tots," he said softly. I stopped moving but didn't turn to look at him. I never wanted to see him again as long as I lived. "I meant what I said." I felt the intent in his voice. The murderous intent. It stopped my heart beating. He would kill me. That's what he meant. *Means.* I got out of the car and ran up the street to the house.

Mom and Dad were walking down the walkway to the car, each in his separate cocoon of withdrawal and preoccupation. "There you are," Mom called. "I've been worried sick. We'll probably be a bit later than usual—Saturday hours are different. I didn't want to leave Becky with Dell—so much trouble, even though she's still asleep and Sister's in there napping with her."

I held the cigarettes out to Dad. "Sorry. Got caught up in a game of touch football in the square . . ." Lying came awfully easily, particularly without Junior's honest brown eyes on hand full of gentle reproof. But even if they had been, I had some awfully good reasons for lying.

Dad took the cigarettes and held his hand out for the change. "Well, you look like you got roughed up a bit." There was a note of satisfaction in his voice. He nodded when I'd handed the change to him and they went to the car for their afternoon vigil with Junior.

As they started to pull away Mom looked at me distractedly and called, "You look a bit peaked. You oughtn't to play so rough in this heat." Her fingers trailed a weak farewell out the window as they drove off.

There was a note on the kitchen table from Aunt Dell:

Roy—
    Gone to office. If you come here, go there. Shopping. D.

I suppose it made sense. I peeked carefully into the sitting room. Sister was dead asleep on the couch near Becky. I flew up the stairs to the bathroom. I'd have it to myself. I needed it. I needed the privacy of the confined space to check what had happened to me—not only what might show physically (I could feel my swollen lip) but what I finally looked like now. There were bound to be visible changes—Dr. Jekyll and Hyde sort of changes. I'd been truly defiled, my body beaten, shaken, and used in the vilest way. If I understood the word correctly, I'd been raped. Ravaged. I'd probably grown fangs where Roy's cock had been. If I'd only had them at the time!

I locked the door, stripped and raced to the mirror. I looked disappointingly like myself. The swollen lip felt worse than it looked. The red slap marks on my cheeks simply gave me a healthy glow. My mouth felt stretched all out of shape, but the skin wasn't broken. My hair hadn't all come out in Roy's hands. As he'd said, it hadn't hurt me much. At least as far as you could see. There was a hidden wide river of humiliation running from the top of my head where he'd yanked my hair down through my gut where he'd knocked the wind out of me, way past that little corner where all the shame was stored. This was new shame, requiring new storage units and more space. It went down even deeper, deep in my bowels causing my stomach to turn. I swallowed hard to keep from throwing up again and to get the taste of him out of my system—I could still smell him. I could actually taste disgrace. It was the nastiest taste of all. But not as nasty as fear. Roy's threat was as real as the bruises on my face. He said he meant what he said and I didn't doubt him for an instant. Life for a life. He'd take mine without batting an eye if I deprived him of his. His new life, his newfound happiness with Aunt Dell he'd searched for all his life. My sense of fair play made me accept his threat as reasonable. Accepting it, made it even more real. He hadn't hesitated to knock me senseless. He'd forced me to perform that act. If he could use and abuse my body the way he had, he wouldn't hesitate to carry it a few steps further. Oh my God. What in the world was I going to do? How in God's name was I going to convince Sister it was a misunderstanding, a joke, anything before she told Aunt Dell what I'd said? If Aunt Dell ever had so much as a hint of what I'd said, I was as good as dead.

In clean, neat, short pants, scrubbed almost to the bone in an attempt to cleanse my soul, I started wandering around the upstairs of the house. I didn't quite know what for. Searching for a way to clear myself with Sister and Roy, I guess.

I stood stock still in the hall and offered up yet another prayer for Junior's recovery—God's batting average had been pretty high when I'd called on him seriously before. I hoped He realized this one was a matter of life and death. Junior's life and my death. If Junior were well, we could get the hell out of here and maybe the whole thing would blow over. For the first time I thought Arkansas might not be all that bad. At least it was a good distance from here. As usual, everything depended on Junior. Things didn't go this wrong when he was here with us where he belonged. We all needed him.

Aunt Dell's room told me very little—the back braces and orthopaedic shoes and bandages in the closet were innocent enough and even pathetic unless one knew that they were used for fraud. The word hit my brain like a gong. Fraud. Fake. Liar. Cheat. *Criminal.* Each word bonged until I shook my head to clear it. Roy was in this with her. He was just as guilty as she. What did she think when she opened the closet door and saw those things? They must be a constant reminder of the years she'd been living lies—swearing false statements, insisting to doctors of nonexistent pain, remembering which foot to limp on, keeping track of where it was supposed to hurt. Didn't seeing the evidence hurt? Perhaps the corsets, crutches, girdles, braces and bandages were all labeled and dated with careful bookkeeping—"Zest-O, 14 June 1937, $1500." "J.C. Penney's, 5 September 1938, $750." "Sinclair Filling Station, October 1939 . . ."—creating a little horror museum of fake injuries. She stored her shame in the closet. At least she could close the door on it.

Sister's room was stifling. No wonder she napped downstairs with Becky. Her suitcase was open on the floor beside a dresser, with bras, stocking suspenders and "half-slips" trimmed with lace frothing up over the edges. I dropped to my knees beside the suitcase. The exotic underwear was as transparent as cellophane and so light you could wad a slip into a small ball in your hand. Even my smallish hand which was now sporting a silver and turquoise ring I'd just found on top of the dresser and put on. The stone was cracked, but the color—it was the color that mattered—held me transfixed. Ever since I'd first seen the Arizona Indian jewelry, I'd longed for a ring. I'd have preferred one a little less damaged—one little silver bead on the side was missing—but it was real silver and real turquoise. It wasn't fake. Damaged, but the elements were honest and true. I was feeling damaged too. Damaged and desperate. Sister was desperate, but how damaged? I held my hand up and stared at the stone, turning my hand this way and that. I had to have it. It was cracked and Sister was so fussy about what she wore, she'd probably give it to me.

I emptied the suitcase in order to fold the things properly and found the bottom layered with photographs—all the nightclub sort of flash photos and all with Sister. Sister always flashing those perfect teeth, eyes sparkling, dark hair pulled back showing off her high cheekbones—Delores Del Ozarkio. She really was beautiful. That crazy bartender was right. I remember how funny he'd been when we were there. "I am blinded by the beauty of Ginny," or something like that he'd said and she'd handed him an envelope. It all came back to me now. She'd come out of the hotel . . . She'd obviously spent the night there, that's why she ran across the street and came back pretending she'd just arrived. Why had she spent the night in the hotel? She wasn't working at the Tucson Bar then, she was still working at The Ship. When she handed the bartender the envelope she'd said, "You take care of me, I'll take care of you." Could that mean . . . Oh damn! Junior! Where are you? You know the word I mean . . . the word for a man that arranges for men to have girls. The word didn't matter. It all fell into place anyway. She was "on the game" herself. That was the expression she'd used about the other girl—the one who'd lie to the judge to punish Sister for something in order to protect herself. Was the other girl what Sister had said? If so, what was Sister?

I rifled through the photos again. The backgrounds were similar—always a bar or restaurant with bottles and glasses on the table. The only thing that changed was the men. They were never the same. Always a different man. I dropped the photos back into the case and absentmindedly folded the gossamer garments.

Could I confront her with what I thought I knew? Could I use that to get myself off the hook with Roy? Make a deal with Sister that I wouldn't say anything about her if she wouldn't . . . The idea was so appalling that my stomach churned. The word blackmail came to mind. That's what I'd actually been contemplating. Blackmail of any sort was beneath contempt. Could I stoop so low? How far was I willing to go to protect myself?

"Totsy, honey." It was Sister's voice from downstairs. "Where are you?" I was still kneeling beside the suitcase, a half-folded slip on my lap. How long had I been like this? The garment on my lap had spots all over it. I blinked and saw more drops hit and darken the sheer fabric—tears were sliding down my face in a steady stream. I wiped them away and stood up. What or who were they for? Sister's lost innocence? Mine? I held onto the top of the dresser and shook my head from side to side. Could I bargain with my beautiful cousin—my favorite cousin? To even suggest to her that I thought she might be a . . . I couldn't even form the word in my mind. What she was doing was her business. Nobody had the right to question her. Bargaining in that way was despicable—the most unmanly thing I could think of. If what she was doing was shameful, it was still her shame. She had to cope with hers like the rest of us with ours.

My own shame was oozing out every pore. There was no more room inside. I'd allowed grown men—granted I hadn't much choice—to play kids' games. And now I was a kid trying to play a man's game. Roy hadn't been just playing around, he'd been dead serious about everything. Dead being the operative word. Starting with the sex. I hadn't known how to accept it or handle it on a man's level and now I was in trouble. Big trouble. Like all of us, he had to do everything in his power to protect himself if caught in an embarrassing or shameful situation.

We were all trying to protect ourselves. Was that what life was about—adult life? Dad was trying to protect himself from disappointment—the dread possibility that Junior might not turn out to be the next Babe Ruth. I was trying to protect myself from a growing and uncomfortable self-knowledge along with things more immediate like threats on my life. Sister was trying to protect her secret life. That's what it actually boiled down to; protecting our secrets. Our guilts and our shame. I had almost unmasked Roy, but he caught me—I hope in time—and he had hit me, hit me hard. He got his message across—I was scared shitless and didn't have a clue how I was going to get my message over to Sister.

"Up here," I called. "Be right down." I couldn't get the ring off. I started sucking on my little finger to get it off as I walked down the hall and slowly descended the stairs.

"Becky's beginning to stir," Sister said as I went into the darkened sitting room.

"Uhumm." I still had my finger in my mouth.

"You still suckin' your thumb?" She laughed. "Come on over here. I thought I broke you of that a hundred years ago."

"I got your ring stuck."

"Well, we'll just have to cut your finger off. Or better yet, why don't you just keep it?"

"Can I? Can I really?"

"Sure. I found it. I don't know why, but it makes me sad. Some young girl lost it."

I leaned up against her and she put an arm around my shoulders lightly. It was too hot for a real embrace but she had always touched me and caressed me at every opportunity. In spite of myself, I melted with joy. As always. How could I believe what I'd pieced together was the truth? This beautiful creature couldn't be anything but my beloved cousin. Adored and revered. Even if she had managed to put my neck in a noose and tightened the knot. The word noose gave me an idea and galvanized me into action. I had to do something. And this was my only opportunity. In order to get a head start, I had to bring up the subject before she did. With an inspiration born of desperation and self-preservation I launched into a monologue—talking as fast as I could, it had to be fast if it would work at all. "Hey, delicious Delores, our conversation got interrupted this morning. By

a dog turd, if I'm not mistaken . . ." She was smiling. "Dog turds in-
terrupting queers—whatever that is—or something like that. What I
was going to say about Ro . . . Uncle Roy was that he was such a cowboy he reminded me of that old movie-star cowboy joke. You know it?
The one where the cowboy's so tough that he never even takes the
woman's hand—well, maybe if she's drowning—or touches her or
kisses her." I started moving around with my legs comically (I hoped)
bowed and holding imaginary pistols. "Ah mean, he's so darned
tough and mean and manly that he can spit a mile through his front
teeth to put out fires when he wasn't biting the heads off rattlers. You
know the kind I mean? Makes Roy Rogers look like a sissy." She was
laughing now. "Well, since this powerhouse won't hardly look at the
girl in the film, at the very end the . . . Oh, what's he called? The man
who tells them what to do?"

"The director. Go on." She seemed to be enjoying my performance.

"Well, the director says to him, 'Well, Stud, what we'll do right
here at the end is just have you throw your arm over your horse's
neck and sort of lean your head next to him and kinda smile up at
the horse like you was cuddlin' up to the leadin' lady.' With that,
Stud starts breaking up the joint. You'd think they were shootin' another barroom fight. He was screaming and hollerin' and carryin'
on like a pig under a gate. When they finally calmed him down, he
was red in the face and sweatin' and still yellin', 'You want me to nuz-
zle up to this here animal? Is that what you are suggestin' I do? What
the hell is the matter with you, you sidewindin' bastard? Don't you
know I cain't do that? What in tarnation are you thinkin' of? Why,
this here beast is a stallion. What do you think I am, queer or something?"

I don't know whether I'd won, but she was roaring with laughter.
"Tots, you are kee-raaa-zy. I never heard that before."

"It's just that I figured Roy is about as un-queer as that guy in the
story—I mean if I understand what queer means. As far as I know,
I've never laid eyes on one. How can you tell a queer anyway?"

"Oh, honey, it doesn't matter." She patted me on the cheek. "I realize that you didn't understand all of *my* story. You're younger than
I thought. If you don't know what a queer is by now, well . . ." she
threw her head back and laughed. "Well, just keep it that way."

I turned to Becky. She was soaking. My hands were trembling as I
changed her. Was I untrapped? Off the hook? Was my head out of
the noose? I thought how things seemed to go haywire when Junior's

presence couldn't be felt. I knew he was up there on the hill and would soon be all right, but I couldn't shake the thought that he was letting me down somehow. Well, all of us down. He'd revealed a weakness, a physical weakness that wasn't allowed him. He wasn't supposed to have weaknesses like the rest of us. That showed him as being vulnerable. The rest of us were the vulnerable ones. He wasn't allowed to have a flaw. While he was healthy, we stayed healthy. Now that he was powerless against his infections, our own personal infections would grow and fester. He was our medicine, our tonic—more than that, he was our rudder, our ballast, our stabilizer. I knew it couldn't possibly, but just suppose something serious happened to him? What would become of us? Dad was already reverting to his irresponsible ways—his drinking was increasing daily and the foolish act of quitting his job went on beggaring analysis. And I knew I'd never—without Junior—be able to live within sight of Dad's reproachful eyes. There was an expression going around, a slang expression that covered almost any situation: Forgive me for living. I'd have to adopt it for my life motto.

Mom's eyes were depthless wells of pain and incomprehension already. Why was this happening to her? Whatever happened to her children happened to her too. But why was any of it happening— Dad's behavior, the constant uprooting? Junior's mysterious illness. If Mom withdrew any more, we'd never be able to find her. With whom would she share books, poetry, those long conversations and deep discussions that were over my head and in Dad's own words "bored the shit" out of him?

I took a deep breath to dispel the gloomy thoughts. Junior is simply too special to each of us for anything to happen to him. Anything bad. A little sinus attack, for heaven's sake. About as serious as "dying with a toothache in his heel."

"Honey, you're going to clog her up," Sister said from behind me, watching me dust Becky's bottom. "Thank God that's powder and not cement." Her teeth flashed. "I'd better go get powdered down and everything myself. Where's Mom and Roy?"

"Went shopping."

"Milly and Uncle Woody still at the hospital?"

"Yeah. They stay later today. Saturday. Visiting hours till six, I think."

Sister started for the stairs and stopped. "Isn't that Roy's car? Yes, it is. I'll go help them unload." She flew past me as I took Becky into the kitchen and put her bottle on to heat. I looked over my shoulder

and saw Sister and Roy with their heads together on the far side of
the car. They were laughing uproariously. Is that all it took to smooth
out the waves? The oldest cowboy story in the world? Mingled with
some barely convincing declarations of innocence on my part? I'd
been beaten up, terrified, raped, threatened with what could be
called terminal punishment, and there they were laughing their
heads off. Some joke. Or was it? Why had she gone straight to Roy
without waiting for an explanation from me? At least she could have
let me try to explain first. I was still faced with a threat on my life no
matter how much oil my tired old joke poured on the troubled wa-
ters. Roy had said I'd planted a seed. Well, seeds can lie dormant for
ages before they sprout. Sister could—as Roy pointed out—get mad
at him for something or need to protect herself (now that I knew her
own dark secret, the danger was like a time bomb ticking away) and
she could always point a finger at Roy to deflect fire from herself.
That could take years or happen any minute. We had to get out of
here. I'd never feel really comfortable with any of them again. By a
foolish slip of the tongue, my lifelong love affair with Sister was en-
dangered. Now it could only be a watchful suspicious relationship.
She watching me for signs that would verify her suspicions and I
watching her for the same reasons. No relationship survives on
doubt or suspicion, as Roy said. Not even one of blind worship. Much
of the sympathy I'd felt for her dilemma with the Vice Squad evapo-
rated. We were both in trouble and couldn't help each other. Never
would be able to.

I was testing the temperature of Becky's bottle by squirting a drop
on my inner arm when I heard Aunt Dell burst into the kitchen with
an armload of groceries. She put them on the table and went back to
the door yelling, "Come on, you two! Git the lead out. Git that stuff
out of the car! Roy! For Christ's sake come git us a beer!" She turned
to me. "Whoooeee! The heat! Totsy, you never seen nothin' like that
market on a Saturday afternoon. Honest to God *hell*. An inferno!"
She sank down into a kitchen chair and bawled over her shoulder,
"Goddammit, Rooooy! Beeeeeerrrrr! I'm dyin', I tell you."

Roy came in, followed by Sister, both obviously still sharing a joke.
I assumed my cowboy joke. Roy put an overflowing cardboard box
down on the floor and patted Aunt Dell's shoulder. "You sound like
a cow that's lost her calf." He headed for the icebox, still smiling and
gave me a big wink. I made a point of not noticing.

"OK. Done my chores for the day," Sister said, putting more groceries on the table. "Off to soak."

"Go lay that child down, Totsy, it's too hot to touch anybody. Even that sweet thing." Roy plunked an open bottle of beer in front of Aunt Dell and she lifted it and drank thirstily. "Couldn't even wait for a glass. Aaaahhh. That's better. I may even live."

I told Aunt Dell about the fiesta last night, how much I'd enjoyed the dancing and might go back tonight since one of the boys I d met was teaching me some steps. I kept my eyes on her and Becky until Roy interrupted. "The boy? The dancing boy? Was he curly haired?" Roy asked. "Named Juan?" His blue eyes were sparkling with mischief. A little secret smile—was it of triumph?—was pulling at the corners of his mouth. What did he know about Juan?

"Yeah, I think so."

"Works at our office." He grinned and shrugged as he headed for the icebox and more beer. His little smile developed into a knowing one as his eyes slid past mine.

That clinched it. I *would* go to the fiesta tonight no matter what happened. I had to find out if Roy did with Juan what he did with me. If so, he was really queer. "I'll go get rid of this sweaty load," I said, taking Becky back to the sitting room, "and then come help you put that stuff away." If Roy really was a queer, I suddenly felt sadly sorry for Aunt Dell. I knew she'd never be able to understand anymore than Dad would Roy's . . . well, Roy's flaw. Roy knew it too. That's why he was so afraid of her finding out. If he took chances of being found out with me and perhaps Juan, how many others were there? There'd been others in the past, he'd said so. But if there were more in the future, how long would it be before he made a really big mistake and got caught with the wrong person. If it were somebody else who blew the whistle on him, some young kid and Roy carried out his threat only to wind up in jail for the rest of his life. Then perhaps I'd be able to breathe easily. He wasn't afraid of jail. He wasn't afraid of anything. He said his life would be over anyway. Oh God. Was there no way out? All I could think of was it was up to Roy to save us all—particularly himself—by keeping his hands off boys. Poor Aunt Dell may be a mess but she is good-hearted and generous and loves us. My thoughts about her earlier seemed harsh in the light of the tightrope existence I now knew she was facing. She'd die of humiliation and shame if Roy created a scandal. Here we all were with our flaws, fissures, weaknesses and shame nakedly revealed. At least revealed to me. I knew too much. Too much for my own good. Was this part of growing up? I knew I was growing up enough to know that our flaws—since we all have them—are supposed not to hurt anybody else. Flaws should be a private anguish, not to be shared. The least we can try to do is keep them to ourselves. I prayed particularly—selfishly, I guess—that Roy would keep his under lock and key.

I say we all have a flaw, but I couldn't think what Mom's was. Perhaps like Junior she was flawless. I didn't want to imagine what Becky's *might* be. She'd already caused me enough worry.

"Mom and Dad not back yet?" Aunt Dell called after me.

"Not yet." Then I saw our Ford pull up to the front of the house as I passed the hall door. "Oh yes, here they are now," I called over my shoulder. I moved down the hall and opened the door. I could hear Aunt Dell and Roy moving in behind me and then heard Sister's house shoes thumping down the stairs. I stepped out onto the porch. Sister stepped out behind me while Aunt Dell held the screen door open with Roy peering over her shoulder. The cement paving slanted from the porch steps down to the sidewalk along the street so we were more or less looking at the tops of their heads, their faces hidden as they got out of the car.

Becky jerked her head away from her bottle, bounced in my arms and reached toward the approaching figures. "Momma! Momma!" she called.

Mom stopped, head still down. Dad took two quick paces and took her by the arm. In a flash I knew what Mom's flaw was. Her only flaw. It was Dad. They didn't look at each other, they looked up at us. It was written on their faces as clearly as if they'd screamed.

"Oh my God," Aunt Dell gasped, hardly audibly.

Junior was dead.